In Theda Bara's Tent

Diana Altman

TAPLEY COVE PRESS

In Theda Bara's Tent is a work of fiction. All incidents and dialogue, and all characters with the exception of some well-known historical and public figures, are products of the author's imagination and are not to be construed as real. Where real-life historical or public figures appear, the situations, incidents, and dialogues concerning those persons are entirely fictional and are not intended to depict actual events or to change the entirely fictional nature of the work. In all other respects, any resemblance to persons living or dead is entirely coincidental.

2010 Tapley Cove Press
Copyright © 2010 Diana Altman
All rights reserved.

ISBN: 0615343279
ISBN-13: 9780615343273
Library of Congress Control Number: 2010924634

Also by Diana Altman

Hollywood East:

Louis B. Mayer and the Origins of the Studio System

For Richard

Acknowledgements

Thank you Jane Murphy, Kathryn Bild, Vanessa Altman-Siegel, Claudia Goldyne, and Barbara Collier for your help and encouragement.

In Theda Bara's Tent, although a work of fiction, is based on many years of careful research. Thanks to all the film historians whose books were so interesting and useful, especially Lawrence Cohn, author of *Movietone Presents the 20th Century* (St. Martin's Press, 1976)

I always bragged of the fact that no second of those contained in the twenty-four hours ever passed but that the name of Fox was on the screen in some part of the world.

William Fox, 1925

Preface

My father, Harry Sirkus, could not walk down the streets of
Manhattan without being stopped for an autograph. He was
the face of television news. Although he was a modest person,
he knew that his own story might have some historical value.
Wounded in 1941 when he was covering the London blitz for
Fox Movietone News, he wrote the tale of his childhood on
Royal London Hospital stationery. It was a labor of love for
me to read those yellowed, handwritten pages. I've never read
a more intimate account of the birth of the American film
industry and of the men who built it. My father was among
them.

Franklin Sirkus, Esq.

Larchmont, New York, 2009

Chapter One

I didn't see my parents die when I was nine but I saw the way they died. I saw others leaping from the flames landing with a thud on the sidewalk. Young girls once vibrant were now a pile of clothes. Thud. Then the next one. Thud. It's that sound that remains with me and the chaos of the scene—the cops linking arms to form a barricade to keep us back, firemen hosing water up the eight stories of the textile factory where my mother worked. The crowds shoved and screamed and knocked over pushcarts, but for one strange moment, I was detached and took a scientific view. Water came from somewhere and went into those hoses. The water came from somewhere outside of my Delancey Street neighborhood, and for a split second, I saw the wide world, saw how everything was really much bigger than I'd imagined. That was a comforting insight. Then someone shoved me, and I shouted for my father, and Oats told me he'd gone in to rescue my mother.

Afterward, neighbors were whispering and looking as if something was lurking behind me. One of the women was cooking at my mother's stove. The men who used to grab and tickle me avoided my eye. But the most frightening thing was that Mr. Goldfarb opened the *pushkas* and gave me the coins that were collected inside. "That's not allowed!" I said, thinking he didn't know the use of *pushkas*. Maybe in his tenement, the families did not put those little boxes on the wall, coins for the homeless, coins for widows, coins for orphans. I knew what an orphan was; it was my job to drop the penny in that *pushka*, but I thought orphans were born that way, deformed.

It was Oats who drove me to the docks in Mr. Goldfarb's wagon. This could not happen unless there was some emergency because Mr. Goldfarb never let anyone drive his dry-goods wagon, especially not Oats, whose racket was protection. If you paid Oats, he wouldn't poison your horse. Now here he was sitting in the wagon outside my building waiting for me to come downstairs with those coins in my pocket and some of my clothes bundled in a shawl. It was early summer, and I was in the middle of a stickball championship, and my team was depending on me. It never entered my head as we clip-clopped along the streets of the Lower East Side that I was going away. We had to avoid a crowd gawking at a juggler throwing flaming pins in the air.

I'd never been to the piers before, and I was excited to see all those gigantic ships, sailing schooners, freight ships and a gaudy three-story side-wheeler like the kind in picture books about the Mississippi River. It was white with red letters near the smoke stacks: "Priscilla Fall River." The pier was dense with activity, families carrying luggage, tractors heaped with cargo, sailors loading freight. It was a madhouse with seagulls overhead screeching, *sheee, yuk, yuk, sheee, yuk, yuk*. A sudden ship-horn blast made Mr. Goldfarb's horse bolt. People rushed to avoid him, and Oats had to stand in the wagon to rein him in saying, "Whoa, Stevie, whoa, big fella," and he said this with a kind of compassion that seemed at odds with his profession. When the horse was again standing in his usual exhausted way, Oats said, "That one," and pointed to the side-wheeler. "You go find him. I can't leave the horse." I assumed he meant my father come back alive somehow.

Passengers were coming down a gangplank to the dock. When I caught sight of my father—tall, shoulders back, head high—I charged through the crowd. What a relief! No more lying in bed at night wondering who was going to take care of me. I threw my arms around his waist, but the hands that loosened my grip were not my father's. Startled, I stepped back and looked up into the face of a young man who said, "You got money for the ticket?" He had my father's face but not the face I knew. He had my father's young face, the one in the photo from Lithuania before my father came to America, the one Mr. Goldfarb tucked into my bundle as I was walking out the door. I held my coins in an open palm as if feeding a horse, and the young man picked out what he needed. His hands were calloused, with black under the nails.

I had made one of the most humiliating mistakes of childhood. I hugged the wrong person. I tried to recover my dignity by saying, "Oats is here," which I thought would show that I had things under control. But Oats had vanished. Now I heard some of the words that had circulated in whispers around me that week: "Who says nineteen isn't old enough?" and "New England? Where's that?"

"Are you Uncle Sonny?" I said. "You're the one's supposed to take care of me."

He looked down at me with grave eyes. "Don't you think I know that?" A whistle blasted. "Come on!"

I ran after him out to the deck where the wind blew my hat off. "My hat!" Uncle Sonny leaned over the rail to watch the wake and the flocks of squawking seagulls being lifted on the wind. "My hat!" I watched it sail out over the water, dip, sail more, then land on the waves.

"Look at the tugs! They're pulling us out!" said Uncle Sonny. He didn't care about my hat. I expected him to scold me and say I should have held it down harder. "Hey! See that?" he shouted above the *plash, splash, whoosh* of the side-wheeler. "It's the Statue of Liberty!"

I couldn't count the number of times at school I had to memorize "Give me your tired, your poor." "Think it will sink?" I asked him. He considered this, then realized I was teasing. He pulled his hand back pretending he was going to cuff me, and I ducked, and our eyes met with a quick hug. I had always wanted an older brother. He would be a shield against bullies. His confident walk would light up the sidewalks, and all the kids would envy me. So this was the Uncle Sonny my father was always looking forward to seeing again.

We spent the night in a room the size of a cell and ate dinner rolls that young women in the ship's galley donated to us after Uncle Sonny flirted with them. We disembarked in Fall River, where mills were belching smoke, and hurried to a train depot. Looking out the window at rural Massachusetts—red barns, black-and-white cows—I waited for bandits with kerchiefs over their noses to gallop close, a familiar scene at the motion-picture hall upstairs in Mr. Goldfarb's store.

Our train stopped in a town of red-brick mills where the air smelled of leather and there was a continual hum coming from the windows of the mills. A large billboard with a picture of a woman's high-buttoned shoe read, "Welcome to Haverhill, Slipper City of the World, population 45,000."

I wondered what happened to the people. There weren't enough of them. Did Cossacks on a rampage kill everyone right and left? No pushcarts overflowing with cabbages, potatoes and lemons. No mangy dogs licking the puddles found under the carts of fish laid out on ice. No organ grinder whose monkey held out a black and shriveled palm and closed tiny humanoid fingers around the pennies he received. No women haranguing merchants on the sidewalk. The stores were lined up, each with its own big glass window, the goods arranged artistically: eggs in a pyramid, butter in terra cotta pots, collars not helter-skelter in the haberdashery. A trolley car not bulging with people hanging off the sides clanged its bell, and the conductor waved to a woman going into a shop. She raised her hand in greeting in a slow, almost dreamy way.

We walked into a neighborhood of dirt streets and triple-decker wooden houses. Clotheslines held up shirts, denim trousers, women's bloomers, socks, diapers. Small children stopped their play to watch us. It was unnerving to see how interesting two people walking by was to them. Did nothing ever happen in this place? Uncle Sonny opened a small gate, and I followed him into one of the identical houses.

The hall was dark and narrow, and the stairs were so steep they were almost perpendicular. The smell was cooked cabbage. People's voices came from behind closed doors as Uncle Sonny and I climbed one flight, two flights, three flights to his room in the attic. A mattress on the floor was covered with a moth-eaten blanket. Books and maps were everywhere. He gave me some of our leftover rolls and said, "Stay here." I heard him go down the steep stairs, and when I looked out the window, I saw him hurrying down the hill as men carrying lunch pails trudged up in the other direction.

His maps were crisscrossed with red pencil, routes to Alaska, Canada and California. Catalogs showed pickaxes, shovels and strainers used for panning gold. When he didn't come back, I went downstairs and stood on the empty dirt street. Then I climbed back up the stairs. A little later, I went down again, hoping maybe a band would march by or an opera singer would belt out some aria, but there was nothing. I went up and down all afternoon, and absolutely nothing happened except the sun began to go down, and then the sun went down, and the street lamps went on, and I stood by the window upstairs looking out and waiting. At last, I heard his footsteps on the stairs and the door open, and he said, "I'm done!" He picked me up, twirled me around and collapsed onto the mattress.

"I'm not a baby," I said and brushed myself off. As far as I could see, he had not brought me anything to eat.

"You'll thank me some day," he said.

"For what?"

"For the fortune I'm going to heap on you."

He packed some maps in his knapsack, stuffed in his hairbrush, took off his factory uniform and stomped on it as if killing a roach. Streetlights illuminated fogs of bugs. Store windows were dark. No music came through the windows of the homes we passed, no raised female voices complained, no male voices defended, no clip-clop of tired wagon horses, no shrill police whistles. I had never been in a night that didn't contain babies crying. A strange bark startled me, so I stopped. "Fox," Uncle Sonny said. I had seen pictures of foxes in books but had no idea what they were capable of. Uncle Sonny didn't even realize I was not next to him. He was half a block away before I caught up with him. When I paused to watch a family of raccoons digging in a trash barrel, he didn't notice.

We stopped in front of a red-brick mansion set back from the road and surrounded by trees, gnarled trunks that seemed alive with shadowy faces. The house loomed there, black at all the windows. The bell on the front door was a bronze crank. Uncle Sonny wound up the handle, and when he released it, a shrill *brriiinnngg* resounded inside. "Let me do that," I said, but I did not wind the handle tight enough, so the sound inside was just a brief *brink*.

A light came on at a window upstairs. Footsteps behind the door, then the porch gaslight whooshed on. The door opened, and a woman with gray hair stood clutching her bathrobe closed and squinting out through wire-rimmed glasses. Behind the woman, sleepy children in pajamas came out to the upstairs landing, then sat on the stairs and peered out between the rungs in the banister. One of them said, "Is it a new boy, Lady Mother?"

Uncle Sonny knelt down so his face was directly in front of mine. For the first time, he spoke in Yiddish. "I done my time," he said. "I signed for two years. I done two years." He stood up, then knelt down again. My heart was racing with fear. "Chick Shoe factory," he said, "don't have no gripe with me." He squeezed my shoulders. "You wouldn't want me to be a stitcher the rest of my life. Your papa, may he rest, didn't mean I should stand in front of that machine until I'm old. I'm going to stake a claim in Dawson City and come right back. You wait for me here. Understand? I'll be back for you." He stood up. "Why are you looking at me like that? Don't look at me like that." Then he turned and ran down the front path and away into the night.

From inside the house, a small voice asked, "How old is he?"

The woman said, "Do you speak English?" Her diction was precise. "Speak English?" She slowed the question way down. "What. Is. Your. Name."

"Harry Sirkus."

"Harry Sirkus, please come in."

"No, thank you. I'll wait here."

The street was empty, nothing but one black dog with a feathery tail trotting by and the rhythmic vibration of crickets. I sat down on the top step with my back to her so I could figure out what to do.

"Harry," she said. "Come inside. Please."

When I stayed put, she closed the door but did not turn off the porch light. I sat on the step, my heart in my throat. How could my mother do this to me? My mother stirring a pot at the stove saying, "Cooking with love is the main thing. Make sure you find a wife that cooks with love. What's love? You see how I love cooking this stuff for you? That's cooking with love."

The sky with filled with stars. I looked up into that New England dome of diamonds and felt like I was falling into it, a speck in the universe. The front door opened. "Come inside, Harry," the woman said. "Come have a cookie. You can't sleep outside. That's for bums and Boy Scouts."

She had a kindly face, and I was hungry. Next to the door was a bronze plaque. I read as I entered: The Elizabeth Home for Destitute Children.

Chapter Two

Day after day, I stood at the windows looking out for Uncle Sonny. Sometimes I saw him and raced downstairs and out the front door just to discover my mistake. Waiting, waiting, hope turning to anger, anger turning to despair, the indignity of helplessness. I could hardly believe this was happening to me, the crown of my mother's head. She said that to me when she tucked me in at night, "Harry, you are the crown of my head." Homesickness was perpetual, like blinking. I went to sleep with it; I woke up with it—the middle of me was encased in a bubble of hurt.

The house was a converted private mansion, so there was no dormitory but separate rooms: a nursery for unfortunate babies, schoolgirls on the second floor, boys on the third. It was my misfortune to be in the same room as an overly developed twelve-year-old named Kyle. He wasn't an orphan but was one of those who came to the home when he needed temporary relief from whatever horror was going on at his own home. Another boy was in that room too, an eleven-year-old named Freckles who was strong enough to scold Kyle for bullying the smaller children.

He could only scold what he saw, and much of what Kyle did was done in secret. For some reason, there was no lock on the bathroom door, and one of Kyle's favorite tricks was to open the door while I was on the toilet. When I protested, he closed the door. Then he opened it and peeked in and closed it again. Then he opened it and came inside and just stood there and when I protested, he departed with a maniacal cackle, leaving the door wide open. Kyle's other trick was shoving you so you'd stumble down the stairs.

The Elizabeth Home was run by volunteers. Each day, self-assured, cheerful, efficient men and women came into the house to attend to something. "And how are we today," they said to me but never waited for a reply. Members of the bedding committee bustled about with sheets and blankets. One volunteer insisted I try a few different pillows to see which one was most comfortable, but since I had never slept with a pillow before, I didn't know how to judge and kept saying, "No, thank you. No, thank you." Her insistence was aggressive as though giving me that pillow was a test to see if she had what it took to uplift someone else. The education committee arrived with books for our library. Men from the fuel committee checked our furnace. The clothing committee brought freshly laundered, hand-me-down trousers, shirts, pajamas and underwear, which filled the clothes chest assigned to me next to my cot. The Lend-a-Hand Circle of Kings' Daughters knit socks and caps for us.

I was of particular interest. "Is this our little Hebrew? My, what eyes! Has a Jewish family been found yet?"

I explained to Lady Mother that it was important for me to remain there so Uncle Sonny could find me when he returned. "When he returns," she said, "we'll tell him where you are." But she did not find a Jewish family. For a while I believed it was my fault. When I became familiar with Haverhill, I realized that most of the Jewish families had eight or more children and lived crowded together on what the city map referred to as Jew Street. Many of those immigrants prospered. Indeed, some of them eventually came to own some of the shoe factories. But when I arrived, no one could afford to feed another mouth. All extra money was used to bring more relatives to America.

I was used to celebrating the Sabbath on Friday nights, a special roast chicken dinner, my father laying his hand on my head and blessing me and my mother silently praying over the candles. Now on Friday nights, I joined the other children in the front parlor where we sang hymns as Lady Mother banged away on the upright. The bold melody of *Onward Christian Soldiers* excited me and so did the odd words "Marching as to war." What were they going to war about? "With the cross of Jesus going on before." They were going to war with a cross? No guns? But I loved that tune and sang with gusto. The words to *Amazing Grace* made me choke up. At first I could not sing "I once was lost but now I'm found." When we came to that part I just had to swallow and bite the inside of my cheeks. Then the evening came when I could sing those words, and I knew that something had shifted in me, and though it felt like a relief that the pain was duller, I worried that I was forgetting my old self.

The public school in Haverhill was about five blocks away. We followed Lady Mother like a line of ducklings. Her final inspection included straightening collars, flattening flyaway hair and making stone suckers spit out their stones. The other children going into school slowed their pace, stared and looked away, embarrassed. They could imagine nothing worse than being us. They had been told to save their outgrown clothes for the orphans and to think of starving orphans when they wasted food. I had been told the same thing by my parents.

All of us, with equal eagerness, watched the transformation of the Haverhill fairgrounds when Buffalo

Bill's Wild West show came to town with eight hundred performers and five hundred horses. Hundreds of Indians in his troupe set up tepees, and we saw Mexicans in big sombreros walking around town. Most of the children in school would go to the show with tickets bought by their parents, and this was bitter to me because I believed that I loved Buffalo Bill better than any of them. Even when I lived in New York City, I read books about him and played being him. I cantered around on Powder Face, his white horse.

I struggled trying to decide whether buying a ticket was a good use of my remaining money and decided that it was. The cash was in a little pouch at the back of my books on a shelf above my cot, except that it wasn't there. I was alone in the room and went to Kyle's space opposite mine to find out if he was the culprit. Kyle had gone home and would stay there, so the others told me, until his father was put in jail again. He had shoved the pouch under his mattress without any of my coins in it. I cried harder than I had ever cried before. It sounded like a wail, and I couldn't stop even when I heard one of the volunteers coming up the stairs. It was Mr. Cogswell from the bank, coming to check the ceiling for leaks. "Say, youngster. That's no way. You don't want me to tell Lady Mother to keep you home Saturday, do you?" He had bought all of us seats right in front, and none of us had to worry about Kyle because he wasn't there. We joined fifteen thousand other fans in the bleachers. Fifteen thousand of us leaped to our feet and cheered when, to the sound of a military march, Buffalo Bill, mounted on his high-stepping white horse, pranced into the arena holding an American flag upright in his gloved hand. His clothes, hemmed with fringe, were the color of tumbleweed; his white hair touched the shoulders of his leather jacket. White mustache, white goatee—his expression was stern. He held black silver-studded reins and sat with ease on a silver-studded saddle. The acts consisted of cowboys riding at lightning speed clinging to their steeds with only one foot in the stirrups and Indians doing rain dances. When an old Deadwood stagecoach rolled into the arena, a cowboy with springs for feet demonstrated how fast a man could change horses in the days of the Pony Express.

At the end of the show, to the sound of cheering, Buffalo Bill dismounted, took off his gloves and walked around the edge of the arena, shaking hands with the children who leaned out over the railing. They begged him to take their hand, calling, "Me! Me!" I did not bother to extend my hand or call his name because I did not want more disappointment. I just stood by the railing, awestruck as he came nearer.

Skin like bark, he was as exotic as a tree come to life. Much to my amazement, he stopped in front of me, looked into my eyes, showed me his grave and intelligent soul and took my hand. His hand was large, warm, with no impatience in it. Quite the opposite. There was something comforting and slow in it. However long it took for us to connect, to really connect, that's how long he stayed. When he moved on to the next child, I felt I had been given a present, that he had lodged a ruby in the middle of me. I smelled my hand and put my palm gently to my cheek. Me, he chose me. There was a bigger world out there and people in it who would see my worth. Such are the encounters from which children draw strength.

Chapter Three

I discovered the Bijou Theater. A hand-painted sign over the entrance read, "High Class Motion Pictures. New Ideas. New Novelties." The coming attraction was advertised by a sign propped on an easel on the sidewalk: "Coming Next. Charlie's Ma-in-Law. You'll laugh for half an hour!"

Lady Mother believed that motion-picture halls were not good for children. She described them as "apothecary shops of the devil" and showed me newspaper stories to prove her point. California passed a law prohibiting moving pictures from showing girls with skirts flying in the wind. Ohio prohibited films that showed anyone pulling off a girl's skirt. The mayor of Boston was making war on the advertising banners outside city picture houses that showed scenes of robbery, safe-cracking, murder or suicide. Lady Mother read with contempt the names of some of the films shown in Boston: *Gaieties of Divorce*; *Old Man's Darling*; *Beware, My Husband Comes*. She had no understanding of the importance of relief for beleaguered people. She seemed to have no compassion for the hundreds of people, thousands of people, who needed to escape from their troubles for at least an hour or two. She didn't see me as one of those people though I was sitting right in front of her.

Her mandate included lifting us up from the lower class, away from the mostly immigrant audience that attended motion pictures. She had never been to a picture hall, and when I suggested it was not as bad as she thought, she said, "There is worthy entertainment, Harry. Haverhill is known as a show city but not because of the Bijou. Our Academy of Music is the greatest legitimate theater north of Boston. All the best people go there, Harry, and I want you to be one of the best people."

In my opinion, all the best people were the ones I used to know, the pals next to me watching the movies upstairs in Mr. Goldfarb's store, mothers haggling at the pushcarts, small older sisters carrying big babies on their hips, the organ grinder combing his mustache, the back-flipping acrobats pulling their tights out of their cracks, opera singers whose high notes startled horses. I was not sure I wanted to be one of Lady Mother's best people. I marked this conversation because I caught a glimpse of how small her world was.

When Lady Mother handed out our allowance, a nickel every week, she warned us of the dangers of the Bijou. Not only would we see things inappropriate for children, but we would ruin our health sitting indoors during daylight hours. I had never been given a nickel for doing nothing and found it confusing. She marched us to the bank on Merrimack Street where we deposited the nickel into our savings account. When the bankers from the frugality committee showed up at the home, they examined our savings book. We didn't dare spend any of those nickels. I misunderstood a savings account and thought we were giving our nickels back to Mr. Cogswell and his friends at the bank.

So it was necessary to earn free admission to the Bijou. I went to visit the manager in his office to ask for work. Mr. Owen looked up over half-glasses and stopped whittling a piece of wood. Wood shavings were puddled on the floor around his chair. The bookcase behind him held carved birds, all shapes, beautifully painted with real-looking glass eyes, some perched on twigs, some balancing on one foot, some with wings extended. They were arranged with care, big with big, small with small, the tidiness of the display a contrast with the disorder in the rest of the room. "Did you make those?" I asked standing at his door.

"What you might call a hobby," he said. He had a New England complexion, ripe apples in autumn.

"You made those, Mr. Owen? All by yourself?"

"All by myself."

"Can I see them close up?"

He gestured for me to enter. "Right now I'm working on a swan. I'll get the general outlines from this book here, then I'll have to find a real one so I can stare at it for a while."

He let me examine the birds, heard my admiring sighs as I noticed how he had painted tiny individual feathers on the canary and vicious talons on the eagle. At last, I came to the point. "I've come for a job," I said. "I'm good at sweeping."

"But I already have a youngster who sweeps," he said. "I can't let two in free." He saw how disappointed I was. "Here's what I'll do, since you're a fellow art lover. You can see the show this afternoon. Just this one time. Our secret."

When I returned later that afternoon, the place was jammed with women, babies, schoolchildren and men. Everyone spoke a different language: Italian, Armenian, Polish or Russian. Children shouted in English to friends, then switched languages to speak to their mothers. Loud ventilating fans blew odors from food baskets—sausage, garlic, cheese. The Bijou Theater had once been a store, and some of the display shelves were still on the walls. About three hundred folding chairs were set up in rows facing a white canvas screen suspended from the ceiling by heavy ropes. Next to the screen was an upright piano. Mr. Owen was inside a metal booth threading the projector.

The piano player, a thin man in a striped shirt, sat at the piano and played the most beautiful music I had ever heard. He told me later it was Chopin. The first reel was a travelogue, *Coney Island at Night.*—the roller coaster lit up like a birthday cake, a glittering world that stayed on the screen for three minutes. Mr. Owen projected a slide: "You Wouldn't Spit on the Floor at Home, So Please Don't Do It Here." Children all over the house translated the English words for their parents. Next slide: "Just a Moment, Please, While the Operator Changes Reels." We saw the Yale football team at practice, a steam shovel digging the New York subway, a locomotive being stoked with coal and a circus elephant being electrocuted because it had killed two men.

I had never seen "actualities" before. At Mr. Goldfarb's store I'd seen only trick pictures and made-up stories about bandits and train robberies. Mr. Owen was showing us real events stripped of smells and sounds. I noticed how detached I felt when the elephant's bulk collapsed. If I had been there, would I have been moved to tears, smelling it and hearing its beastly moan? As for the digging of the subway, I had seen that myself when I lived in New York. How different it was on the screen—no dust in your eyes, no men shouting to each other, no lift of the stomach at the thought of falling in, no deafening machinery. The event had been sanitized by making a movie of it.

Something else was going on, too, that was the reverse of everyday life. The death of an elephant was trivialized, and college boys playing football were made to seem important. I found this confusing and exhilarating. As I was struggling to understand why this was exciting, the screen lit up with *Hunting Big Game in Africa*. The film starred our former president Teddy Roosevelt who went to the Belgian Congo to collect specimens for the Smithsonian Institution. Onscreen were scenes of dense jungle and several Negro gun bearers. Teddy, in his customary safari outfit, led everyone through thick underbrush, then—oh, no! A lion! Teddy aimed, fired, and the lion dropped. The boys in the audience jumped up cheering; the girls moaned in pity. The last title card was "The most noteworthy collection of big animals that has ever come out of Africa."

As luck would have it, the boy who swept the peanut shells off the floor of the Bijou moved away, and I got the job. Lady Mother reminded me that she did not approve of motion pictures, but she did not stop me. She had a relaxed attitude toward me because I didn't really count. All the other children at the home had a history in Haverhill. Freckles, for instance, was the child of a prostitute who worked on Essex Street. Another child was the daughter of the town drunk. The parents of the twins were killed in a train wreck that everyone still remembered. No one was looking over Lady Mother's shoulder about me. It was as if I had been dropped from the moon.

The snow melted, the crocuses made their yearly mistake of sticking their pointed caps up too soon, daffodils made the same mistake, and soon they were all joined by the bilious yellow of forsythia. I'd never seen groves of trees covered with neon green leaves shaped like closed umbrellas or horses stampeding across a field of tiny blue flowers. And then heat bugs filled the air with their metallic vibration, shades in shops were closed like sleeping eyelids, the lower leaves of trees were covered with dust. Horses twisted against their harness to snap at flies. The beaches filled, and the seesaw in the playground at school waited with one foot in the air.

The Bijou closed for the summer even though a sign outside read "Coolest Theater North of Boston!" Mr. Owen gave a speech at the last show, his shirt plastered to his body: "Ladies and Jelly Beans, the Bijou has not been built just for a little while and then after the craze of moving pictures is over shut up and abandoned. In the fall, expect the New Bijou, especially fitted up for women and children, everything modern. In the ladies' parlor, a maid will be in attendance at all times. There will be a smoking room for gentlemen. The theater seats will be the collapsible kind, arranged so you will all have a perfect view."

Later, in his sweltering office, he said, "Son, here's a little bonus." He handed me a carved swan that fit in my palm. "Now, go outside and play. Go 'head." I wanted to hug him, and he saw that. "Go! Go! Go on!"

I carried my treasure to the river where it was cool, and I could watch people fishing on the riverbank, barges loaded with leather goods destined for Europe, sailboats with their jibs puffed out. I looked at the carved swan, the black around its orange bill, its black eyes, its black webbed feet tucked up under its belly, the perfection of the carving of the white feathers. I brought it to my lips and held it there for a long minute, then put it carefully in my pocket. That night I put it under my pillow where it would sleep every night.

Kyle returned, his arms covered with bruises. His lower lip hung down like an unattached shoe sole. Because he came and went so often, Kyle did not have a permanent spot but was given whichever cot was empty, and this time it was the bed next to mine.

For the first week, Kyle was withdrawn and fell asleep the minute he lay down. One night, as I was getting into pajamas, he said, "Holy cow! What's that? Your dick looks like a thumb!" I had compared before with uncircumcised boys, so I knew this was an interesting subject. But when I looked into his face, my heart lurched. There was something wrong with him. "Let me see that thing," he said, coming too close to me. He bent down and put his face too near.

"Get out of here!" I yelled and backed away. His laugh was maniacal. Later, lights out, he whispered from the cot next to mine, "I'm gonna cut off your freaky dick." Heart thumping, I lay awake. Each time I felt the tug of sleep, I yanked myself awake to be ready. To stay awake, I made myself get up and go to the bathroom. Kyle whispered, "Where do you think you're going?" and he reached across the aisle and clamped his hand on my knee. My body recoiled as if touched by a branding iron.

When I returned from the bathroom, I reached under my pillow to get strength from my swan. It was not there. "Hey! Give it back to me." I looked across the room for Freckles, but he wasn't there that night.

"Make me."

"Give it back."

"Be quiet,"came a sleepy voice from one of the other children.

"Give it back to me right now!" I cursed the tears that he could surely hear in my voice.

"Make me," he said. "Try, Freaky Dick."

I flew at him with my fists, while he chortled an unnatural, demented laugh and held my hands. I tore my hands free and began to pummel him. He grabbed both my hands in his and stamped on my bare feet until I fell. I got up and lunged at him as lights went on in the room. Lady Mother stood there in her bathrobe. "What is the meaning of this," she said. "Have you no consideration for others?"

"He has my swan," I said throwing the cardinal rule of childhood to the winds. "He took my swan."

"Did not."

I flew at him again, and for the first time, I knew how it felt to be consumed with rage. It was the worst feeling I had ever had, worse than sorrow or disappointment because it took me over. I was lost in it, blind from it. I knew it was Lady Mother's hands that pulled at me, and I knew why her hands were pulling at me, but I did not come entirely back into myself until I was separated from Kyle for what must have been a long time because Lady Mother was already winding down her lecture with: "Last chance for you, Kyle."

She resolved nothing. We heard the slap-slap of her slippers going down the hall and her bedroom door close downstairs. Through the dormitory windows came the tinny percussion of crickets. Kyle whispered, "Hey, look at this, Freaky Dick." I peered through the dark and saw something sticking up under his sheet. He made the sheet wiggle and said in a lewd voice, "See? See how big it gets? See what it does?" and he pulled the sheet away, exposing himself.

I bolted out of the room, down the stairs and out the front door of the house. I imagined Kyle right behind me, and I ran until I stumbled, then ran more until it seemed my insides would explode. I ran toward the lights in town and collapsed from exhaustion on the weeds between the pool hall and the burlesque house. Raucous hooting came through the open windows of the burlesque hall. A man whistled through his teeth as a piano played honky-tonk.

My inhalations were so noisy, a man came out of the pool hall. "Hey! What the..." I picked myself up and ran into the burlesque house, a room full of men sitting on wooden benches or leaning against the walls smoking. On the stage, a plump woman in bloomers was doing splits and thumbing her nose at the audience. The men hooted at her until she got up. I was sitting on the floor catching my breath when a man whispered down to me, "You got money, kid?" I couldn't answer; my breath was still gone. "This one time," he whispered. "You understand me? Just this one time and keep your trap shut about it." He gestured for me to move against one of the walls, and when I got up to obey, he said, "It ain't proper to come in your pajamas, kid. You should show some respect." I sat on the warped floor next to the wall and worried about my swan. A man sitting on the bench spit a wad of tobacco that thwacked against the wall right next to me. There were tobacco stains all up and down the wall, and I could hear someone outdoors pissing against the clapboards. "Ladies and gentlemen!" an announcer called. He had a waxed mustache and wore a suit of black with white polka dots. "Miss Blanche Fernandez will now sing *White Wings*!"

"Blanche Fernandez is a whore!" a sailor shouted.

"Nevertheless," said the announcer, "Miss Blanche Fernandez will now sing *White Wings*."

A tiny field mouse couldn't have had a smaller voice. "You're worth more flat on your back!" a sailor shouted. She stuck out her tongue and flounced off stage.

A plump girl in a corset came from the wings, and the men applauded wildly. She put a dollar bill in her stocking. The announcer said, "What are you doing?"

"I just put money in the bank."

"Is that,"—he pointed to her leg—"your bank?"

"Yeth," she lisped and rotated her leg so the audience could get a better look at her thigh.

"Gee," the announcer said with a wink. "I'd like to be the bookkeeper in that bank!"

Another comic appeared with a suitcase. He bet the announcer that he could not pick up the suitcase without saying "Ouch." Every time the announcer tried to pick up the suitcase, the comic kicked him in the pants, and he cried, "Ouch!"

Mine was the convulsive kind of laughing that was almost crying. I noticed a young man across the room eyeing me through wire-rimmed spectacles that perched on the bridge of his nose without earpieces. He was not slovenly like the rest of the audience. He was clean shaven and dressed in a suit, vest and starched collar. When our eyes met, he looked away so fast that I knew he had been watching me for a while.

Four girls dressed in opaque nightgowns ran onto the stage singing, "College girls, college girls, we are the college girls." Their voices were so shrill that I put my hands over my ears. The announcer held a piece of paper. "I've just received this letter from two millionaires, Mr. Clancy and Mr. Goldberg. Shall we show them a good time?"

I woke up on the burlesque-hall porch being shaken by the man who had been watching me inside. Men's voices were saying, "No, never seen him before," and "Don't he got no mother?"

"Scram. Leave him to me," said a stranger.

The stranger's eyes, magnified behind his lenses, were vast caverns of feeling. I scuttled backward away from him. He shrugged and went to sit on the porch steps with his back to me. The burlesque hall was now quiet and darkened. "I run away once," the man said without looking at me. "Got so sick of my old man slapping me around, me doing all the work, him taking all the dough, I said good riddance to bad rubbish." He was short, stocky, his upper body the muscular result of physical labor. His shoes were polished but needed new heels, trousers pressed but cuffs frayed. "What's your opinion of the show?" he asked, turning to look at me.

"What show?"

"What show? The show you just seen." I hunched my shoulders. "What's your opinion of the theater?" I shrugged again. He imitated me. "Is this all you do?" He hunched his shoulders up and down fast. "You don't talk?"

"What theater?" I said.

"What theater? The one you was just in."

"You mean the Germ?"

"The what?"

"The Germ."

"That ain't the Germ. It's the Gem. Can't you read? Read the name over the door. Read me the name. Go on."

"Says the Gem."

"Case closed."

"May say the Gem, but we call it the Germ. Or the Garlic Box."

He took a cigar stump out of his pocket, lit it with a match, watched the flame flare and flicked the match into the street. "Well," he said, "meet the new owner." He sighed. "I'm twenty-two years old, and what do I have to show for it? I quit school when I was twelve. Should of quit when I was ten." A rat scurried across the road and disappeared under some bushes. "What do you want to do," he asked me, "worry your mother to death? Don't you know your mother is the best friend you'll ever have? She's sitting at home, and she don't know where you are. You only have one mother. You ain't going to get another one. You have one chance to treat her good, and what do you do? You run out in your pajamas and go to a dirty show. Where's the smartness in this kind of behavior?" He took a puff on his cigar. "Do you know what I'd do to see my sainted mother one more time? For even a second? I'd give you this arm. That's what I would do to see her for a split second." He took a few more puffs, tamped the cigar on the porch steps, dropped the butt in his jacket pocket and stood up. "Come on. I'll walk you home."

As we were cutting across the square, I saw Freckles with a woman who looked like him, straw hair, freckles all over her face. Her lips were painted bright red and her cheeks were painted like a doll's cheeks. Before we turned the corner, I saw her cuff Freckles on the forehead, and he wilted.

The stranger had a fast, choppy walk. I ran along next to him planning my escape but wondering where to sleep. "First thing I'm going to do," the man said, "is change the name. Going to call it the Orpheum. Give it some class."

I selected one in a row of sleeping two-family houses. "This is it. Thanks a lot, mister."

"The name's Louie. Louis Mayer. Louis B. Mayer. Remember that."

"Okay," I said and walked down the front path to the dark backyard. A watchdog lunged at me with a roar and jerked itself against its collar. Lights snapped on as I ran past Louie and down the street. I ran until I collapsed behind some milk cans.

"Couldn't be that bad, could it?" Louie was looking down at me. "What could be so bad? What did he do? Beat you with a belt? That's what mine did. One day I turned on him. That ended that. Come on," Louie said. "It's after midnight. What are you, six, seven?"

"No! Nine and a half."

He held up his hands in mock surrender. "Tell you what. Sleep at my place. Tomorrow's another day." He smacked a mosquito by his ear.

"No, thank you," I responded. If I could just put my head down on the grass for one second, just one second, I could think clearer.

I woke up on a blanket in a cramped room, a baby crying, a toddler making cymbals out of pot lids, which did not wake a bearded man on a mattress on the floor. In the room were an old table, chairs, a crib, a sewing machine, logs stacked next to a woodstove, an icebox dripping into the pan under it, a washtub and a basket of coal. A breeze made the gauzy dime-store curtains huff inward. Outside, I heard the clang of the trolley and shouts of children playing.

A young woman with dark hair coiled atop her head was sitting in a rocking chair with her blouse unbuttoned, placing a baby to her breast. When she noticed I was awake, she covered her breast with a shawl and said to me, "So. You're awake. You can call me Maggie. Louie's wife.

And you could earn a blessing, if you would. You see the pan under the icebox? Dump out the water. Will you do that for me?"

The young woman was lost in her nursing baby, smiling down at it, in a world of perfect and exclusive contentment. Until the toddler forced her to come back by banging on her knee and saying, "Up. Up." Maggie showed the toddler a dreamy smile. "Up!" the toddler commanded and stamped her foot.

"Wait a minute, Edie," Maggie said. Trying to accommodate the toddler, she pulled herself away from the baby, who protested. "Wait, I…tsk!" There was a jumble of babies and crying, but Maggie got it arranged: one child on her knee and the baby resettled at her breast. "It's like I don't even own my own body," she said to the air. "But I was born for this. This is the reason I was put on this earth." I could hear the baby sucking, a distinctive sound I remembered from my old neighborhood. The man on the mattress snorted loudly and turned over. "My cousin," Maggie whispered. "From the old country. I think I have a job lined up for him."

I stood up, went to the icebox, pulled the pan out from underneath and carried it carefully to a soapstone sink, dumped the water and replaced the pan. I used to empty the icebox pan for my mother and was proud of the way I kept the water from sloshing onto the floor. "Thank you, dear," Maggie said. "That's a big help." Her gaze was soft, unchallenging. "You're very thin," she said. "My Louie was a very thin little boy too. His mother, of blessed memory, told me. No matter how much she fed him. People used to say to her, you don't feed him enough, but she did. He was just thin, like you, boychick." She stopped paying attention to me and fell to kissing the toddler's cheek. As I went to the door, she said, "Maybe you'll have a nosh before you go home? There's some challah in the bread box." I sat at the kitchen table and chewed the taste of my past, and a wave of hopelessness washed over me. "You'll come Friday night," Maggie said, and I realized she had been regarding me for a while. "You'll come have dinner—roast chicken, tsimmis, which is a stew of carrots, and..."

"I know what tsimmis is," I said in Yiddish.

"Well, what do you know!" Maggie exclaimed.

"Where's Louie?"

"Come Friday night, you'll see your friend. Whatever he's doing, wherever he is, we have Sabbath dinner together. Are you acquainted with Shabbat?" I nodded and walked toward the door. As I opened it, she said, "Boychick, what's your name?" I told her, but she couldn't pay attention because the toddler jumped off her lap and fell and starting screaming, and the baby started crying, and the man on the mattress woke up. I went out and found myself on a dirt street of identical two-story wooden houses. A cow had wandered into someone's yard. A child pointed at me, which made me remember I was wearing pajamas. Would people start calling me Pajamas, as we did the soiled drunk on Orchard Street who didn't have any other clothes?

Maybe this was the day that Uncle Sonny would arrive, and he would see me walking around in my pajamas. I ran from dirt roads to cobblestones and through town. When I got to the Gem, I was surprised to see Louie there in the middle of a hubbub of construction. Men were tearing clapboards off the building, pounding nails into the roof, unloading wood from a wagon, tossing trash out the windows. Louie was gesturing wildly to another man. "Don't talk to me about code! A marquee has to cover the sidewalk. You want my patrons to stand unsheltered in the rain? You want people to say Louis B. Mayer runs a low-class establishment? The marquee has to extend forty-six and one-half inches and it's got to be lit up with four thousand bulbs."

"It ain't my call, Mr. Mayer."

"Ain't this your town? Don't you got pride in your own town? I come here, I try to uplift the people, and this is how you repay me. Listen, Frank, I'm in debt six hundred dollars. I come here with the intention of bringing the finest in motion-picture entertainment to the people," Louie said, taking off his spectacles and pinching the bridge of his nose. "I know you're just doing your job, Frank. But the public ain't stupid. You can't throw any old thing at the public. The public is smarter than I or you are."

A wagon horse, bored and hot in its harness, pierced the air with a sharp whinny. Louie, in his abrupt and choppy way, strode toward the wagon and, like one possessed, unloaded lumber and stacked it. His energy inspired the others, and they picked up their pace.

I crept along the edge of town, trying to stay out of sight, and ducked into an alley. Soon there would be no cover, and I would have to be a boy in his pajamas walking through town. The pajamas were one piece with a buttoned flap over the backside. At the end of the alley a pair of legs was sticking out from behind a trash barrel, and the sound of crying came from there. It was Freckles, sitting against the building with his face in his hands.

He looked up. "Oh, hi, Harry." He sniffed and wiped his nose with the back of his hand and rubbed the slime on his trousers. He wiped his eyes with his hand and tasted the tears. I stood there looking down at him, then sat down next to him. After a while, he said, "I wish I was you."

"Me? Are you kidding?"

"No, I ain't kidding, Harry."

"But why, Freckles?"

He fished a dirty handkerchief out of his pocket, wiped his forehead, showed me the dirt that came off. "You read real good. Everyone knows that, Harry. Everyone knows you're the smartest boy in the whole school."

"No, I'm not, Freckles."

"How come you come out in your pajamas, Harry?"

A vision of Kyle in the dark swamped me with shame. "I don't know," I said.

Freckles looked directly at me with his pale eyes fringed with white lashes. I tried to meet his gaze in a steady way, but my eyes flicked away. Once again, I was surprised by how eyes had a life of their own and always told the truth, separate little moral orbs that didn't compromise when I was pretending. Tactful, Freckles did not press me.

Flies buzzed around the trash cans lined up in the alley. "I could help you, Freckles," I said in what I thought was a jaunty voice. "When school starts, you show me your homework and I'll try to help you."

"They're keeping me back." His fingernails were chewed to the quick. "I done fifth grade already, Harry."

"Then it will be easier this year. You'll see. You'll fly right through it."

He yanked at a thumbnail for a while. "Guess what, Harry?"

"What."

"I never had a best friend before."

Had it come to this? My place was supposed to be among the brightest and best. Neighbors used to smile when they saw the gang of us. "With such boys," they used to say, "What's to worry?" But at my new school, the children whose great grandparents had settled Haverhill, who lived in stately houses with private stables, were royalty. One of them, Elsie Cogswell, was the prettiest girl I had ever seen, but when I talked to her, she was painfully polite. She and her friends included me in their games at recess but never invited me to their parties. Even the nitwits in that crowd were treated with deference by the teachers.

Now here I was being offered friendship by a boy I wouldn't have looked at a year ago. So this was need. This was humility. I gratefully accepted his soiled and sweaty shirt and buttoned it over my pajamas. For me, he would walk through the streets in his undershirt. We arrived at the Elizabeth Home in time to see Lady Mother gathering the rest of the children into a bus for an outing. I was afraid to see Kyle and held Freckles back with me behind a tree. Lady Mother did not see us, and the bus pulled away.

The house felt hollow with the children away. Freckles and I went to the kitchen expecting Cook to be there, but she wasn't. We raided the icebox, ate ham left from Sunday dinner, cold mashed potatoes, freshly baked cookies right from the cookie sheet. When we heard Cook in the front hall, we ran upstairs two steps at a time and collapsed on our beds, laughing. It felt so good to laugh like that, belly shaking, the ice inside breaking loose. It was the first big laugh I'd had with anyone since arriving in Haverhill. I marked it and thought, I will never forget this boy.

The bedding was gone from Kyle's cot, and the shelf where he kept his school books was empty. The chest for his clothes was cleaned out. Not a trace of him. I put my hand under my pillow hoping Kyle had returned my swan and pulled out pieces: head, wings, amputated feet and a tiny orange beak severed from its head. This was too much loss. I gave in, and Freckles patted my back in a tender, awkward way.

Chapter Four

On Thanksgiving, members of the Children's Aid Society came through the front door bearing holiday bounty: turkeys, cranberries, mashed potatoes, gravy, stuffing and pecan pies. They invaded Cook's kitchen and bustled around heating things up and arranging food on platters. Their confidence was impenetrable. They reeked of comfort and the conviction that God was praising them. They spoke to me in a cooing voice.

They believed their example was beneficial, so they brought their children. This was the day those children were to learn that it is better to give than to receive. But the children were not strangers. I knew them from school. They were dressed in satin and lace while I sat in my secondhand clothes at a long table with my hands folded in my lap, as instructed.

Elsie Cogswell was among them, looking even more beautiful than she did when the sun shone through her golden hair as she played jacks on the playground. Now she could see with her own eyes where I lived. I knew her house. Everyone did. She lived in the Cogswell estate, and once, when I was exploring Haverhill, I walked by her street and rested for a moment on a stone wall. Just then she cantered bareback across her meadow on a white pony. Did she think these ragamuffins at the table mirrored me? Did she imagine me grateful to her?

She was not the only reason I didn't want to be there. This was the day that Louie was opening his new theater.

A banner at the entrance read "Your Orpheum Theater! Grand Opening Thanksgiving Day! Come see *The Life of Christ from the Annunciation to the Ascension in Twenty-Seven Beautiful Scenes.*" Lady Mother was horrified that I wanted to spend the day inside a motion-picture hall, especially one that had so recently been a burlesque theater. She put her palm over her heart and said, "No. Absolutely not. Out of the question. Simply out of the question." She said this as if I'd asked her to lift her skirt in public.

So I sat smoldering at the table in the dining room as Elsie, her blue velvet sash matching the blue velvet ribbons on her braids, lowered a bowl of mashed potatoes next to me and said in an unnatural, practiced way, "Won't you have some mashed potatoes?" She had been schooled, obviously, on how to behave toward the less fortunate—polite, correct and keeping a kindly distance. The hands that held that heavy stoneware bowl were trembling slightly from fatigue.

Furious, humiliated by finding myself at such a disadvantage, I punched the bowl upward, and white blobs of potato flew out. The bowl crashed and split apart. The sound made everything go dead for a second until Mrs. Cogswell called across the room in a scolding voice, "Elsie!" The other volunteers filled in the silence with reassuring clucking: "That's all right. Accidents happen—no harm done." During the flurry of mops and sponges, for the first time, though we were in the same advanced reading group in school, Elsie met my eyes and did not flick hers away. She knew it wasn't an accident. She glared at me, waiting for me to be chivalrous, to speak up and take the blame. When I said nothing, she put more energy into her eye beam, which she imagined would wither me. We were locked in combat with our eyes. Yes, I am not grateful. Take your food and shove it. Right, I am just like you. I'm as proud as they come. She lowered her eyelids and blushed.

Lady Mother shot me the hard eye and pointed upstairs, but I did not accept banishment. I pretended to, just to avoid a scene, but when Lady Mother's back was turned, I grabbed my winter jacket, snuck out the back door and ran into town under a cold, white November sky.

The streets of Haverhill were almost deserted because most people were home celebrating Thanksgiving. Downtown, on the sidewalk, a scratchy-sounding automatic barker blared out, "Step right up, folks. Come inside. Step right up, folks. Come inside." The old Garlic Box had a fresh coat of white paint but no marquee over the sidewalk. The box office was a separate little closet with Maggie inside, looking cheerful behind the window. "Harry, dear," she said putting her mouth next to the open slot, "come around here and look at my ledger book." I was surprised she remembered me because I had not seen her since I woke up in her house that time in the summer.

There was barely room in the box office for Maggie alone. She was about twenty-four, though to me at age ten, she seemed a mature matron, soft with a slight smell of soap. When I opened the box-office door, she welcomed me by putting her arm around my waist and pulling me close to her so we could fit. She did this with no shyness, just hugged me close to her as if it was perfectly natural. She had no reserve at all, nothing in her held back from me, and she took this so much for granted that I dared to cuddle next to her. "Each day," she said, opening a black book with the hand that wasn't holding me close, "I will enter on the debit side our expenses, such as rent, electricity, film rental, slides, advertising, salaries. And each day on the credit side," she pointed to red margins, "I will enter our earnings. That's called bookkeeping." She tore a ticket off a large roll of tickets and gave it to me. "Friday night, you'll come to us. Put some meat on those bones."

"I can pay for my ticket. I saved a nickel from my job at the Bijou."

"The Bijou? Don't mention the Bijou. We don't want to know from the Bijou." She opened the box-office door and gently shifted her body so I was forced on the other side of it. She pulled the door closed behind me, blew me a kiss and looked down at her ledger book.

Dressed in a three-piece suit and stiff white collar, Louie was at the theater door. "Welcome to the Orpheum Theater, the little theater 'round the corner," he said, as he accepted tickets from four lumberjacks in plaid jackets who towered over him. When I gave him my ticket, he said, "Welcome to the Orpheum Theater, the little theater 'round the corner," but then he recognized me. "Don't be such a stranger," he said, as I went inside. The theater was still lopsided, with a warped floor. Tobacco stains on the walls showed through coats of whitewash. Three women in large hats were already sitting in the front row. The three women opened their compacts and sneaked backward peeks at the lumberjacks. When some sailors entered, the women opened their compacts again. The town drunk wobbled in, pressed his ticket into Louie's palm and walked tipped backward to a seat on the aisle.

To start the show, Louie pulled a switch on the wall. The automatic barker stopped abruptly: "Step right..." The house lights dimmed, and a player piano, keys bouncing up and down by themselves, played *Bicycle Built for Two*, as Louie projected the lyrics onto the screen. He sang the loudest of everyone: "Daisy, Daisy, give me your answer do! I'm half crazy, all for the love of you..."

When he projected the slide "Ladies, We Like Your Hats, but Please Remove Them," the sailors called out, "That means you, girls!" One of the women turned around and said, "Excuse me, sir, where are your manners?" Louie projected another slide: "We Aim to Present the Pinnacle of Motion Picture Perfection." One of the lumberjacks took a swig from his flask. Louie threaded the projector but didn't do it correctly, and the image jumped in a frenzy of misaligned sprocket holes.

Projector threaded, the screen lit up with a Biograph newsreel of the San Francisco earthquake. We saw parched earth, a mosaic of cracks with wide fissures where the earth had pulled apart. Office buildings and houses in the background went up in flames, and the flames spread to the next building, which exploded in fire. Soon all the buildings were in a roaring blaze. There were no people in the picture, no police barriers holding back frantic crowds pushing forward for news of their mothers or fathers, no placid people just watching the sight, no horses, no trolleys on tracks, no automobiles. There were no fire wagons shooting water through hoses. Luckily, the reel lasted only three minutes because I was about to shout, "Louie! Turn that off!" I couldn't have stayed in my seat for another second, and it took all my self-control not to start crying. Sometimes, as I was falling asleep at night, I saw those girls at the windows leaping out. Once, much to my chagrin, I woke up to find Lady Mother shaking me, and I came out of a nightmare into her rigid arms that pulled me close to her scratchy bathrobe while she murmured, "There, there. There, there."

Louie projected his main feature, a series of tableaux about the life of Jesus, who seemed to be wearing a diaper. He lugged a cross as people in togas, their eyes heavenward, followed after him. The audience was hushed when the lights went on, as if they had seen Jesus in person. I was a bit confused myself. Was Jesus still alive?

"Thank you all for coming," Louie said above *Oh! Susanna*, racing away on the player piano. "Remember! When it comes to entertainment you can trust, you can trust the little theater 'round the corner."

The sailors eyed the women, the lumberjacks eyed the women, and they all walked out to the renewed sounds of the mechanical barker outside: "Step right up, folks. Come inside…" Louie rewound the film, but he did it incorrectly, and the reel slipped off the projector, film blossoming all over the floor. I ran to help gather the loops of film. I disentangled it while Louie wound it back on the reel by hand. A rash the color of a baboon's bottom flared across his cheeks. Maggie entered holding the cash box. Her husband was now sitting on a theater seat pressing his fingertips into his temples. "There's too much light," he said in a weak voice, eyes closed. "Maggie, get rid of the light."

She whispered to me, "You'll come, too. Take the girls out. He can't take any noise when he gets like this."

Louie tried to appear fit and buoyant in case people were looking out the windows in the houses we passed, but Maggie and I heard his intermittent groans. Once home, Maggie guided him to a bed in a tiny bedroom, and he lay flat on his back, eyes closed, as she pulled the shades down. Then she held a washcloth under cold water, wrung it out and placed it on Louie's forehead. She closed the door softly. The mattress in the kitchen where the cousin with the beard had been sleeping was vacant, covered with children's clothes, sewing equipment, blankets. "They're downstairs," Maggie whispered. "Go get them now."

"Is he sick?" I whispered.

"It's his sinus."

"What's a sinus?"

"What's a sinus? It's in your nose someplace."

"Like a bugger?"

"No. Not like that. I don't know. He gets terrible headaches. Just go, Harry. Take the girls outside."

"Maggie?"

"What? What now?"

"Is Jesus still alive?"

"Who?"

"Jesus."

"Harry, I can't leave Louie alone right now. Please go downstairs, and give some relief to Mrs. Cohen. She has six of her own. Please."

"Was that really him in the photoplay?" She was done with me and went into the bedroom to adjust the cloth on Louie's forehead.

I collected Edie and Irene from the apartment below and pushed them in their carriage on the street outside. It was gratifying to see how they flirted with me even though they were so little. They made me share their cookies and seemed to think I was the funniest person who had ever lived. Maggie, noting how happy they were when I returned, bartered with me. I could attend every show at the Orpheum for free in exchange for babysitting at least one afternoon a week so she could go to the meetings of the Blossoms of Zion.

I became comfortable at Louie's house, sitting at his table on Friday nights inhaling the cozy fragrance of roast chicken. Maggie and he did not ask me about my parents or where I lived. I understood this reticence to be tact.

Louie's theater had been open a few months and still people stayed away. Maggie had a straight forward solution: "Go invite them, Louie." So he did. He visited the Blossoms of Zion, the Workmen's Circle, the Sons of Italy, the Ladies' Helping Hand Society, the German, Irish and Russian clubs, speaking to some through translators. He told the various memberships that there was no better way to teach children American ways than to let them see American players doing American things on the screen. As for learning geography, a picture was worth a thousand words. He admitted that his theater had a bad reputation but promised to show only pictures he would show to his own little girls. He promised big donations to each organization.

"There ain't no country in the world better than the United States of America," he said one Friday night after another profitable week. "Don't you ever forget that. What other country has such opportunity? What other country welcomes the tired and the poor?" Instead of setting the drumstick on my plate, he withheld it, and I understood this was a quiz.

"None."

"You're telling me. You know the name of the president?"

"Me? Of course. William Howard Taft." Louie put the drumstick on my plate.

"Did you vote for him, Louie?"

"What kind of question is that? How could I vote when I ain't a citizen." Through a full mouth, he said, "You didn't know that, right?"

"Where do you come from?"

"St. John, Canada. It's a hilly town. Up and down, up and down. I lugged scrap metal up and down. I come to Boston where I met Maggie. I vow to her we will never live with her parents again. My mother kissed the hem of Maggie's garment."

"Why?"

"Why? Here, eat some challah. Why do you think? She was so happy I found a good wife. I talk to her every day. She's with me all the time, right on my shoulder."

"Who?"

"My mother, who do you think? I ask her advice. I listen when she tells me do this, do that, trust this one, don't trust that one. You can accomplish great things, son. I listen when she tells me that."

"But if she's dead, how does she tell you?"

"I don't know. I don't know how it happens, but she talks to me from the other side of the grave."

I sighed so deeply it made a squeak. "Mine doesn't," I said.

Louie and Maggie exchanged a look. "Not all of them do," Louie said. "Don't mean she's not watching over you. Maybe she was a quieter person than mine. Was she quiet?"

"Sometimes."

"You ever hear her scream at anybody?"

"Oats."

"So then, that's the answer. Screaming wore out her voice. That's all that means. Believe me, it don't mean she's not watching out for you."

"Then how come she let Kyle break my swan?"

"How come? What do you think, she's God? She ain't God. And how do you know what she's going to do to what's-his-name Kyle. How do you know? Do you know everything that's going to happen? Do you? Do you know everything that's going to happen?"

"No."

"You're damn right you don't. So don't tell me she ain't going to punish what's-his-name." That night I took the photograph of my father from my pocket and showed it to them.

Chapter Five

A few years later, when the wooden stables on Merrimack Street came up for sale, Louie and two investors bought them. They constructed one of the largest theaters in New England, the fifteen-hundred seat Colonial for movies and vaudeville. The Colonial was important enough to have its program listed in New York trade journals. It was an opulent show palace, marble staircase to the balcony, paintings in rococo gold frames. Louie's favorite was a recumbent lion in profile. A stuffed moose's head protruded over the door to the auditorium. The mayor and other prominent citizens attended opening night and made speeches about Haverhill's industrial growth. To wild applause, Louie marched onto the stage as the orchestra played *Hail to the Chief*. In his speech, he said, "The Colonial is the zenith of my ambitions."

A full orchestra accompanied every movie while a sound-effects man stood behind a screen clanging bells, slamming doors, galloping horses, popping Champagne corks, firing guns. We never thought of our movies as silent. They weren't.

The biggest names in vaudeville came to the Colonial: dancer Bill "Bojangles" Robinson, singer Eva Tanguay, Hardeen the Handcuff King who escaped from the Crazy Crib—a crate used to confine lunatics in asylums. Gertrude Hoffman, the dancer, earned $3,000 per week. J. Robert Pauline, the hypnotist, earned $2,000 per week. The salaries were mentioned in *The Gazette* so audiences understood that Louie was bringing them something special.

In eighth grade, I joined the staff of *The Thinker*, the school newspaper. I made up a job called entertainment editor and wrote a column entitled "Don't Applaud, Just Throw Money." My pieces about each female entertainer began "Miss So-and-So never looked lovelier..." followed by a description of her clothes, "in a cunning hat and a light opera cape from her varied wardrobe," words copied directly from the press release that accompanied each film tin.

None of the stars would talk to a schoolboy except for Jimmy Durante. He was not yet the famous "Schnozzola" and was still performing at Diamond Tony's in Coney Island. Wearing a silk bathrobe that exposed thin, white legs and socks held up by garters, he spoke to me while I took down his words as fast as I could. "Every time I went down the street, I'd hear, 'Lookit, the big-nose kid!' And when anybody'd stare, I'd just sneak off. Even if they said nothin', nothin' at all, I'd shrivel up and think they was sayin', 'What an ugly kid! What a monster!' And then I'd go home and cry. Even when I am makin' a fortune on account of the big beak, and while I am out there on the stage laughin' and kiddin' about the nose, at no time was I ever happy about it."

The title of my interview with Durante was "I Don't Want Nobody to Put Me on a Pedasill." After it was published, a kid in sixth grade with a gigantic nose showed me a letter he had written and wanted me to send to Durante. "I've got a big nose, Mr. Durante. Everybody laughs at it. But then I saw you at the Colonial, and you kept laughing about your nose. That made me feel good all over." By then Durante had finished his run. I managed to find out where he was performing and forwarded the letter to him. I don't know if he ever received it, but after that heartfelt encounter with the sixth-grader, I felt as if I was contributing to the greater good.

When describing female photoplayers, I only wrote about their clothes. I didn't really know burlap from linen. Movie stars were responsible for their own wardrobes, so women in the audience were really seeing the personal taste of their idols. One of the most popular fashion icons was fifteen-year-old Anita Stewart, employed by Vitagraph, a major studio in Brooklyn. All across America, little girls, Louie's included, were cutting out Anita Stewart paper dolls.

When Louie showed one of her films at the Colonial, I wrote a review, half copied, half original: "Miss Stewart wore an attractive bathing cloak in the beach scene where she posed on the sands. In the parlor scene, she looked very striking in a cloak of ermine tied shawl fashion 'round her shoulders. Anita Stewart stands second to none in popularity among the moving-picture stars. She is a true daughter of the films, for unlike most of her rivals, she has never appeared in the spoken drama."

Never entered my head that one day I'd laugh with her about this piece.

Chapter Six

The Elizabeth Home was required to provide for children in need until the age of fourteen, the age when it became legally possible to quit school. For most of my house mates, this was not a problem because they wanted to leave school. Freckles, for instance, was pursued by the truant officer until the day he turned fourteen. He then packed his bag, hugged the living daylights out of me at the train depot and said I was the best friend he had ever had and that he would never throw away the orange swan beak I had given him.

After the train pulled away, filling the sky with smoke, I saw his mother in the shadow of the maple tree next to the station house. She was a bedraggled creature, too young to have a fourteen-year-old son. She stood there forlorn before coming toward me, probably for consolation. She assumed I was sad about Freckles leaving, but I wasn't. Now I had other friends, Oscar and Bruno, two energetic pals who lived with their parents in town. They were impatient with Freckles, with his slowness and his devotion to me. Freckles waited at the edge while we talked about the books we read, *Wrecked on Spider Island, Search for Silver City, Captured by Apes.* Freckles tagged along when we dug mushrooms and compared them to pictures in our guidebook, delighting most in the ones that would kill us. He tried to contribute when we discussed Lieutenant Robert E. Peary, the Arctic explorer photographed with icicles in his beard. Peary was searching for the North Pole and believed he would find it sticking out of the earth. Freckles asked, "Why don't he ice skate to the pole?" I am ashamed to report that I pretended not to see his mother the day Freckles left Haverhill.

When I was thirteen and about to graduate from elementary school, my teachers encouraged me to work hard in high school so I could earn a scholarship to college. None of them mentioned the inconvenient fact that I couldn't stay at the Elizabeth Home past the age of fourteen. I assumed, because I vaguely believed all adults were in some sort of club together, that the teachers had spoken to Lady Mother and that some special accommodation was being arranged for me. Maybe they were going to let me stay at the home in exchange for tutoring the younger children. Then I would go to Yale and come back to visit wearing a beanie like Elsie Cogswell's brother.

The population at the Elizabeth Home was always transient—kids coming in, kids going out—but lately, there were many more coming in than going out. I was surprised to hear that they were not from Haverhill but from Amesbury, Newburyport, Georgetown and other cities close by. At the same time that there were more mouths to feed, it was obvious that our volunteers had lost interest. The women who had bustled about when I first arrived were now championing the cause of women's suffrage. Members of the bedding committee, instead of showing up with more sheets, now marched in parades holding signs that read "Good Wives and Good Mothers Make Good Voters." When the comedian Felix Honey performed a skit called "The Suffragette Family," the women picketed Louie's theater. "Felix Honey Belittles Women" and "Women's Suffrage Is No Joke" read the signs. Volunteers who had brought food to the home now stood on the street holding placards for the opposition: "Suffragists Are She-Males" and "The Vote Is a Burden" and "If Men Have Failed in Government, It Is the Fault of the Women Who Trained Them." One stout woman stood on a soap box saying, "We are not afraid of the masculine woman but have grave fears for the woman who confuses the work of man and woman and attempts to do both."

The population of Massachusetts was growing so fast that orphanages across the state were overcrowded. The rule, when I arrived in Haverhill, was that each town had to take care of its own. In wealthy towns, the orphanages were well supplied and comfortable. In towns where the citizens were too poor to be generous, the orphanages were less than adequate. So the wealthy towns had to take in children from the poorer towns. The problem with this was it took away the feeling of personal responsibility from the good citizens of prosperous towns. Our benefactors resented having to support the children of strangers. The bankers, coal magnates and shoe-manufacturing tycoons of Haverhill ceased to feel that the Elizabeth Home was their personal cause. I remember Lady Mother's distress when our roof began to leak and no one came to fix it.

Since most people preferred to adopt a baby rather than an older child, the state, in its effort to empty the orphanages, came up with the idea that it should be possible for a family to give shelter to a child without having to legally adopt the child. Lady Mother called foster care the child-rental system. "If a family has to be paid by the state to take in a child, that family cannot be trusted. They will use the money for drink." In some cases, overcrowding in orphanages was relieved by sending children out West to help on farms. Reports claimed some of the children were treated like slaves.

The Elizabeth Home was in such financial trouble that the acreage it sat on had to be sold. Bulldozers and steam shovels dug up our playground and ball field. There was no front yard anymore. We heard hammering and sawing all day long. The tree where I had seen a robin's nest with three blue eggs in it was replaced by a new house almost identical to the new house next to it. A grid of new streets was named for presidents Hamilton, Lincoln and Adams.

Louie and Maggie lived in one of the new houses. Maggie was delighted that there was more room for relatives who arrived from the Old Country lugging their own featherbeds. There was a continual parade of strangers on Friday nights at Sabbath dinner, four or five women with babushkas on their head and men with long beards.

One day, Lady Mother, flicking her fan in an agitated way, beckoned to me as I was going out the door to school. "Harry," Lady Mother said, "I have something to discuss with you." A rotund man I had never seen before was sitting in the front parlor. His clothes were shiny but not from wear. They were supposed to be like that, silky jacket, silky white shirt, tan shoes made of pimpled leather. He appraised me when I entered, evaluating my every move. "Harry," Lady Mother said, "it has been decided to close the Elizabeth Home."

"Excuse me?" Lady Mother did not repeat the words, just waited for them to hit bottom. "But I have another year," I said.

Lady Mother took a lace hanky from her sleeve and patted her nostrils. "You know my feelings about foster care. I have made my feelings known throughout the community." She snapped her fan closed and snapped it open *flick, flick, flick*. "We've located an excellent family for you, respectable and hard working."

"But I'm only thirteen. I have another year." My heart was thudding against my ribs. Let me out of here! Let me out of here!

The man stood up, took a watch from his pocket, looked at it and said, "You be ready to go by three, son." Through the window I saw him get into his Model T, put on goggles and leather helmet, and drive away.

"They value education, Harry," Lady Mother said, fanning, fanning. "They are farm people, but they value education."

Farm people? Did she think I didn't know what farm work was? Every year at haying time, I was required to help local farmers. We had no choice. This was the way we paid back the citizens of Haverhill who supported us. We were roused at dawn and driven to the fields. There we pitched hay into horse-drawn wagons as the sun rose in the sky—hotter, hotter, hotter—until I wished I was dead instead of scalded and pestered by gnats. The mounds of hay that had to be brought in before the rain were endless. Our whole world was the color of straw and the smell of cured grass. I hated that work and suffered headaches from the unrelenting sting of the sun. Anyone who complained was branded a sissy and an ingrate. It was a relief to find out in school that Nathaniel Hawthorne detested farm work too.

"You will want to withdraw your savings," Lady Mother said. "You will need it on your journey to Kansas."

"Kansas?"

She stood up–fanning, fanning–walked across the room and walked back. "These are difficult times. You're one of the lucky ones, Harry. I don't know what I'm going to do with the other boys. I just don't know. You'll have a roof over your head. You should be grateful for that. The Elizabeth Home is going to close within a few months. Our citizens know about this, but I do not think they know what it means. I have lived to see indifference in Haverhill."

Photographs in schoolbooks showed me Kansas farms: thousands of acres of wheat to the horizon, exhausted men with pitchforks lifting wheat into wagons, cattle pens full of droopy bovines waiting to be slaughtered.

"We cannot always do as we wish, Harry. Do you think this is easy for me? Do you think I will be allowed to stay on here? Is that what you think? Do you think they are going to let me continue living in the house where I have lived for the past thirty-five years?" She turned from me, and her posture melted. "No, of course you do not think about me. No farmer has agreed to take me in, Harry. I can assure you, no farmer has agreed to take me in."

Her? What did I care about her? I cared about me! I turned from her and ran upstairs. Some new boys were in the room playing cards, and they paid no attention to me as I stuffed some clothes into my pillowcase. I would go to Louie. He would save me. His new house was on the next block. But when I got there I remembered that he and his family were vacationing on Cape Cod. All the shades were pulled down, and his car was gone from the driveway.

I gathered myself together, emptying everything out of my mind except what I'd need to solve this problem.

First, get my savings. When I presented my bankbook, Cora, the teller, said, "I can't give you all your savings, Harry, without Lady Mother's permission."

"It's mine, isn't it?"

"In a way. But you're still a minor."

"Cora, I need that money."

I watched her go into the bank president's office, saw him listen to her and saw him peer around her to look at me. I'd known Mr. Cogswell for years, had presented my savings book to him every month since I was nine. I could hardly breathe. The helplessness of childhood made me claustrophobic. I watched the bank president talk on his phone, nod his head, then set the telephone earpiece back on its hook.

"All right, Harry," Cora said, taking her position behind the window. "You just have to sign here." I was so relieved, I felt tears threatening to swamp me. She finished counting the money, and I put ten dollars in my pocket. I went outside and retrieved my pillowcase bundle from behind a tree. No house in Haverhill was safe. Lady Mother was one of the most respected women in town. If she thought a farm in Kansas was good for Harry Sirkus, it was.

I recognized the Model T in front of Willet's Chop Shop as the one that the man in the silky clothes had driven. Now he emerged from the restaurant cleaning his teeth with a toothpick. He stood there on the sidewalk as two other men I had never seen before approached him. They conferred, then got into his car and drove toward the Elizabeth Home. I imagined them waiting for me there, binding me and hauling me away.

I ran to the train depot. The stationmaster knew me because I had interviewed him for my steam-engine project in the fifth grade. I was afraid he would send word to Lady Mother, but he sold me a ticket to Boston and went back to his word puzzle.

When the train pulled away, I was disappointed that no one cared enough to chase me. Even Freckles had someone to wave goodbye to him. I reminded myself that no one knew I was leaving, but that did not make me feel any less sorry for myself.

The conductor punched my ticket, eyed my satchel and continued his rounds. I moved to a window seat hoping that passing scenery would lessen my melancholy. New England farms, usually so picturesque, made me envision farms in Kansas. The train chugged along until Lawrence, where it stopped. I felt hungry and remembered one of my friends saying he was going to invent a pill that would take the place of dinner. "Hey ho, pal," said a warm voice from the aisle. "Mind if I join you?"

A hearty young man smiled down at me, a factory worker in lace-up boots. I was sitting in one of those enclosures that train seats make when you turn one around to face the other. My bundle was on the seat facing me. I did not feel like company and found it annoying that he sat down across from me when the whole car was practically empty. I reached for my bundle. "Leave it, leave it," he said. "I don't mind." He put his bundle on the seat next to me. I continued to gaze out the window, but the view was not the same because his reflection was in the window. I tried to peer beyond his reflection but gave up and watched him mirrored in the window. He did not catch my eye in the glass and paid no attention to anyone, just opened his satchel and took out salami, cheese and bread. He began to chew with his mouth open. The aroma of garlic and smelly cheese shot longing into my belly. He cut off a piece of cheese and handed it across to me. I hesitated, but he offered it with more insistence. Finally, I put it in my mouth and was grateful.

"Butch," he said, pointing at himself with his thumb. "What can I do you out of?" I planned to remember this greeting, which sounded tough and cool. He cut a coin of salami and handed it to me. "Friends call me Butch. You play cards?" He took a deck from his breast pocket and shuffled in a dramatic cascade from one palm to the other. The showy shuffle was something my friends and I admired. Practice, however, reminded us that we were still children because our hands were not yet big enough to control the cards. "Gin rummy?" He sat down next to me using the space between us as a table. I fanned my cards, saw that I had a great hand, let him play a card and went out. "Already? I have nothing," he said, showing me his hand, adding up out loud. "Keep score in my head." We played several more hands, chitchatting about the new features of various automobiles. "Your parents meeting you at the station, Pal?"

"I don't have any parents."

"On your own, are you?"

"I guess so."

By the time we arrived at North Station, having discussed player by player the merits of the Red Sox as opposed to the Boston Braves, Butch had promised to help me find a place to stay. In the crush of passengers getting off the train, we walked down a long platform to the terminal, an enormous space where hundreds of men and women hurried this way and that, speakers full of static announced arrivals and departures, and skycaps pushed luggage carts. "Wait here," Butch said. "I'll go con a cabby." I obeyed, passing the time by reading the headlines of newspapers at the kiosk: "Austria Formally Declares War on Serbia," "Russia Threatens, Already Moving Troops," "Peace of Europe Now in Kaiser's Hands."

Perhaps I misunderstood Butch. Maybe he said I should wait for him outside. I followed one of the ramps and found myself outside on the sidewalk, surprised that the air smelled of fish and stunned by the enormous activity of the city: rush-hour traffic, horses, automobiles, police whistles, sirens, office buildings made of red brick, billboards everywhere demanding attention all at the same time. Now it hit me. I'd been rash. I was too young and inexperienced for this. I'd been hasty. I'd been foolish. Butch would know what to do; he was a savvy guy. But he wasn't there. Every face was a stranger's face. Should I turn right, left, go straight across the wide cobblestone street? Crows pecked at horse manure, flew up out of the way, came down for another peck, flew back up over and over again. The squawk of seagulls mixed with car horns and trolley-bell clangs. Everyone seemed to have someplace definite to go as they hurried past me. I sat down on the curb to wait for courage.

At last I could focus and noticed a pretzel vendor on the corner. Even he seemed sinister, but I was hungry so I approached him. He held the pretzel until I could fish some coins from my pocket. I turned my pockets inside out, looked into my cap, dumped out my pillowcase. Gone. All of it. How? When? Butch didn't leave me a penny. How does a person like that get into your pocket and you don't even feel it? Panic threatened to mount its cannon. I stood very still and spoke sternly to myself. You must find a place to sleep before it gets dark. You must put one foot in front of the other. You must avoid the policeman directing traffic because he might know you are a truant. You must go now. Go now.

I might as well have been in Cairo or Tehran. It was as if I didn't even speak the language. Cobblestone streets wound around, twisted and ended up as dead ends. The sky darkened, and street lamps popped on, casting sinister shadows in doorways. Raucous laughter burst from the taverns: men went in; men lurched out; women in groups hurried by. If someone caught my eye, I wheeled around and headed off in the opposite direction. Dogs rummaged in garbage cans. I wondered if I had been on this street before. Was I walking in circles? How was I supposed to know if I was walking in circles? So this was what it meant to be blind with fear.

At last, too sleepy to take another step, I turned into an alley between dark warehouses and almost jumped out of my skin when a cat leaped from a window next to me. Palm over my heart to still its furious pounding, I noticed that the window was open, but there were no lights inside. Whatever was inside couldn't be worse than wandering around outside, so I crawled in. When my eyes became accustomed to the dark, I saw rolls of carpet stacked floor to ceiling. There was a woolly smell, and the stacked carpet muffled the street sounds outside. I sat on broadloom and finally lay down.

Sunlight and loud clattering woke me as well as a man's voice: "What the..." Then another voice: "You leave that window open again, Jed?" *Smash, rattle, jingle.* "No, suh, not me." Horse smell, rumbling horse lips. Two black men dressed in red military caps and jackets were looking down at me. When I scrambled backward to get away, they were alarmed and stepped back too. "Aw, he be all right," one of them said, and they ignored me and went back to hauling rolls of carpet out to the alley where eight Clydesdale horses wearing patent-leather harness were hitched to a brightly painted wagon. The horses stamped ponderous hooves fringed with white feathers. Harness bells jingled, and red pom-poms jiggled on black bridles. White manes were tightly braided; tails were cropped like shaving brushes. The wagon was silver with poppy red letters that read "Coleman Levin Carpets Will Surely Stand the Test of Hard Usage."

The men, dressed more like guards at Buckingham Palace than wagon drivers, heaved carpet into the wagons, saying, "Whoa, Bill" or "Easy, Ben." Then the wagons moved out of the alley, bells jangling, thirty-two massive hooves clattering on cobblestones—the sound of a regiment.

"Boy, you can't stay in here no more." A man dressed in drab worker's clothes was moving his hands in a hurry-up motion because he was waiting to lock the warehouse door. I stood next to him in the alley as he turned keys in several locks. "What you doing here, boy? What you doing sleeping in amongst carpet? Ain't you got no sense? They's rats eat a boy's foot off at the bone. I seen it. That's how rats is."

I ran to the end of the alley and out into the morning streets of Boston. Pedestrians hurried into buildings; merchants turned signs on front doors to "Open" and unrolled their awnings. Billboards on roofs advertised "Washburns Clothing, No Money Down", "Magee Furnaces and Ranges", "Walkers Kitchen Utensils", "Welsh Corn Salve." I came to a market square where dozens of wagons stood while sacks of flour, logs for stoves and slabs of beef were unloaded. Overhead, seagulls squawked; sparrows bounced on the cobblestones looking for crumbs. I wondered what I always wondered about sparrows. Do they look different to one another?

The perfume of bacon drew me to a coffee shop. Men in working clothes were eating in wooden booths. Waitresses shouted orders to a cook behind the counter. It seemed the most wonderful thing in the world to sit inside a restaurant and eat. I would say, "Bacon and eggs, please, scrambled. Three or four would do, and I notice you have muffins, two or three of those and..."

A muffin landed near my shoe. It was a corn muffin with a crusty brown border. I looked to see who had tossed it and caught the eye of a workman sitting at one of the tables. He saluted me and looked away. I considered being proud and leaving the thing on the floor, but deeply embarrassed, I grabbed it and ran to the nearest alley and gobbled it like a starved rat. So this was hunger.

I went in and out of stores and restaurants asking, "Do you have work for me?" Sometimes I passed a boy in similar straits. Our eyes locked, first asking if it might be possible to team up but deciding the other was just a tramp.

From history books at school, I recognized the golden dome of the Massachusetts State House and the manicured acres of the Boston Common, a park with gentle pathways and a pond where boats shaped like swans glided along. In shop after shop, I offered myself. By midday, I was tempted to steal food from an unsuspecting merchant. But if he nabbed me, the police would send me back to Haverhill and life on a Kansas farm.

At twilight, I found myself at the Boston Harbor, submerged in the putrid smell of low tide. Maybe I could stow away on one of the sailing ships docked there and end up in Borneo among good-hearted savages. The water in the harbor was a black cauldron, thick as oil. I could jump in there. Wouldn't Lady Mother be sorry at my funeral, all of Haverhill weeping at my grave and turning on her with pointed fingers. "You are to blame. You! You drove him off!" they'd say. Would the water freeze me or suffocate me first? What if I changed my mind, tried to climb out and couldn't get a grip on the seawall, fingers slipping on seaweed slime. Were there sharks in there? Was Moby Dick in there? Perhaps someone else decided to jump. His dead body would still be in there, and I would feel his hair against my arm. I ran back through the narrow streets of Boston.

I came to a stop in front a miniature display replica of the gaudy wagon I'd seen that morning. On the side were the words "Coleman Levin, Wholesale. Exclusive Distributor in New England of Bigelow Carpet." Through the building window, I saw a carpet showroom. Two men examined a piece of carpet, ran their hands back and forth on the pile and tried to tear the sample. They sat on a carpet roll and did some figuring with a pad and pencil. I went inside and took off my cap. "Excuse me, sir?"

Both men stood up, startled. The shorter one took charge by stepping forward but not in an aggressive way. He was a pleasant man with shy eyes. He called toward a door at the back of the showroom, "Ethel?" Then he turned to me. "Go on back, son. She'll give you something. Next time use the service door." Full of shame, I tried to cross the floor without stepping on any carpet. I had to tiptoe along narrow paths, step over wide rolls and make a fool of myself until I finally arrived at the open door of a small office.

A plump woman in middle years was sitting at a typewriter. "You know better than to go in the front way," she said. "Shame on you." From a desk drawer she extracted a nickel and held it toward me. The gesture was so practiced and fluid, I realized it was a policy of this place to have coins ready for giving to the needy.

Finding myself in the company of the lowest of the low, having eaten a muffin thrown on the floor that morning, was so excruciating that I stumbled backward. I was shocked by that view of myself, me, the crown of my mother's head. "I'm not a beggar," I whispered.

"Don't be silly," she said. "Take it. You need it. Don't be proud. That's foolish." She set the nickel near the edge of the desk, in easy reach. I stood as straight as I could. She went back to typing, and I stood there listening to some horrible hum inside my head.

After a while, the man from the showroom came in. "Jed deliver that chenille to Filene's?" he asked.

The secretary flipped through an appointment book. "At two-thirty, Mr. Levin."

He looked at his pocket watch. "Call over there tomorrow and tell them the dye lot isn't the same. If they aren't satisfied, I'll take it back." Then, much to my amazement, he said in Yiddish to Ethel, "Why is this chutzpanik still here?"

"Because I need a job, sir," I replied in Yiddish. "I may look like a bum right now, but I'm not. I'm competent at many things." By mistake I used the word brilliant.

Mr. Levin and Ethel exchanged a surprised eyebrow lift. "What, for instance," he said in Yiddish, "are you so brilliant at?" The phone rang. Ethel picked it up and handed it to Mr. Levin. "It's Mr. Gordon."

"Nate," Mr. Levin talked with half of himself, the other half thumbing through order forms, handing one every now and then to his secretary, who looked it over and filed it. "That's good news. I knew if anyone could convince him, Sally could. Say, Nate. Could you use a kid? I don't know. Just showed up here. Righto. Just thought I'd ask." He hung up, started flipping through the order forms again and said to me with his eyes lowered, "Where did you say you landed from, son?" I remained silent, though I liked this man. He was gentle and reminded me of an early day in summer when baby ducks were on the lake. "Don't you think it's my obligation to get in touch with your parents? I can see by your pillowcase that you've run away. What are you, ten, eleven?"

"No! Thirteen."

"Do you have someplace to sleep?" His voice was so kind it made my eyes sting, and water blurred my vision. To make the swelling tide stop, I clamped my back teeth together. I walked as proudly as possible out the back door and ran to the end of the street, where I sat down to compose myself. Lights went off in Mr. Levin's office, and I saw him and his secretary emerge. They said goodnight, and she walked away, but he just waited there. A limousine rolled slowly down the street and stopped. A chauffeur in uniform, a big, slow man who moved as if one false step would pinch some injury, held open the back door, and Mr. Levin ducked inside. The car door slammed with an expensive sound. I stood up to get a better view. Was it a Buick Model 25, a LeZebre Torpedo? No! It was a Peugeot 145S Torpedo Tourer Chassis No. 20644 Engine No. KC20644! In person! My favorite car!

The car stopped in front me, and Mr. Levin rolled down his window. "Come on," he said. "I'll find you work." He gestured for me to get in the back seat next to him, but I was cautious. "Don't fear. Get in. You need a bath, some food and a good night's sleep." He rolled up his window and waited. The only time I had ever seen a motorcar to compare was when Lionel Barrymore had come to Haverhill to perform at the Academy of Music. That car had dark leather front seats, corduroy back seats and headlights like protruding eyes. Now it was me who got into an interior of caramel leather. Mr. Levin, tired from his day's work, put his head back against the seat and closed his eyes as the automobile purred out of the city.

We drove to a suburb of big houses with hardly any land around them. I was used to stately homes sitting on wide skirts of meadows and ponds. Here in Brookline, the houses stood one right next to the other, almost no front yards and so little land surrounding them they seemed like people with heads that were too big. We turned into the driveway of a stone-and-clapboard mansion. The chauffeur, in his deliberate way, held the door for Mr. Levin, who said, "Give him something to eat, and put him to sleep in the carriage house."

The kitchen staff were all black people: cook, maid and a gray-haired butler. The chauffeur said, "Boss said give him some eats." He sat down at a table, picked up a racing form, lit a cigarette, opened the top buttons of his jacket and yanked his collar loose. The cook was mashing potatoes. The butler, wearing an apron over a black uniform, carved a large roasted chicken. The slices of white meat were symmetrical and lined up neatly when he set them on the platter. "I never saw anyone do that better than you do, sir," I said. There was so much saliva in my mouth I could hardly talk.

"This?" he said. "Oh, this ain't nothing. My daddy, now he's the one could carve."

The maid set down before me a plate of chicken, mashed potatoes and squash. I never imagined that a family might routinely eat like this. When I finished wolfing the food down, the chauffeur offered me a cigarette, and I sat at the table, smoking comfortably with him, while the cook put the finishing touches on dishes that the maid and butler carried on trays through a swinging door. I caught a glimpse of two children at a long table, a woman and Mr. Levin in a velvet smoking jacket. The boy was about my age, and once, just before the swinging door thwacked shut, his eyes met mine. I envied the aura of comfort that radiated from his scrubbed and polished face. He made me feel defeated.

Later, I followed the chauffeur to the carriage house in back where we climbed to the floor above the garage. He opened the door of a bathroom, gestured toward the tub and gave me a shove as if I might be reluctant to wash myself. "And use soap," he said through the door after closing it. I had never taken a bath alone in a bathtub. Here you could stretch your whole body out and not sit with your knees to your chin in a washtub.

I tiptoed to the door. Did I dare turn the lock? I turned the key as silently as possible. I took off my clothes and climbed in. When the water came over my thighs, I turned it off, not wanting to be greedy. The warm water soon turned cool so I dared let more hot in, and then I let the water run until it blanketed me, suspended me in liquid warmth. Heavenly.

When I got out, I felt slightly weak and vague and longed to lie down. But I didn't dare stay because when I pulled the plug and the water drained out, the dirt from my body left a ring around the tub, and there was no brush to scrub it off. Fingers didn't work, and I didn't want to get the fluffy towels dirty by using them for rags. I was not worthy of Mr. Levin's kindness. I'd messed up his bathroom. Clothes on, I turned the lock slowly so it would not click too loudly, tiptoed downstairs and ducked behind some bushes outside in front of the carriage house. I managed to get to the main house without being seen, and through a space in the heavy velvet drapery, I saw into the dining room where Mr. Levin sat at the table playing chess with his son. The young daughter was rolling a tennis ball to a black poodle. The mother sat knitting and looked up to hear what her daughter was saying. I had a moment of intense longing: the lighted house, the residents so comfortable and unconscious, at least right then, of anyone else's loneliness.

There was no place to go but back to the carriage house. I climbed upstairs to the chauffeur's bedroom, a space full of masculine objects, big shoes, uniform jackets, caps and long underwear. The smell was hair pomade and marijuana, smells I recognized from backstage at the Colonial. I sat on the floor and waited to be told where to sleep.

Chapter Seven

The chauffeur shook me awake the next morning. I'd slept on the floor of his room without realizing it. When he was dressed, he went with me across the driveway to the back door where dozens of sparrows were pecking at crumbs someone had thrown out to them. Breakfast was not oatmeal but eggs, bacon and thick toast with as much butter as you wanted. Did the children who lived here eat like this every morning?

After breakfast, I drove downtown with Mr. Levin who sat next to me in the back seat reading the *Boston Post*. The car came to a stop on a narrow street of livery stables. Stable boys pushed wheelbarrows, and a few spiffily dressed equestrians rode away on good-looking saddle horses.

It was obvious which was Mr. Levin's stable because his Clydesdales were out front, dwarfing the handlers who dressed them in patent-leather harness. Because of their size, the complicated assemblage of reins and the narrowness of the street, hitching the team to the wagon created a commotion: a staccato composition of hooves striking cobblestone, harness bells tinkling, horses snorting and seagulls screaming overhead. There was a cacophony of smells too: leather, horse, sea, hay.

Mr. Levin in a straw hat and a seersucker suit, escorted me inside. There were rows of empty box stalls. Barn swallows swooped down and returned to the rafters. In the hayloft above the stalls, a young man was shoveling hay through a trapdoor. It crashed onto the barn floor and sent up clouds of dust. "Niko," Mr. Levin called, stepping back fast from the cascading hay. "Knock it off!" The young man came to the edge of the loft and looked down. "Come meet the new boy."

Niko was framed on the platform by rafters overhead and hay all around him. In bib overalls and a sleeveless undershirt, he just stood there, yet the space became a stage, and he alone existed. Mr. Levin felt it too and was agape next to me. Here was the handsomest young man I had ever seen—and I mean even in the movies. His face was not typically American, more like that of a god on an Aztec coin, with shapely lips and chiseled cheekbones. Maybe he was eighteen or twenty. "Come meet Harry Sirkus," Mr. Levin called up to him. The young man came to the very edge of the loft, spread his arms wide and said in a stentorian voice that filled the barn, "In thy face I see the map of honor, truth and loyalty. I'll note you in my book of memory." The vibrations of his voice were still bouncing around as Mr. Levin laughed and said, "Get down here, Niko. I've got appointments."

Niko jammed his pitchfork into a hay mound and climbed down the ladder. He stood before me as if presenting himself. Here I am, and you may gaze upon me. His eyes were intensely blue, and they held mine so boldly that I looked away and felt confused and slightly diminished. "A goodly lad and fair," he said, grabbing my hand and shaking it up and down, which forced me to look at him again. I pulled my hand away before he was ready to let go. Mr. Levin said to me, "Do what Niko tells you and you'll be all right." From outside, we heard the horses clatter away. Mr. Levin walked into a patch of sunlight on the barn floor. "Show him the ropes, Niko." With his back to us, Mr. Levin went out to his waiting limousine, his goodbye wave a hand held up straight.

I stood there hoping I would be able to endure the smell of hay and that I would not be trampled by the giant horses when they returned. Niko handed me a shovel, pointed to a wheelbarrow, nodded toward the empty stalls with their filthy straw and manure and said, in a normal voice, "Dump it out back." Then he returned to the loft, and I made sure I was out of the way when hay thundered down. I mucked out stalls and pushed the heavy wheelbarrow out to a steaming, fly-infested heap at the end of the alley where other stable boys from other barns were doing the same thing. My arms trembled from the weight of the wheelbarrow, and I wished that I was stronger and taller. Niko showed me how to spread sawdust on the stall floors, and we pitched clumps of hay into each one.

At dusk, clattering hooves on cobblestones signaled the return of the Clydesdales. My heart was pounding at the thought of having to lead those titanic gods into the barn, but it turned out they did not need to be led. They walked by themselves into their stalls and put their noses in the feed buckets that Niko and I had filled with grain. Niko went from stall to stall bolting the doors—*ker klatch, ker klatch, ker klatch*—as the drivers carried jingling harness back to the tack room. One of the drivers tossed me a brush and said, "You clean up Ben, child. Stand on a stool if you gots to." Later I heard him say to the man grooming in the stall next to him, "What he get such a pip-squeak about? He don't look no bigger than twelve year old."

The other driver said, "So long as he ain't lazy."

I watched as the men picked mud from the horses' hooves with a sharp tool and groomed the animals with a quick *whiff, whiff, whiff,* of the brush. I pulled the bolt back on Ben's stall and went inside. I had never been so close to such a big creature and had no idea how to lift its hoof to pick the mud out of its shoe. The shoe was the size of a beret. I started brushing, *whiff, whiff, whiff* and the dried mud came loose from its fur. There was so much of him! He went on forever, the long back, four legs, a chest as wide as the Pacific and the head. The brush bristles were hard and sharp, and I wondered if the horse would allow it on his face. "Niko?"

"Did you call?" He had been watching me. He opened the stall door and came in. "Hey, Ben," he said patting the horse. "Hey, fella. How's my big baby?" The horse greeted him with a rumble. Niko reached up to scratch behind the ear, saying, "Yes, you love this, don't you, don't you, ooooh, feels so good." He kept that up for a while. Then he said to me, "Hand me the brush, my good man." I moved away to watch, and he said, "Not back there. You'll get kicked. Don't ever go behind a horse. Even the gentle ones get spooked. Even Ben here, and he's more pussycat than equine specimen."

That first night I ached so bad I wondered if working on a wheat farm in Kansas might have been the better choice. We slept in the tack room on two army cots on either side of the room. Patent-leather harness hung from pegs; oak chests were full of currycombs, hoof picks, brushes and hoof polish. Reins, bits and halters were stuffed in cubbyholes, each one marked with a horse's name: Ben, Andy, Baron, Bill, Buck, Captain, Dean. Hoses were coiled up on the floor. It was hot in there, and the only fan was turned to blow directly on Niko. I didn't have the nerve yet to demand that he share that breeze.

A marmalade cat with balls the size of walnuts and an ear bent over by ear mites, delivered a dead mouse to Niko, who was sitting on his cot in his underwear reading, of all things, *Variety*. The cat dropped the broken mouse on the floor. Niko said, "Felix, lad, you do good work." He stroked Felix long enough to bring out a loud purr. "Take it to the mess hall, lad." Felix picked up the mouse and trotted away with it swinging from his mouth. Niko turned the pages of the newspaper with a snap and a let's-see-what's-on-the-next-page *hmmm* sound, making even the simple task of reading the paper an occasion to draw attention to himself. He was an eye magnet, but I was growing tired of having to pay attention to him. I was homesick, lonesome for my friends Oscar and Bruno, for my job at the Colonial, for Louie and Maggie who would be wondering what had happened to me. Maybe they would go to Lady Mother; maybe they would blame her for making me run away. I was so afraid of being sent back to Haverhill and from there to Kansas that I didn't dare contact anyone. I arranged my clothes on pegs near my cot and wondered who else had slept in the sleeping bag that was now mine.

When he had finished reading *Variety*, Niko took an instrument case from under his cot. Inside was a guitar. After he tuned it, he leaned some sheet music against the case, peered close to it and strummed. He sang in a voice so musical my mouth gaped. Sound cannot be represented by alphabet anymore than a photograph can ever capture a flower. I gave up before I could begin to describe how beautiful Niko's voice was. Warm cocoa. The sound went directly into my chest. When I applauded, he smiled broadly and said, "Thank you, my good man. So very kind."

"Encore!"

"Certainly." Could one person be so talented and so handsome? God overdid it. Niko had another job, I soon discovered. He was a song plugger. The songwriters of Tin Pan Alley hired pluggers to sing the new songs in theaters and music shops across the country. If the audiences liked the tune, they bought the sheet music to play on their own pianos at home.

Every Saturday night, Niko sang in music halls and left me alone in the barn. At first, I was afraid of the noises and creaks; of rats, bats, fire; and that something might happen to one of the horses. But soon I looked forward to those nights alone for two reasons. First, it was very tiresome to be with someone who always demanded attention, and second, I was now responsible for my own education and needed time to read. I arrived at the barn with one book, *Helping Himself* by Horatio Alger. I had intended to return it to the lending library at the back of the candy store in Haverhill, but now I couldn't. I had a good reason for the lapse, but it still felt like stealing. What was worse than possessing the book, which I didn't even like, was not having another one to read and not having enough money to buy one. Luckily, Niko kept me supplied with *Variety*, which I read from cover to cover. I was following the careers of Marcus Loew in New York, who kept opening new theaters, and William Fox, whose star Tom Mix was America's favorite cowboy. I read fan magazines like *Photoplay, Screen World, Motion Picture News* and *The Inside Scoop*, so I knew that Mary Pickford grew up backstage in a trunk and that Anita Stewart went to Erasmus High in Brooklyn. Niko and I read the theater sections of the local newspapers and followed all the arguments against making pictures talk. It was said that acting for the screen brought the art of pantomime to new heights. "Why have words," the head of Vitagraph said, "when any well-made picture tells the complete story?"

Mr. Levin delivered our generous paychecks in person on Friday evenings and spent some time in the cozy atmosphere of his barn, going from stall to stall calling each animal by name. He loved his horses and knew the particular requirements of each one. Niko dropped all theatrics when he conferred with Mr. Levin about whether the sore on King's back required the vet or whether Baron should have more bran. I hoped that, one day, I would know the horses that well and Mr. Levin would confer with me in that serious voice of his. One evening, he came into the tack room to examine Ben's broken halter and noticed my book. "Are you a fan of Horatio Alger, Harry?"

"He's too easy."

"The words or the philosophy?"

"Both."

"Don't you believe that if you work hard, you'll prosper?"

"I don't know. I hope it's true. But there is the fist of life too."

"Yes, indeed. I suspect you've been punched by that fist."

When you're trying to hold yourself together, there's nothing you want less than sympathy. "Yes, sir. But no more than others."

"What are you going to read next?"

"I was just worrying about that."

"We're very proud of our library here in Boston. It was the first large library open to the public in the United States, the first library to trust people to borrow books, take them home, and bring them back. Do you understand how radical that concept is, Harry? The founders got together a collection of books and let total strangers take them away, trusting that those strangers would bring them back. How's that for an idea?"

"Is the store near here, sir?"

"They're free. You don't have to buy them. And you don't have to go all the way to the main library in Copley Square either. Ours is the first city to have branch libraries. Think of that, Harry. Bringing books right to the people where they live." He wrote down the address of the nearest branch. It turned out to be a whole building and not just a counter in the back of a store. So after that, I had two or three books to read when Niko went out on Saturday nights.

Niko wanted me to take more time off. It annoyed him that I was always there, that he never could have our room to himself. "They'll catch me," I said.

"They aren't looking for you."

"How do you know? It's the truant officer's job to catch me."

"From Haverhill? Come searching in the big city from the boondocks? You're not that important."

"Thanks a lot."

"Do your parents vote in that place? Does the mayor depend on your parents for his job? Are your parents pounding down the doors of the school begging the truant officer to find you? Those bureaucrats can hardly find the toilet. Do you like this color on me?"

"It's okay."

"Which is better, this or this." And he held up two different shirts next to his face and waited for my opinion as if his life depended upon it.

Sometimes Mr. Levin arrived with a friend of his, Nathan Gordon, who owned high-class movie palaces in

Boston. When he came, Niko set down the buckets of water he was carrying and sang for Mr. Gordon, who was always surprised, annoyed and seduced. Like the rest of us, he could not resist listening, though he was an impatient person with one foot always out the door. "Give him a regular audition, Nate," Mr. Levin said. "Look at the kid. He's bursting with talent." It happened at last, and Niko got a regular Sunday-afternoon gig plugging songs at Mr. Gordon's biggest theater, the Olympia.

One Sunday afternoon, I heard, "Whoa, Nelly!" The barn door opened, and in a rush of winter air, Dr. Sam and his middle-aged son came in leading a bony bay nag attached to a wagon that read "Dr. Sam & Son, Horse Dentists." Both men were dark black, tall and unusually skinny. "Who's this boy?" the old man said, looking at me as if I had done something wrong.

"Harry Sirkus, sir."

"Where's Niko at?" I told him about the new gig. "You need some new trousers, boy," he said. "You done sprung up out of these here." Then he and his son got to work taking the horses one by one from their stalls, hitching them in the barn aisle, then filing down their teeth lest they grow too sharp and cut the insides of their cheeks. There was nothing much for me to do while Dr. Sam was there, so I asked to leave. "Go on. You go on. Have yourself a day, boy."

Wrapped in scarf, wool hat and jacket bought at Goodwill, I trudged through slushy streets banked with mounds of dirty snow to the vast Olympia Theater. I wanted to see Niko, sure, but I really wanted to see Theda Bara who was starring in a movie called *A Fool There Was*. Rumor said her sex urges were uncontrollable and even the most faithful husbands could not resist her. The producer

William Fox had discovered her on the sands of the Sahara and brought her to America to appear in motion pictures. Her father was an Arab, her mother his French mistress. With such a background, Theda Bara could not help being bad. I had seen photos of her in fan magazines and on posters, eyes outlined like a raccoon, bracelets snaked up bare arms and gossamer skirts that showed bare legs. Reporters who interviewed her said she showed up in a white limousine driven by a Nubian slave and she received them in a tent reclining on a satin bed surrounded by incense, human skulls and candles on the floor. She spoke in whispers about her longing for Arabia.

I climbed and climbed, getting vertigo on the way to my inexpensive seat in the top balcony. I sat, jacket folded on my lap, under a domed ceiling painted with clouds and angels. There were hundreds of seats and tiers of balconies. People in dressy clothes walked down the aisles next to uniformed ushers as the orchestra warmed up: a tuba, violins, the strangled sound of oboes, all playing different notes—discordant and exciting. I had never been in such a beautiful theater. Here was the patina of age and Old World charm. It was a legitimate playhouse that had been converted to accommodate motion pictures.

The lights dimmed, the orchestra played some rousing music, and people squinted down at their programs. Yes, as usual the night would start with a singalong. The stage lights went up, and Niko, dressed in skin-tight black leotard from neck to foot, with a bright-yellow cape sparkling with sequins thrown around his shoulders and knee-high black boots, entered from the wings like a matador entering the bull ring—chest high, head thrown back. Song pluggers never looked like this. They wore suits and ties and conservative shoes, their mandate being to put the song forward, not themselves. The audience hushed at the sight of him. A screen slid smoothly down in front of the curtain and the lyrics to *Let Me Call You Sweetheart* were projected:

Let me call you sweetheart, I'm in love with you. Let me hear you whisper that you love me too. Keep the love light glowing in your eyes so true, Let me call you sweetheart, I'm in love with you.

Niko sang the song slowly as if his heart was breaking, as if his love was impossible, as if the love light in the lover's eyes was not for him. He did not signal for the audience to join in, as expected, but sang the chorus through again. Not a sound was heard when he finished. Finally someone began to clap and someone else joined in, and pretty soon the applause was thunderous, people shouting, "More! Sing more!" The man next to me whispered to his wife, "Who is that kid?" She whispered back, "Adonis." Niko let the applause rain down on him. A woman behind me whispered, "How old do you think he is?" Her friend replied, "Old enough, I hope."

The lyrics on the screen switched to those of *Aba Daba Honeymoon*. This time Niko sang with so much upbeat energy that the audience burst out singing too. Then Niko introduced *La Cucaracha*, adding sexy, hip-swinging as he sang. The crowd went wild. To get Niko off the stage, an announcer jogged out from the wings and shouted, "Ladies and gentlemen, Nikos Adrianos! Isn't he fabulous? Isn't he splendid?" The spotlight moved to Niko who put his hands up like a victorious prizefighter.

Then a magician released doves into the air, acrobats balanced on one pinky, and a dog trainer brought out scruffy mutts dressed like hobos with bandannas around their necks. The dogs disobeyed every command, went left instead of right, sat instead of playing dead, ran instead of staying, and threw themselves at their trainer so that at the end he was covered with dogs. I laughed so hard that the brittleness left my shoulders.

The film began. The orchestra played music expressly written for it. At Louie's theater in Haverhill, the sound-effects man spoke all the film's dialogue, male and female parts. Here, there were live actors behind a screen: men for the male parts, women for the female. From the first moment that she appeared on screen, I was captivated by Theda Bara, her Oriental eyes, her slow way of moving, the thrilling way she touched her milk-white arms. I wanted to kiss her and see her naked. Many times during the film, I was glad my jacket hid what was going on in my lap.

Lights up, I filed out with the rest of the audience to the lobby, face averted just in case the truant officer was there. This was a matinee, so children were there, and I overheard some parents complaining about the picture and reminding their children that marriage was sacred. A woman said to her husband, "Don't blame me. How was I supposed to know what it was about?"

Crossing the lobby, I was surprised to see Elsie Cogswell with her parents. Her father was running for governor of Massachusetts and was shaking hands with various people. Mrs. Cogswell was smiling at the well-wishers in a strained way. Elsie, in a blue coat with a blue velvet collar, was shifting her weight from one lace-up boot to the other, back and forth, until her mother nudged her, and she stood still and put on an exaggerated smile, which made her mother nudge her again. Mrs. Cogswell, I imagined, would report me, but I couldn't run away because too many people were hemming me in. Elsie saw me, and her face lit up. She bolted away from her parents, zigzagged through the crowd and presented herself to me like an eager puppy. "Harry! What happened to you? What are you doing here?" Would she have beamed at me so freely in front of her friends? Could it be that she had loved me all along? Her skin had the glow of rose petals. "How come you're here, Harry? All your paramecium died in science class." Her eyes were chocolate velvet. "Guess what? I won the blue in Pony Club equitation. What are you doing here?"

"I don't know. What are you doing here?"

"I don't know. What are you doing here?"

"I don't know."

"How come your hair's so long?"

"It grew."

"Are they looking for me?" she asked.

"Who?"

"My parents. Is my mother looking around for me? She is so impossible. They said I never should have seen that picture. Isn't that silly? I said, 'It's just a picture. It's not real.' They wouldn't let me go see Fatty Arbuckle when he was at the Colonial. All the kids went except me. Anyway, what are you doing here? When are you coming home?"

"Never."

"No, really..." She examined my face. The acorns on her chest were now oranges, and even though she was being childishly animated, there was a new womanly caution in her, like a pointer sniffing the wind and deciding which way to go. "Because of me? Because I wasn't nice enough to you? Because I ignored you that time?"

"Yes."

She slapped my arm, and we just stood there looking into each other's eyes until Mrs. Cogswell strode across the lobby. "Harry! What a surprise! How are you?" But she did not wait for an answer, put her arm around

Elsie's shoulders and lead her away. I heard her whisper, "Of course I know who he is. I know who he is better than you do, Elsie. Let's not keep Daddy waiting." Elsie kept her head turned in my direction so our eyes could keep hugging.

I just stood there until she was out of sight and hated the longing and hopelessness she generated in me. Seeing Elsie made me realize that I had not been sad for a long while. I had broken free of the constraints of the Elizabeth Home and Haverhill, and the wide world was waiting for me again. I was a man among men. Elsie's cheerfulness—partly a result of her nature and partly of her feeling protected and loved—her radiant complexion, her delicious smell, her expensive clothes brought back that old Haverhill feeling of worthlessness. Of course I loved her. Who wouldn't? But I wasn't the one she would choose, me in my clothes that reeked of horse barn, my muddy lace-up boots, my hair that had not been cut in months. Me who had dirty, filthy, unspeakable, exciting thoughts about Theda Bara.

I worked my way through the crowd and went outside to wait by the stage door for Niko. Others were waiting for him with tensed readiness, and when he emerged, the wool scarf he had found on the street transformed into ermine just by being around his particular neck, they thrust their programs at him for his autograph. When he saw me, he called, "Hey, Harry! Wait for me!" I was proud to be singled out by Niko. His fans turned to see who merited his attention, and for a second, I was a celebrity by proxy. I was not jealous of Niko because by now I knew too much about him. I could walk next to him and feel no envy when all eyes turned to stare. His mother was confined to some loony bin in New Hampshire, and his father was a lout responsible for the scars showing on Niko's thighs. "Broke my index finger one time when I wouldn't stop playing the piano. Said I was banging." Niko held up that finger for me to inspect, and it was, indeed, a little bit crooked. No, I was not envious of him. His lot in life was no easier than mine, and I thought he had some character faults. He could not pass a mirror without turning into Narcissus, and he could suddenly become imperious and petulant. "You do it," he would say to me at night when one of the horses needed attention. "I'm practicing."

"You are not," I would reply, glancing up from my book. "You're sitting there looking in the mirror."

"But I have a blemish," he said in his most annoying whine.

However, I did enjoy the benefits of his magnetism. The Oyster House, where we stopped for clam chowder, was packed with no available tables, but as we took our place among the waiting patrons, the captain came over to Niko and whispered, "I think I have something for you," and we were seated right away. The waitress saw him, turned abruptly away from the customer she was serving and rushed over to take his order. She peered at him. "Can you be real?" Tired when he sat down, depleted by his performance onstage and a supposed slight from one of the stagehands, he preened under her admiration, and by the time we left to go back to the barn, he had shared his big personality with the whole room, everyone hearing his infectious guffaw. We departed to the sound of applause for the song he stood up and sang free of charge.

Several months later—when the snow was gone and we didn't have to pick ice out of hooves, and I no longer feared the truant officer because I had turned fourteen—a scout from the Victor Record Company in New Jersey heard Niko at the Olympia and signed him. Niko packed his few belongings in a suitcase and was gone. And not too long after that, the sheet music for *I Didn't Raise My Son to Be a Soldier* was in the window of music stores with a photograph of Niko on the cover. It was captioned, "As Sung by the New Sensation, Nick Meadows!"

Chapter Eight

Niko was replaced in the barn by a series of immigrant men whose wives delivered lunch in string bags while their many children, dressed in Old World clothes, waited in the alley. Mr. Levin knew I had outgrown my job and understood that it wasn't so pleasant sleeping in the tack room with grown men who didn't understand enough English for a conversation. When he delivered the checks on Friday he made sure to sit with me on a bale of hay and talk. Sometimes he arrived from a meeting with other philanthropists, and his conversation was full of the progress of his pet cause, establishing a Jewish hospital in Boston. "There are three hospitals in Boston," he told me, "St. Elizabeth, Carney and Massachusetts General, all supported by the church. About ten percent of the patients are Jewish, but the wealthy Jews here don't contribute to the Christian charities that support those hospitals. They use the hospitals, but they don't contribute to them financially."

"So they're mean to them there?"

"No. Not at all. Not intentionally anyway. Boston is home to hundreds of Jewish immigrants who sometimes get sick. When they go to the hospital, no one understands their Yiddish, and they can't eat the food because it's not kosher. They suffer not only from their ailment but from fear, so they usually rush to leave the hospital before being cured, and their minor problem turns into something chronic. Ah, but I'm boring you. That's the trouble with being in the grip of a cause. You turn into a big bore."

"No, sir. I like it when you talk to me."

"Most big cities already have Jewish hospitals. But here in Boston, it's considered bad form to call attention to your Jewishness. Being an American and a citizen of Boston, the city of culture, is supposed to be enough. But slowly we're convincing the community. We now have two hundred thirty-one members on the Beth Israel Hospital committee, and we've purchased an estate in Roxbury that can house twenty-five beds." He looked around the barn. "You do a good job here, Harry. But the work is beneath you. I wish I could help you more."

Like many people who are tired of their job, I started taking too much time off. My new stable partner, a father of six, scolded me in Armenian, his bushy eyebrows knitted together, his finger wagged in my face. He referred to me as a *vochil*, which I discovered meant maggot.

One day, lilacs blooming on the Boston Common, my attention was called away from ecstatic sniffing by the approaching sound of a parade, a slow crescendo of snare drums rat-a-tat-tatting, bass drums thumping, a majorette's shrill whistling and fifes screeching. I hurried to Tremont Street to watch the marchers, who carried signs: "Stop the War" and "No One Can Fight on an Empty Stomach." A speaker's platform set up on the Common was draped with American flags, and Mayor Curley was up there shouting, "This American peace rally is one of the great events of the century! It is my opinion that the best and surest way to stop this war is for the American nation—North and South—to place an embargo on food products." Some people cheered; others hooted. "No man can be a good soldier with an empty haversack. As Napoleon put it, the army travels on its belly. Sooner or later, wheat will be more valuable to our friends across the sea than cannon. If you should ask my advice, it would be that we adopt resolutions today favoring the appointment of a commission to work with President Wilson and Secretary of State Bryan to bring together the presidents of the South American republics in an agreement to establish an absolute embargo on every necessary of life while the war continues." The crowd cheered.

I could not envision the war in Europe. It was all about some Serbian who had shot Archduke Franz Ferdinand in Sarajevo, a city that annoyed me because it was not pronounced the way it was spelled. I didn't know what an archduke was or why anyone except his own subjects cared if he was assassinated. I didn't know what a Serbian was either.

The speaker after Mayor Curley was the president of the Boston Bar Association. Dressed in top hat and tails, he had a thick white handlebar mustache. "I have called together this antiwar demonstration here on the Boston Common," he shouted, "to show President Wilson how many of us there are who hate this war in Europe. The movement for peace will now become irresistible. The world will soon say, Lay down your arms! Armaments must be limited and no longer a menace to the peace and comfort and progress of the world!"

To the sound of wild cheering, I was carried along by the crowd to Tremont Street, where I ducked into the entrance of a building to get out of the way of a troop of Boy Scouts. While I waited for them to pass by, I perused the names on the building directory and saw one that had the word film in it. I decided to investigate and climbed three flights to a closed door that was lettered "American Feature Film Company." When no one responded to my knock, I walked into a tiny office with a view of a brick air shaft. A no-nonsense woman in a blouse buttoned up to her chin was sitting behind a desk typing. She took me in at a glance but did not stop typing. A man's voice from the adjoining room called through a closed door, "You got it done yet, Fanny?"

"Hold your horses," she called back.

The door to the adjoining room opened and out came a man who looked exactly like Louie Mayer. "Don't forget to say it's a sure thing. He can't lose. Say that, Fanny. Don't forget to say Metro's a sure bet." He flicked his eyes toward me as he strode back to his own office in that choppy way of his.

"Louie?"

He turned and waited for me to state my business. Suddenly his face changed. "Harry?" We ran to each other and hugged for a long time. I'm not sure I've ever hugged anyone as hard as I hugged Louie then. "Is it really you?" he said, setting me away, looking at me, then clasping me again. When he let me go, he took off his glasses, wiped his eyes and said, "Fanny. Call Maggie. Tell her I found Harry." He clasped me again. "Here," Louie said to Fanny, "is the son I never had." Then he said to me, "I imagined all kinds of things." He took out his handkerchief and loudly blew his nose.

"Don't blow your nose like that," Fanny said. "It's not good for the sinus passages. God didn't mean you to blast your delicate membranes like a fog horn."

"I went to the school," Louie said, touching my arm, my cheek. "None of them knew." He blew his nose more softly and stuffed his handkerchief back in his pocket. "How can they lose a boy? This is the question I asked them. How can you lose a boy? How can that be possible? You grew. You're a man. Fanny, look at him. Taller than me." The telephone on Fanny's desk jangled.

"If that's Lasky," Louie said, "tell him the check's in the mail."

"You tell him," Fanny said. "I'm tired of saying that." She lifted the receiver and said in an entirely different voice, cheerful as spring robins hopping on the lawn, "Good afternoon. American Feature Film Company." She listened. "Thank you. One moment please." She clamped her palm over the mouthpiece and whispered, "It's that Kinetophone salesman again."

Louie made a dismissive hand flap, and I followed him into a small office. I noted an oak desk, a swivel chair, theater programs, movie posters and a photograph of Louie's mother, the frame draped in black. "Have a seat." He gestured to an elderly wingchair in front of his desk. He sat behind his desk and swiveled right and left slowly. "You ask what's been going on with me. I'll tell you. I own not only the Colonial and the Orpheum but also the Academy of Music. I'm the biggest entertainment person in the whole city. None can compare. I have my brother Jerry managing the Colonial. The Cozy Nickel burned down in a mysterious way, and I have the former manager looking after the Academy of Music for me. Maggie says to me, 'Why isn't this enough? Why can't you be satisfied?' I don't know the answer. It's a drive I got deep in my heart," he pounded his heart with his fist. "It says do more, more, more. I don't sleep. I'm up all night thinking, plotting."

"What is this place, Louie?"

"Distribution. Jesse Lasky's making feature-length pictures, and I got the exclusive right to distribute them in New England. I'm in the right place at the right time. Tell me about yourself." He swiveled around, looked up at the portrait of his mother and said to the image, "See who's come back, Ma? Didn't you say not to worry?" He swiveled to face me, took a cigar from his breast pocket, put it in his mouth, showed me a strange little device and said, "Watch this." He scratched a metal rod that ignited a wick soaked in fuel, and a flame shot up. He lowered his cigar tip into the flame and puffed. "See?" he asked, as smoke leaked out of his mouth. "See that?"

"Why don't you just use a match?"

"What if you don't got a match." He considered me for a minute while asking himself some question I was not able to hear, then reached into his pocket, and I knew the answer. Yes, Harry was old enough to smoke. I put the cigar he offered me into my mouth and waited for him to ignite his Wonderlite, its name printed on the base. The flame shot up, and I drew back. Louie held the thing steady as I lowered my cigar into it. "See?" he said when the tobacco caught. "What'd I tell you. Huh?" I nodded approval as he set his lighter in its place of honor next to his inkwell. "I always keep up with the times, Harry." I hoped Louie noticed what an experienced smoker I was.

"This war in Europe," he said, "bad for them, good for us. Nothing coming out of there now. Exhibitors here screaming for feature pictures. You think the public wants to sit in those expensive movie-palace seats and see the crap that's coming out of New York? One-reel slapstick and shoot-'em-ups. I go to a meeting of exhibitors, and they argue over how long people can pay attention. They say a motion picture is a short story, not a novel. They say no one wants a picture longer than ten minutes."

"Ten minutes is not enough of Theda Bara," I said, puffing.

"Is that who you like? Is that who the young boys want to take to their beds? With them snake bracelets all up her arms?"

"And what about *Cabiria*? President Wilson sat on the White House lawn and watched all ten reels of it."

"Maybe he had to. Maybe the Italian ambassador was sitting next to him." We both laughed in a way that meant it was fun to be cynical. "Point is, they ain't sending nothing here now—no *Cabiria*, no nothing. Kaput. You know what's in the film studios over there now instead of cameras and scenery? Ammunition. You know what them actors wear now instead of costumes? Uniforms. You know what's on the fields where they used to build stage sets? Bloody bodies, that's what."

"Lasky and Fox have the right idea," I said, tapping my ash into a souvenir of the Flume.

"You been following the trades? You still interested?"

"Theater owners have invested thousands converting legitimate theaters into picture palaces. They're begging American producers to create longer pictures. I read about it all the time, Louie. I know a fellow here, Nathan Gordon. His audiences are complaining. They say he's still charging them big at the box office and showing them shit."

"You swear now?"

"I am up to my neck in shit, Louie."

"Yeah? You look good."

"The producers here in America, Louie, they've got to take the next step. They've got to take more risk. They've got to dare invest in more film and find scenario writers who can map out longer photoplays. You're right to throw in with Lasky. Lasky, Fox and Griffith are the only ones with their heads screwed on right."

"Nathan Gordon," Louie said. "I know Gordon. His people buy Lasky's pictures from my people." It felt so wonderful to be with Louie that I got up, ran around to his side of the desk, kissed his big cheek in a noisy, comical way and went back to my chair. He wiped his cheek and laughed. He said, "My immediate problem, Harry, is the lack of forty thousand dollars." He swiveled to the window, looked out at the brick air shaft and swiveled back. "Here is an opportunity, and I cannot seize it." Through his open window, we heard the remains of the parade outside fading away. "Some of the boys in the distribution business in New York," he said leaning across the desk so he could talk closer to my face, "have pooled their money so they can make pictures. What we are discussing today, me and you, is not unknown, Harry. Now is the time to make feature pictures here in America. Why should I have to buy pictures from Jesse Lasky when I can make the pictures myself? And let's say, just for the sake of discussion, that I not only make the pictures, but I distribute them too. You see the advantage here? I will own what I sell. William Fox already does this. He has his Fox Film Company and his distribution company and, on top of that, Harry, he owns the theaters that show his pictures. He's got it sewn up top to bottom, bottom to top. Vertical integration is how they call this. Remember that. Vertical integration. Now I don't got no vertical integration. All I got is pieces. I got theaters, and I got this distribution company, but it ain't vertical. They ain't connected together." He puffed on his cigar for a moment. "This new venture they're calling Metro Pictures Corporation, and they plan to acquire one new motion picture per week, each picture costing between fifteen and twenty thousand dollars. They want me to buy in. To do so, I need forty thousand dollars." He handed me "Moving Picture World" magazine with a classified ad circled in red. "Read it. Go on. Read it out loud."

"Responsible producers possessing or contemplating features of quality desiring immediate marketing, wide distribution, through an organization composed of exchange men of acknowledged standing submit their products to Metro Pictures, 1465 Broadway." I handed the magazine back to him. "You want to make movies, Louie?"

He took off his glasses, huffed on them and cleaned them with his handkerchief. "You say the word *movie*. I like the word *movie*. It's catchy. From now on I use the word *movie*. You see how important it is to have young people around?" He did not include himself among the young, though he was only twenty-eight. He swiveled to look up at the photograph of his mother. "Is this why you sent him back to me, Ma?" He swiveled back. "Let me ask you something, Harry. Who is the most important person in the teamwork that is required to produce a motion-picture movie?"

"The photoplayer."

"Do you think the photoplayer is more important than the story play in a motion-picture movie?"

"Yes."

"And is it your opinion that the photoplayer is more important than the director?"

"Yes."

"So it is your opinion, Harry, that the public pays to see the player and not the play or the director?"

"Yes. That is my opinion."

"And if I was to tell you, Harry, that this opinion is not the current opinion, that Sam Goldwyn out there in California is banking on the story carrying the load and that Vitagraph in Brooklyn is making a fortune of money ballyhooing the director, that most producers of motion-picture movies believe the actors are interchangeable, would you change your mind?"

"No."

"Whatever he's paying you, I'll pay you double."

"Who? Mr. Levin? He's very rich, Louie."

"Rich? What's rich? I'll tell you what rich is. Rich is having first of all health, a wife like my Maggie, two daughters like I got and a son like you."

"Rich is having a stone mansion like Mr. Levin's, a limousine, a chauffeur who lives in a carriage house behind the big house and a kitchen full of maids."

"Levin?"

"My boss."

"He don't happen to be a banker?"

"He does two things, Louie. He runs a carpet business, and the rest of the time, he's trying to establish a Jewish hospital in Boston."

"My poor mother, may she rest in peace, would be with us today if they had a Jewish hospital in St. John. She went in for a routine gallbladder. Nothing to it. Routine. They killed her." Louie's chin quivered. "What gets me," he said, eyes filling, "is she couldn't even talk to those butchers. She was a religious woman, Harry. She couldn't eat that food." He honked his nose in his handkerchief and sighed. "Ah, well. She's here with me now." He tapped his heart three times with a closed fist. "She watches my every move. Tells me yes, this is right— no, that ain't right."

"How come she couldn't eat the food?"

"How come? It wasn't kosher. They don't got kosher food in the hospital. They don't got anyone understands Yiddish. They got nothing but nuns all over the place."

"That's how it is in Boston too."

"Nuns, and then some priest comes in and asks her if she wants the last rites. Some priest comes in and asks my sainted mother if he should say mumbo jumbo over her, and I wasn't even there. I was hundreds of miles away. Do you know what she did? Can you guess what my mother said to that priest? I'll tell you what she said. My sainted mother. So sweet. She said, 'Yes, of course, give me your last rites. You got a job to do like everyone else. You got a mother wants you to do good. You do good, and give me your last rites.' Do you think my mother knew what last rites were? Believe me, she didn't know from last rites." He sighed. "What I need, Harry, is private financing. I've been to the banks. They all say no."

"Why?"

"Why? I'm a Jew. Why do you think?"

"Oh. How did you do it in Haverhill?"

"How? You present your plan to someone with means, convince that someone, give him a piece of the action—usually too big—and there you go."

"Why don't you ask them to help you buy into Metro Pictures?"

"They only think Haverhill, Harry. Anything outside Haverhill don't exist."

"You should ask Mr. Levin."

"It ain't that easy. He don't know me. My investors in Haverhill, they all know me. And not from the Pentucket Club. Hell, I had that Orpheum up and running two years before they give me the time of day." He sighed remembering his struggle.

"There are Jewish millionaires in Boston," I said. "Mr. Levin and Mr. Gordon and all those other millionaires meet every month. You should join the committee."

"What committee?"

"The Beth Israel Hospital Committee. You're interested in starting a Jewish hospital, right?"

Louie turned from the window and regarded me for a while, puffing. "You able to bring it up?"

"Sure. I'll mention you to Mr. Levin. I'll tell him about your mother, may she rest in peace."

"You're working for me now, right?"

"But I sleep there, Louie. I don't pay rent."

He opened the door and said to Fanny, "How much your mother asking for that room?"

She looked at me. "On condition you buy him some new clothes, you pay for him to get his hair cut at a barbershop, and he promises to eat Mommy's breakfast."

Chapter Nine

Nathan Gordon's wife Sally was the moving force behind the Jewish hospital movement in Boston. Louie and I stood at her front door in Jamaica Plain cowed by the size of her house. Louie straightened his tie, brushed the dust from his shoes, fidgeted, rebuttoned his jacket and smoothed his hair. We expected a butler, but Mrs. Gordon herself opened the front door, a plain person entirely without vanity. She led Louie and me to a sunporch full of flowers in Chinese vases, indoor trees in pots and wicker furniture upholstered with stylish blue dragons. She sat on one side of a coffee table, and Louie and I sat together on a love seat on the other side, both of us so intimidated by her wealth that we perched on the edge of the seat. From a shapely teapot, she poured tea into delicate cups, and I winced at having to accept that ladylike cup in my calloused hands stained by black hoof polish. Mrs. Gordon offered us sugar cookies on a tray that was obviously the work of a child in shop class. It was made of wood with a rooster painted in the middle, and the handles had been glued on unevenly. Seemed an odd choice for company, considering the valuable trays she probably owned. Did she use this tray because she thought Louie and I were not good enough for the antique Wedgewood? "Several of us have been fortunate in America," she said.

"I love America," Louie said and wiped the sugar off his lips with the back of his hand before he remembered he had been given a linen cocktail napkin and patted his lips in the dainty way he thought correct.

"We have formed the Jewish Hospital Association for the purpose of raising money to erect, equip and endow a Jewish hospital in Boston." Just then a door slammed, and we heard a child shout, "Mamma! I'm home!"

"Marion," Mrs. Gordon called turning toward the sound, "please do not slam that door!" A little girl of about eight ran into the room and stopped when she saw us. "Come meet Mr. Mayer and Harry Sirkus. Come on." The girl came shyly forward and was introduced. Then she said, "Hey! You're using your birthday present tray!"

Mrs. Gordon said, "Of course I am. I'm serving tea." The child squirmed with pleasure and ran out of the room. "Excuse us, please," Mrs. Gordon said. "Now where was I? Oh, yes. At first, we went upstairs and down, door to door soliciting. Then we sold miniature bricks at fifty cents a piece. Each brick was inscribed "Brick for Jewish Hospital." Now we have many prominent Jews contributing." Her eyes were deep brown, full of intelligence and intensity. "But there are still Boston Jews who believe it is a breach of honor to mention creed or race in a city where all are served by the existing hospitals."

"Jew ain't a dirty word, Mrs. Gordon," Louie said.

She burst out laughing, "Call me Sally, please. You know, we don't own this place. Nathan rents these gigantic houses all furnished, and the children and I adjust. You see those big urns over there? They're the same ones that are in that John Singer Sargent painting of those little girls, *The Daughters of Edward Darley Boit*. Can you imagine if my children broke them? I tiptoe around this place. I used to be a nurse and had an apartment of my own. Since I've been married, I have never lived in a house of my own. You should have seen the size of the place before this one!" She laughed. "Maybe that's why I want a hospital of my own!"

Louie and I settled back more comfortably. "Sally, I'm going to tell you something," Louie said, setting down his cup and leaning toward her. "I'm sitting here, and I see you, and I know, sure as I'm sitting here, a Jewish hospital is going to be established in the city of Boston. How do I know this? Because," he pounded his heart with his fist, "it is right. He who saves one life—so my mother of blessed memory said to me—is considered as though he saved the world. I will turn my pockets inside out for you."

"Thank you," she said.

"I pledge to you fifteen thousand dollars." What? Where was he going to get that? She was surprised too. "You have my word. If there is anything else I can do, just ask."

"Would you consider being on our board of directors?"

"Me?"

"Yes, of course. All that's required is a willingness to do the work. Volunteers, I've discovered, are enthusiastic for about two years. Then we need new blood. Consider yourself a member of the Beth Israel Hospital board, Louis."

And that's how Louie came to mingle with the millionaires who would eventually launch his career as a movie producer. One of them was my boss, Mr. Levin. "Motion pictures are a risky business," he said when I told him I was going to quit my job at the barn. "I'm not saying you should continue working here. I'm just saying that if things don't work out, you always have a job with me."

"Thank you, sir." Behind us was the clang of the blacksmith banging molten iron rods into horseshoes, fitting each hoof individually, clanging some more, fitting again, clanging again—the horses amazingly patient.

"I know you've always been interested in motion-pictures and the entertainment world. We got a little taste of it first hand with Niko."

"Yes, sir. We did."

"Of course, you would have to move on. It's only natural."

"Thank you, sir," I said, my voice trembling as I extended my hand, "for saving my life."

Mr. Levin took my hand and pulled me against him for a quick, shy hug. "I expect we will continue being friends."

"Yes, sir. I expect so too."

"You have my telephone number. You know where I live."

I moved from the tack room to a house on Washington Street owned by Louie's secretary, Fanny. Fanny slept in her childhood room, dolls and stuffed animals still arranged on her pillow. Fanny's mother, Mrs. Mittenthal, was about seventy. She was so nice and such a good cook that most of her boarders had lived with her for more than ten years and contributed their skills to the upkeep of the house. One was a carpenter so the roof never leaked. Another was an upholsterer so the chairs and sofas all looked new. Another was a plumber. An Irish maid lived in a room off the kitchen. She made our beds, did our laundry and kept the house clean.

Mrs. Mittenthal believed that breakfast was the most important meal of the day, so she included it in the rent: coffee, corn muffins, cinnamon rolls—all baked each morning. She was a timid little person. If someone was behind on rent, Fanny took care of it. Fanny dealt with the gasman, the milkman, the coal vender, the garbageman. They were a great team, Fanny and her mother. Fanny and I shared the front office of the American Feature Film Company, but I don't think I got in her way too much because I was always out running errands.

Louie met Nathan Gordon at the hospital-board meetings and persuaded him to invest the forty thousand dollars required for partnership in Metro Pictures. This seemed a good idea to Nathan Gordon because he, too, wanted control over the product he sold. Owning a share of Metro Pictures would allow him to influence the kind of pictures produced and the price of those pictures. He knew what Boston audiences wanted to see and the price they were willing to pay at the box office. Mr. Gordon's contract stated that he had exclusive rights to Metro's movies in New England; they could be shown only at his theaters. I knew what his contract said because I had to deliver it to him after Fanny finished typing it, and I read it on the bus and understood the gist of it.

It's always hard to imagine great stars at the beginning of their career working freelance and wondering about the next paycheck. Such was Charlie Chaplin once, and that time coincided with Louie and Nathan Gordon's becoming partners in Metro Pictures. Charlie Chaplin, not under contract to any particular studio, signed on to make pictures for Metro. So did the heart-throb Francis X. Bushman, voted a favorite film star by the readers of *Ladies' World* magazine. The pictures that those two stars made for Metro paid Mr. Gordon back more than double his investment. The Gordon-Mayer Theatrical Company moved to bigger quarters, and Fanny got an office of her own. I learned about booking vaudeville acts, making arrangements for them when they arrived in town, distributing motion pictures, calculating box-office returns and juggling the myriad costs of show business.

Louie also met Mr. Levin on the hospital board, but Mr. Levin could not understand Louie's enthusiasm for motion pictures. He couldn't understand at all why movies were so popular, why anyone would prefer them to stage plays. Louie didn't argue with him about artistic merit. He simply showed him statistics to prove that motion pictures were a developing business and a good opportunity for investment. More than half a billion admissions were paid at the box offices of motion-picture theaters. More than seventy-five thousand miles of film were manufactured and exhibited. The return on investment for *The Squaw Man*, a picture Louie distributed, was almost sixteen fold. *The Whispering Chorus* grossed three times its cost.

Mr. Levin was inclined to be convinced because he was somewhat bored by the carpet business. When I worked for him, he often talked to me in a nostalgic way about the challenges he had faced as a young man when mass-produced carpet was a new invention. Wealthy people scorned it. They covered the holes in their wooden floors with hand-woven Oriental rugs, each one an expensive example of good taste. Mr. Levin knew that middle-class homeowners and merchants would welcome carpet manufactured on power looms in mills in Clinton, Massachusetts. At age twenty-two, he went to Clinton to convince the Bigelow brothers to ignore his youth and allow him to distribute their product in New England. What heady days those were! How scary not to know the outcome. How marvelous when he received a big order from the Boston Public Library, from Shreve, Crump &

Low, Trinity Church in Copley Square, the Hotel Vendome, the State House, Filene's department store. How clever he'd been to make the delivery of the carpet glamorous by using Clydesdale horses.

Mr. Levin identified with Louie. They were the same age when they had taken their daring first step, when they had risked all. They both understood that their product was not for the very wealthy but for the middle class and for those who longed to become middle class. Mr. Levin's enthusiasm escalated when Louie took us to New York to see how pictures were put together. We traveled by train through Connecticut where swamps of cattails like hot dogs on poles stood in reedy pools by the edge of the tracks.

From Grand Central Station, we took a taxi, and I was surprised how deep my reaction to New York was. I didn't even know I had missed it until I saw it again: the massive buildings; people on crowded sidewalks rushing to appointments, wrapped in cloaks of privacy; people not rushing but strolling, stopping to buy nuts from a vendor; billboards shouting for attention: "The Edison Phonograph Puts Music in Every Home." Poor people, rich people, black people, white people. There was construction everywhere, gaping foundations, walls part way up, awnings being affixed to windows, men handling pickaxes, shovels, teams of unkempt horses pulling wagons of lumber. Haverhill was sleepy compared with Boston, but Boston was sleepy compared with this.

In Brooklyn, on a street full of children playing stickball, we stopped at a nondescript building. It was impossible to imagine from the outside the frenetic activity inside. Five motion pictures were in production at the same time, each with its own cast of actors, stage sets, cameras, lights and technical men hurrying here and there with coils of wire, film reels and costumes. Next to some of the stages were musicians, mostly violinists, playing sad music to help actors cry. Louie was greeted by several men and went with them to a meeting in another part of the building, while Mr. Levin and I were escorted to one of the sets where we sat at the edge and watched. I was surprised how well Louie knew the men who greeted him, how comfortable he was at that studio. Louie had a way of making you feel important and that his very life depended on your opinions and your help. Now I was reminded how much of his life had nothing to do with me at all.

Mr. Levin and I sat by the edge of the stage surrounded by actors in costumes lounging around. The director, script in hand, gave out the roles: "Mr. Evans, you are a lover. Miss Miles, you are his affianced bride. Mrs. Marsh, you are the mother."

"A mother?" she said. "How can I play a mother? I'm not old enough to play a mother."

"A young mother," the director said. "Mr. Conway, you are the father. Mr. Washburn, you are a villain." He walked onto the stage, a raised platform with oversize electric lights set up around it. "Miss Miles, you stand here. Mr. Evans, you enter stage left through the door and tell Miss Miles that you must leave for a long time. You're going to jail for something you didn't do, but you don't want her to know that. Miss Miles, you ask him why he has to go just when your wedding is planned. He doesn't tell you, you insist, and at last he explains that he's been unjustly accused of a robbery. It's mistaken identity. Ready?"

The actors walked through the scene, the director adding business and building the tension. Then the lights were blasted onto the stage, the cameras were cranked up, and the scene was filmed. The next scene was the inside of a fabric store. "Miss Miles, you work in the store," the director said. "Mr. Washburn, you own the store. You love Miss Miles, that's why you've connived to get rid of her fiancé by staging a robbery and getting him sent to the clinker. Where are those bolts of fabric?" A young man hurried onto the stage with bolts of fabric. I sat there enthralled. Being an actor seemed such a strange profession, how they could switch on and off, how they blew up the details—a lift of the hand, the eyebrows, the edges of the mouth—how they could make themselves burst out laughing when nothing was funny.

In the cab going back into Manhattan, Mr. Levin said, "Why, it's noble, it's worthy. It's a whole world of make-believe, all those people working just so we'll be entertained."

"Not just us," I said. "Poor people too."

We arrived back in Boston that night and walked together to Tremont Street, where our progress was arrested by a crowd of angry people, at least five hundred of them, in front of the Tremont Theater. Protesters held signs that read "Fight Race Hatred" and "This Film Panders to Depraved Tastes." *The Birth of a Nation* was playing here after forty-four consecutive weeks in New York. Louie said, "Let's see what all the fuss is about."

"You can't cross those picket lines, Louis," Mr. Levin said as we were jostled by a protester holding a sign that read "Griffith Foments Race Antipathy." People screamed at us as we stood in line and kept screaming when it was our turn at the box office, where Louie exhibited his

Gordon-Mayer pass that got us into all movie theaters free. Mr. Levin turned in the other direction and left us. For a second, I was affected by his scruples and wondered if I should go with him. But I was too curious about the picture to miss it.

Louie said, "Look at this, Harry. They're lining up to pay two bucks. All these people. Did you ever think you'd see the day when they'd pay the same for a motion-picture movie as for a stage play? Was I smart to get into this business, or what? Huh?"

"We."

"We?"

"We're in the business."

"That we are, my boy. That we are," and he had to reach up a little to put his arm around my shoulders.

We entered the gorgeous Tremont Theater where Sarah Bernhardt once played Tosca on the stage. Under twinkling chandeliers, ushers, some dressed like Confederate soldiers and others like Union soldiers—caps, boots, epaulets—stood at attention. We were escorted to our reserved seats by a female usher in a long, frilly plantation dress. She handed us both a souvenir program full of illustrations and photographs. "This cost a fortune of money," Louie whispered. "Read it to me."

"Says the music is made up of classical pieces and popular songs arranged especially for the picture."

The lights dimmed, the orchestra played an overture, and the picture began. A white woman reached out to hug a black child but drew back in disgust because the child smelled so bad. I did not like seeing that and expected that the next scene would show the woman being punished for hurting the child's feelings. Or that it would show the black child taking a bath and then being hugged. It took several more scenes before I realized that we were supposed to think she was justified in not wanting to get near the child and that nothing, no amount of bathing, could make the child attractive because it was a black child.

The camera took us to the South before the Civil War, where we saw happy slaves, white actors in black face. They had easy hours, plenty of time for tap dancing, comfortable quarters and kind masters who played with puppies and kittens. This also struck me as strange because I believed that I had got a glimpse of slavery in Haverhill during the summer days when I had worked in the hay fields. I expected a scene to show how exhausted the slaves were, how burned by the sun, but there were no scenes like that. It was in Haverhill, pitching hay, that I first understood the Passover service that my father had conducted every year in which we gave thanks for being released from slavery in Egypt. As the movie continued, I was sorry for the soldiers who died but glad that the North was fighting the South to end slavery. I was impressed, as the movie reviews said I would be, by the spectacular cast-of-thousands battle scenes. The actor soldiers spread over hills seemingly as far as the horizon. When the slaves were freed, the first thing they did was lust after white women and dominate the state legislature. In the House of Representatives, they dressed in clownish plaid suits, guzzled from flasks, sat with their feet up and danced around like idiots. To save themselves from the power-hungry and sex-mad Negroes, the white men organized the Ku Klux Klan. The music became rousing, and a bugle blast from the theater orchestra announced the valiant riders of the Klan as they swept across the screen, saving white girls from the terror of the black mob. Negroes subdued, the final scenes were supposed to be a kind of Utopia in which people—some looking like Koreans, others like early Romans—were blessed by Jesus Christ. The orchestra played *Gloria* from Haydn's *Mass in C*, the lights came up, and I turned to Louie and met his astonished gaze. I said, "Have you ever seen anything so..." And before I could finish his face lit up. He thought he was agreeing with me when he said, "You're damn right, Harry. A gold mine!"

Back at the office, he said to Fanny, "Find out what it costs to get the New England rights to this golden goose." Surely Louie knew what he was doing. I was probably wrong about the picture. Everyone seemed to love it. They lined up at the box office. And surely the director, D.W. Griffith, deserved the benefit of the doubt. Fanny said, "What do you want with something that appeals to the basest passions of the semiliterate?"

"What are you talking about. You don't know nothing. President Wilson showed this picture at the White House."

"But he regrets it."

"Who says?"

"He says," said Fanny rattling a newspaper on her desk to show she'd read this information. "He didn't have any idea what the thing was about. He did it as a favor. Thomas Dixon used to be his student."

"Aw, what do you know? You ain't ever seen battle scenes like that before, did ya? Huh? Did ya?"

"I'm telling you, Louis," she said, "even President Wilson has come out against this picture."

Louie looked at me to see if I agreed, but I was too confused to respond. Anyway, maybe he would not be able to get the rights. And even if the rights were offered to him, he might not be able to afford to buy them. So there was plenty of time to argue about the morality of *Birth of a Nation*.

When the picture finished its run at major theaters and came up for sale, most of Louie's investors refused to give him the fifty thousand dollars required for New England distribution rights, not because they thought the picture objectionable but because they believed there wasn't any money left in it. They said the picture had played itself out.

But Louie knew differently. He and his family still lived in Haverhill where most people did not have the time or the money to travel into Boston. Neither did the citizens of Bangor, Rutland, Waterbury, Concord, Hartford, Augusta or Montpelier. They, too, wanted to see the picture that the whole country was talking about. They had read the reviews in newspapers: "The march of Sherman from Atlanta to the sea made the audience gasp with wonder and admiration. Nothing more impressive has ever been seen on the screen."

When I overheard Louie say to Nathan Gordon, "I'm putting in twelve thousand dollars of my own money," I got to work finding out as much as I could about the picture. I wanted to prove myself wrong. Surely I had misunderstood the intent because, if the picture really was as racist as it seemed, why would my friend Louie, who knew discrimination firsthand, want to distribute it to even more people?

I discovered that the film was based on a novel written by Thomas Dixon who, like his father before him, was a member of the Ku Klux Klan. The original title of the film was *The Clansman*, and it opened with that name in Los Angeles. The black members of the audience became enraged, and before the picture opened in New York, the National Association for the Advancement of Colored People tried to prevent its being shown. They exerted so much pressure that the director, Griffith, agreed to cut a few of the shots of white girls being attacked by wild Negroes, and he cut most of the epilogue in which an actor dressed as President Lincoln declared that he did not believe in racial equality and suggested that the solution to America's race problem was to send Negroes back to Africa. Dixon, the author of the original novel, shared in the profits of the picture and openly discussed his reasons for writing it.

"It was written by a member of the Klan, Louie," I said one day when we were going over hotel arrangements for various vaudeville players. "I understood it correctly, Louie. The author is quoted as saying that he thinks the dominant passion of colored men is to have sex with white women." Louie was only half listening. "He said the purpose of his book was to create a feeling of abhorrence in white people, especially white women, against colored men. He wants to prevent the mixing of white and Negro blood by intermarriage."

"Stop *hocking* me. What's this? You don't need to put Will Rogers into such an expensive room. He's a cowboy. He don't know from luxury. You should marry your own kind. Remember that."

"Dixon claims the NAACP wants to lower the standard of American citizenship by mixing white and black blood."

"Harry, will you shut up? How the hell am I supposed to know what the NA whatever you call it does? Huh? What are you saying for God sakes? You think Negroes should marry white people? They got laws against that. It ain't natural. Are we going over these bookings, or are you spouting nonsense?"

"I'm saying it's a nasty picture, and you shouldn't have anything to do with it."

"What? Why not?"

"That's what I'm talking to you about."

"What's to talk? The picture broke all theater records in every city it played. You don't know a fortune of money when you see it, after all I've taught you?"

"Dixon wants all black people in America to go back to Africa."

"So? What do I care what they do?"

"He says they want to go back to Africa."

"So? Maybe they do. How the hell should I know? You think they like the snow? Did you get a car to meet Houdini at the train?"

"You'll be showing racist propaganda, Louie."

"Harry, will you calm down? What's the matter with you? He don't portray them all as bad. You see good ones in there. You were sitting next to me. You seen them. The ones who were ready to die protecting their white friends. Griffith applauds them characters in the picture. He applauds their devotion."

"Louie! You're a Jew! How would you like it if all those black people in the picture were Jews rampaging around. You wouldn't be showing it all over New England if they were Jews!"

"If they was Jews? What are you talking? Jews don't act like that!"

"Neither do Negroes!"

"How do you know? Were you in the South when them things was going on? What do you think, the slaves were smart? You think they knew how to make laws?"

"Louie!"

"Harry, will you sit down? What's got into you? Why are we even talking about this?"

"Because you can't go around making people look worse than they are. How would you like it if Griffith made a picture showing all the Jews in their yarmulkes rubbing their hands together going into the banks and grabbing all the money and taking baths with money while all the farmers lose their farms."

"Aw, don't talk stupid."

"It's the same thing. It's the same principle."

"Principle? Listen to yourself. The principle is freedom of expression. That's the principle. Didn't you learn nothing in school?"

"You're defending it based on freedom of speech?"

"I ain't defending nothing! Especially not to you, you little pisher. I don't got to defend one goddamn thing! Now either we're working, or we ain't! Go on, go on. Get outta here! Get outta my face. I can't stand the sight of you."

"I can't stand the sight of you either! You'll do anything for money. You don't care about justice!"

"How dare you say that to me! Goddamn it! Me, who has tried to uplift the public with everything I do. Me, who brought the Boston Opera all the way to Haverhill, brought the real opera to the people, and now you accuse. You stand there and accuse me. Get the hell out of my sight!" His face was red, and his eyes bulged. "Get out of my sight before I break your skull!" Then he lunged and would have caught me, but I ducked in time and ran out and slammed the door shut. He came after me, and I ran but stopped when I heard a loud thud. I turned and saw Louie collapsed on the floor. "Fanny! Fanny!" She came running, saw him and said, "Oh, for heaven's sakes. Not again."

"What's the matter with him? What's the matter with him?"

"He's just fainted. It isn't anything. Go get a towel in the bathroom and put some cold water on it and lay it on his forehead. Go head. I've got to finish typing the contract for First National."

I did as she said, and when Louie came to, he looked up at me and said, "What have I ever done to you that you should hurt me so much?"

Mr. Gordon gave him the money he needed to buy the New England rights to *Birth of a Nation*. He and Gordon formed a company, Master Photoplays, with Louie owning twenty-five percent. He distributed *Birth of a Nation* to towns in Maine, Connecticut, Rhode Island, New Hampshire and Vermont, earned a quarter of a million dollars, moved Maggie and the girls to a big house in Brookline and set about organizing the Louis B. Mayer Film Company, although he had no actors, directors or screenwriters.

Chapter Ten

Money flowed into our Piedmont Street offices not only from *Birth of a Nation* but from theaters, too. Louie and Mr. Gordon soon owned at least a piece of fifty of them in New England.

But Louie was restless and wanted to get started producing pictures. When I was sixteen, he took me with him to the Actors' Fund Fair in New York City. He had no films to sell yet, but he rented a booth, and we draped it with a banner: "The Louis B. Mayer Film Company." All the major film studios were represented at the fair, Vitagraph, Biograph, Kalem, Essanay, Keystone, Mutual Film, Victor Film, Eclectic Film, Solax, Thanhouser and Fox Films. Motion pictures were fast becoming big business in America, and even at sixteen, I knew I'd find a way to be part of it. Except for some of the major theater owners who were in their forties, it was a young person's game. I did not think of myself as being too young to be taken seriously. This attitude made me bolder than was appropriate, no doubt. My voice was now deep enough to fool adults on the phone, and I conducted some pretty serious business with men who would have been surprised to see that I only had a little fuzz on my upper lip.

The war in Europe, which stopped the flow of feature films from there to America, had forced our industry to mature until most of the studios were producing multi-reel pictures. Full-length stories showcased the talents of actors who were now named in the credits. Movie stars arrived at the Actors' Fund Fair to promote themselves and their studios. Francis X. Bushman, the barrel-chested matinee idol, walked by our booth with four pony-size Great Danes. America's sweetheart, Mary Pickford, paraded by surrounded by an entourage. Our booth happened to be next to the Vitagraph booth, and there before my eyes, real as anything, was Anita Stewart. Her hair, a mass of brown waves, was held in place by two strands of pearls twisted together around her forehead. She had the gangly delicacy of a fawn or foal, and her abashed expression further enhanced the air of vulnerability that made her so popular. She signed autographs, smiled for hours and was gracious to everyone.

While Louie worked the room by shaking as many hands as possible, I manned the booth handing out brochures that explained our philosophy: the star is the most important member of the team. I discussed our plans to make family entertainment. I spoke the name of Louis B. Mayer as much as possible, describing him as a comet in the heavens and repeating what he often said about himself—that he was going to be the most important man in the movie industry. There were lulls in the crush of people, and during one of them, Anita Stewart and I exchanged hellos. It surprised me that she was as star struck as I was. "He breeds them on his estate," she said about Bushman's Great Danes. "He has twenty-eight of them."

"Did you read that in *Photoplay*?"

"Or *Motion Picture World*," she said. "One of them."

"It was *Photoplay*," I said, to show her I was up on things. "It showed him with that puppy."

"That puppy! Was that cute? Those paws?" And right before my eyes, she turned into that puppy, held her hands the way that puppy held its paws in the photo of it sleeping on its back and made her mouth into a sleeping puppy's mouth. It all happened in a split second, but it was so accurate, all I could do was stand there in awe.

When the cowboy star Tom Mix walked by with spurs jingling, she put her hand over her heart and whispered to me, "Be still my heart!" Another time she whispered, "My feet are killing me!" Our age connected us. She was a teenager too.

On the third day of the fair, I saw Anita sway, then grab one of the poles holding up the Vitagraph banner to support herself. No one else seemed to notice; they thrust their programs in her face and looked adoringly at her. She must have felt my eyes on her because she turned and showed me the panic in her eyes. I hurried to her and said to the line of fans waiting to approach her, "Thank you, thank you so much for coming. Yes, yes, I know you've been waiting," and other such words, while Anita managed to get herself to the only chair available, the one behind our booth. She was hidden from the crowd back there. When I had persuaded the last person out front to return in an hour, I found her sitting on the chair bent in two, her face on her knees.

"Anita, should I get your mother?"

"Harry," she said lifting her head—she was the color of putty. "The people are blurry."

"What people, Anita?"

"All the people."

"Blurry how?"

"Like you right now. Distorted. In a fun-house mirror." She grabbed my arm. "I'm scared."

I abandoned my post, ran from booth to booth looking for Mrs. Stewart, a round woman in a floor-length chinchilla coat. She was at the Fox Film's booth talking to a medium-size man with a dark thick mustache who had tried to hide his bald dome by combing his side hair over it. While Mrs. Stewart spoke, he tidied brochures on his counter, but in a way that was so awkward, I looked harder. He used only one hand. The other hand remained stuffed in his jacket pocket. "Mrs. Stewart!" I called rushing to her. Then I froze in my tracks when I saw a sign "Theda Bara in Person This Afternoon!"

Mrs. Stewart was saying, "Motion-picture fairs ain't in her contract. She don't get compensation for this. On her feet from morning to night, and she don't get nothing for it. We drive down Broadway; we see Clara Kimball Young's name in electric lights. They don't put Anita's name nowhere. She's worked years with no vacation. When she asked for one, they said she could retire for all they..."

"Come with me," I interrupted her.

"Pardon me?" She stared, then remembered me from the booth, and we hurried through the crowd. Anita was bent over on the chair, her face on her knees. "Annie!" Mrs. Stewart rushed to her daughter. Ours was about the least popular booth at the fair, so I was free to attend to Anita.

"Ma," she said in a tiny voice. "What is this place?"

"This place? You know this place."

"How do you do," Anita said. "Very heavy, thank you."

"Annie!"

"Leading man, four hundred dollars a week; cameraman, seventy-five dollars a week. Four weeks to complete an average production. Yes, I do have a pet. I bleed every month."

"Annie!" She took her daughter's greenish-gray face in her hands. "Harry, darling, get my car. Hurry. I'm taking her home to Long Island."

I ran to the building entrance wondering how on earth I was going to know which car of the hundreds parked outside belonged to Anita. They were lined up out there by the curb, each one the latest model. My attention was arrested by a white limousine with tinted black windows that purred to a stop at the curb. The chauffeur, in Moroccan blue uniform, knee-high black boots and a blue cap with a snake insignia above the visor, opened the back door and stood at attention so rigidly it was dramatic. Two people hidden under black tent-like Arabian garments—with only slits in the veil to see through—got out of the back seat and stood next to the chauffeur. An Arab in a red fez, white bloomers, red vest and golden slippers with pointed toes emerged from the car and stood at attention next to the chauffeur. All the chauffeurs from the other cars parked near the curb were now standing next to their vehicles watching. Everyone on the sidewalk was watching too.

All of us knew who would emerge next. But she didn't. She didn't. She didn't. And then... she did! Theda Bara, moving as if in an opium dream, slowly got out of the car. She wore a gold-and-black-striped headpiece like a pharaoh's, with a golden snake above her forehead. Her arms were bare with bracelets not on her wrists but on her slender, snow-white upper arms. Her eyes were very large, outlined in black brought to points at the sides. She jingled when she moved because of the ankle bracelets under her long, almost transparent, billowy culottes. The veiled Arabian attendants stood on each side of her and waited while the chauffeur reached into the car. Out pranced a magnificent white Borzoi in a diamond collar with a ruby leash. Theda Bara accepted the leash, and the entourage entered the film fair.

"If I died now," said one of the chauffeurs, "I wouldn't care. I seen it all."

Another kept repeating, "Holy moly. Holy moly. Did you see that?"

"She's from the sands of Arabia," a young girl on the sidewalk said. "Her mother was a mistress. That's why she can't help being bad."

I was spellbound too, but remembering my mission, I found Anita's chauffeur and had him waiting with the Packard when Mrs. Stewart came out with her arm around her daughter's slender shoulders. Anita kept her face down as they hurried to the car.

I returned to the booth and stayed there for the rest of the afternoon. This was my job. I knew it was unreasonable to be mad at Louie, but I didn't think it was fair that he got to wander around. I wanted to see Theda Bara close up in the tent that William Fox had erected for her at the back of the auditorium. It was Friday, the last day of the fair. I had never met an Arab except in books—Scheherazade, Aladdin, Ali Baba. Some of the people who stopped at our booth told me that the tent was dimly lit, draped in velvet and perfumed with incense. They said Theda Bara reclined on a circular bed surrounded by human skulls and crystal balls, that she spoke in hushed tones about her exotic childhood along the Nile and her triumphs on the stage in Paris.

Louie returned to the booth as the fair was closing. No one had shown up at our booth for more than an hour. He said, "What's eating you?"

"My turn," I said and regretted the sound of childish petulance. I hurried through the auditorium to stand in line to see Theda Bara. But it was too late. The black candles that lined the walkway into the tent no longer flickered.

A black skull-and-crossbones banner blocked the tent entrance. All around me, booths were being disassembled and one-sheets packed in boxes. Actors and producers no longer smiled but now were free to show their fatigue.

Not fair. Not my fault that I had to work the booth all day. There should have been an after-hours meeting for those of us who couldn't get there on time. I could understand closing the tent to the public, but those of us in the industry should have been able... What was the worst that could happen if I just barged in? They'd say get out of here. It would be embarrassing but not tragic. So I ignored the skull banner blocking the entrance, lifted the tent flap and went inside.

A table with a white cloth was in the middle of the floor. Four men in yarmulkes sat around it. On the table were a wine goblet, a loaf of challah bread and a candlestick. Waving her hands in a circular motion above the candle flame, as my mother had done every Friday night, was Theda Bara saying the Sabbath prayer: "Barukh ata Adonai Eloheinu melekh ha-olam..."

All eyes turned to me. "Gut Shabbes," I said. "Shavua tov." The words came from my bones. It was my father wishing us a good week as he had done every Friday night. I had not heard those words for more than ten years. The Borzoi, resting on the floor, put his chin back down on his outstretched paws.

Theda Bara said, "Shabbat shalom. Please. Come in." She wore no pharaoh's headpiece now, just a piece of lace on top of her head and instead of exotic clothes, a muslin smock. "Look at his eyes, Papa. So full of soul. Come in. Don't be shy."

"Like Uncle Moishe," Papa said. He was a slight, round-shouldered, harmless old man, the sort of man a mouse would have conversations with in a fairy tale. On the floor next to him was the black burqa he had worn when he got out of the white car that afternoon.

"You got a lotta nerve," said the man Mrs. Stewart had talked to that afternoon. The hand that had been in his pocket when he rearranged one-sheets was on the table, and I could see that it was paralyzed.

"Please," said Theda Bara, gesturing toward the table. "Papa's about to say the prayer over the wine. Do you know it?"

"Yes. I do."

Papa said the prayer and passed the wine goblet around. Theda Bara handed it to me, and when I hesitated, she said, "Go on. Don't stand on ceremony." Papa said the prayer over the bread and broke off a piece to hand around too.

"I am astonished at the balls of this boy," the man from that afternoon said. He was portly with an egg-shaped head. His thick eyebrows met above his nose. His eyes were suspicious and shaded by heavy lids. The corners of his mouth turned down. "Just like that, he walks in. I never saw nothing like that in my life. What is the reason for your entering this forbidden tent?"

"I'm Theodosia Goodman," said Theda Bara. "This is my papa, Mr. Goodman, my Uncle Yonah, my cousin Shimmen and my employer, Mr. Fox." Shimmen was still in his Turkish bloomers and wore his fez instead of a yarmulke.

"You should pardon me for telling you this," said Papa to me. "But your trousers need to be let down."

"Papa!"

"I could do this for you."

"Papa! Stop!"

"You go behind the screen, take them off, I'll fix them. Takes two seconds."

"I had a growth spurt," I said, now thinking that maybe Louie was right to complain about my lack of interest in clothes.

"Forgive Papa."

"What's to forgive?" said Papa. "I won't even charge him a penny."

"You don't have time to mend trousers," said Uncle Yonah looking down at a gold watch on a chain. "Look at the hour. We'll be late to the theater."

"Irving Berlin," Cousin Shimmen told me. "Have you seen it? *Stop, Look, and Listen.*"

Uncle Yonah said, "I didn't come here from Cincinnati to sit in a tent. Who knows when we'll go to the theater again?"

"Answer me," William Fox said to me.

"Shimmen," Theda Bara said, "you had a growth spurt about that age too." She ducked behind a Japanese screen painted with white chrysanthemums. The Borzoi lifted his head, followed Theda Bara with his eyes, then got up, trotted to the screen and sat in front of it. "Papa, please get the maid for me. She's out there somewhere." Papa exited through a flap at the side of the tent.

"State your business at this fair," said Mr. Fox, drawing a long cigar from his pocket, lighting it, setting the match carefully in an ashtray on the table and taking a puff. He was wearing white cotton socks more appropriate to a tennis outfit than to the three-piece suit he wore. Uncle Yonah and Cousin Shimmen got up from the table and began to put things away in satchels made of Oriental carpet.

"I work for Louis B. Mayer," I said.

"Who?"

"Louis B. Mayer."

"Never heard of him."

"He's the foremost exhibitor and distributor of high-class entertainment in New England."

"No, he ain't. I would of heard of him. William Fox knows everyone who is of importance."

"I would be happy to introduce you to him," I said.

"His booth is next to Vitagraph," Theda Bara called from behind the screen. "I was hoping to get over there to meet Anita Stewart. I'm a big fan. Did you get to meet her, Harry?"

"Yes," I called to her. "She's just like on the screen."

"That's more than I can say about me," said Theda Bara. Papa entered the tent through the back flap with a small, thin black woman dressed in black clothes. She went behind the screen, and the star said, "Golly. You were supposed to be here half an hour ago. You know I can't work this get up without your help."

"I invented her," Mr. Fox said to me, puffing his cigar and leaning back on his chair. "I took a tailor's daughter from Cincinnati and made her a worldwide star. I am the first film man to do that. Name one other who has done that. You cannot. They tell the truth. They tell you Anita Stewart went to Erasmus High School in Brooklyn. Is Erasmus High School interesting? They tell you Florence Turner eats a soft-boiled egg for breakfast. This is not interesting. This is not theater. It is only William Fox who has applied the lessons of vaudeville ballyhoo to the making of films." He tapped his cigar ash carefully into the ashtray. "The public don't want the truth. They want a vamp."

"You should see the angry letters married women send me," Theda Bara said from behind the screen. "They think I go around stealing husbands."

"The public don't want the truth unless the truth is dramatic. Take Tom Mix. You like the cowboy Tom Mix?"

"Yes, I do."

"I know you do. Everyone does. He is a real Westerner. He was the U.S. Marshal in Oklahoma. Tom Mix performs all his own stunts. His horse Tony can perform twenty tricks, including stamping on villains and jumping a thirty-foot chasm. Does William Fox ignore the merits of this animal? No. He includes his name in the credits. Name one other film man puts the horse's name in the credits. I do this for two reasons. One, it makes Tom happy, and two, it sells pictures." He took another a puff on his cigar. "At the age of sixteen, I appeared on the stage with Cliff Gordon under the name Schmaltz Brothers. Listen to one of our jokes: I say, 'Someone wanted to buy my blind horse.' Cliff says, 'No one would buy that.' I say, 'Why do you say that? Irving offered me two hundred dollars for him yesterday.' Cliff says, 'Why, he hasn't got two cents.' I say, 'I know but wasn't it a good offer?'" Mr. Fox eyed me, waiting to see if I would laugh. When I didn't, he continued. "I was the first to open a moving-picture theater in Brooklyn. It was the old Unique, which, by an outlay of sixteen thousand dollars, was transformed into a beautiful playhouse. In that place, I combined vaudeville with motion pictures. We changed acts three times a week. I mastered the difficulties of booking artists. I created four booking offices, and today thousands of theaters all over the country are operated on the William Fox lines, vaudeville and motion pictures. By the age of thirty-one, I had twelve theaters on Manhattan Island. Can the individual you work for say the same?"

Out from behind the screen came Theda Bara, pharaoh helmet in place, eyes outlined in fierce black, bracelets on her bare upper arms. She was aloof, regal and stood there looking into the distance. Her father and uncle pulled their burqas over their clothes; her cousin adjusted his fez and straightened his red vest; the maid stood back to appraise her work, came forward and gave a quick tug to straighten the vamp's culottes, picked up the dog's leash and handed it to the star, nodding approval at her work and disappearing out the back. Uncle Yonah opened the main tent flap, and Theda Bara, flanked by her Arab attendants, the white Borzoi trotting ahead of her, went out to play the role of the vamp driving away in her limousine.

Mr. Fox took down the skull-and-crossbones banner. I thought it would be more polite to look away when he folded it because he did it so awkwardly with his one good hand. I don't know why I followed him across the floor to his booth, but I did. While a crew of workers disassembled the Fox Film's booth, he said to me, "I was a poor boy on Stanton Street. My home was in a tenement. And now Fox Film Corporation is a public company, the first film company listed on the Curb Exchange. Answer my question." He stopped walking and looked me full in the face, standing too close, a bullying tactic. I defied him by not stepping back as he expected me to, as most people probably would. It felt like an aggressive act for him to get so close to me, to break right into my aura and invade my illusion of safety. We stood almost nose to nose in the middle of the chaos of the closing fair—workers hurrying by, people barking orders, men pushing loaded dollies. He smelled of cigar smoke but also cologne. "State the reason you entered the tent."

"I wanted to see Theda Bara."

"So you could get her away from me?"

"What?"

"She's under contract. Tell that to the person you work for."

"What?"

"Do you know what a contract is? Do you know what happens to people who break them?" Now I stepped back. "Listen," he said taking a step forward so my space was reinvaded. "You keep your trap shut. No one wants to know the truth."

"Well, I certainly didn't," I said stepping back again and to the side. "I liked it better thinking there was such a person as Theda Bara."

This time he stood where he was. "You got balls, kid," he said. "I like a kid with balls. You want a job with me? You got one."

Chapter Eleven

"But Anita Stewart's under contract," Louie said the next day at breakfast in the Astor Hotel. "Why would she break her contract with Vitagraph?"

"You saw her."

"But how do you know that has anything to do with Vitagraph?"

"Because her mother was complaining to William Fox."

"You don't know. You don't know, Harry. Maybe she complains all the time to anyone who's around. Maybe the girl has a disorder. Look at my daughter. She stutters. Why does she stutter? Is it a bad environment at home? No. She stutters." He handed me another roll and indicated with an authoritative gesture toward my mouth that I should eat it. He was still trying to fatten me up. "Why would a star like Anita Stewart give up a contract with Vitagraph, one of the biggest studios in the country, and come work for the Louis B. Mayer Film Company that never even made one picture yet."

"Because we'll promise her happiness," I said. He laughed and took a noisy slurp of coffee.

After breakfast, he went to an exhibitor's meeting, and I was free to wander around. I took the trolley down to the docks to visit the place where I first met Uncle Sonny. Maybe I was looking for a clue to solve the mystery of his disappearance but it couldn't be found there because all was different. No sailing schooners, side-wheelers, or passengers with luggage but horses, at least twenty thousand of them assembled in a grossly overcrowded makeshift stockyard. Soldiers were loading them into transport ships.

Most of the horses did not wear halters so when a terrified animal broke from the herd and galloped away, it took a long time for the soldiers to catch it. A couple of the smaller horses were so frightened they ran right off the dock into the black water and drowned, their wide eyes horrible to remember. Some were so scared of stepping onto the gangplank that they fainted, and the soldiers had to haul them back onto the dock where they stood over them cursing and hosing the manure off them. The men had to manage thousands of animals that were as scared of one another as they were of the place, and fights broke out: ears pinned back, teeth bared, hind legs thrust out and landing with a smack.

Much to my amazement, no one stopped me when I walked up the gangplank. Above deck, there were hundreds of wooden wagons being mended by soldiers. Other soldiers were sorting acres of leather reins, bridles, saddles, woolen blankets, sacks of feed and piles of laundry. Some were tearing old shirts into rags. Below deck were the corrals, hundreds of animals bunched together, some soldiers forking hay to them and others shoveling manure into wheelbarrows. It seemed a very dangerous assignment to take care of horses that were seasick and frightened. A young soldier, sitting on a bale of hay, noticed me, raised his eyebrows and waited for me to explain myself. "I wouldn't like to have your job," I said.

"I wouldn't like to be you when they catch you," he said. "What are you doing in here?"

"I don't know."

He snorted. "Maybe you're a volunteer come to help us quote unquote get the job done "

"Is this where you sleep?"

"Go on, kid. Get out of here. You don't want to be down here when the rest of them come in."

"Don't they get sick?"

"Takes us twelve days to get across. Usually about one hundred fifty of them die and maybe forty will get sick or injured."

"So what do they do with them?"

He made a gun out of his hand and shot himself in the head, "*Tchoo*!"

"Did you ever kill one?"

"One? Try dozens."

"You've killed dozens of horses?"

"You'd kill them too, kid, if you saw what they looked like—half a face, some of them. You think the Boche artillery discriminates? You think those minnies say to themselves, 'Oh, let's not strike there. That's a poor defenseless horse?' When the *minenwerfer* burst close by, the noise is so terrifying that some of the horses die of fright." He took off his cap and rubbed his shaved head and slapped the cap back on. "The Huns use a shell that contains gas. But our gas masks are so uncomfortable and hot, some fellows don't put them on, and others put them on, but the masks don't work." He sighed, stood up and sat down. "Go on. Get out of here," he said to me.

"What happens when the masks don't work?"

"You go blind. You get burned." He had been comfortable sitting on a bale of hay, and I came along and made him remember things he didn't want to think about, and now I didn't know how to back away. This trip to New York was quite an eye-opener. One day Theda Bara gets stripped of her make-believe, and the next day I see cavalry horses not as the gallant steeds of the screen but as pathetic food for the cannon. "You get good at identifying the shells," the soldier said. "There's a certain sound to the ones that will whiz on by and another sound to the ones that will drop near you. Some of the shells explode with a sound of crockery being broken. Some shells sound like a fast train. We know when to ignore machine-gun and rifle bullets and when a steady *phew-phew-phew* means the Boche are right next to us. Sometimes our own men fire machine guns at us by mistake." He took a watch out of his pocket, looked at it, wound it and put it back. "You can't tell me the *Lusitania* wasn't carrying munitions," he said. "Claim it was an innocent passenger ship. The State Department warned all those tourists. They knew it was carrying munitions to England. You ask me, the Boche had a right to sink it. It wasn't enough reason to get us into this war."

"What do you do with all the horses?"

"We deliver fresh horses and mules to the front and return wounded animals to the veterinary hospital. Over there we sell the dead ones to an old farmer who comes by in his wagon, lifts two or three at a time cranking a winch he made. Sells the hides. We set out from the remount station about four in the afternoon and travel at night. We use Missouri mules as lead animals, a team of them before and a team behind. Hitched to them are eighty horses divided four abreast all roped together. The mud comes up to your knees. Some shadow or flapping fabric spooks one of them or a bee stings one, and they all go crazy because they're roped together, and the spooked one spooks all the others. They go crazy. The whole hitch goes wild. When they see smashed armored tanks upended in the mud, they get terrified. Sometimes we have to tread on a new cemetery, acres of wooden crosses set in rows, the earth freshly turned. They don't like soft footing. Traveling at night makes matters worse because the horses stumble over stones or spent munitions or sink a foot in a rabbit hole, and when one goes down, it pulls others down."

"Hey, Al," a soldier called from the horse pen, "you're on break, not on vacation. It's my turn."

"When we arrive in France," Al said to me, "another remount division meets us on shore, and while the officers sort the horses, we enlisted men scrub the ship so it will be clean for the next cargo. It takes us four days to get the horse shit out of here, and then they load us into Army trucks and take us to headquarters. Last time I was in a little town called Claye Souilly." He saluted me and said, "Give my regards to Broadway, remember me to Herald Square," and walked away.

I hurried up to the deck and managed to navigate through the crowd of soldiers and horses out to the street. I was possessed by the idea that this young man was going to die, that he was almost a ghost, almost just a photograph that his family would look at with regret. I wanted to scream up to God, "Why are you always so unfair?" I walked as fast as I could uptown along a pathway next to the Hudson River where barges were being towed by tugboats. The tugs reminded me of Uncle Sonny. Where was Uncle Sonny? It was a beautiful fall day—blue sky, warm—and I thought that if I went to Central Park and wandered among the autumn trees, I could get the gloom out of my head. It was a long walk from the pier uptown, and I found myself pretending to be a soldier slogging along mile after mile, waiting my turn to take revenge on the Boche.

Central Park blotted out the city, and it was with some relief that I wandered on leafy paths and came at last to a lake that had been co-opted for a movie shoot. About twenty young actors, all too young to be drafted, were lounging around in military uniforms, some American, others German. The uniforms were too big for most of them, the cuffs of the sleeves and trousers turned up. They were eating candy and horsing around. Parked on the road next to the lake was a truck with a sign on the side: "Biograph Newsreel Service."

One of the crew, a small wiry boy who looked about my age, was wearing a black beret, knickers and lace-up boots. He was testing bayonets to be sure the blades retracted when he jammed them into a leather trunk. Some of the film crew were wading into the lake, planting bladders filled with gunpowder, while others practiced tossing soldier dummies into the air. The director put his megaphone to his lips and shouted, "Attention! Get up you sluggards, and let's see if we can get it right this time." The soldiers stood up and put on their helmets. "You enter the water here and charge across to that outcropping of stones like we practiced." The boys arranged themselves and the crew member who had been testing the bayonets gave the few that he had to some of the actors, most of whom couldn't resist jabbing him. The boys who did not receive a bayonet complained and tried to grab bayonets from the others. The cameraman put his eye to the lens and said, "What the hell is that glinting over there?" The director looked through the lens and shouted, "Kenny! Go over there, and pick up that candy wrapper."

Kenny, the young man in the beret, said, "Let me see it first."

The cameraman clapped his palms on his cheeks and said, "Holy Mary, mother of God, I am going to go crazy with this. I am going to go crazy."

"I'll do it fast," Kenny said running to the camera and peering in. "Oh, I see what you mean," he said and ran to the edge of the water and got the candy wrapper, which he held up for the actors to see as an example of bad behavior. When all was arranged, the director shouted, "Action!" The boys charged into the water, the bladders of gunpowder exploded underwater making it seem as if bullets had struck. Pop! Pop! Some of the soldiers stuck bayonets in others, while dummies were thrown into the air as if blown to bits by gunfire. "Cut! How'd that look?" The cameraman held thumbs up, and the boys rejoiced by splashing one another and playing catch with the dummies.

Kenny shouted, "Hold on, Irwin! You have to take it again!"

"Why, may I ask?" said the cameraman, who was about twice Kenny's age.

"Why? You didn't see that?"

"Oh, may the holy mother preserve us."

"You didn't see that American kid stick another American kid? How could you not see that? You were looking through the lens. This is supposed to be a newsreel. It's supposed to be true. You think our boys over there kill each other while they're running across a brook? I don't know. Maybe they do. But I don't think so. I don't know. What do you think, Frank?" he asked the director. "You think they go around killing their platoon mates? You don't think they know each other? Haven't they been sleeping in the same trench together for weeks?"

The director heaved a sigh and called through his megaphone, "Take ten. We're doing it again, you boneheads, and this time, only kill Germans. Get it? Look at the helmets before you jab." The crew dispersed to various lounging spots, and it happened that Kenny chose a spot of grass near me to lie down flat on his back. He pulled his beret over his face, clasped his hands on his narrow chest and lay there like he was in a casket.

"Why don't you take pictures of the real war," I asked. "Why don't you go down to the piers and take shots of those horses drowning in the Hudson?"

He was as surprised as I was by the belligerent tone of my question, and he pulled the beret off his face and squinted up at me with one eye closed. Then he sat up, took a package of French cigarettes out of his pocket and offered me one. I sat down next to him and accepted a light. "Military won't let us anywhere near it. The only boys who get real footage are military cameramen. That footage never reaches the theaters. If it isn't destroyed during combat, it's destroyed by military censors."

"So none of those newsreels about the war are true?"

"Sure. Some of them are. But it takes a long time to get the reels back here, and we have a theater schedule to keep. We make one of these a week." Cigarette dangling from his lower lip, he extended his hand and said, "Kenny Anderson," and pumped my hand up and down.

"Harry Sirkus."

"I'm a cameraman," Kenny said.

"Really?"

"Well, a cameraman in his youth."

"Have you been with Biograph a long time?"

"My whole life, if you count being my sister's baby brother. She runs the art department over there. She makes those tiny rubber people they throw out of ships when they fake a naval battle. She makes little clothes for them, depending on where it's supposed to be. Like that bomb that went off on Wall Street? She made some little briefcases for the corpses. You ever see that reel of the San Francisco earthquake? I was, maybe, ten when she did that. Even the mayor of San Francisco was fooled. No one noticed there were no people in the shots. The real footage is crowded with people, horses, automobiles, trolleys. My sister was upset there wasn't time for her to make some fire trucks."

"It wasn't real?"

"Pathé got some real shots. They were there, but we got ours to the theaters first. We got the scoop. By the time Pathé got theirs ready to go, it was yesterday's news."

"Those fires weren't real?"

"I take it you found it memorable. I'll tell her."

"But I saw it. I saw the buildings burning."

"She is going to be so happy when I tell her this." He saw I was confused. "It was all shot in the studio. She made those buildings out of cardboard. The ground was made out of clay that dried, and when they pulled the clay apart, it looked like a fissure in the earth. The crew set fire to the cardboard buildings. All these years, she's been embarrassed about how there were no trolleys or horses or anything."

"You mean it was fake?"

He looked at me in a way that made me feel too young. "Must have moved you. That's the goal. If you aren't moved, it's not entertainment."

"But how can boys being killed in the war be entertainment?"

"Good question."

"What's your answer?"

"I don't know. Ask yourself." He squashed his cigarette butt into the grass.

"Are you going to fake their mothers crying?" I said aggressively, my tone the result of feeling humiliated by my innocence.

He pulled his beret straight down over his wing-like ears and stood up. "If we do," he said, "I'll backlight it so the hair looks like a halo, sort of Virgin Maryish." He did not smile, but I knew he was teasing me for being so earnest.

I wished I could be Kenny's friend. I missed having friends my own age. As he walked back to the lake, I called after him: "Kenny!" He turned, but all I managed to say was "Good luck!"

Chapter Twelve

Anita Stewart came to Boston to make a personal appearance at Nathan Gordon's Olympia Theater, where one of her pictures was playing. The Gordons gave a gala party for her at their mansion in Jamaica Plain, and I went there dressed in my first tuxedo, a present from Louie who was always saying to me, "If you look like a million, you'll feel like a million." I spent quite some time admiring myself in the mirror, a decidedly prosperous, good-looking young man, tall, lean, muscular—a commanding fellow with curly dark hair and no beard yet, just fuzz no matter how many times I rubbed my pink cheeks.

Butlers at the entrance doors accepted top hats, scarves and fur capes worn more for show than necessity because it was a warm spring night. The sound of a Viennese waltz filled the grand foyer.

In the ballroom, men and women in formal attire were lifting Champagne flutes from silver trays carried by waiters in white jackets. Chandeliers sparkled light on everyone. Banquet tables were heaped with food. Anita stood in one corner as if backed there by the crowd that surrounded her. She was greeting everyone with a smile and an extended hand sheathed in a white glove up to her elbow. The dark circles under her eyes were the color of bruises. Nearby, her mother hovered, alert as a she-wolf.

Men in cutaway tails and gray muttonchops smoked cigars and talked business. Matrons in gowns sat on love seats around the edge of the floor appraising those who passed by and holding fans before their lips so no one except their immediate neighbor could hear what they said. Waiters passed around trays of miniature food cut in interesting shapes. In front of a mirror in a gilt frame was a group of girls in ball gowns, some with flowers twined in their hair, others with jewels sparkling around their waist and neck. How lovely they were! They had erected a barrier of giggles about themselves broken now and then by quick eye darts around the room to see who might be admiring them. Secretly, they peeked in the gilt mirror for reassurance.

I had always wanted and not wanted to be included on the guest list of this sort of party. I wanted to be among the swells, but I worried that I wouldn't know how to behave. My classmates in Haverhill who had attended the formal shindigs in the ballrooms of one another's houses were trained year after year in the etiquette of such things—how to stand before adults without shrinking when introduced, how to ask a lady to dance, how to perform the dances, what to speak about while dancing and how to return the lady to her seat when the music stopped. In movies, I'd seen dashing cavaliers with perfect manners twirl about with perfect girls in wedding-cake dresses. It never occurred to me that in real life, the girls had to wait to be asked. The movies never showed the wallflowers or, if there was one, she was shown as so unattractive, she deserved to be sitting by her self. The audience was encouraged to ridicule her. But now I saw that even pretty girls had to face the humiliation of waiting to be asked. If I invited them to dance (even me!), they would be grateful. There they were in their dresses, purebred kittens, brave little creatures trying to put the best face on their predicament, which was that their future depended upon finding a man willing to take care of them. Maybe he would be at this party. They were as trapped as I was, as everyone was, in their stage of life. They would soon be old enough to hire the girls I grew up with at the Elizabeth Home, girls who, at the age of six, began to scrub floors, lug water buckets, shine brass, mend clothes, darn socks and wash dishes, so that when they were fourteen, they would be competent domestics. I stood in that glittering ballroom and hoped that Katie O'Reilly whose job was washing the breakfast dishes, and Maria dePasquale, who had to take care of the crying babies, might, by some miracle, be doing as I was, picking up a crystal flute and tasting for the first time a carbonated drink that wasn't exactly delicious but produced an expansive feeling.

One of the girls by the mirror was willowy in a soft yellow dress cut so the tops of her breasts were exposed. Her hair was pulled up and held in place by jewels. She seemed composed, listening to her friends with her head inclined in a charming way. I would have to cut her out of the flock and herd her over to the banquet tables. It could be done. Our eyes met. She was adorable! Was that a blush? Did she blush?

To fortify myself, I worked my way across the room to the banquet tables where there was an array of cheeses, meats and patés. A chef in a white coat and a tall white hat presided over a hunk of beef that he stabbed with a long fork. He placed a slice on a plate and handed it across the table to me. How was I supposed to cut it standing up? While trying to figure that out, I tried to look busy by adding other things to the plate: cookies, dainty sandwich triangles and sausages wrapped in pastry. I still didn't know how to manage, so I set the plate down and walked away hoping no one had seen me waste food. I went to another banquet table where there was no intimidating chef and found delicious tidbits to nibble.

"Harry!" It was Sally Gordon dressed in a drab gray gown, her brown hair parted in the middle and pulled back into a bun. I was flattered that she remembered me from the one time we met. "You look so handsome!" She was looking up at me with a face that was not her normal face. Age had fallen off of her, and I saw before me the flirtatious girl Mr. Gordon had married.

Flummoxed, I said, "I thought so, too, when I looked in the mirror." She laughed, and her age reappeared. "I've never been to a party like this in my life, Mrs. Gordon. Thank you for inviting me."

"You schmooze, you nosh, you schmooze. Nothing to it. Eat. Go on. Don't be shy." I chewed a mushroom tart, swallowed, picked up something else, tasted it, nodded approval and took a sip of Champagne. Mrs. Gordon's attention was drawn by other guests who stopped to greet her. She thanked them for coming and stood abashed when she couldn't think up replies to clever remarks. I wanted to get Anita's attention. I would wave, she would wave back, and when the crowd around her became thinner, I'd go to her and tell her that I had managed to see Theda Bara and that Theda Bara said she was a fan of Anita's. Then I'd defy William Fox and tell Anita the truth about Theda Bara. She probably already knew. I'd tell her anyway, and we'd have a good laugh. Mrs. Gordon came close to me, stood close enough so it made me nervous and said in a low voice, "Anita Stewart is seriously ill. I am a nurse, Harry, so I know symptoms. You must arrange her departure now."

"Me?"

"Sally!" An older woman in a gown trimmed with fox hurried toward us. "There you are! I've been looking for you. Come meet my sister. She's in town for the suffragist parade. I thought you said you weren't going to wear that old dress again," and she led my companion away into the crowd. I worked my way closer to Anita and saw that her eyes were strange and unfocused and that her mother had taken on the task of greeting star-struck guests. Though she was smiling, Mrs. Stewart's face was strained, and her plump body, encased in a beaded gown like a bejeweled knockwurst, was poised for flight.

I eased my way through the crowd and hurried toward the actress, saying, "Anita Stewart! I've been looking for you!" She turned toward the sound of her name as a blind person might with a drifting head, searching in the air. "Come on!" I said. "You have to meet my sister. She's in town for the suffragist parade!" I put my arm around her shoulders and escorted her through the crowd, her mother saying to the disappointed guests, "Yeah, yeah, we'll be right back. Don't go 'way—we'll be right back." Anita hurried along next to me, docile as a frightened child, her eyes on the floor, my protective arm around her bony shoulders. In the foyer, Mrs. Stewart whispered, "Get the car." I ran to the driveway, found the chauffeur and rode with him back to the entrance where Mrs. Stewart was holding her daughter's hand. Mrs. Stewart was talking to some invisible person whose job was to hear complaints, "She's got typhoid, and they tell her she has to finish the picture while the leaves are still on the trees. They give her two weeks. She has typhoid fever, and they give her two weeks to recover. She says to me, 'Ma, I don't know what I'm doing or why.'" Mrs. Stewart walked down the front steps and said to the chauffeur, "Drive straight to the clinic."

"The same place?"

"Of course the same place. She knows the doctors there. You sure you know the way to Stamford from here?"

"Two, three hours."

"I knew this would happen, Annie. Didn't I say cancel Boston? Boston ain't in your contract."

"Ma," Anita said in a weak, scolding voice, "they were expecting me."

"Who listens to their mother?"

The chauffeur held the back door open, but Anita had forgotten how to get in, so he had to urge her forward. He demonstrated how to lift a leg to get inside. When she was seated, Anita bent forward and put her face down on her lap. "You get lost," Mrs. Stewart said to the chauffeur, "you're fired."

I found Louie inside surrounded by people listening to the story of how his mother died of a botched gallbladder operation in a hospital where no one could understand Yiddish. I took him aside. "She's having a nervous breakdown. They're taking her to a clinic in Stamford."

Louie looked around the room and saw that Anita was gone. "Now?"

"Just now."

Louie lit a cigar, took a puff, flicked his head in a way that meant I should follow him, and we worked our way through the crowd and outside where we walked out to the street in front of the mansion. It was a cobblestone street lit with gas lamps and canopied by giant sycamores silhouetted in the night.

"Her mother blames overwork," I said. "You offer her same pay, less work, she's yours. Picture it, Louie. The Louis B. Mayer Film Company presents Anita Stewart, a beloved star with international fame and a following of millions of devoted fans."

Louie eyed me with approval. "You should always dress up. No need to play down your good looks. Don't make any sense at all." Frogs—some like piccolos, others like cellos—serenaded us from the Charles River nearby. "That clinic will be crawling with Vitagraph people," Louie said taking a puff of his cigar. "She's their bread and butter. They'll be hanging around making everyone line up to get her autograph. The place will be crawling with guards."

"Or else they'll keep it secret." An owl called *hoo, hoo, hoo.* "Ruin her reputation and theirs. They're the ones made her sick. She didn't make herself sick."

"But that don't mean they won't be at the clinic."

The idea of Louie securing one of the most popular movie stars for his first venture into film production was so enormous, we continued walking so we could settle down. "You'll get to her through her mother, Louie." As we strolled on the banks of the Charles River, newsreel titles formed in my mind: "Anita Stewart Breaks Down!" or "Vitagraph Blamed for Film Star's Illness!" On our way back to the house, I made up copy for fan magazines: "Anita Stewart looks demure in her bed jacket of pink, pink what, silk?" Zoom to her bedroom slippers. "Sick from exhaustion, the beloved screen star insists upon having her own golden bedroom slippers." No. "Anita Stewart's dainty feet, a mere size five, tiny..." I chastised myself for thinking of her discomfort as paint on a pallet.

The party was winding down, and chauffeurs were behind the wheel in cars lined up at the entrance waiting. As Louie and I climbed the front stairs to go in, my chosen one and her parents came out. Her shoulders were wrapped in a white fox stole, which must have been difficult to close because she kept trying to find the clasp, her face lowered. Rooted, I stood there. Should I go to her and say, "Allow me," and put my hands in that fluffy stuff? She looked up, our eyes met, my stomach jumped over a cliff, and she blushed. The look lasted a second, but it turned into a full-length play night after night as I lay in my bed. Finally, one night about two weeks later, I noticed that I didn't remember that girl's face but had replaced her in my imagination with some girl I saw earlier that day on the bus.

Chapter Thirteen

There was no mention of Anita's breakdown in any of the papers so that's how we knew her studio was keeping it a secret. Louie decided to visit her at the Stamford clinic and to take me with him. "Young people like young people," he said. "Me, she could do without. You, she'll welcome."

Dressed in his automobile clothes—a long duster, goggles and cloth helmet—Louie cranked up the engine of his Ford Model T, and when it started, he shouted, "Get in, get in, get in!" He raced around to get behind the wheel, I jumped into the passenger seat, but instead of going backwards out of his driveway in Brookline, we lurched forward. He put the car in reverse again, tried to back straight out but ended up on the lawn, pulled forward, tried again, and we shot forward. The pot of chicken soup packed in a picnic basket sloshed dangerously but didn't spill because Maggie had secured the lid with one of Louie's belts. When we were on the street, at last, Louie said, "I'm an excellent driver."

We drove on the Boston Post Road past tobacco farms with acres of gauze stretched over the plants. Louie said, "Levin said he'd invest enough to get us started, if I can get her," and once again, I pointed frantically to the windshield to remind him that he could talk and look ahead at the same time.

The Hotel Davenport in Stamford was a five-story brick structure with hundreds of rooms. When we checked in, Louie said to the clerk, "I am Louis B. Mayer, president of the Louis B. Mayer Film Company. Give me the finest room in the house. Our stay is indefinite." We were assigned a two-bedroom suite, dreary but clean. From the window, I watched a child kick himself along the sidewalk on a scooter.

After freshening up, we walked down five flights because we were afraid of the rickety elevator that hauled us up by fits and starts. On the sidewalk, while Louie cranked the car, I absently read a poster tacked to the electricity pole next to me: "Are you Protestant? Join The Ku Klux Klan. Chapters in New Haven, Bridgeport, Darien, Greenwich, Norwalk and Stamford." So! Here was evidence of what was predicted, a resurgence of the Klan after Griffith's movie *Birth of a Nation*. "Did you see this?" I asked Louie, then read aloud about the next meeting at the Lincoln Republican Club, home of the local Republican Party. "All those with un-American names need not attend. What do you have to say for yourself?"

He looked up. "You think a moving picture makes people hate shvartzas?" He started cranking again.

"You could think of it as encouragement, couldn't you?"

Within months of the release of *The Birth of a Nation,* we read in newspapers that the "second" Klan was inaugurated by a cross-burning ceremony on top of Stone Mountain outside Atlanta. The Klan was growing in New England and had a statewide membership in Connecticut of at least fifteen thousand. Most of them were big fans of Griffith's movie, seen at their local theaters because Louie had brought it to them, and the car he was now cranking had been bought with some of his profits.

"You don't believe in propaganda?"

"It's make-believe. It's a motion picture." The engine caught, and Louie vaulted in behind the wheel. "I don't hear enough about censorship without you shooting off your mouth? Get in, get in, get in already!"

After stopping to buy flowers and a box of candy, we drove to the Stamford Rest Home, a brick mansion set back on nicely manicured lawns. Steel bars on the lower windows changed the aspect from a house that would make a tycoon proud to something foreboding. We parked behind an ambulance and went inside, me carrying the flowers and chocolates, Louie carrying the chicken soup, which he considered cargo too precious to entrust to anyone else. At the end of a corridor with wallpaper of shepherds and Little Bo Peeps was a nurses' desk. With no hesitation or fanfare, a nurse pointed down the hall. "She's in Daffodil, our finest room."

In a bright, airy room, Anita sat up in a starched white bed plinking on a ukulele. Two other people were in the room, her mother knitting and a preppy young man, about age twenty, reading. There were no floral bouquets, no get-well cards lined up on the windowsill, no boxes of candy. "Well, look who's here!" her mother said, pausing her needles but not getting up. "It's about time someone showed up." The young man—straight brown hair over one eyebrow, small straight nose, blue blazer—stood up and waited to see what was expected of him. Anita, pale as a wafer in a pink bed jacket, kept plinking the strings. "Annie," her mother said, "look who's here. Look who came to visit you." She didn't look. She kept trying to pick out *She'll Be Coming 'Round the Mountain,* missing notes, testing for the right one, finding it, then rehearsing the passage correctly. "That's what she does all day," her mother said.

The young man, taking it upon himself to act as host, spoke to Louie and me: "Thank you for coming. I'm Rudy

Cameron." His handshake was vigorous but ended too abruptly, so I wondered if that meant you could count on him but not for the long haul.

"I'm Louis B. Mayer," Louie said, "president of Louis B. Mayer Film Company, and this is my assistant, Harry Sirkus. What's in this pot is my wife's chicken soup. You eat this, Miss Stewart, and you will feel better." He set the pot on a table, and I set the candy and flowers next to it.

At the sound of my name, Anita lifted her head. "Harry?" She didn't seem to know where to direct her eyes, but when they did land on me, she said softly, "Come sit next to me." She said this in a conspiratorial way as if we were children in a room of grownups and had to be careful how we managed them so we could get our own way. She looked no more like a movie star than a wet puppy looks like a winner at Westminster.

"You came to visit me," she said when I was next to the bed. "I'm sick." She held up her hand, and I took the limp little thing in mine. "Can he sit on the bed, Ma?"

"Yeah. Why not."

"Can he, Rudy?"

"Of course he can, baby."

She hunched her shoulders and smiled with delight as if Santa had said yes. She patted the bed next to her, and I sat down. "I'm so sick," she whispered.

"I can see that."

"I'll play you a song."

"You don't need to entertain me, Anita."

"Yeah, I do."

"No, you don't."

"But I like entertaining people."

"Okay. Entertain me."

She strummed *She'll Be Coming 'Round the Mountain*, while singing along in a raucous voice. "She'll be coming 'round the mountain when she comes, when she comes, She'll be coming 'round the mountain when she comes, when she comes, She'll be coming 'round the mountain, She'll be coming 'round the mountain, She'll be coming 'round the mountain, she'll be coming 'round the mountain, she'll be coming 'round..." Rudy Cameron and Mrs. Stewart exchanged worried looks. "She'll be driving six white horses, she'll be driving six white horses, she'll be driving six white horses..."

Rudy hurried to the bed. "That's enough for now, baby," he said, taking the ukulele from her. "That was splendid. Absolutely splendid."

"Did you get it on the first take?"

"Yes, baby. It's in the can."

"Did I get to the wearing red pajamas part?"

"We're going to rehearse that after lunch."

"I'm so tired, Rudy. How come I'm so tired?"

"It's nothing, baby. It's nothing."

"I'm having a rest cure, right?"

"Right."

"Well deserved, if you ask me, "said Mrs. Stewart. "Bunch of animals over there."

"I didn't get to the part she'll have to sleep with Grandma when she comes. I do a snore. She'll have to sleep with Grandma..." Anita inhaled two vulgar snorts. "See? That makes it interesting. You know why I do that? Because it's so unladylike. Yeah. It's a sure laugh when a dainty person makes a crude sound." She leaned back against her pillow and closed her eyes, and the rest of us tiptoed out.

From the visitors' sunporch with views of the lawn, patches of snow still held out against the early spring sun. We sat on wicker furniture while Mrs. Stewart reviewed the various injuries her daughter had suffered at the hands of Vitagraph studio executives. "Mr. Smith said if any of his employees told about Annie's breakdown, they'd ruin her reputation. Everyone would think she was unreliable. They're mad at her for collapsing."

"Her fans have no idea," said Rudy. "They see her moving around on the screen, so they think she's fine."

"The studio sold a calendar with her photo on it to promote *The Girl Philippa* and didn't even mention her name," said Mrs. Stewart. "The caption under the photo said 'The Girl Philippa.' When that picture opened at the Rialto, the line was around the block. They had to call in the cops to keep order."

"Set a record for a single day's receipts at any motion-picture theater in the world," Rudy added.

"Anita Stewart is a great star," said Louie. "I go down on my knees to talent."

"You know her serial The Goddess? They release the damn thing one reel at a time. Fan mail pours in each time. I seen it. Bins of envelopes, little girl handwriting on the outside. Did you see the poster they stuck up in the theaters? A full-length photograph of Annie dressed in long robes with words all around her, 'Beauty, Hatred, Revenge, Love, A Continued Photoplay in Chapters, the Interest Increases Every Week,' all that crap. Biggest words on the poster were 'The Vitagraph Company of America.' Don't mention Annie's name. Not even in little letters."

I noticed that Louie had spirited the box of candy out of the sickroom. He held it up in an offering gesture, and

Mrs. Stewart shrugged in a why-not gesture. One piece wouldn't hurt. Louie proffered the assortment, and she selected a square caramel and put it in her mouth in a small, ceremonious way as if it were precious. "She not only should have her name in lights," Louie said, holding the box toward Rudy who waved it away. "She should have a film company of her own. Anita Stewart Productions."

"That's what I keep telling her," said Mrs. Stewart. "Like Norma Talmadge." She swiped her tongue across her front teeth. "Norma don't got more talent then Annie. They know each other from Erasmus High."

"Norma Talmadge Productions," said Louie. "Joe Schenk set her up. Now I like Joe Schenk, everyone likes Joe, but I know talent. Anita Stewart is a greater star than Norma Talmadge."

"You're telling me," said Mrs. Stewart.

Rudy, smoking a pipe in the wicker armchair across the room, came to attention. Louie selected a peanut cluster and bit into it.

"You're the only one in the whole goddamn industry who bothered to come see her," said Mrs. Stewart to Louie and me. "She works her heart out, and that's the treatment she gets. Bunch of hoodlums." Out the window, we saw patients wrapped in shawls being wheeled by nurses in capes along the paths that crisscrossed the lawns.

Louie said to Rudy, "Haven't I seen you on the screen?"

Startled, as if caught doing something bad, he said, "I've been in one or two pictures."

Mrs. Stewart said, "Rudy's a graduate of Georgetown University." She pronounced each syllable separately, "grad-u-ate," and said it proudly. "Civil engineering. He was on the Broadway stage."

"Once," he said.

"Not once."

"Okay, twice. Bully for me."

Louie said, "Acting on the stage is more challenging than playing in a motion- picture movie. The stage actor don't get two, three takes. One chance, that's all you get on the stage. The audience don't just see you from the head up or shoulders up. They see the whole body. The whole body's got to emote. Plus the scenarios can't be compared. What photoplay can compare to Ibsen or Shakespeare? Might as well compare Irving Berlin to Verdi."

Mrs. Stewart was not interested in this conversation. "She don't make half the dough Mary so-called Pickford does," she said. "Pickford's cute, but she ain't that cute. Annie worked four years straight for those bums without a vacation. They says to her, 'You wanna rest? Go retire.'"

"I'd double her salary, if I had the chance," Louie said. "I started from nothing—used to be in the junk business. Why? Because my old man was in the junk business. You see these shoulders? That's from hauling steel since I was nine years old. My old man never said a kind word to me. Never. But my mother, of blessed memory, that was a different story. Later on, you'll taste her chicken soup, the recipe handed down to my wife."

"I remember the first time you saw Anita," I cued Louie.

"I said, 'That's a great star.' And where was she? Standing in the background. Didn't have one line of her own. Fifteen years old. The public sees her, responds to her, writes letters. 'Dear Vitagraph, Who was that pretty girl in the background?' It's the public makes a star. Not the studio. A film company is only as good as its star. It ain't the director. It ain't the story. It ain't the setting. It's the star."

"It sure is," agreed Mrs. Stewart.

"And the star should choose her own stories, her co-stars, her director," said Louie.

"Yeah."

"Why should Norma Talmadge, who started at Vitagraph when Anita did, went to Erasmus High same as Anita, why should she, a good actress but not great, have a production company of her own and not Anita? I am offering to Anita Stewart what Joe Schenck offered to Norma Talmadge. But what I ask you to consider is why shouldn't the star's mother be on the board of directors of the star's company? Who besides her own mother would look out for her interests?"

"Yeah. Yeah. That's right."

"Have I seen any of the Louis B. Mayer Film Company productions?" Rudy asked, frowning. He reminded me of the boys who had excluded me in Haverhill.

"Now that's an astute question," Louie said. "That's the sort of question a true friend of Anita's would ask."

"He ain't a friend," Mrs. Stewart said. "He's her husband."

"Ma!"

"Oh, it don't matter with Louie and Harry. Who are they going to tell? Wouldn't do them no good to damage Annie's girlish reputation."

Louie, to cover his surprise, busied himself with his watch, took it from his pocket, wound it and straightened the gold chain attached to it. "The time has come, my friends," he said, standing up.

"Don't misunderstand," Rudy said to Louie in a hushed voice as we walked down the hall. "My wife has done all right for herself. She earns one hundred twenty-seven thousand dollars a year plus ten percent of the profits of all her films. We live in a lovely home on Long Island, have a staff of six, a motorcar and closets full of clothes."

"You ever see ten percent of the profits?" Louie asked.

"Well, it's true that..."

"I didn't think so. They ain't going to account to you, no offense. My offer stands. Whatever you get now, I'll double it."

"But she's under contract, Mr. Mayer."

"There ain't no contract I ever heard of says a company's allowed to push a young girl into a nervous breakdown. Nineteen years old and she's in the hospital."

"But Vitagraph's a huge studio, a multimillion-dollar concern. They'll take you to court and claim Anita's a figment of publicity. They paid Hearst fifty thousand dollars for those rave reviews of *The Girl Phillipa*. They'll say she's high strung, use this hospital stay as evidence that she's difficult to work with. They'll say she's lucky they employ her."

"That's why she needs you to look out for her interests. That's why you should consent to being a member of the board of directors of Anita Stewart Productions."

"Me?" Rudy laughed. "That would certainly shut my parents up." They continued walking close together down the corridor, Rudy at least a foot taller than Louie. "I'll admit to you, Mr. Mayer, they're somewhat appalled by the direction I've taken."

"That so?"

"There are no actors in my family, Mr. Mayer. It's not one of the options. We're businessmen." They both nodded to a nurse passing by. "Cameron isn't even my name. It's Brennan. I'm a Brennan from Connecticut."

"A Brennan," said Louie. "A fine old family."

"They won't even talk to Annie. 'How can you bring a film actress into the family,' Mother said. A girl with no background, no education.'"

"Maybe they don't see her worth now," said Louie, "but they soon will. Anita Stewart Productions. Rudolph Brennan on the letterhead. Take it from me, a son needs his mother's approval."

Louie and I returned to Boston and waited. April, the unreliable, turned cold again and threatened to freeze the crocuses. Coat-check rooms at the theaters continued to be full. In May, magnolia blossoms blended purple and cream. Duchess Margot, a vaudeville star at the Olympia Theater, walked her dancing poodles in the Boston Garden without their hand-knit sweaters. Then we bought mothballs and stored our winter coats. Anita was wheeled around the grounds of the hospital without a shawl covering her shoulders.

One day, Louie handed me a letter. Part of it was a copy of a letter sent to Vitagraph by Anita's lawyer. "By reasons of the continued violation on your part of my contract with you, I have severed my relation with your company." Her signature was under those words.

"This ain't going to hold up," Louie said. "Since when can a sick person sign anything?" The other part of the letter said that if Louie was sincere, he should prove it by putting up ten thousand dollars.

Louie showed the letter to his friend Mr. Levin. "She's a big star, Louie," he said. "That's not too much to ask. Do you really think we can get her?"

Mr. Levin, Louie and I drove to Stamford, this time in the comfort of Mr. Levin's limousine. Anita was now strong enough to stroll the grounds with us. At first, Mr. Levin was star struck, overwhelmed by shyness. Then he began to trust Anita's straightforward way of talking. "We got carpet," she said. "I think it's Bigelow. Ma, is that Bigelow we got in the *foy-yay?*" Mr. Levin dared take Anita's hand and put it through his arm, a gallant escort. I had never seen him so happy.

He put up the ten thousand dollars needed to launch Anita Stewart Productions, though he knew that Vitagraph would not give up without a fight. The studio could afford a lengthy court battle. Anita still had several pictures in the pipeline. Her contract was not due to expire for three years.

Instead of seeing this as an obstacle, Mr. Levin saw it as a challenge. He had already built one business up from nothing. Now he wanted to see if he still had what it takes. He read everything he could about the motion-picture industry and convinced himself that it was full of promise and riches. He would have two careers, carpet merchant and film-company executive. Here was the excitement missing from his life. His enthusiasm gave Louie confidence. If a man of Mr. Levin's stature thought Anita Stewart Productions was a good investment, it must be.

As soon as Anita was well enough to return home to Long Island, Anita Stewart Productions was incorporated. Coleman Levin and Louis B. Mayer were its chief executives. Thus began *Vitagraph Co. of America v. Stewart et al.,* a court battle that became front-page news. Never before had a movie actor's contract been tested. Here was a young woman, Brooklyn's best-known moving-picture actress, who had started at twenty-five dollars a week and five years later was receiving a salary of two thousand five hundred a week from the same studio. According to the newspapers, she was to receive ten thousand a week from

Louis B. Mayer. "This must be a misprint," I said to Louie when I read that in the *New York Dramatic Mirror*.

"It don't hurt to exaggerate," Louie said. "If she costs a lot, she must be worth a lot. Remember that."

"But did you promise her that much, Louie?"

"Promise, schmomis. You think they have a right to push that girl into illness? Is that what you think?"

While Anita's lawyers claimed she was inadequately compensated by Vitagraph, the company's lawyers claimed Anita would not exist as an actress without the studio. Her success was owing to her schooling at the studio and to the money spent in promoting her.

The Supreme Court in New York took months to decide—lawyer bills, court dates, papers to sign—and then it decided for Vitagraph. Yes, the young woman's success was a result of Vitagraph's investment in her, and she must fulfill her contract. Yes, two thousand five hundred dollars per week was adequate compensation. Louie and Mr. Levin appealed. More attorney's fees. More days of riding the train from Boston to New York to sit in the corridor of a New York court building waiting, waiting, waiting. The appellate court took months to decide, and then it, too, found for Vitagraph. Anita was forbidden to work for the Louis B. Mayer Film Company, and Louis B. Mayer, specifically named, was not allowed to further entice her.

The loss of this court case was not a secret shame. It was front-page business news as well as entertainment news, and Mr. Levin found himself publicly humiliated. He cursed his misguided dreams of glamour and blamed Louie for misleading him. Now the board of directors of the Beth Israel Hospital noticed that they never received the fifteen thousand dollars Louie had pledged. This Louis

Mayer fellow, they decided, was just a scoundrel. They kicked him off the board.

Like most young people, I heaped more blame upon myself than was appropriate. It was my fault Mr. Levin got involved with Louie. He never would have met him if it weren't for me. He never would have invested in the project if I hadn't been so enthusiastic. He wouldn't have liked Anita so much if I hadn't liked Anita so much. I went to his showroom to apologize. "Now you need a job, right?" he said. "Well, you've come to the wrong place."

"No, sir, I..."

"Take my advice, Harry. Get as far away from Louie Mayer as you can. Do you understand? He is not an ethical person, and he will do you no good. As far as a job is concerned, I can't help you there."

"No, I came here..."

"I've neglected my business, my name is splashed all over the newspapers, I've been made a fool. I wish you well, Harry. But please don't ask me for help again." With that, he turned his back on me and walked to the other side of the showroom.

Chapter Fourteen

Louie used to love publicity. He courted newspaper reporters and said to me, "Always be good to the men who write." He was news in the Haverhill *Gazette* and now and then in a Boston paper, but he longed for the day when his name would light up New York newspapers, and the whole industry would know his name. Now he got his wish but backward.

The whole industry knew his name: he was that idiot from New England who had tried to steal Anita Stewart from Vitagraph, the largest and most important movie studio in the country. If Anita Stewart could walk out of Vitagraph, then actors could walk out of every other studio too. Studio contracts would be meaningless. Didn't that New England fool know this? Rumor said he went to Anita's sick bed and tempted her while she was still too weak to make sound judgments.

Metro Film Company, whose pictures we distributed, severed ties with us. Gordon-Mayer Theatrical Company closed its doors, and I was out of a job. I had to say goodbye to Mrs. Mittenthal and Fanny.

"You'll stay here," Maggie said. "My uncle's cousin is in the guest room, but you can have the sofa in the front parlor until my aunt's friend arrives. If she schleps her featherbed, we can put her in Edie's room. Louie, tell him. Tell him he'll stay here."

"Do what you want," said Louie, the rash on his cheeks flaring. To buoy himself, he drove every day to Haverhill where he was still a big shot. His brother Jerry, now manager of the Colonial, threatened to quit and return to Canada if Louie didn't stop his kibitzing.

Louie convinced the mayor of Haverhill to let him film local boys setting off to war. We watched the footage in his living room in Brookline. "You see this?" Louie said as he threaded his new projector. "This is the Bell & Howell Filmo 75, the latest in home projection." We saw the boys assembling at city hall and marching to the armory. I knew some of them from the upper grades at school, and Louie knew them as customers at the Colonial. He filmed their mothers crying helplessly as the boys climbed into trucks that took them away. Maggie started crying, saying, "Oh, there's poor Mrs. Rubin. You'll take me with you tomorrow, Louis. I'll bring her my coffee cake, even though it's not so good with Karo syrup. I'll be thankful when the government lets us use sugar again."

Louie's was the first home movie I'd ever seen, and it taught me about editing and camerawork. I got bored watching some of the scenes and annoyed during other scenes. I kept wanting to point the camera at what was more important than the image on the screen. For instance, we had to endure frame after frame of truck wheels spinning in the mud when what we wanted to see was the boys looking back at their mothers. Was Louie bad at everything he did?

I was jealous of those boys on the screen. They would go fight the Boche and make the world safe for democracy. They would go overseas and have adventures, visit Paris and see can-can girls dancing with no tops on. I wanted to fight the war that would end all wars. Patriotic songs filled the taverns, and Niko's voice on phonograph records flowed into the streets from open windows. "Over there, over there, send the word over there, that the Yanks are coming, the Yanks are coming..."

The Army got Rudy. Newspapers carried photos of Anita sobbing at the train station in New York, and so the public learned that their perpetual young thing was actually a married woman.

The Selective Service office in Boston said I was too young. If I could bring in a birth certificate proving I was eighteen, I'd be allowed to sign up, but of course, I couldn't since I had just turned seventeen and had no idea where my birth certificate was anyway. Downhearted, I turned into the nearest movie theater and sat down just as the orchestra played a rousing march and the screen lit up with the words "Fox News, Mightiest of Them All."

First title: "**Daredevils!**" A man roller-skates on the edge of a high-rise building. Will he fall? Then men racing motorcycles leap from the cycles onto speeding cars. A man clinging to the wing of an airplane is photographed by a Fox cameraman also balancing on the airplane's wing.

"**Women Over 30 Get the Vote in Britain.**" All the women on the screen shaking hands with each other are unattractive and mannish. One of them ignores the crying child next to her until the little boy tugs at her skirt, and then she just pushes him away.

"**U.S. Post Office Torches** *Ulysses*!" Several men in front of a post office building hold up copies of James Joyce's book. They set fire to it and watch the pages burn while nodding approval.

"**Airmail Service Established Between New York City and Washington!**" We see bags of mail loaded into an airplane. A handsome pilot shows us an airmail stamp that was just issued.

"Daylight Saving Time Introduced in America!" Images flash onscreen of women shaking sleeping men and men setting their pocket watches.

"Disaster in Hong Kong! Jockey Club Racetrack Grandstand Collapses, 600 die!" Panicky people and horses rearing and charging.

"President Wilson Presides at League of Nations Meeting in Paris." Shots of him sitting at a desk surrounded with dignitaries.

"Race Riots in Chicago! 38 People Dead! 537 injured!" Black people rush into stores and hurry away with clothing, phonographs, washing machines. White members of the state militia shoot rifles into the air, fires rage, white people beat black people, black people beat white people, and chaos reigns in the smoky streets.

"A.D. Juilliard Dies. Leaves $20 Million to Endow Juilliard School of Music, New York!" A young pianist tickles the ivories and audiences applaud.

"Babe Ruth Belts 587-foot Home Run!" The Boston Red Sox play the NY Giants at Tampa, Florida.

"Who's The Fairest of Them All?" Girls in bathing suits line up to be judged at a beauty pageant in Atlantic City. They walk slowly toward the camera wearing sashes across their bathing suits. We see one of the girls crowned and two cameramen standing in front of a car decorated with a banner "Fox News, Around the World in Pictures." The younger one, wearing a black beret, takes a comical bow, and with a jolt, I recognized the boy I had met in Central Park, Kenny Anderson. In the same amount of time that it took me to lose my job and become stuck in the mud, he was flying forward and had become a cameraman at Fox News. Now was the time for me to make a change. Now was the time to remind William Fox that he'd promised to hire me.

"You can't go to New York, boychick," Maggie said. "There's flu there."

"There's flu here too."

"My house ain't good enough for you?" Louie said. "You need some place better to stay?"

"Come on, Louie. I need a job."

"I told you. Come to Haverhill. You'll work at the Colonial."

"I don't want to work at the Colonial."

"I don't wanna work at the Colonial," he said in a singsong voice that was supposed to mimic mine. "What's wrong with Haverhill? Go on. Tell me."

"I don't know."

"So it's settled. You'll come with me in the morning." We were sitting in the living room in the Brookline house, Maggie darning socks, the girls sprawled on the floor doing their homework. "We don't feed you enough? You need more food? The bed ain't soft enough?"

"What bed?"

"Oh, so now you object to helping the relatives? So now you want to take the pillow out from under the head of Auntie Rivka?"

About a week later, when I told Louie I had decided to move to New York, he blew up. "This is what you do to me? Me who taught you everything you know? This is how you treat me? This is what you do when things don't go just right? Now you go, now that you're old enough to be some use to me you go. What's the matter? I ain't good enough for you, you little pisher, you little piece of worthless crap! Go on. Go on. Let's see you find anyone who would be so good to you. Go on. Let's see you find someone like me, you, you, ingrate!"

He knew the day I was leaving. I had told him, so it was on purpose that he wasn't home, on purpose that he insisted Maggie and the girls go with him to Haverhill so there would be no one at the train station in Boston saying goodbye to me. Sitting on the train with my pathetic worldly possessions fitting in one knapsack, my savings in an envelope taped to my chest, not knowing where I'd sleep that night, I felt so lonely, I wished I could just cut my heart right out of my chest.

At Grand Central Station in New York, I watched a grisly sight. Men wearing surgical masks over their noses and mouths unloaded coffins from the very train I'd been on, and grim-faced relatives, also wearing surgical masks, came forward from the crowd on the platform to claim their own. I thought maybe the coffins held flu victims, but then I noticed that each family got a folded-up American flag. I wondered who would come forward to claim me if I came home dead from the war.

Knapsack bending me forward, I trudged on slush under a steady sprinkle of snow. When I needed to rest and dry off, I stopped in a barroom. There was no one in there except the bartender who said, "Sorry, Johnny. I'd like to serve you, but I'd lose my license." I was flattered that he thought I was a soldier come home. He gestured toward his supply of liquor bottles, then toward the empty stools at the bar. "Can't congregate in bars anymore. When the armistice was signed in November," he said, wiping the counter out of habit, "the city went wild. You should have seen them whooping it up, marching down the streets banging tin plates, church bells clanging, people in office buildings throwing confetti out the windows, people torching effigies of the Kaiser strung up on lamp posts. The flu bug had an orgy, Johnny. You've come marching home at a bad time. I can sell you a pitcher of beer to take home, if that will help any."

I walked across town past pedestrians with handkerchiefs tied over their mouths, policemen patrolling in surgical masks. Carriage horses, heads down, stood at the curb stamping their hooves, shaking their harness, the jingle of the reins a pleasant sound that mingled with taxis blasting their horns and ambulance sirens. Most of the people on the street were young men, soldiers home from war. The scene had a surreal quality, ghostly uniforms wandering around in the snow dwarfed by the tall buildings that lined the streets. An insurance company poster read "Spanish Influenza! Can you afford sudden death?" I wrapped my scarf around my mouth and walked past closed theaters, dark marquees, black wreaths hung on apartment-building doors. A truck pulled up to a townhouse, and two orderlies in surgical masks hurried inside. I didn't wait to see what they brought out but rushed away and turned onto another street.

I paused to look into the window of a music store. The display was an artistic arrangement of the sheet music for *Pack Up Your Troubles*, a portrait of handsome Nick Meadows on the cover. At the bottom of the cover was written "The Victor Talking Machine Company, New Jersey." I wondered where Niko was living. Maybe I could find him. Maybe he'd let me sleep at his house. Maybe he'd help me find a job. Here I was again, now almost eighteen instead of thirteen but in the same position, wandering around an unfamiliar city with my heart pounding with apprehension. Again, I emptied my mind of everything but what was necessary and said to myself, step one, find someplace to sleep before it gets dark.

The weather became steadily colder, and I walked under a blanket of falling snow, ducking my head against uncomfortable gusts of wind. At dusk I came upon a "Room for Rent" placard in the window of an antique tavern on Broadway. A sign in front read "Filpot Tavern, Washington Slept Here." It was a half-timber cottage from the days of the Revolutionary War—wide floorboards, wooden beams, a fire blazing in a massive stone fireplace. I entered on a blast of cold air that made the flames all bend in one direction, and a fat man sitting in a rocking chair in front of the fire turned to see who had come in. A bottle of whiskey and a half-filled glass was on the wooden table next to him. I shut the door as fast as possible and stood there covered in snow.

The fat man regarded me for a minute before turning away to face the fire. "Glasses are behind the bar," he said. He was about fifty, dressed in baggy clothes, his belt unbuckled for comfort. I sat in the armchair next to him, poured myself a glass of whiskey and prayed I wouldn't choke as I usually did when I tried to get booze down. We sat there sipping and not talking, the logs crackling, the fire dancing up blue tips. I dared to peek at him and saw that he wore beat-up slippers rather than shoes, that his heels were crusty as peach cobbler and that his fingers were fat as sausages. If I sipped the stinging liquid slowly and waited patiently for it to burn a path down the middle of me, it produced a warm sensation that was very agreeable. My companion made no attempt to be cordial. We sat without talking until the bottle was empty. Then he gestured for me to follow him up a flight of worn wooden stairs. Here was a scene from slapstick: his elephantine rear end above me on the stairs, his hand grabbing the banister to steady himself, his intoxicated weaving, his leaning way back with backside looming, his regaining his balance until we reached the second floor, where I chose from all the empty rooms the one with a view of Broadway.

Despite the flu epidemic, the lights of Times Square were dancing and blinking as if celebrating, a beautiful sight in the snow. Pedestrians throwing all caution to the wind, women wrapped in furs, men in storm coats walking under umbrellas, heads bowed against the cold.

I lay down under a crocheted blanket, a remainder of someone female? A tenant? Former wife? A dead person? When I woke up, the room was dark. I couldn't remember where I was. Orphanage? Stable tack room? Mrs. Mittenthal's? Louie's house in Brookline? An ambulance siren screamed *roy roy roy roy* on the street outside. I pulled the chain on the ceiling light bulb, and a tide of loneliness washed over me. What was I thinking, coming to New York? I opened my knapsack and ate the cookies Maggie had given me, but I wanted something more substantial so I went downstairs to see if my host served food. I assumed we were alone so I didn't bother putting on shoes or trousers and found myself standing at the foot of the stairs in my long winter underwear in front of a table full of men playing cards. They all lifted their heads to look at me from under green eyeshades. Then one of them, cigarette dangling from his lip, said, "Go on, deal, deal, for Crissakes."

Another said, "Who the hell's this?"

"Hey! Now we got seven!"

My host said, "You play poker, Johnny?"

"I don't have any pants on," I answered.

"You don't need your pants, kid. You got any money?"

"Deal him in. Look at him. Shell-shocked. It's a mitzvah. I'm telling you. Deal him in."

"And what, may I ask, Mr. Generosity," said the one with the bushy mustache, "is he going to use to ante?"

"Wait a minute," said another player. "He don't got the grippe. Tell me he don't got the grippe, Filpot."

Filpot took a drink of whiskey and tapped his cigarette ash in a coffee can. Then he dealt the cards as if I was not there, and the men took their eyes off me.

"Would you take an I.O.U?" I asked. If there was one thing I knew how to do, it was to play poker. You couldn't live in a room full of other boys without knowing how to play cards, and you couldn't hang around backstage waiting for an interview without knowing how to pass the time.

They all looked up at me, discussing the pros and cons. "Leave him alone, leave him alone," said the guy with the mustache. "What he's seen should not be seen by anyone. Am I right, Johnny?"

"Harry," I said. "Harry Sirkus. I'm an excellent poker player, and I always pay my debts." They made room for me at the table. I started the game very sincerely, only playing the hands that were sure to win and folding most of the time. I came on spineless, so at the end, after a few hours, when I did bid high, they all assumed I had the cards. Every time I won, I acted amazed. By the end of the game, they all resented me and told Filpot there should be a new rule, no playing without your pants on. They cleared out after midnight, and Filpot and I sat drinking in front of the fire.

"What'd you say your name was?" Filpot asked keeping his eyes on the fire. I told him. "Harry, my friend," Filpot said, "now you can pay me your rent."

Chapter Fifteen

Fox's newsreel factory was a five-story brick building on the corner of Tenth Avenue and Fifty-fourth Street, the roughest area in New York City, known as Hell's Kitchen. The neighborhood was blighted by the elevated railway that blocked sunlight and canopied Ninth Avenue with noise.

When I was a child, if anyone complained about conditions on the Lower East Side, the typical comeback was, "Give thanks. Could be Hell's Kitchen." Our tenements were crowded and falling apart, but on the sidewalk, at the pushcarts or applauding the skill of a juggler, we mingled with our neighbors. They fasted during Lent; we fasted on Yom Kippur. They celebrated Easter—the Greeks one way, the Italians another. We celebrated Passover—the Polish one way, the Germans another.

In Hell's Kitchen, people avoided the streets. The sidewalks were owned by the gangs. Each clump of thugs hung around on their own corner harassing everyone who passed by, especially women even if they were pushing a baby carriage. On every block there was a bar, a fanny on every stool even in the morning, and each ethnic gang claimed a particular bar. The Irish Catholics hated the Irish Protestants. Their gangs were always beating up somebody, often men unlucky enough to work at the nearby railway yard.

My plan was simply to present myself to William Fox and remind him of his offer. I would suggest that he place me in the publicity department or in the news department writing titles. The studios were in flux, some of them merging with others, some just dropping dead. It was far from prestigious to be associated with motion pictures. Those associated with the legitimate stage were considered vastly superior to movie people. Most Broadway stage actors believed it would ruin their careers if they appeared in motion pictures, and they spurned the film scouts who tried to recruit them. So it wasn't that scary to present myself to Mr. Fox, though he was one of the most powerful men in the business. My attitude was that he should be grateful that a young man with his future before him believed the movie business was worthwhile. I was sure that Mr. Fox would find it reassuring that someone young wanted to throw in with him.

His voice was staticky coming through the secretary's intercom. "Who?" She repeated my name. "What's he selling?"

"Says he knows you, sir."

"He's a liar."

She looked up at me with a blank expression, as if to say, you heard for yourself. She seemed stubborn, as hard to move as a breakfront.

"I'm not a liar," I said. "He is. He promised me a job."

She pushed a button on the intercom and spoke into it. "Says you promised him a job, sir."

"Get ridda him."

She pointed her face up at me, then down at her typewriter. To the sound of her renewed clackety-clack, I strode across the office and yanked open the door to his office, but it wasn't his office. It was brooms and mops, and there I was in a ridiculous position. The secretary paused, looked up at me with an infuriating lack of interest, then continued typing.

I strode to another door, yanked it open, and there was Mr. Fox in a cloud of cigar smoke working by the light of a gooseneck lamp, all shades drawn. The office was large, furnished like an English gentleman's club: dark paneling, leather chairs, Oriental carpet. If you objected to the smell of cigars, you were in trouble here. None of the windows were open, no cross-ventilation at all. Mr. Fox, sitting on a swivel chair at a massive desk, looked up. He was dressed in a suit, vest and tie, with his side hair brushed over his bald dome and his hooded eyes looking at me with a direct, strong beam. "Oh," he said, "the kid who don't take no for an answer."

"You promised me a job."

"Get outta here."

"No. You said."

"So I said. So what?"

"So I need a job, that's so what. I'm not ashamed of needing a job."

"Shut the door, for Chrissakes. You want the whole office to know your business?" I had to turn my back to him on my way to close the door, and I felt very childish walking across the carpet. When I turned back, he was watching me from under those hooded eyes, the eyelids closed over more than half of the eyeball, and I had to walk toward him feeling self-conscious. He gestured at the chair facing his desk and said, "Siddown." The minute my bottom touched down, he swiveled away and said, facing the wall, "State your case."

"I can write titles, I can write publicity, I can book vaudeville. I've been in the motion-picture business my whole life."

"This is a newsreel factory, kid. This ain't motion pictures. You want motion pictures, go to the Coast. New York's finished. It ain't here anymore."

"How come you have all the shades pulled down?"

"I don't want to know what time it is, that's why. I don't know if it's day or night. I never carry a watch. My workday ends when my work is finished." He put a cigar in his mouth, lit it and placed the match carefully in an ashtray full of cigar stumps. Then he faced me. "Do you know what makes a successful newsreel?"

"It's probably the same thing that makes a successful newspaper. Being the first to arrive. I'd say it's about getting the scoops. Is that the right answer?"

"You tell me."

"Okay. I'll stick with that. You have to get the scoops and get the footage to the theaters before the other newsreel companies do. I don't know how you do that, but I'm willing to learn. I think it would be fun and interesting to do that. I want you to hire me. I want to work here."

He pressed a button on his intercom. "Faye. Take this pest up to news. Tell Fred he's got a new grunt. Same salary as the others." He waved his cigar in a dismissive way and said to me, "Get outta here. Prove yourself." Then he was done with me, as if I had evaporated.

His secretary, Faye, led me along some corridors and into an open warehouse space where models stood on stage sets. Some were dressed in golf clothes and holding golf clubs while a cameraman looked through the lens at them. I had to be careful not to trip on coils of cable. At the freight elevator, Faye planted herself in front of me and turned into an anonymous tour guide. "On the first floor we film fashion shows. The stages are fully equipped, even including a small swimming pool for underwater shots." She heaved back a brass gate that opened and closed like an accordion and stepped into the freight elevator. "Today you see a Burberry shoot, the latest in golf wear." She waited for me to dare to step across the gap between the elevator and the floor, a pit seemingly to the center of the earth.

It took some nerve to get into that freight elevator because it had no roof, and the cables trembled and groaned. "The second floor," Faye said, "is devoted to short subjects that deal with music, travel, adventure, transportation and rural American life. We produce about twenty-six shorts a year and sell them to theaters along with feature films and newsreels." She had played this role so many times, the lines came out automatically, but all the while, something in her was shrinking because being a tour guide focused too much attention on her. "The news department," she said twisting slightly so my eyes would leave her alone, "is on third. On the fourth floor is the art department. The library is on the fifth, where we store all the newsreels Mr. Fox has ever produced as well as outtakes and dope sheets that record the film footage, subject, names of the people and location." The elevator stopped before it was flush with the third floor. The gate, if it had opened, would face a dirty wall. I knew it! I knew this thing wasn't safe! We were trapped. I was going to die. Faye varied the pressure on the lever, and we arrived, at last, lined up with the third floor. She tried to push the gate back, but it stuck. Oh, no! Then the gate opened, and we stepped out into the madhouse that was the Fox news department, men running around in a frantic effort to meet deadline. "Fox releases two issues a week," Faye said, "on Wednesday and Saturday, to an audience of about thirty million. William Fox was the first to affiliate with a wire service. United Press makes its reporters and photographers around the world available exclusively to Fox. He has cameramen and representatives in Tokyo, Shanghai, Peking, Hong Kong, Manila, Honolulu, New Zealand, Australia, New Guinea,

Borneo, Sumatra, Tibet, Russia, Alaska, Sweden, Dublin, Liverpool, London, Paris, Madrid, Rome and Manchuria."

"Wow! That's a mouthful!"

She did not acknowledge my attempt at familiarity, and I regretted interrupting her because it was an effort for her to resume her memorized lines. "Fox is served by more than a thousand cameramen with about sixty thousand feet of film pouring into Fox's laboratories each week from around the world. The news department is open twenty-four hours a day, seven days a week." Her manner forbade complimenting her as she stepped back into the elevator. "You want the third office on the right," she said through the gate. And so began my career at Fox News.

Chapter Sixteen

I was hired as an assistant contact man, which meant I did the legwork for all kinds of shoots and secured various permissions or permits so that the filming process could proceed efficiently. It was up to me and the other contact men at the studio to make sure cameramen, who lugged tons of equipment, could set up as quickly as possible when they arrived on the scene.

One of my first assignments was to figure out how to pirate the Astor Stakes at Belmont Park racetrack. Hearst News had paid fifty thousand dollars for the exclusive rights to film the race, and those rights were sold to only one newsreel company.

The most obvious solution was handheld cameras. We would buy twenty of them for cameramen who would pose as fans and shoot from the grandstand while mingling with the crowd. A few weeks before the race, I went out to Belmont Park and rented the roof of an old factory beside the track where we could post cameramen with telescopic lenses. At the other end of the track was another old factory with a wooden water tank on the edge of the roof. I rented the roof and got permission from the owner to drain the water out of the tank, bored a hole through it and put a cameraman inside.

I took a few carpenters to the track with me. They earned about six dollars a day, and they built platforms at both ends of the track, which we camouflaged with trees. Another contact man leased two airplanes and equipped them with cameras for aerial coverage. The cameramen stationed in the buildings and on the platforms would go to the track a few days before the event and camp out there. We made sure they had enough decks of cards and whiskey to keep them amused at night. The cameramen were as eager to get a scoop as Mr. Fox was, and they loved playing the pirate game.

The track hired freelance security guards for the big races. I thought it was a good idea to have some of them on our payroll as well so they could ignore our cameramen. Hell's Kitchen was full of muscular men who might qualify as Belmont Park racetrack security guards.

I was not afraid to prowl for candidates because Fox Studio seldom had trouble with neighbors. Our two doormen, Vinnie and Pasko, would just as soon kill you as talk to you, a reputation cultivated when they worked as goons for Big Tim Sullivan. They alternated patrolling the sidewalk to clear away troublemakers, a ritual more than a necessity not only because of their reputations but also because our neighbors were proud of us. They loved movies. Mr. Fox made sure that at least twice a year, a movie star strolled the sidewalks. Tom Mix was there with his horse when the building opened, and a dog rumored to be Rin Tin Tin arrived to delight crowds of ill-kempt children. Theda Bara came by in her white limousine with her Arabian entourage.

So it was with confidence that I entered Paddy's Saloon at Fifty-fifth and Ninth under the elevated tracks. There was no legal drinking age. I could go into any bar and be served. Paddy's was a long, narrow space with a warped wooden floor littered with peanut shells. Everywhere, on all the walls and above you on the ceiling facing down, were framed portraits of prizefighters. There were Irish flags tacked to the wall behind the bar and an American flag draped around a portrait of President Wilson. The men sitting at the bar did not take their eyes off me as I made my way across the floor. Their faces were either belligerent or vacant, with an abundance of big stubbly jaws and pug noses. Their coloring was on a descending scale of rosé wine to peeled potatoes.

I expected to be harassed. My plan was to wait it out, then ask the bartender in a low voice if Jack Dempsey had stopped by yet. Dropping his name would get everyone's attention because Dempsey was a very popular fighter. His boxing style consisted of constantly bobbing and weaving before attacking furiously. He knocked out most of his opponents in the first round. Fox was planning to do an on-camera interview with him because he was going to attempt the heavyweight championship. The first title would say "Rage in Motion." I was pretending we were doing the shoot that day.

All eyes at the bar bored into me. Against the wall was the usual arrangement of liquor bottles: artistic labels, amber, caramel, silver, in shapes, squat, rectangular, round, long necks, lit from above—a beautiful display of temptation. A train thundered by overhead, and all the bottles rattled. It was a long train, and waiting to see if the bottles might be jiggled onto the floor was a moment of live animation in Technicolor. I liked the sight so much I forgot caution and sat down on a stool. "Taken," said the thug on the next stool and with one swat knocked me off. I fell to the floor, bumping my thigh hard on the footrest. For him, it was a moment of live slapstick comedy. I flew at him shouting, "You idiot! How dare you hit me!"

Not a good idea. He pinned my arms behind my back and whispered, "Say uncle." Of course I didn't until I was almost maimed, but at last I gave in, and he let me go while guffawing his stupid head off. Here was the perfect security guard. If any of the real guards tried to stop my cameramen, this hooligan would know a million undetectable tortures to inflict. I stood at the bar and ordered a beer from the bartender, who hesitated, waiting for permission. I slapped some coins down on the bar. "Gimme a beer, will ya? I come in here from the Fox Studio looking for Jack Dempsey, and this is the welcome I get."

"I wouldn't sit down on that stool if I was you, buddy," said the thug next to me. "Kikes ain't welcome in this place. You got kike written all over you. Whad' ya think, boys? He's a kike, ain't he?"

The moron on the next stool said, "He got kike eyes."

Some of the men on the stools could see my reflection in the mirror behind the bar, but others had to lean forward. "This here's a private club," said one of the men leaning. Our eyes met for a second, and then he sat back. A zap of confusion.

"Yeah," said another. "This here's a private club. You gotta have a membership card. Ha ha ha ha."

The one who said it was a private club leaned forward again. Our eyes locked. Could it be? "Freckles?"

He ran to me, threw his arms around me, lifted me off my feet and danced me around the room. "Harry! It's Harry! Look how he grew up! Look how he grew up!" He set me on the floor, picked me up, set me on the floor, hugged me hard, let me go and gave me a squeaky kiss on the cheek. "I still got your present, Harry," he said, wiping his eyes with the back of his hand, sniffling hard, then hawking a gob on the sawdust floor. He fished in his pocket. "Look." He held the broken swan's beak on his palm and stood beaming down at me with his pale blue eyes. "Did Uncle Sonny ever come back, Harry?"

I couldn't speak. I just stood there.

His face was the same, covered with freckles, slivers for lips, white eyelashes, but his body had ballooned, and he was now about six foot three with massive broad shoulders. "Look at me not procuring you a drink. Paddy! Did you see? Did you see, it's my best friend Harry? Did you see how he come looking for me? I knew he wouldn't forget me. I knew it. I says to myself, if there's one person in the whole wide world I can count on, it's Harry." He couldn't keep his hands off me, like a child with a puppy. The bartender slid a mug of beer down to me. "Move over, you apes," Freckles said to the other men. "Let Harry sit down."

"This here's my stool, Freckles," whined the man on the stool next to Freckles.

"Yeah?" said Freckles, standing behind the man. The man skulked to the other end of the bar, and Freckles patted the leather on the stool next to him. I sat down, amazed by what life gave me. Why Freckles? And why did seeing him make me want to weep? Freckles wasn't the least bit ashamed of being overwhelmed. "You got a mustache, Harry," Freckles said and wiped foam off my upper lip with his finger.

By the time I left the bar, five men had promised to help me at Belmont. I was overcome while walking back to the studio and had to duck into a doorway and turn my back so I could cry without being seen. I had no idea until then how much strength I'd been using to hold myself together and how futile had been my resolve to put my past life out of my mind.

The next day, Freckles and five of his friends went with me out to the track, where they were hired as security guards. Then I gathered them around me in the studio and showed them a handheld Sept camera. "This, boys, is one of the great inventions of our day. Look how small it is. It uses what we call 35-millimeter film. Why do we call it 35 millimeter?" I showed them a piece of film. "Because that's how wide this film is." I passed around an inch or two of film, and they regarded it intensely. "It's a spring-motor-driven camera that makes single exposures, rapid sequences and short movies." I handed it to Freckles. "Pass it around." He held it gently and passed it to the next thug, who held it the same way. When this greatest of God's miracles was carefully handed back to me, I held it to my eye in imitation of our cameramen so they could see what to ignore at the track. "Just turn a blind eye," I said.

"I understand that expression, Harry," said Freckles.

On the day of the race, about twenty cameramen with cameras under their coats entered the stands as ticket-holding spectators and mingled with the crowd. We smuggled other cameramen onto the track in a horse trailer. The cameramen on the neighboring roofs and on the camouflaged platforms readied their equipment, and the hired airplanes whirred their propellers in a farmer's field nearby, waiting for the okay to take off.

At the starting gate, horses fidgeted, bolted forward and went back, as the jockeys tried to keep steady at the gate. Then *clang*! "They're off!" They burst out, and so did the smoke pots set all around the track by the Hearst News people who had anticipated our shenanigans. Gray clouds obscured the view of the Fox cameramen in the stands. Just as our airplanes flew overhead, so did a Hearst plane, which laid a screen of smoke over the entire track. At the same time, mirrors angled to catch the sun's glare were aimed directly into the lenses of the Fox cameras on the rooftop. Hearst sent cops to get my cameraman out of the water tank, which was fine with me because it set up such a commotion that none of them noticed the Fox cameraman stationed in a window below. Some of the masquerading cameramen in the stands were arrested and their film confiscated. However, in the end, five thousand feet of film covering the race from beginning to end got back to our studio. Fox's newsreel of the race was exhibited in the United States and Europe a full week before Hearst.

Chapter Seventeen

Now came a big change in Louie's life. The war caused coal shortages, so the studios in New York were cold. The resulting electricity shortages made it impossible to use the strong lights needed for shooting indoors. The flu epidemic shut down many theaters, so box-office receipts declined. Most New York film studios began moving to California to take advantage of the warmth and perpetual sunlight. Vitagraph moved from its Brooklyn studio to the Coast. Fed up with Anita Stewart's absences and complaints, the Vitagraph executives gave her permission to sign with Louis B. Mayer of Boston even though her contract had not expired. Not only did they give Anita to Louie but they also gave him permission to film his first feature at their studio in Flatbush. I had been corresponding with Maggie so I knew that Louie had set up an office on West Forty-fifth Street and that he wanted to see me. So I went to his office one day. After hugging me as if nothing bad had happened between us, he accused me of liking Mr. Fox better than him. "What's he ever done for you? Tell me that."

"I like newsreel work, Louie. It's exciting. It has everything. It's real, it's fake, it's important, it's trivial."

"Come on, you little pisher," he said. "I'll buy you lunch." I didn't feel like a little pisher, and I didn't like being called one. He saw my annoyance and made fun of me with a roll of his eyes that suggested I was pretending to be a big shot.

He took me to his favorite place, Shanley's Grill on Forty-third Street and Broadway. At a table in the corner were two film tycoons, Adolph Zukor of Paramount and Marcus Loew of Loew's Theaters. Their children had married, Loew's son to Zukor's daughter, and the families lived near each other on estates by the ocean on Long Island. They were laughing with Sime Silverman, the editor and founder of *Variety* who wrote about them all the time. That table was for the In crowd, and Louie kept glancing over there to see whether they were paying any attention to him, which they were not. They had greeted him, of course, when we came in. They knew him as a fellow theater owner, from New England, and perhaps, they remembered the Anita Stewart lawsuit. But Louie was such small potatoes, and he was an out of towner, so after their initial, "How are you, good to see you," they turned away and went back to having fun with each other. Louie liked to go to Shanley's and believed it was important to be seen there by the other movie men, but I could see that it was painful for him.

"I'm going to be the biggest picture man in the business," Louie said to me, taking a brutal bite out of his pastrami sandwich. Russian dressing and cole slaw dropped out of the rye bread onto his plate. "I'm paying her eighty thousand dollars per picture plus a percentage for the first six pictures with an option for six more at one hundred thousand and a percentage. It's a three-year contract with an option for another two years. Anita is one of the biggest stars in the firmament." His eyes darted to the corner table, then back to me.

I ate my corned beef and cabbage and didn't say what I was thinking, which was that Louie's new venture with Anita was flimsy and could leave me stranded. I was done with that. I didn't like Mr. Fox better than Louie—no one could like Mr. Fox better than Louie—but I liked my new life, and I believed that I could depend upon Mr. Fox to pay my salary. His newsreel company in New York was flourishing, and his feature-film production company in California was making a fortune producing cowboy movies starring Tom Mix. Mr. Fox owned some theaters and bragged that one day he'd own a chain of them that reached across the country. I had seen for myself how he never stopped working.

Sitting in Shanley's with the movie millionaires in the corner ignoring us, I began to see Louie as limited. Louie thought being the biggest movie man in America was the height of ambition. He had no idea that I was working for a man who intended to be the biggest movie man on earth. When we finished eating, we collected our hats from the coat check and went outside into the hot August afternoon. Perhaps Louie imagined that the men in Shanley's would greet him more warmly now that he was producing a movie. He was a member of the big boy's club in his own mind, and I think he wanted me to see that. Instead, I saw the head of Loew's Incorporated and the head of Paramount Pictures greet him indifferently and then ignore him. As we walked to Times Square, Louie said, "I'm offering you the opportunity of a lifetime, Harry. What's a newsreel? It don't compare to a motion-picture movie."

"I appreciate what you've done for me, Louie."

"This is appreciation? This is what you call appreciation, telling me I'm a nobody?"

"I never said that."

"You thought it."

"Who said? How do you know what I'm thinking?"

"How do I know? How should I not know? I brought you up. I say come work for me, and you say no, I'm

not going to work for you. You're nothing but a two bit
operator. I want someone bigger. That's what you say to
me after all I've done for you."

"I didn't say that."

"You think those fellas in there have something on me?
You think just because they got gold toilets now they'll
always be on top? Well, you listen to me, you little pisher."
Now he stopped and poked me in the chest as he said, "I'm
going to be bigger than the both of them put together, and
don't you forget it. And when you come to me—after I've
buried that William Fox of yours along with the rest of
them—when you come crawling to me asking forgiveness,
asking, 'Please, Louie, give me a job. Please, Louie,' then
we'll see who's what. Then we'll see. And don't you forget
it." With that he turned and strode off in that choppy way
of his. I stood, heart pounding, and watched him weave
in and out of the crowd on the sidewalk, an anonymous
fireplug of a man. I walked back to the Fox Studio raging
against Louie's injustice and was happy to lose myself in
the work of that day.

Louie's film opened that winter at the Strand Theater
on Broadway, the marquee ablaze with lights announcing
"Virtuous Wives, Anita Stewart in a Louis B. Mayer
Production." I decided to put an end to our feud by going
to the opening. I missed Maggie, and maybe Louie would
be in a better mood now that he'd completed his project.
It was not a gala opening because people were still afraid
to go out. Anita and the other actors stayed away. Louie
and his family weren't there.

A uniformed usher wearing a surgical mask escorted me
to my seat and handed me an elaborate souvenir program.
Those who dared venture out sat in the red velvet seats
wearing gauze masks over their mouths. When I tried to
lower my scarf, I got angry looks, so I wrapped it around

my mouth again even though it was too hot. I opened the program and saw a portrait of Anita on every page. The words on the cover were "And the Wise men shall secure unto their houses Virtuous Wives, sayeth the prophet." Sayeth?

The lights dimmed, and a man with no strut in his stride came from the wings and stood in front of the curtain, always an ominous sign at the theater. He said he was sure we would applaud management's decision to cancel the vaudeville part of the show. More than half the orchestra was out sick, and most of the girls who danced were ill.

Louie's movie was about people who are stupid, vain and vicious but reform themselves at the end because a little boy is nearly drowned. But even a worse story could not dim the appeal of Anita. When she was on the screen, you couldn't take your eyes off of her. I would phone her and say hello.

Long Island was a long-distance call from Manhattan, and Mr. Fox would surely catch me if I used the office phone. He followed every penny that was spent at his studios, pored over the bills and called people into his office to defend themselves if he noticed an unauthorized expense. So I gathered a pocketful of change and called Anita from a public phone. "Wood Violet," a voice on the other end said.

"I'd like to speak to Anita Stewart, please."

"I know you would, honey. But so would everyone else."

"Tell her it's Harry Sirkus."

"Aw right. You hold on, hear?"

Footsteps on marble came from a distance. Sounded like her house was huge. "Harry? Is that you?"

"Hello, Anita." The operator interrupted me to tell me my time was running out.

"Harry! Where are you? Why haven't you called me before? Louie said you were in the city. Said you're working for Fox. I kept thinking you'd call me. Ma said I should call you. I said, 'How should I call him when I don't even know where he's staying.' I said to Louie, 'Where's he staying?' Louie says to me, 'How should I know?' What happened? Did you two have a fight or something? You know we're moving, right?"

"Call me back. I'm at a public phone. You got a pen?" I gave her the number, waited and when the phone rang, I picked it up. "Where to?"

"To the ends of the friggin' earth. California."

"Why?"

"Because Louie rented a studio out there. I don't have a choice. Do you think I would have signed a three-year contract if I thought he'd move to Timbuktu? He thinks it's more healthful."

"What's more healthful about it?"

"He has this idea his daughter needs the sun."

"Why?"

"She got the flu."

"Who? Edie? Irene?"

"The one that's twelve. Gosh, you and Louie really did have a split. They thought she was going to die. Happened right before the picture opened. Did you see it?"

"Edie's okay, right?"

"Yeah. She got cured. So what'd you think?"

"You were good."

"It's got legs. It's boffo at the box office."

"I know. I'm surprised. I thought the story stunk."

"I know. Me too. But I looked good. I liked that dress in the scene where the kid drowns."

"Edie's okay, right? She got over it, right?"

"I think so. He's out there now. He's been out there for months. I have to go out to start shooting *In Old*

Kentucky. He got Lois Weber to direct. I'm all balled up. I don't want to leave New York. Ma's having a fit. She's had the same mahjong group for twenty years. They play every Wednesday night. Now what's she going to do? Rudy's parents are giving him a hard time. Telling him there's no one to know out there, and this is what comes from marrying a show girl. How do you like it over at Fox?"

"I do."

"Can you imagine me in California? There ain't any stores out there. I'm supposed to be so well dressed, and where the hell am I going to buy the clothes? I said this to Louie. He says, 'You'll take the train back now and then.'"

"Tell Louie I'm sorry about Edie."

"You tell him."

"No, you tell him."

"Okay. You want him to call you?"

"Yes."

"Okay, Harry. I probably won't see you for a long time."

"Write to me."

"No. Then you'll see how ignorant I am."

"Don't be silly."

"I ain't being silly. I never did good in English. Teacher said I wrote like I wasn't born in America."

"That's not a very nice thing to say."

"You should of seen her. She looked like a man. And she wore this belt that had two big balls hanging off of it. Boy, did I hate her."

"Write to me anyway."

"Okay. But only postcards."

"That's fine with me. Did Louie buy a studio?"

"No. He's renting from Colonel Selig. We're shooting in a zoo."

Chapter Eighteen

When the flu epidemic lifted and all the regulations meant to protect us from one another no longer applied, Filpot's business returned. He played host all day and night to the many people who appreciated the generous size of his whiskey shots. Travelers rented rooms next to mine and I had to share the bathroom at the end of the hall. The cook returned, and fumes from the kitchen rose to the top of the house, so my sleeping hours were plagued not only by bursts of laughter from the bar but by the overwhelming smell of fried onions. I opened the window, but it didn't help, and once when I was on line at the bank depositing my paycheck, the person close behind me said, "I smell onions."

I worked on many different projects at Fox, but a couple of them stand out. One was the Hammond circus-train wreck. A locomotive engineer fell asleep and plowed into a circus train near Hammond, Indiana. Eighty-six people died, some burned beyond recognition, and one hundred twenty-seven were injured. We rushed cameras out there but had to supplement some of the real footage with fake shots of trains in flames and kerosene lamps igniting because much of the fire was caused by the lamps that lit the sleeper cars of the circus train. I had an argument with a woman in the art department about whether or not to show an elephant wandering around lost. There were no elephants on the train, but she said it didn't matter. It would add pathos. "You must be new," she said. "We're not in the business of journalism here. It's entertainment." We compromised by editing in footage from our archives of frightened monkeys screeching. I was proud of the resulting newsreel because for the first time, one of my titles was used: "Circus of Horrors." I liked it because it described the crash as well as the crowd of spectators watching the charred bodies being unloaded.

I was still living at Filpot's when the Volstead Act was passed in 1919 over President Wilson's veto, and Prohibition became the law of the land. Shanley's Grill closed. They couldn't make a living without selling alcohol. Filpot's business disappeared. His brother in Florida convinced him to get in on the real estate boom there. "Don't believe it, Filpot," one of his poker buddies said. "They're selling you swamps. It's just swamps. Pay off the cops here like everyone else does, and keep on serving booze." But he put his tavern up for sale.

The bars in New York turned into speakeasies. At Paddy's, we had to say the password "Lorraine," the name of Paddy's wife, before Goo Goo Maloney would open up. We endured periodic raids by local cops who lingered for a free drink or two.

Prohibition was a popular newsreel topic. Fox News filmed an anti-Prohibition rally in Boston at Faneuil Hall, men carrying signs proclaiming the "Death of Liberty." They filmed G-men dumping liquor onto the street and carting bottles out of saloons as well as G-men destroying a moonshine still in Alabama.

I asked Freckles and his gang if I could join them on a rum-running operation. "You're going to put me in the movies, Harry?"

"Hold on," said Fists, the one who had knocked me off the stool. "They'll snag us."

"I always wanted to be in pictures," said Goo Goo. "I got the looks for it."

"You boys set it up, and I'll come along with our best cameraman."

"He know how to keep his mouth shut?" asked Milo whose nose was flat against his face. The others glared at Milo for daring to question me.

The problem was finding a cameraman. "It's done at night, Harry," they said to me. "It's dark. And dangerous. You know the kind of people these are? They aren't pretending to be crooks. They are crooks." I was baffled that the same cameramen who put themselves in the middle of brawls during labor strikes would not take a chance with my idea. "They take the hooch from a ship in the pitch dark, they put the hooch in a truck, they drive the hooch to a warehouse. Period. End of story. It's not theater. Wait a minute. Why don't you ask that rookie?"

A few days later, I was passing the screening room, and the door was open, so I went in to view what was supposed to be footage explaining the meaning of the term bootlegging. On the screen was a small house on a residential street with two young women in front. Along came an older woman wearing a dress that looked like a prison matron's uniform. "That's my mother," a voice in the dark said. "We've told her for years she looks like a prison guard in that thing." The older woman on the screen stopped in front of the girls, frisked one of them who acted blasé, then frisked the other one and *Voila*! She found a flat bottle of Old Crow whiskey stuffed into the knee-high stocking of the girl. This was bootlegging, carrying the stuff next to your calf.

Though the cameraman was looking through the camera lens, he hadn't noticed a cat in the window of the house behind the girls. The cat looked straight at him, washed its face, stared out again and scratched its ears with a vigorous hind foot. It was a comical cat that made crazy faces, especially when digging into its ear with its hind foot. We were all laughing, and the cameraman said, "That is one of the best cats we've ever owned." The lights came on, and Mr. Fox stood up and said in a loud voice, "You won't think it's so funny when I take it out of your pay. You don't waste my film, pal. Not my film." He stalked out, leaving a sickened wake behind him. The other people in the room shuffled around and departed and the cameraman, his face red, pulled on his black beret. He stood up and sighed. "I thought my sister looked pretty good," he said. This was the first time I'd seen Kenny since I'd been working at Fox.

"Hey, do you remember me?"

"There's not going to be anything left in my check. My sister's going to brain me. She told me not to do it. She said there's a shortage of raw film stock. You think he's going to fire me?"

"I don't know. Don't you remember me?" I reminded him about our meeting in the park, but he only pretended to remember. "Oh, right. Sure." I told him my idea of shooting a rum-running expedition.

"I own lights that could do that," he said.

"But the problem is they're gangsters. Maybe they aren't going to want to be all lit up while they're smuggling booze."

"Are you kidding? Everyone loves to be in the movies. They'll eat it up."

He showed up on the appointed evening in polka-dot bow tie, black beret smashed straight down over his forehead, rust-and-white-striped jacket, black jodhpurs and brown lace-up boots. He was skinny with a narrow face, eyes set close together, and when my gang of thugs saw him, they fell for his celebrity getup and imagined they were in the presence of a great cameraman, even though he was only about my age. "He wouldn't wear them clothes," Milo whispered to Freckles, "if he wasn't famous." We began to load Kenny's camera equipment into the back of Milo's truck, and I noticed that Kenny had brought along his prized possession, a French airport light made of metallic mirrors that reflected a brilliant eight hundred million candlepower beam. I took him aside and said again, "These are criminals. They will not enjoy being illuminated while committing a crime."

Kenny whispered, "Says who?" We climbed into the truck for our three-hour drive to the coast of New Jersey.

Freckles' gang was responsible for picking up the contraband at the beach, loading it into their truck, then delivering it to a warehouse in Hell's Kitchen. Unlike other couriers in New York, Freckles' gang never filched the bottles, and that's why they were employed by the most successful and famous smuggler, Captain William McCoy, a former boat builder and excursion-boat captain from Florida, who charged more than other smugglers because he never added water to the booze. He was caught by the Coast Guard once, so he began to anchor his schooner, *Tomoka*, outside U.S. territorial waters and employed men with small boats to shuttle the "real McCoy" to shore.

These excursions happened once a month on the moonless night. We drove to the beach at Raritan Bay and waited inside the truck until dark. Once Kenny's lights were turned on, the gang would balk for sure. So I resigned myself to just having an adventure rather than getting exciting footage to show Mr. Fox. There would be no expense to justify because Kenny wouldn't be able to expose any film. Just after midnight, the gang, having exhausted the topic of which was more constipating, cheese or sausage, came alive. Kenny and I followed them to the edge of the water, where he set up his tripod and lights. "Ahoy there, Freckles," Kenny yelled from the water's edge. "What happens next?"

"Shut your pie hole!" said Goo Goo.

"I have to point my camera somewhere, Goo Goo. What am I going to be pointing it at?"

"Shut your trap," hissed Fists.

"You hear anything?" whispered Milo.

Suddenly, we heard a motor speeding toward us across the dark bay. Freckles said, "That's him!" and Kenny blasted his light and started filming, just as a flat-bottomed speedboat fitted with armor-plating and packed high with cartons ran up on the beach. The captain, standing at the wheel, a bearded man with stringy black hair down to his shoulders, wearing clothes that looked like he'd slept in a coal bin, squinted into the light and said, "Que pasa?"

"It's a movie," said Freckles. "We're in a movie, Joe!"

Joe put his palms over his eyes and said, "Stings my eyes, amigo."

"Come on, you idiots," said Fists. "Get this stuff into the truck. How many loads tonight, Joe?"

Kenny, still cranking his camera, said, "Joe? Is this Havana Joe?"

The captain got out of his skiff. He was a small, weasly man who looked at people sideways. Kenny was still filming. "Havana Joe?" he asked again.

"You heard of my name?" asked Joe.

"Heard of you!" Kenny said, eye to the lens. "You're the star of this film!"

Havana Joe took a bow for Kenny, who then turned the camera on the gang loading the cartons into the truck.

"Andale, muchachos! We got three loads, rum from Bimini and Irish whiskey."

"Is Captain McCoy's schooner out there?" I asked. "We have a smaller camera. Could we put Kenny in your boat? He doesn't take up much room. Could we go with you to pick up the next load?"

"Amigo," Joe said, his body was tensed like a flyswatter as he watched Freckles and the gang unload the cartons from the skiff and lug them to the truck. "You do not want to get near the machine guns."

"I don't mind," Kenny said, cutting his light and coming to where we stood near some beach bushes.

"Oh," said Joe, "you would mind, amigo."

"Let's ask him," said Kenny. "Tell him we're making a news picture, and ask him if he'd mind if we got some footage of *Tomoka*."

All cartons out of the skiff, Joe shoved it into the water, climbed in and sped away into the blackness. "Let's make it look like the bootleggers wouldn't cooperate with us," said Kenny. "Get some shots of me being disappointed. No! Wait! Better! Get some shots of one of the boys pushing me around."

"Are you sure, Kenny?"

"Freckles!" Kenny yelled. "Come beat me up."

"Oh, no, Kenny. I wouldn't do that. You're my friend."

"I know. I know. Just a little. Come over here. Harry get behind the camera. Okay, Freckles, when I say go, I'm going to turn on the lights, and when Harry says Action! you give me a big push, and I'm going to act like I'm scared."

"I don't shove my friends, Kenny. I don't do that."

"It's acting, Freckles. Don't you want to be an actor?"

"Fists!" I called. "Come over here, and give Kenny a push." Fists swaggered to us and shoved Kenny so hard he fell backward onto the sand. "Not yet!" I said. "Wait for the word *action*, you big palooka." Kenny was stunned but pretended he was okay as he got up and dusted beach sand from his jodhpurs.

"Ain't going to do it if you call me names," said Fists. "Sticks and stones break my bones, but names don't hurt me."

"Palooka's a good name, Fists," said Kenny, sending me a scolding look. "It means a strong and handsome man. Let's do another take." He explained the procedure, but we forgot to tell Fists the purpose of the shot. Kenny blasted the beach with his light, and I got behind the lens. "Action!" Fists, thinking this was a game, burst out laughing and gave Kenny another shove that sent him backward a few feet. I kept the camera on Kenny while he was seeing stars and acting frustrated like a big fish just got away. "Shoot Fists again," he said to me as he got up. "Fists, can you pretend you're angry? Can you growl into the camera? I'll cut it in later. Come on, Fists. Let's see an angry face."

When Havana Joe returned with the second load, he said that Captain McCoy wanted to meet a representative of Fox News, so Kenny loaded his lights and his handheld camera into the skiff and sped away with Havana Joe across the choppy black waters of the bay.

Mr. Fox was at the New York studio on the day the rushes were ready. We sat in the screening room and saw the most spectacular sights: Havana Joe looked even more like a weasel than he did in real life, a crew of thugs lugged liquor cases and then smacked the poor daredevil cameraman, and Captain William McCoy himself posed on his famous rum-running schooner. He took the camera on a tour of his boat, the fish pens below refitted to hold as much contraband as possible, stacks of Canadian whiskey plainly visible in Kenny's light. He held up bottles of French Champagne and showed how the label was secure, meaning it hadn't been changed. The camera panned the crew as well as the prostitutes onboard. The last shot was of Fists growling like a maniac into the camera as if furious that he was being photographed.

When the lights came up, Mr. Fox sat nodding his head and puffing his cigar. "That was your work?" he said to Kenny.

"Sure was. Did you see that shot of *Tomoka* from the water? I thought that was going to be a bust because the skiff was wobbling around so much. That was some great shot. That is my masterpiece as of this date."

"You got nerve, kid," Mr. Fox said to Kenny, looking at him steadily from under those hooded, suspicious, deeply hurt eyes of his. He kept his gaze on Kenny long enough for Kenny to feel uncomfortable and begin to smile in a childishly ingratiating way. Then Mr. Fox drilled the beam into me. "This was your idea?" he said. I considered spreading the blame around, but the third degree was in his gaze, so if you didn't tell the truth immediately, he'd get it out of you soon.

"Yes, sir."

"I am asking you something I already know. They were laughing at you about this."

"Who?"

"Don't matter who. It come to my attention." He put his cigar stump back in his downturned lips, smoothed his side hair over the top of his egg and went out with his paralyzed arm stuffed in his suit-jacket pocket.

Kenny and I slumped in our seats, disappointed and frightened for our jobs. We met by accident as we were leaving the building that night. "I don't know about you," Kenny said, "but I'd like to get smashed. You ever been to the Red Head in Greenwich Village?"

My future seemed a black pit. I would never amount to anything. "I've never been anywhere, Kenny." Filpot had a buyer for his tavern, and I had to move, but so far, I hadn't been able to afford any of the rooms I'd visited from ads in the paper, and I didn't like any of them anyway: roach-infested cells on dark hallways.

Chapter Nineteen

I was used to drinking at Filpot's with companions twice my age who talked about their blood pressure or at Paddy's with a bunch of professional bums who didn't talk, so it was a surprise to enter a speakeasy full of college kids with bright, straight teeth and stylish flapper clothes, all crowded close together at small tables in a dim basement in a cloud of cigarette smoke. Dixieland jazz rang out from a phonograph behind the bar and mixed with the pleasant tinkling of ice cubes and the buzz of intense conversation.

Kenny and I worked our way through the smoke to a couple of empty seats, and all eyes swept our way for an instant to see if anyone interesting had just come in. The tables were so close that conversation was not confined to those sitting together but included three or four tables, and the minute Kenny and I sat down, we became part of it and were expected to join in. Our companions were discussing pending legislation about female clothing. A bill in Utah would mandate fines and imprisonment for women who wore on the streets skirts higher than three inches above the ankle; a bill in Virginia would forbid evening gowns that displayed more than three inches of female throat. A bill in Ohio sought to prohibit any female over fourteen from wearing a skirt that did not reach to the instep.

"Now that women have the vote," one of the flappers said, "we no longer have to endure such silly laws." She fished a packet of cigarettes from her purse, lit one and scrutinized me to see if I was shocked. She thought she was being modern by smoking, a Jazz Age baby rebelling against the Establishment. She smoked self-consciously, waving the cigarette dramatically after each puff but not inhaling.

Another woman said, "Women are masochists. They'll vote for that legislation. Let's face it. We women have an inferiority complex." They agreed that women were their own worst enemies. Then they debated whether Sacco and Vanzetti were guilty of murder, the merits of Eugene O'Neill's new play *Anna Christie* and whether self-control was out of fashion.

"Freud says if you inhibit your libido," a girl in blood-red lipstick said, "you'll become mentally ill."

"I'll help you keep it uninhibited," one of the boys said, and they all laughed.

I was secretly depending on Kenny's social ease to cover my shyness. But like me, he shrank into himself, intimidated by the softness of these young people, the comfort they exuded. It was bitter to think of the money and love that propped them up. Kenny lived in Flushing, Queens, with his mother and sisters who all worked. He had never gone to college and never expected to. He searched the room for a waiter, saw one, waved his arms, and one of the young men said to him, "Order the Champagne. It's the real McCoy."

"None of the giggle water in this gin mill is watered," another boy said, taking a sip of whatever was in his coffee cup. "Charlie and Jack wouldn't dare." He was referring to the cousins who owned the Red Head. "Are you fellows Columbia or NYU?"

Kenny said, "Don't ask," as if answering would remind him of something horrible. The conversation turned to prudish parents and how the older generation was to blame for ruining the world before passing it on.

"Hit me again, Jose!" one of the young women said when the waiter finally worked his way over to our table. I could see by Kenny's expression that he had no idea what to order, and I realized his inviting me to get smashed was just tough talk. He had never been to a speakeasy in his life. "Bourbon," I said to the waiter. "For my pal and me. Straight up." These words I learned from Freckles.

"What exactly does compare and contrast mean anyway?" one of the girls asked. A discussion began of the merits of various professors they all knew. When the waiter brought the drinks, he set them down and said, "Enjoy!" But he was Spanish speaking, so he pronounced the *j* as a *y*, *enyoy*. When he was out of earshot, the people at our table made fun of him by clinking coffee cups and toasting one another, "Enyoy!" This offended me, the son of immigrants. These fools would probably make fun of my father who said "peanuts butter." I learned the term was not correct only when I moved to Haverhill. Let them try to earn a living in a foreign city. Let them try to earn a living at all. What could any of them do, other than open a book and memorize the contents?

Kenny took a sip of bourbon and cried, "Holy mackerel! What is this crap?" He wiped his lips with the back of his hand, opened his mouth wide saying, "Ahhhh," as if hoping the taste would escape. He said, "Water! Get me some water! My mouth's on fire!" Why this was funny, I had no idea, but everyone at the table started laughing. Kenny stood up, saying, "You're just a big bunch of idiots," and turned to leave. By the time he got to the door, I realized I was going to have to pay for him, so I peeled off some bills, left them on the table and followed him outside. He was way down the sidewalk, walking along with his hands jammed deep into his pockets, his head bent forward.

"Kenny!" He didn't stop. When I caught up to him, I said, "You owe me a buck."

"What for?"

"For the bourbon."

"I didn't drink it."

"You still have to pay."

"Why? I didn't drink it."

No use arguing. I'd get him some other time. We took separate subways home, and he, too, probably went to sleep with a heavy heart expecting to be fired the next day.

But the opposite happened. Our rum-running footage was chosen for the next issue and was shown to thousands of people in hundreds of theaters. We both got raises that allowed us to move together to a fourth-floor walk-up in Greenwich Village, above a tattoo parlor, and there we practiced the Charleston in front of our mirror, so we'd be ready if we ever met any girls who would go out with us.

Chapter Twenty

The Waldorf-Astoria Hotel was a world-famous palace of luxury, a massive granite wedding cake at Fifth Avenue and Thirty-fourth Street. Host to celebrities, pashas, kings and rajas, the Waldorf-Astoria, with its thousand guest rooms and opulent restaurants, was designed to prove that New York could be a world capital. The hotel was proof that Americans were not hicks compared with Europeans, that we understood luxury, comfort, service and magnificence. A cuckoo clock, a caliph's palace, a Bavarian castle—it challenged the brownstone monotony of the surrounding neighborhoods. The concierge had the reputation of Cerberus and was known to turn away visitors who did not enhance the image of the place. I assumed this meant me, so I had a problem.

A messenger had delivered a note to me one day at work written on Waldorf-Astoria Hotel stationery. "I'm in town. Mum's the word. Come see us. Anita."

There was a young woman in the fashion department at Fox named Etta, a mighty twig with a boyish body. Her black hair was cut short with severe straight bangs down over her eyebrows, like an upside-down bowl. Instead of being ashamed of having weak eyes, she emphasized her spectacles and wore owlish, round black frames that dominated her little face. Her clothes were so fashion forward that even I noticed them. "Did you see Etta's ugly shoes?" I heard the women in the lunchroom whisper. "Did you see how short her skirt is?" Six months later, the whispers changed to, "I never thought I'd be wearing these shoes." Or "My mother said I can't go out in a skirt this short, and I said but all the girls are wearing them." Like so many tiny women, Etta was afraid of being treated like a child, so she made her voice deep and forceful, and her posture was sternly erect.

She was responsible for setting up fashion shoots and was always lugging around armfuls of garments. I visited her on the first floor and explained my dilemma. "What are you saying?" she asked, frowning up at me. "You want me to dress you?" I tried very hard to keep my expression blank because my face wanted to go all tender looking down at her littleness. "Why don't you just buy yourself some nice clothes?"

"That's what Kenny says."

"So why don't you?"

"Makes me uncomfortable to spend money on clothes. They used to give them to me free when I was kid."

"What else is new? Every child gets clothes free."

I was in fifth grade again, and John Hale, at the desk next to mine, was screaming with delight: "Hey! He's wearing my old shirt!" I wished I had the kind of face that no one could read, but I didn't and whatever washed over me while I was remembering that humiliation, Etta must have seen because her tone softened. "As what?"

"As someone who could get by the concierge at the Waldorf-Astoria."

"As what? A prince? Businessman? Yachtsman? Be specific."

"Man about town."

She pursed her lips then swung the pucker over to the side and looked up at me with her eyebrows raised. "No," she said. "You don't have the face for man about town. Too sensitive. You're a wealthy Yale post doc in town to see your financial people."

The next day, after everyone else in the fashion department had gone home, Etta rummaged around and came up with some gray flannel trousers. She didn't have an office but claimed territory of her own by erecting a Japanese screen across one corner of the floor. When I tried to duck behind the screen to try on the trousers, she said, "Don't go back there. Put them on here. I have to see. Think of me as a doctor. I see men in their drawers all the time."

"Etta," I said, "I'm very shy. I always have been. Let me go behind the screen."

"No. You can't."

"Why?"

"Because."

When I tried to walk across the floor to the screen, she tried to hold me back. I had no intention of taking off my clothes in front of Etta, so I pulled her along across the floor and went behind the screen where her desk was cluttered with fabric, seam tape, tailor's chalk, shoes and fashion sketches. Next to the desk was a suitcase full of women's clothes. "Just borrowing," she said, stuffing the clothes in and shutting the suitcase fast. "I'm going to bring them back." Her face was so worried, I bopped her on the head lightly with a ruler. "I always bring them back." I bopped her again. She turned her back and became very quiet.

"I won't tell, Etta." I turned her toward me and saw her eyes were filled with tears. "I won't tell. Honestly. Who would I tell?"

She snatched her glasses off her face and wiped her eyes impatiently with the butt of her palm. "Now you're happy."

"About what?"

"About having something on me."

"Let's call it even. You know I'm a big phony who goes to the Waldorf-Astoria in clothes from the costume department."

"Okay, okay. You think I have all night? Try on the trousers. I'll get you a jacket and shirt." When I came out from behind the screen, she switched her lips to the side and appraised me. "Stripes," and went to get me a striped tie.

Limousines were lined up on Fifth Avenue at the entrance, but I was not intimidated because I was wearing the armor of expensive, stylish clothes: a felt hat, dove-gray leather gloves, a blue cashmere coat with a silk ascot and dove-gray spats fastened with pearl buttons. Well-dressed young women in furs turned to give me a second look. The lobby gave way to a long corridor studded with marble columns. Peacock Alley stretched a full city block, chandeliers were lit even during daylight, palm trees stood tall, uniformed bellboys rushed around with luggage. Guests, with the self-confidence that comes from being able to afford almost anything, promenaded in furs and diamonds. The legendary concierge was not more haughty to me than to the other guests. He asked my destination, and when I said, "Anita Stewart," he scanned his leather notebook and discovered that I was, indeed, a person she wanted to admit. Her privacy was so well guarded that the elevator man needed special permission from the concierge to take me up to her suite on the top floor.

In a grand room, gold and burgundy, with high ceilings and large vases of flowers everywhere, Anita was reclining on a satin chaise longe, the leftovers from room service on a rolling cart next to her. She still had that beautiful delicacy that the public loved, but she was ashen with purple crescents under her eyes and too thin. To hide the concern that I knew showed on my face, I quickly made a deep courtier's bow and said, "Miss Stewart looks lovely in a fur-trimmed bed jacket."

"He's cheating on me," she said as if we had just seen each other the day before.

Her mother came in from one of the other rooms. "Harry!" She pulled me against her softness, then set me away. "Look at you. You're a grown-up man. Look at you!"

"You know who with?" Anita asked.

"Annie," said Mrs. Stewart, "look at Harry. Look how he's grown up!" Then she said to me, "Did you ever see so many fruit baskets? You'll take some home. Sit. Sit in the armchair. It's got down cushions. Every cushion in our house in California is made out of down. Every one. And there's a fig tree in our backyard. Figs! You go outside, and you pick figs!"

"And that's about it," said Anita.

"There's plenty to do there, believe me," said Mrs. Stewart.

"Right, Ma. You can also pick oranges."

"She doesn't like it there," said Mrs. Stewart.

"It's the sticks. There's no stores, no theaters. There's not even any sidewalks! Adobe. The whole place is adobe. They have to send back East to get props. Every piece of furniture in our new house we had to wait months for because it all came from New York. I'm supposed to be the best-dressed woman in the world, and there's no place to buy clothes. I have to get on the train and come here just to buy a decent dress. I should of stayed at Vitagraph."

"They have fig trees, orange trees," said Mrs. Stewart.

"Ma, you sound like Louie. He loves it out there, Harry. We're working in a friggin' zoo, and he loves it."

"They got cactus," said Mrs. Stewart.

"And guess what? They come in different shapes!" Anita turned herself into a cactus, arms at right angles up, arms rounded down, and I wondered what it must be like to be able to mimic something so exactly.

"Harry," said Mrs. Stewart, "I have to keep staring at you, you're so grown up. And prosperous! Look at them clothes! Tell me. You got a girlfriend?" I shook my head.

"Leave him alone, Ma."

"I'm just asking. Have you ever been in love, Harry?"

"Ma! Will you get down off that horse?"

"He's a good-looking young man. He should have lots of girlfriends."

"Maybe he does, Ma. Look how he's blushing. Go 'head, Harry. Guess. Guess who Rudy's fooling around with." Anita jammed a cigarette into an ivory cigarette holder.

"She didn't used to smoke. Now she smokes. Like that's going to do her any good."

"Mae Murray," Anita said, lighting the cigarette. "She of the two expressions. Fully asleep and half awake. He had a bit part in *Idols of Clay*. Met her on the set. Doesn't even know she's fooling around with Chaplin. My life is subpoenas and court dates."

"He wouldn't be anything without you," I said, throwing caution to the wind because maybe they would get back together.

"Even with me, he's nothing," she said. "The public don't take to him. We made him leading man in *Rose o' the Sea*. Didn't even know it was charity. Started giving orders to everyone on the set like a big shot." Her chin quivered. "So who cares, right? Who cares?"

"How 'bout some Champagne?" said Mrs. Stewart going to a sideboard. "Will you look at the glasses? Real crystal. In a hotel, no less."

"They're the right kind of glasses too, Ma." Anita's chin was quivering faster now.

"Oh, Anita," I said and went to her on the sofa and held her in my arms while she sobbed. I could feel her bones under my hands, especially the knobs at the end of her shoulders.

"Enough, enough, enough," said Mrs. Stewart, coming to the sofa with two flutes. "Have some bubbly. Time for bubbly! Drink up!"

Anita kept her face against my chest. She was so thin and fragile that it was like holding a marionette. "He used to be so nice to me."

"And you to him," I said smoothing her hair.

She lay against me until she wasn't crying anymore, then pulled back. "I got your new suit all snotty." She wiped her face gently with polished fingertips. I fished my handkerchief out of my pocket, gave it to her, then remembered that it told the truth about my wardrobe. It wasn't linen but pure crap from the dime store, and Anita would know the minute she felt it. But I remembered that she was like me and a cheap handkerchief would feel like home. She took it, blew her nose hard on it, wiped her eyes and handed it back to me crumpled up and soggy.

"Tell me," I said stuffing the rag in my pocket, "how's Louie?"

"They call him L.B. out there. Are you in contact with him?"

"Maggie sends me postcards now and then."

"California ain't her cup of tea," said Mrs. Stewart. "She pretends for the sake of Louie and the girls. But once we were at the beach standing with our feet in the Pacific Ocean, and she says to me that when she closes her eyes, she can pretend it's Cape Cod." We raised a silent toast to Maggie.

"And what about Louis B. Mayer films? I never read anything. The trades keep referring to him as Louis B. Mayer of Boston."

"He ain't got distribution," said Mrs. Stewart. "That's his problem."

"Why not?"

"He don't own enough theaters. What does he got, Annie? Three houses in New England some place?"

"The way it's going," said Anita, "you don't got a national theater chain, you don't amount to nothing. Marcus Loew owns Metro Pictures, so he shows them in Loew's theaters. Zukor owns Paramount and shows Paramount pictures in his theaters. Fox shows Fox pictures in his theaters. What do they want with Louis B. Mayer pictures?"

"Even though you're in them?"

"Me? I ain't the draw I used to be, Harry. I don't kid myself none. Ever since they found out I'm married, they don't want to see me so much."

"It ain't you, Annie," said Mrs. Stewart. "It ain't your fault at all. He don't even got a studio of his own. Sam Goldwyn's got that big spread in Culver City. Fox has a lot on Western Avenue. Paramount took over some citrus grove in Hollywood. Universal is over there with the chicken farms. What's he got? Selig's Zoo. It's full of animals. It's a zoo!"

"The monkeys escape all the time, and they find film and play with it. It's funny, but it ain't funny because it's expensive. When we were shooting *In Old Kentucky*, we lost a day because some lion spooked the horses, and it took all day to catch them." Anita sipped Champagne and sighed. "I'm allergic to horses, Harry. That don't matter. Nobody cares. There's a scene, I'm supposed to save my lover's prize mare from a stable fire, so I have to lead the thing. I broke out in hives. Didn't I, Ma?"

"The size of grapes."

"I'm a New Yorker. What can I tell you. They got this dump out there called the Hollywood Hotel, and the big thrill is you go and sit on the veranda and watch everyone. Everyone's an extra. They get five bucks a day: misfits, outcasts, runaways. Then you see these would-be character actors with beards parading around in sandals and a toga. And all the pretty girls have curls like Mary so-called Pickford."

"I don't mind them so much," said Mrs. Stewart. "I don't like them mothers pushing their little kids. You should see it, Harry. Tiny kids with peroxide hair. Tiny."

"Is he discouraged?"

"Who, Louie? You mean because he's renting from Colonel Selig? Hell, no. Says he's going to be the biggest movie man in the country. I'm supposed to tell you he's coming to town next month. Wants to see you. You heard about the merger, right?"

"Lasky and Zukor?"

"No, Marcus Loew's deal. Hey, Ma, maybe it's not in the papers yet."

"Maybe. Everyone out there knows about it, Harry."

"About what?"

"Well, you know how Metro went from nothing to a gold mine after Loew bought it, right?"

"Because of Rudolph Valentino."

"Oh, do I love that Rudolph Valentino," said Mrs. Stewart.

"Ma, control yourself. Anyway, Metro's so big now it's busting out of its space, so Loew bought Sam Goldwyn's facility. Sam paid fourteen million dollars for fifty acres of nothing in a place called Culver City, put up forty-two buildings including bungalows for dressing rooms, planted magnolia and fir trees, made an entire miniature city that's almost a half-mile long. They built a street there that's exactly like a street on the Lower East Side of New York. I walk down it, I get homesick. So now Louie's talking about running the new company, Metro-Goldwyn."

"It's ridiculous," said Mrs. Stewart. "Why would Marcus Loew—who has more dough than God, who can hire anyone he wants—hire Louie? What's Louie got? Not meaning any disrespect, mind you, but what's Louie got to offer? So he owned a couple of theaters, and he made a few pictures."

"Wait. You mean Louie wants to ditch his production company?"

"It ain't easy to own your own business," said Anita, "always worrying about the payroll."

"He works her like a dog. No better than Vitagraph."

"Ma, do me a favor. Put on that Nick Meadows record."

"No, Annie. I won't. You listen, you cry." But she walked into one of the bedrooms. "Especially with all that Champagne in you." Mrs. Stewart came back from the bedroom holding a record in a cardboard envelope, a picture of Nick Meadows lit from the side on the cover. She cranked the phonograph, and when the turntable was spinning fast enough, she set the needle on the record. Out came Niko's beautiful voice singing Irving Berlin's song:

I'm so unhappy, What'll I do? I long for somebody who will sympathize with me. I'm growing so tired of living alone. I lie awake all night and cry. Nobody loves me, that's why. All by myself in the morning, all by myself in the night...

We sat there while Mrs. Stewart puttered around picking up glasses, straightening pillows on the sofas, moving around as loudly as she could to distract her daughter. Niko's voice brought back Mr. Levin's stable and me at thirteen on the train running away, lost in Boston, alone. As for my parents, that memory always came back more as a feeling than an image. It was the feeling of being scooped off my feet and carried by Oats as he ran through the crowd to get me away from there. My legs were useless. I was without strength.

"Enough of that," said Mrs. Stewart, abruptly lifting the needle. "That ain't doing nobody no good."

"He makes me swoon," said Anita.

"His real name's Nikos Adrianos," I said so I could hold on to something real.

"You know him, Harry?"

"Used to."

"You mean like really really, or you wish you did. You should see all the people think they know me."

"I used to work with him in Boston."

"Don't play with me about this, Harry," Anita said, becoming comically dramatic. "I adore Nick Meadows. I'm not kidding. So tell me before I faint, yes or no about meeting him in person. Ma, did you hear? Harry knows him!"

"When you say know him," asked Mrs. Stewart, "do you mean in person?"

"I used to work with him."

"In Rome?"

"No. In Boston."

"But he's Italian. He's the son of an Italian count."

"Maybe now, but he used to be Greek."

"You mean he ain't?"

"Harry, invite him here," said Anita.

"He'd be thrilled to know Anita Stewart wants to meet him," said her mother. "Who doesn't want to meet Anita Stewart?"

"When are we leaving, Ma. Saturday?"

"Depends on the court date, Annie. I told you. Rudy ain't signed them papers."

"Ma, get that eight by ten of me by the pool. We really do got a pool, Harry." She signed her name as carefully as a child just learning script. "It's me in my charming bathing costume." She handed it to me. I promised to contact Nick Meadows, and I went home trying to figure out how I was going to do that.

Chapter Twenty-One

Because newsreels lasted about twelve minutes, only seven or eight stories were selected from about two dozen possibilities. Most of our footage went unused; the outtakes and cut negatives were sent up to the archives. Sandwiched between cartoons and the feature, newsreels could show nothing that might threaten the parents and children sitting in the dark. Our job was to entertain. Those of us who worked at Fox were forever having to calm down the new employees who angrily maintained that we were feeding pabulum to the public. Newsreels were blamed for being trivial. I was always perplexed by the people who thought the public should get hard information about the world in the same movie show in which they paid admission to be entertained. If they saw scenes of real torture, would they buy another ticket? I remembered how bitter Kenny was when his footage of Lenin's funeral was rejected. It was his first overseas assignment. He flew to Moscow, not an easy task, photographed Lenin embalmed on a slab while lines of Russians filed by to look at the body. The theater reps wouldn't show it. They said the footage was too controversial. There might be a communist sympathizer in the audience who would applaud Lenin. That would cause someone else to hiss Lenin, and a fight might erupt and ruin everyone's night out.

When I was considering a story, I asked myself just one question: What does everyone like to see? Here's my list:

1. Laughing baby, especially when the baby is with a kitten or a puppy.

2. Unusual people: midgets, giants, Siamese twins and athletes with one leg.
3. Pretty girls: beauty contestants, fashion models and starlets.
4. Daredevils: a brother and sister balanced on a board for twenty-four hours, fifteen stories above Fifth Avenue. A man tightrope walking between skyscrapers.
5. Celebrities, including statesmen, kings, actors, comedians, authors, dancers, musicians, scientists and sportsmen.

Based on the mail we received every day, I learned that the public liked to see silly things. I did too. I'd never forgotten myself as a boy going to the movies in Haverhill, so sad, so angry at Uncle Sonny, so frightened of the bullies at the orphanage, sitting in the dark carried out of myself by the images on the flickering screen.

An interview with Nick Meadows would be well received. We'd use the fan- magazine format: he has fame and fortune, but underneath he's just a regular guy. We would show him at home in weekend clothes relaxing among his things. I hoped those things would include a bewitching dog with a perky face, cut to him in public surrounded by swooning females and finish with a closeup and a long gaze directly into the lens that would last long enough for the women sitting in the dark to feel their hearts twitch.

Most singers refused to be photographed for newsreels in the silent days because they looked strange singing with no sound coming out. "Hearst has asked him, Universal has asked him, Pathé has asked him," said Bernie, Niko's agent. "The policy with Nick Meadows is no newsreels. Period. As for meeting Anita Stewart, he won't do it. You know how many people want to meet Nick Meadows? Do you have any idea at all? You know how many fan letters he gets every day? Imagine a mail truck. Then imagine a convoy of mail trucks, and that's only the half of it. You should see what they send him. Naked pictures, begging him. You wouldn't believe it. We have a staff hired just to answer the fan letters, and half the time the girls quit from what they see when they open the envelopes. I'm sorry to disappoint you, but my hands are tied."

"Do me one favor, Bernie. Tell him Harry Sirkus phoned. See what he says." Bernie agreed.

One of the secretaries hurried to my desk. "Your Stalins are here."

"Did you weed them out?"

"I sent four home. One of them looked like Abraham Lincoln."

The purpose of the Stalins was to find someone to stand in for the real man when we faked segments about Russia. We already had our caption for the Stalin segment: "Joseph Stalin, a political name adopted when he was thirty-four, meaning Man of Steel. His real name? Dzhugashvili. Son of a shoemaker."

I distributed photographs of Stalin to Freckles and his friends. Their job was to find a man who looked like the photograph and persuade that man to go to the Fox studio for an audition. They would get five dollars for each candidate we chose to audition. They scoured the docks and the railway yards, and here was the result: twelve Stalins wandering around on the first floor, tripping over cables, getting in the way of a fashion shoot with models wearing capes made of feathers. We tried to get the men to stay in a cluster off to the side, but some of them didn't understand English.

It was a funny sight, if you weren't one of the people working there and getting interrupted. At last, the Stalins gathered at one end of the studio and lined up. Why all those men looking slightly like Stalin with big mustaches and dark hair seemed so funny to me, I don't know, but I did know that what was amusing to me was amusing to others. "Get me a cameraman," I whispered to my assistant. He found Irwin Meggins, who had just returned from the Gobi Desert shooting skeletons of Mesozoic dinosaurs that were found there. "This is a segment called the Stalin look-alike contest," I whispered to Irwin when he lugged his camera to the set. "That's the only caption." Irwin set up some lights, and the Stalins began to preen, smoothing their mustaches, their hair and straightening their clothes. "Just keep cranking," I said.

"You sure?" Irwin said. He knew how angry it made Mr. Fox when we used too much film. I lined up the Stalins, had them put their arms around one another's shoulders and take a step left, step right, step left. It was mean of me, I guess, to take advantage of them that way, to make them look like chorus girls when they were earnestly thinking that maybe they would become movie stars, but I did it anyway. Much to my surprise, some of the Stalins broke from the line to show us their specialty. One squatted down, folded his arms and thrust his legs out, yelling "Hoopa! Hoopa!" Another balanced on his hands. Another played his accordion. As the shoot progressed, the people on the neighboring sets wandered over to watch and applaud. Irwin turned his lens on the models who were watching in their feather capes. One of the Stalins grabbed a model and danced her around the floor with so much energy, she was weak from laughing.

My assistant signaled me from across the room. I waved him away. He knew not to interrupt a shoot. He gestured in a more insistent way. I mouthed, "Who?"

"Nick Meadows!"

"Keep the shoot going," I said to the cameraman and hurried to the telephone. I was not sure how I felt about a reunion with Niko. Our memory lane was so full of ruts. Bad enough to remember all that surrounded my fleeing Haverhill and the terror of my first day alone in Boston picking up that tossed corn muffin and cramming it into my mouth. But I remembered Niko as someone entirely self-centered, and I wasn't sure I wanted him in my life now that I had a choice. My assistant was so starstruck, he just stood there until I gave him the "get lost" face. "Nick!" I barked in my least favorite slap-on-the-back voice, strident manliness.

"Mr. Sirkus?" A pleasant male voice asked. "This is Nick Meadow's personal assistant. Is this a convenient time to speak?"

He couldn't even call me himself? "Fine, fine. In the middle of a shoot but fine."

"Mr. Meadows has asked me to telephone you."

"So I see."

"He is sorry to disappoint you, but he does not appear in newsreels."

"I know. His agent told me."

"Mr. Meadows has extended an invitation to his home. Is tomorrow night convenient?"

"Tomorrow? Where does he live?"

"I am not at liberty to divulge that information."

I knew it was silly to resent Niko not calling me himself. He was a big star. People from his past were probably always wanting special attention from him.

"If you won't divulge, how am I supposed to get there?"

"There is a train from Grand Central Station to New Rochelle. He will send a car to meet you there. Is eight o'clock convenient?"

"How will I recognize his car?"

"Oh, it's easy to spot. It's a Rolls-Royce Silver Ghost. Will it be possible for you to dine with him at his home? Just one more thing, Mr. Sirkus. Mr. Meadows does not allow any photography or camera equipment of any kind. He is sure you will understand his caution."

"Naturally. He is jealous of his privacy."

"Exactly. Thank you so much."

I ran back to finish the Stalin shoot. My Stalin look-alike contest, nestled between shots of Knute Rockne at Notre Dame and J. Edgar Hoover who had just been appointed director of the F.B.I., was shown in more than three thousand theaters.

The white Rolls-Royce driven by a uniformed chauffeur was a gleaming show dog among mutts parked at the New Rochelle station, where wives at the wheel of ordinary cars waited for commuter husbands. The chauffeur looked up from his newspaper and showed me an angelic face, pink cheeks and full lips. "I'm Harry Sirkus. Are you here for me?" He sprang out, held the back door open for me, and I settled into plush gray upholstery. We drove by small houses with their porch lights on and past acres of farmland with wilted cornstalks. A dot of light in the middle of the street became a shepherd's lantern when we got close enough to see. He was urging his flock across the road, an unusual sight at night. A black-and-white border collie ran from one side of the flock to the other, keeping the sheep moving in an orderly fashion until they were all the way across North Avenue. Eventually, we turned onto a winding road, then onto a dirt road. At the end of the dirt road was an iron gate. A uniformed guard came out of the brick gatehouse, nodded to the chauffeur, and we passed through. There were no lights on the dirt drive, but in the dimness, I saw tall trees in silhouette on either side. The narrow driveway opened out to reveal a clapboard mansion with a mansard roof. "Wow! What a house!" I said to the driver.

"These are the stables, sir," he said as we passed by.

At last we came to a brick Tudor-style mansion that had a fountain in front with water cascading from a huge marble seashell decorated with naked Greek warriors. The chauffeur opened the car door for me, then drove away. The door knocker was a lascivious satyr's face made of brass. I lifted it and let it thud against the door, which set off a herd of dogs yowling, woofing, arfing *wa, wa, wa*. There was scrambling behind the door, toenails clicking on marble, and finally someone shouted, "Enough! Lay off!"

The din stopped, and the door opened onto a foyer paneled with mirrors. Six boxers—caramel colored, sturdy chested, handsome if you liked jowly dogs—all looked at me about to spring at my throat, so it seemed, until I stepped inside. They cringed toward me, whining, turning in circles with their tail stumps wagging, longing to leap up and show me an enthusiastic greeting but trained not to. To be polite, I touched one and noted how silky clean its fur felt. The butler, yet another handsome young man in uniform, said, "Be good doggies. Go to your beds." They obeyed as if they understood English, toenails clicking on marble as they retreated down the hall. The butler said, "Good evening, sir. Please forgive this unusual welcome. Mr. Meadows is expecting you."

I followed him down the corridor. There was nothing wry in the way he delivered his lines or the least bit familiar, though we were probably close to the same age. He wasn't pretending to be a butler; he really was one, without any hint that he thought he was too good for the job. He wasn't like the waiters in Greenwich Village who were really actors or artists and made sure you knew they were equal to you, if not better. I took a calming breath to prepare myself for the crowd that awaited me, Niko's entourage: admirers, sycophants, business people, fellow performers. The butler opened the door to an art-deco living room, white and ebony, and announced, "Mr. Sirkus, sir," and softly closed the door behind me.

Niko, brushed and polished, glossy as a thoroughbred, sat in a forest-green leather armchair sipping a martini. He was alone, dressed in a paisley smoking jacket, white silk ascot, white jodhpurs and black boots. His hair was coifed—no other word for it. The room was spectacular, a stage set of the latest in streamlined design.

At the sight of me, his mouth opened slightly in surprise, probably because he remembered a much younger boy. He set the martini glass down and came toward me. "I can't go out," he said. "I'm a prisoner." He stopped before he was close enough to shake hands. I remembered this greeting from the first time we met, the steady gaze of bright blue, the slight smile meant to show patience as he absorbed the admiration he saw on everyone's face: Here I am—gaze upon me. He turned away, walked back to his chair and lifted the drink that waited on the table. "They mob me. They pull off my buttons. They want pieces of my hair." He sat down, gestured to the leather chair across from his. "Fame is a curse."

"Pays well," I said, sitting down and noticing how much more comfortable this chair was than the one

Kenny and I found on the street and lugged up to our apartment.

He erupted in a loud guffaw, a sound I remembered. It was a laugh that came from somewhere very deep and was almost alarming. "Mirror, mirror on the wall," he said, taking a sip of his drink and raising his eyebrow at me, "who's the richest of them all?"

The butler opened the door. "You rang, sir?"

"Fix our guest one of these," he said holding up his martini. The butler went to the bar, made the concoction, shook it vigorously, brought it to me on a silver tray and departed. "Here's to Nick Meadows," Niko said, holding his glass toward me. "Whoever that is."

"It's not you?" I took a sip and said, "Delicious!" with my eyebrows though I'd never had a martini before. It was bitter, and its action was immediate.

"He makes a good one. Aren't you wondering how he knew to come in here?" Niko moved his foot. "It's under the rug. It's a bell under the rug. I can call him just by pressing my foot down. My parents had the same thing, only it was by my father's chair in the dining room. He could never find it. He'd try to call the maid, and he'd stamp here, there, here—my mother getting irritated, until finally I'd drop down from my chair, crawl to where he sat, find the bump under the carpet and press it while my mother said, "Nicholas. Sit down. Get out from under there." Again the loud guffaw. Wait a minute. Wasn't his father a brute and his mother confined in a hospital in New Hampshire? And wasn't he so penniless he had to work in a stable mucking stalls? "Catch me up. You're at Fox News."

"Well, I left the barn about a year after..."

"And now you want me to pose for Fox News. Don't write it off yet. I'm thinking about it. Did you see that fountain when you came in? Guess how much that cost."

"A fortune of money?" Louie's phrase.

"Everyone thinks I want to be in pictures. I don't want to be in pictures. What kind of life is that, sitting around all day. Clara Bow sends me a telegram: What a team we'd make. Gloria Swanson, same thing. DeMille came in person to beg me. I said to Bernie—he's the best agent in the business—I don't give a damn if it is DeMille. You don't give my address to anyone unless I say so. Everyone wants a piece of me. See these pants? Rudolph Valentino wore them in *Blood and Sand*. These very pants. I bought them from a friend of mine in the costume department at Lasky. Look at these boots. They aren't boots, see?" He wiggled his toes. "They're like slipper socks. Had them made for me. Got the idea from the American Indians, but mine don't have the beading. Do you think I should have them beaded?" He brushed his hair with a sweep of fingers. "Hope you didn't eat. My chef is brilliant."

The door opened, and a young man breezed in wearing white silk trousers and a white silk shirt. He had blond hair and was good looking in a delicate way and tan as if just back from a sunny resort. "Toby," said Niko, "say hello to Harry."

Toby walked toward me like a model, one foot directly in front of the other, extended a limp hand, let me squeeze it and proceeded to the sideboard. "No more olives," he said. "How can a person have a martini without an olive?"

"Where do you think they all went?"

"I haven't had that many."

"He drinks too much," Niko said to me.

"I do not."

"Do too."

"Do not."

"Do too. But isn't he gorgeous?" Niko looked to me for confirmation, and I hoped I was hiding my embarrassment. "Come see my art collection." We left Toby nursing his martini and walked down the marble corridor. Niko opened a door and switched on lights in a cavernous space with walls covered with modern paintings, each one with its own small light shining down on it. "Come," he said. "I'll introduce you. This is Picasso. You see how he doesn't even try to make the face like a photograph? It's called abstract. This is Miro, here's Braque, here's Paul Klee—don't say *klee* but *clay*. These are my friends, Harry. They all come down for the Masked Ball. You'll come this year. New Year's Eve. Can you afford a costume?"

"Yes," I said, annoyed. "I can afford a costume."

"Everyone goes all out. Have someone in the costume department at Fox make something for you."

"I'm not a pauper."

"No? Then you need a new tailor." We strolled around the gallery pausing to give each painting its due, me wondering what exactly was wrong with my clothes. They fit; they were comfortable. "I'm just warning you, that's all. You'll feel out of place if you don't go all out. It's a big event."

"I'll bring a cameraman," I said to annoy him.

"Iksnay on that. And I'm not kidding." As he turned off the lights he said, "My agent, Bernie, tells me you know Anita Stewart. Do you know her well enough to invite her?"

"Yes."

"Then do. Bring Anita Stewart."

"Why?"

He lowered his voice as we walked down the corridor. "Toby's crazy about her. A birthday present. He turns twenty-one that day. Just between us, okay?"

"I can't promise you, Niko. I have no idea what her schedule is. Far as I know, she's going back to the Coast on Saturday." Could this be why he asked me here? "If she can't come, am I uninvited?"

"No, no, no. Of course, come," he said.

"Why don't you just invite Anita Stewart yourself? She's a big fan of yours. Listens to your records."

"Then I'd have to extend myself to everyone, wouldn't I? I'd have to do something equal for Mae Murray, Clara Bow and Florence Turner. Things get around. Nick Meadows invited me to his house. You? Why didn't he invite me?"

We walked down the corridor and into the dining room where we came upon Toby, melancholy at the table. Instantly, he changed his expression to perky. "I like to surround myself with good-looking people," Nick said, sitting at the head of the table, Toby on one side, me on the other, the rest of the table stretching away from us. "I can seat twenty-five in here," he said. "Had the cast party here when Toby played in Eugene O'Neill's *Desire under the Elms*. What a performance! The critics singled him out."

The butler served dinner while Niko told us about the important people he met in Milan, London, Paris.

Toby said, apropos of nothing, "I'm an orphan."

"His aunt brought him up," said Niko. "She preferred her own children."

Toby said, "She'd come into the breakfast room and say, 'Who wants to go to the carousel in Central Park?'

We'd all say, 'Me, me, me!' And guess who she wouldn't take. She'd say, 'The maid can't handle so many children. Toby, you can go next time.'"

I looked across the table at Toby, everything about him so soft, smooth and pampered, and I hated his whining until he lifted his eyes to mine, and I saw him pleading with me to like him. "May she rot in hell!" I said holding my glass toward him.

"I'll drink to that!" said Toby, and we clinked glasses, *ping*! The note hung in the air.

"They were going to send me to a farm in Kansas," I said, loosened by drink.

"I played Kansas," Niko said. "The Baltimore Hotel. You want to hear jazz, you go to Kansas City. In one district of the city alone, there are over fifty night clubs. All the greats play there: Jack Teagarden, Ma Rainey, Bessie Smith, Duke Ellington, Benny Moten. I've seen them all." He tore a roll and mopped up gravy. "The Novelty Club had a band that consisted of Count Basie, Jo Jones, Hot Lips Page and Lester Young. Anyone can just walk in to the jam sessions."

After dinner, we staggered into a wood-paneled library with an upright piano against a wall. A small projector was set up on a table aimed at a movie screen. "Toby, get the lights." The machine whirred, clacked, clicked with images of Nick clowning in front of the Arc de Triomphe in Paris, clowning in front of the Tivoli Fountain in Rome, Nick and Toby sitting at a café wearing berets.

Toby went to the piano. "Don't mind me," he said. "I've seen these a billion trillion times." He began to play a jaunty popular song and sing,

"*Masculine women, feminine men. Which is the rooster, which is the hen? It's hard to tell 'em apart today! And, say! Sister is busy learning to shave, brother just loves his permanent wave. It's hard to tell 'em apart today! Hey, hey! Girls were girls and boys were boys when I was a tot. Now we don't know who is who, or even what's what! Knickers and trousers, baggy and wide. Nobody knows who's walking inside. Those masculine women and feminine men!*"

I applauded. "I told you he's talented," said Niko, threading yet another home movie.

"I've had a long day," I said getting up. "That's probably enough for tonight."

Toby said, "I'm going to have a nightcap for medicinal purposes" and swayed across the hall to the living room. Niko touched my shoulder and beckoned for me to follow him, putting his finger to his lips, a secret. I followed him upstairs to a bedroom of satin pillows and a circular bed. "This is Toby's room," he said. "Just wanted to show you something before I send you to the station."

In Toby's dressing room, with walls of mirror, he opened a closet. "Recognize any of these things?" I didn't. He lifted out a fur-trimmed evening cloak. "Anita Stewart wore this in *The Combat*. Not this very one. An exact copy."

"Toby wears that?"

"When he goes to pansy clubs, sure. Look." He took out gowns and capes, naming the movies, from *The Lucky Elopement*, from *A Million Bid*. "Remember this from *The Glory of Yolanda*?" I was speechless. "You can see for yourself how beautiful Toby is. Why shouldn't he have clothes he likes?" He shut the closet door. "So now you can see what a swell birthday present it would be to introduce him to his idol at the New Year's ball. Not too much to ask of an old friend, right?" He gave my arm a comradely punch, but it stung and I rubbed it for comfort all the way to the station. I had no intention of going to his party or of ever seeing him again.

Chapter Twenty-Two

A few days later, William Fox summoned me to his office for a scolding. He was angry because a cameraman from the features department had gone out to the Ford Motor Company in Michigan to get footage of an assembly line. I secured the permissions for that shoot, a mistake given Mr. Fox's feelings about Henry Ford, who published anti-Semitic diatribes in his newspaper, *The Dearborn Independent.* There was overt anti-Semitism everywhere in America. We took for granted that some hotels wouldn't let us in, some neighborhoods wouldn't sell us a house, some clubs wouldn't let us join, most colleges would accept only a few of us, many law firms would never hire us. Bigotry was all over the place, but we just got around it as best we could and set up our own clubs, colleges and banks.

Sitting behind his desk hunched over ledger books, Mr. Fox didn't look up. Shades drawn, he wrote by the light of a gooseneck lamp and chewed on the stump of a cigar. I stood uncomfortably before him in air thick with smoke. "Siddown." He continued doing his paperwork as if I was not there. When he lifted his hooded eyes, he shone them into mine. "Explain yourself," he said.

"It was a mistake, sir." I sat there with my eyes on my shoes thinking any minute this torture would end. All I had to do was not say anything, just wait it out, but it went on and on, until I began to wonder if he'd gone back to his ledger books, so I looked up. His eye caught mine. "The Fox Film Corporation is my company. I have built it block by block from the workings of my imagination. If you put together all the executives who work for William Fox and ask them what to do next, they could not begin to fathom the depth of what is necessary to succeed. I am accused of running a one-man operation. This is true. I do. Now you send Fox News to Henry Ford's place of business to commemorate a product that brings in the money that allows him to say mean and dirty things against an entire race of human beings." He took his eyes away, re-lit his cigar stump and kept it in his mouth as he spoke. "Henry Ford is waging an anti-Semitic campaign through the pages of the *Dearborn Independent.* He is telling farmers that there is a conspiracy of Jewish bankers who wish to take away their farms."

"I understand your feelings," I said, "and regret sending our cameraman there."

"Our? *My* cameramen."

"Yes, sir."

"Understand the difference. I am Fox. The trucks that were at his car factory said 'Fox.' I was at his factory."

A knock on the door and Faye poked her head in. "Your grandson is here, Mr. Fox." A pudgy boy of seven or eight ran through the door dressed as a miniature military cadet but stopped short, seeing that his grandfather had company. Under the brim of a cadet's cap was a clouded face. Mr. Fox held his good arm out to the boy as if happy to see him but that gesture was too late because annoyance had swept over his face when the boy came in. The boy walked reluctantly to him. Mr. Fox said, "Grandma didn't tell me you were going to visit."

"It smells in here."

To Faye, "Get the trains." Mr. Fox drummed his fingers. The boy looked at me with a mixture of interest and resentment.

Faye returned quickly with a carton and said, "Mrs. Fox said she will pick him up in an hour." She set the box down on the conference table. The child ran in a klutzy way to the table, climbed on the chair and sat on his knees taking out pieces of track, a locomotive and freight cars. He set up a train depot while whispering the dialogue of his play.

Mr. Fox said, "Ford is circulating pamphlets entitled *The International Jew*. His intention is to set the whole world against us. He sees there is straw in every country, and he wants to drop the match. All the words in the world will not put out that conflagration."

"It is my intention, Mr. Fox," I said, "to scrap all the permissions. But I don't know how we'll undo the impression that Fox News supports Ford's activities. His employees saw our trucks and cameras."

We heard *choo choo choo* and the child's whispered voice, the tinkle of a miniature bell and the clack of a miniature gate.

"Here is what I did," Mr. Fox said, raising his eyebrows in a flick of self-congratulation. "When I learned that Fox News trucks were on the Ford premises..." The intercom on his desk buzzed and Faye's staticky voice announced, "Telephone call from the Coast." He picked up his telephone: "Go on, Sol." He listened, chewing his cigar, his chair swiveled away from me. "I have a complete understanding of what you want." He listened more. "I have made changes to the story. We build up the man to a big height of power and influence so that when he does fall, his fall will be a direct contrast, and a tremendous lesson will be taught by the story." Mr. Fox listened for a while and said, "I will decide on the salaries to be paid." He hung up.

"Grandpa," the little boy said, "where's the caboose?"

The phone call had put Mr. Fox into a reverie, so it took a moment for the boy's words to penetrate. "It's in there."

"No, it isn't."

"No one has taken your caboose. Look harder."

"I did look harder."

"Go ask the secretary." The boy got down from the chair and went out. Mr. Fox ignored me and began to write something. I didn't know whether to get up and go out or just sit there and wait. The door opened, and his grandson came back. "Grandpa, she doesn't have it." He walked across the Oriental carpet and stood next to Mr. Fox in his cadet uniform and cap—a soft, pallid little boy, more like a lapdog than a soldier.

"Play without it."

"I don't want to play without it."

"What do you want me to do about it? I don't have it."

"But I need it."

Mr. Fox got up from his chair. He took the boy's hand and led him back to the conference table. "Make a game without the caboose. Put this car next to the silver car. Pretend this is a train without a caboose."

The child was making *choo choo* sounds again as Mr. Fox sat down across from me at his desk. He ground his cigar stump into an ashtray in a fastidious way so not one speck of ash got on the desk, took another cigar from the humidor on his desk, clipped the ends, lit it and stared at the edge of my face. "When I learned that Fox News trucks were on the Ford premises, I personally phoned Henry Ford and spoke to Henry Ford on the telephone. Here is what Mr. William Fox said to Mr. Henry Ford. I said if

Mr. Ford does not stop his attacks against the Jewish people, I will include in my biweekly newsreels the results of every accident involving a Ford car."

A loud thud washed his face with alarm, and I turned to see the child on the floor twitching, his legs in the air. His eyes were pinched, his whole body jerked as if electrocuted, and he moaned as if some invisible demon was saying intolerable things to him. Mr. Fox hurried across the room and stood above the boy looking down. "Nothing helps," he said, seeing that I was about to run for help. "Just plays itself out."

"Won't he swallow his tongue, sir?"

"No," he said. The seizure propelled the little body a few inches across the floor, and his legs lowered. The sounds that came from the child were heartbreaking. He was a closed system, a locked vault, teeth clenched, everything held impossibly tight. It was a shock to see urine come out and leave a puddle on the carpet the size of a saucer. "He loses his bladder," Mr. Fox said. I was sickened and fascinated. At last, the dybbuk released the boy, and he opened his eyes and looked around as if just waking up from a nap, groggy. He focused on his military hat and said, "Grandpa, I need my hat. They get mad when I forget my hat."

Mr. Fox called, "Faye!" She came to the door and looked in. "Clean this up."

Faye held her hand out to the boy, led him to Mr. Fox's private bathroom at the other end of the office, closed the door, and we heard water from the faucet. Faye came out, closed the door quickly to preserve the child's privacy, went to a credenza on one side of the room, opened a drawer, took out some small clothes and carried them into the bathroom.

"Well, sir," I said, "I think it's time for me..."

"Siddown," he said and walked in a painfully erect way back to his desk. "Anti-Semitism," he said when we were seated opposite each other, "is rampant throughout the country. It behooves every man, woman and child who has the blood of a Jew running through their veins to stand firmly together." But the heart had gone out of his diatribe. He stood up, paralyzed hand in his pocket, walked to the window, pulled the shade back and gazed down on Tenth Avenue.

The little boy came out of the bathroom in clean trousers that did not match his military school jacket and went back to the table to continue playing with his trains. Faye carried the soiled clothes out of the office and closed the door, not in a gentle way that would have said something about the sympathy she felt, not in an angry way that would have said something about her idea of the proper parameters of her job, but in a perfunctory way as if nothing had happened. Mr. Fox continued to stare out the window. The sight of the child convulsing had sickened, frightened and confused me. Everyone at the office knew that Mr. Fox had a grandson he sent to military school to fool a kidnapper who had threatened the child. Kidnapping was on everybody's mind because Charles Lindbergh's son had been kidnapped and murdered. Mr. Fox bragged that he was clever to think of putting his grandson into a uniform so he'd be indistinguishable from the other cadets and the kidnapper wouldn't know which boy to snatch. But I never imagined the boy to be so young and afflicted. I wanted to say, Take him home, Mr. Fox. Don't abandon him among strangers. When I glanced back, Mr. Fox was still staring out the window. He had shut himself away from me thoroughly. He was not a man who asked for help or received comfort from others. I couldn't help but compare him there, holding still like some bird with camouflage feathers who doesn't even know you're looking at it, with Louie who would have talked to almost everyone about an afflicted grandson if he had one. It would comfort Louie to sorrow out loud and turn the problem into something dramatic that he could act out. Before I opened the office door to go quietly out, I peeked at the child, a little pudge just about the same age I was when I'd been yanked from everything I knew. I wanted to tell him things would get better and he'd be okay. But I didn't say anything. I just opened the office door and went out, leaving the little wreck by the side of the road.

Chapter Twenty-Three

Outside, New York was decorated for Christmas, lights strung everywhere, Christmas trees for sale, the smell of pine perfuming the air around them on the sidewalk, a New England smell. Salvation Army volunteers rang insistent bells. My plan was to walk off my agitation, just be by myself, but then I found myself near the Waldorf, and it seemed a good idea to be miserable with my friend. I knew she'd be there because she couldn't go out. If she did go out, she'd be mobbed by fans. I arrived when her mother was out running an errand.

"Look!" she said and handed me a Pomeranian puppy. "It's name is Fluff Ball." She laid down an exercise mat.

I took the puppy to the sofa and allowed it to cover my face with licks while Anita lay flat on her back, raising and lowering one leg at a time. After a few moments, the puppy settled down against me, leaning its little chin on my thigh, the weight of a finger.

"What's eating you?" Anita said in a pinched voice as she curled up and down.

"Oh, I don't know. I'm just sick of everything."

"What did Nick Meadows say?"

"Oh, I don't know. You don't want to see that guy."

"Yes, I do."

"No, you don't."

"So the truth comes out," she said, still doing sit-ups. "You don't really know him."

"You calling me a liar?"

"Yeah."

"When did you get Fluff Ball?"

"A few days ago. A fan left him for me. Read in the Inside Scoop that Rudy and me was splitting up and felt bad for me. Came in a cute little basket. What is it, Harry? What's eating you?" Now she stood on her shoulders, legs in the air, and started pedaling.

"I don't know." My mind was full of that child writhing on the floor. I was weak from the sight. "Life stinks, that's all."

"You're telling me. I don't got nothing to look forward to."

"Sure you do. You're a big star."

"Come on, Harry. What's that supposed to mean."

"I did see him, Anita. He invited us to his big shindig New Year's Eve. Acted like I couldn't afford a costume."

Now she was all attention. "Are you kidding me, Harry? I can't believe it!" She got up, took the puppy and danced the sleeping little thing around the room. "Do you have any idea what people go through to get an invite to that thing? Do you have any idea at all?"

"Who cares. I'm not going."

"I can't go by myself, Harry. Did I ever ask you for anything before?"

"I'm telling you, Anita. You don't want to go."

"I do too. I'm cooped up here all day long. What did he say?"

"He wants you to be a birthday present for his boyfriend."

"How sweet!"

"I don't want to go."

"You only think about yourself all the time."

"Everybody only thinks about themselves all the time."

"Gandhi don't."

"How do you know?"

"All I'm asking is to go to this one party. That's all I'm asking. I just want to meet Nick Meadows in person. Wasn't you ever a fan of anybody?"

"Theda Bara."

"What?" She handed the puppy back to me. "You fell for that?"

"Hook, line and sinker."

"She's a nice girl. She knows about Rudy and me. Wasn't she at that film fair where I met you?"

"That's where I found out."

"How?"

"I went into her tent after hours."

Anita laughed. "Harry, you're a hot sketch!" She walked to the mirror. "Do you think my arms are getting fat?"

Her arms were toothpicks. "Hardly, madam."

"I could go as Little Bo Peep. You could be the devil you are. Only trouble is I can't go out to get a costume. You'll have to get the costumes, Harry."

"Don't have time."

"I'm cooped up in here day in and day out waiting for them lawyers. Please! Don't you understand? I won't have to play Anita Stewart there. The place will be swimming with celebs bigger than me. He ain't a teetotaler, is he?"

"Not at all."

"So it'll be fun. We'll get fried." She leaned in close to the mirror. "My dark circles are the color of eggplant."

"New Year's Eve is a lonely night," I said, putting the puppy on a sofa pillow. "It comes around each year and asks the same question, How many friends do you have? The answer is always the same: too few."

Anita came to the sofa and sat next to me. "Don't talk like that, Harry. You ain't in that orphanage no more."

Back at the office, I found Etta in the costume department and asked if she would find costumes for Anita and me. "For free?" the mighty twig said, standing before me loaded down with garments. "You want me to dress you and Anita Stewart for free?"

"Don't you want to meet Anita?"

"I do intend to meet her but not this way."

"What way."

"Not as a peon in the costume department at Fox News. As equals is how I'm going to meet that dame."

"So call it a freelance job."

"I'm not going to just call it that. It has to *be* that. Which involves money, in case you forgot what job means."

"How much?"

She looked up at me through her owlish glasses, then closed her eyes and I thought she was calculating. "I see you as Titania and Oberon," she said with her eyes still closed.

"Which one am I?"

"Very funny, very funny." She continued toward her desk, me towering next to her.

"What would the king of the forest wear?"

"What do you think he'd wear? He'd wear the leftover costumes from *Midsummer Night's Dream* that just closed. My friend works over there at Hammerstein's."

We did not discuss this again. Just when I began rehearsing the words I was going to use to disappoint Anita, Etta arrived at the studio with both costumes made entirely by herself in her spare time at home. She made the masks too—intricate feathered things with sequins.

Anita hired a limousine that drove us to New Rochelle on New Year's Eve. As the fairy queen Titania, she glowed in a gown of white satin and a tiara of white foxtails. My crown was a ring of ermine, my cape white velvet. We sat in the back seat of the car smoking cigarettes. "Then he says he has a right to everything I earned from the time we got married because if it wasn't for him, I'd be in some loony bin somewhere. Can you beat that?" She opened her beaded bag, took out a hip flask, tipped it back into her mouth and handed it to me. I took a swig without wiping as a sign of friendship. Anita put the flask in her bag. "I'm already tired."

"What's Ma doing tonight?"

"Ma? She's going out to Long Island to her friends. She really misses her mahjong club. Paramount called today. Did I tell you that? Offered me a picture."

"Are you going to take it?"

"Sure. I like Adolph Zukor. Treated Mary so-called Pickford fair."

Nick's house was aglow with lights. People were bundled against the cold as they descended from expensive cars. When it was our turn, Anita said, "I can't. I can't. I cannot."

"Sure, you can."

"I can't. Really, I can't."

"Of course you cannot. But Titania can. She can do anything. She's queen of the forest."

Anita touched my hand. "No, wait a sec. Not like that." She touched my hand again, and we both laughed because it really felt like a fairy had touched me, delicate as a spiderweb strand.

A team of butlers at the door, dressed as sheikhs, took coats from Carmen, Cleopatra, the devil, a Chinese Mandarin and an Eskimo.

The ballroom was Egypt: sphinxes, an ice pyramid and wall hangings of Egyptian design. A full orchestra played the triumphal march from Aïda. Niko was Horus, the sun god, resplendent in a metallic gold costume—so handsome that Anita and I had to pause for a moment with mouths hanging open. "Oh, my shoes!" Anita whispered. "Hold me up before I faint." Next to him was Toby as a vulture, the sacred bird of Egypt. His costume was of shining blue-green silk painted with iridescent feathers of gold and peacock blue. His legs were painted to represent iridescent tail feathers, and he wore no mask. "Holy moly!" Anita whispered taking my arm. "Did you ever see anyone prettier than that? Is it a boy or a girl?"

When I greeted Niko, would I call him Niko to remind him of mucking out stalls? "Nick Meadows," I said. "This lovely Titania is Anita Stewart."

He turned to Toby. "Sweetie, guess who this is."

Toby turned, saw us and said, "A king and queen?"

"But who's the queen?"

"Her?"

"But guess who's under the costume."

Toby stood there perplexed. "I'm Anita Stewart, you gorgeous thing," she said, lowering her mask and holding her hand out to him.

His mouth fell open. He put his long, slender fingers to his chest and pretended to sink down. "No. No you are not. No! Are you? I can't believe it! I love you! I've seen everything you ever did! I love you! I just love you!" Then he did a most girlish thing: he jumped up and clapped his hands and came down with them still clasped, his eyes pinned to Anita. "Nicky! Look!"

"I know, sweetie. Happy birthday."

"You're adorable," she said as we were swept into the ballroom by the crush of new arrivals. Again, I felt stung by Niko. He hadn't even said hello. Did he actually imagine I wanted to come to this stupid thing? I was doing him a favor.

The waiters, culled perhaps from chorus lines, were dressed as man slaves, their bodies painted brown. They wore short skirts of striped material and no shirts. They circulated with trays of Champagne. Tables along the edges of the walls were heaped with food. Working our way toward the tables, Anita said, "I'm exhausted," and leaned heavily on my arm. This, I knew, was a reaction to seeing Lillian Gish in the crowd surrounded by admiring fans, dressed as a shepherdess but easily recognizable because she wasn't wearing a mask.

"Maybe you're too hot. Take off your mask for a while."

"Should I?"

"Sure."

Anita unclipped her mask and held it down by her side. "Yeah, that's better." As we walked through the crowd, people fell back. "Is that Anita Stewart?" and, "Hey! There's Anita Stewart!" and "Who's with her?" We paused to lift Champagne from a passing tray, and the man next to us, dressed as a French king, said, "Could this be Anita Stewart?" She was delighted and put her mask up as if he had caught her doing something naughty. "George Peabody Converse, at your service," he said, bowing in an easy, charming way. He was older than we were, gray at the temples. The orchestra began to play a waltz, and he offered his hand to Anita after saying to me, "May I?" I walked away trying to recall why his name was so familiar, then remembered that his father was the president of U.S. Steel.

This party was making me feel even worse than I thought it would. When I looked in the mirror at home, I thought the costume enhanced my handsomeness, but here I felt invisible. When I left the apartment, I was Oberon, king of the forest, on his way to a party given by one of the most famous men in America and accompanied by one of the most famous women in America. Last year Kenny and I had gone to the Roosevelt Hotel to usher in the New Year with the Guy Lombardo Orchestra, both of us too shy to ask any of the girls there to dance. We made a pact that the following year, we would make ourselves ask five girls to dance before the stroke of midnight. But Kenny was in Chamonix, France, shooting the Winter Olympics where an eleven-year-old figure skater named Sonja Henie was making headlines.

It seemed as if everyone at this party had someone to talk to except me. There was Anita twirling around with a French king. She might have told me she would abandon me the second we walked in. I hadn't even wanted to come. I was doing it just for her, and she let me wander around the stupid place getting jostled by all those hysterical revelers. High-pitched shrieks were supposed to be laughs. Ha, ha, ha, everyone was so happy. Why not. Free eats in a mansion the size of a castle. I should have stayed home. Couldn't have been worse than this, with everyone yukking it up all over the place. I downed one glass of Champagne, accepted another, downed that and looked around to see if there were any girls standing around waiting to be rescued. Maybe that Statue of Liberty over there. Too many people around her, and she was laughing in a phony way—sounded like a machine gun. I hated people. I hated everyone in the world. Might as well just spend the night stuffing myself with gourmet tidbits. I moved forward to the smoked-salmon roses and paté scarabs. There was a tray of tiny pyramids, and when I reached for one, my hand landed on the same one as a shapely female hand that belonged to a swan. She wore a white mask, her copper-colored hair dotted with white feathers. "After you," I said.

"No," she said, "please. You first." She was graceful with a long neck, long arms and a graceful way of moving her head. She had a feathered mask over the top part of her face, but you could see her eyes, which were as clear as a lake in Maine. They were shiny with intelligence. "Let's do it together," she said. "One, two, three," and we extended our hands over the plate, "go!" We each lifted a small pyramid and popped it in our mouths, then wondered what it was. "Caviar," she said, tasting her lips. Her mouth was shaped like a bow with a defining ridge around the edge, and inside was one of my favorite imperfections: a slight overbite.

"Do you know many people here?" I asked, wishing I'd said something that didn't sound like misery wanted company.

"A few." Her lips did not return to home base immediately but stayed slightly puckered on the *eeeuuuu* of *few*. I was captivated. I was helpless. The eyes behind the mask flicked to mine and then away, like a glimpse of a white-tail deer in the woods. "The harlequin over there inching his way closer to Lillian Gish is *Modern Screen*," she said, "and let's see, that Cleopatra is from *Photoplay*. And let's see, the Brunhilda near the chocolate fountain is Louella Parsons, movie editor at Universal News Service."

"You know everyone."

"I know who they are anyway."

"How old are you?"

"Nineteen. How old are you?"

"Twenty-one. You're really pretty."

"Thank you. But how do you know?"

"It's leaking out around the edges of your mask. Take off your mask, and let me see."

"No."

"I thought Nick didn't want any publicity. The whole press corps is here."

"Nick not want publicity? It is to laugh. Who are you supposed to be, some kind of king? Is that real ermine?"

"He told me he'd break the camera if I brought one."

"Why? Where are you from?"

"Fox News."

"Oh. That's different. There are no cameras here. He can't control pictures. Can you imagine if his fans saw him right now dancing with Toby? I did a piece once about his romance with Clara Bow."

"But she's a girl!"

"That's what I mean."

"I used to be a writer. I was entertainment editor of *The Thinker*."

"*The Thinker*?"

"Eighth grade, Haverhill, Massachusetts."

"Really? I'm from Newton, Mass." We looked at each other for a long while.

"I can't stop looking at you. Why is that? Are you always so smiley?" She tried to pinch off her smile, but it broke out again. "Oh! It's a Charleston! Come on!" I took her hand and led her through the crowd to the dance floor as the orchestra played *Ain't She Sweet* in a rollicking way. I had not done the Charleston with too many partners. Mostly I just did it alone in front of the mirror or with Kenny who made up hilarious steps, but for some reason, I was not at all reluctant to show all my moves. My swan stepped back with the right foot, kicked back with her left foot, swung her arms, knocked her knees together while crisscrossing her hands, seemed to touch the ground with no weight, raised her leg and smacked her knee, raised the other leg and smacked that knee. We grabbed hands, pulled back, pulled close, wiggled to the side, let go, twirled around, and when it was over, we fell into each other's arms laughing and panting. I should have let her go. I knew I should not hold her beyond catching our breath, but she smelled so delicious!

"Oberon," she said, pulling back and adjusting her costume. "I think you have fairy dust in your eyes."

"Is that what it is?"

"Or Champagne on the brain," she said. Even though there were hundreds of people there and now and then we were getting bumped by a tail or a wand or a wing, it felt as if we were alone. I took her in my arms again for a fox-trot, which I didn't know how to do, held her close and whispered, "You are so beautiful." When the song ended, we stood there awkwardly. I shouldn't have squeezed her so hard. I probably had hurt her. And I stepped on her toes twice. I should have put on some of Kenny's cologne. "Who do you write for?"

"*Inside Scoop.*"

"Have you ever had an inside scoop?"

"No," she said, "boo hoo." And she put her forehead on my chest before pulling back and laughing.

"Maybe tonight will be your big break."

"I saw you come in with Anita Stewart. Do you love her?"

We smiled and looked into each other's eyes. "Do you care?"

"I don't know."

"Yes, you do. Do you care?"

"I don't know."

"Your chin's blushing."

"It is not. Chins don't blush."

"Yours does.

"She could use some love."

"You mean because of Rudy?"

"The rat."

"Are you trying to pump me?" A mistake. She pulled back abruptly and turned away. How stupid I was! I broke the spell! "Swany. Don't be mad. Come on. Tell me your name. Tell me your name. Come on. Turn around. Don't be mad. I shouldn't have said that."

"A perfectly reasonable assumption," she said.

"Come on. What's your name? I'm Harry Sirkus. I work at Fox."

It took her a while to accept my extended hand. Finally she did and said, "Molly Tepper."

"Molly."

"Yes."

"Take off your mask."

"You."

"Okay." I took off my mask and watched to see her expression. I passed. She liked me. I had never smiled so much in my whole life. "Now you."

She unhooked her mask, and she was so beautiful, a sound came out of me, *ohhhh*. She laughed. "I used to be an ugly duckling," she said.

"Me too."

"You? I bet you were an adorable little boy." She blushed and changed the subject. "I did a piece about Nick Meadows one time. The story was called The Price They Pay for Fame. It began, 'In the glittering world of international fame, health, friends, beauty, even life itself, are sacrificed on the altar of terrible ambition.'" Our eyes seemed to have a life of their own. They just fixed on each other and stayed there searching, searching. "Fame imposed on Nick Meadows the curse of nerves," Molly said. "He forced himself through performance after performance when he should have been resting."

The orchestra played a waltz, and I took her in my arms and pretended I knew how to waltz. She felt exactly right, fit against my body as if we were two halves. "George will never get over this night," she said into my shoulder. "He adores Anita Stewart." We twirled around a few times, but I didn't steer well, and we kept bumping into other couples. But even that was cause for fun because each time we collided, we said, "'Scuse me!" at the same time. The music ended, and I was afraid she'd walk away, so I tried to hold her with a question. "How do you know George?"

"He's my boss. He owns the *Inside Scoop*." She did not move away. "Look, he's having to share her." We stood close together and watched Anita across the room talking to Toby, who hugged her, let her go, hugged her again and turned her around so he could examine her costume. Niko, the sun king, stood next to him, Toby's proud lord, his guffaw ringing out over the music. George was waiting for Toby's gushing to be finished so he could dance again. I hadn't seen Anita so happy in a long time.

I kept thinking that any minute, Molly would have had enough of me and move on, but she didn't, and we found ourselves on the dance floor at the countdown to midnight. Forty, thirty-nine, thirty-eight, everyone chanted together, all of us on this earth not knowing what fate had in store and most of us tipsy. When the drum banged and the orchestra played *Auld Lang Syne*, we looked at each other and didn't know what to do. All around us, people were kissing and slapping each other on the back. Some woman, laughing, threw herself at me and planted a kiss on my mouth. Then another woman did the same thing, and from the edge of my eye, I saw that some man was kissing Molly, so I pushed the woman away and tore the man away from Molly. I took her in my arms and kissed her, and she did not pull away. She stayed there, and I could hear her breathing and taste her. I felt like swooning. When we pulled apart, we both staggered for a moment.

The band switched to *Happy Birthday*, and a gigantic birthday cake—the size of a wading pool with twenty-one candles in the shape of obelisks and each about a foot high—was pulled by Roman gladiators into the middle of the floor on a rolling cart made to look like a chariot. We all started singing *Happy Birthday*, and Toby came forward to blow out the candles, but he couldn't get them all, so he threw up his hands and said, "Help! Everybody help!" and dozens of people in costume went forward and blew on the cake.

Molly whispered, "Yuk."

From across the room, George waved and walked over to us with Anita. "Happy New Year, Molly," he said, giving her a peck on the cheek, then turning to introduce Anita, who stepped into my arms and sunk her weight against me. Confetti sprinkled down from the ceiling, white balloons were released and rose up, the orchestra blared, horns tooted, people were shouting. Anita whispered, "Rudy didn't even call to wish me Happy New Year. He didn't send flowers or nothing." I gave her little skeleton a sympathetic squeeze.

"Molly," George said, "allow me to introduce Anita Stewart. Miss Stewart this is Molly Tepper."

She extended her hand to Anita. "It's a great pleasure, Miss Stewart," she said. "I've admired you since the first time I saw you in *The Wood Violet*."

"Okay," Anita said.

"Are you having a good time?" Molly asked Anita.

"I guess so."

"You like to dance, I could see that. George is a great dancer, don't you think?"

"For an old guy, sure." Our laughter showed her mistake so she gave him an apologetic kiss on his cheek. His surprise and delight was endearing. "I'm pooped, Harry," Anita whispered, turning me away from Molly and George. "I been gracious and down to earth all night. Can we go?" We shook hands with George and Molly, but I didn't let Molly's hand go, and she had to tug it away.

I took Anita by the arm and escorted her across the floor toward the door. In the back seat of the car, speeding along the Henry Hudson Parkway, Anita said, "You really liked that swan girl, didn't you?" I shrugged. "You wanted to have nookie with that cookie."

"She's a reporter for *Inside Scoop*."

"I know. He owns it. His father bought it for him. He's loaded."

"Did he get anything out of you?"

"I fed him some crap about my new picture. No such thing as too much publicity, right?" Anita lit a cigarette. "I'm taking a bath when I get back. They got bath salts there. Free. Ma's staying out on the island." She took off her foxtail tiara and scratched her head. "Rudy thinks he's better than me. Comes out in little ways. Makes reference to vacation spots that only the hobnobs go to and if you showed up there they wouldn't let you in. I don't mean you, I mean me too. Even now I'm Anita Stewart they wouldn't let me in. My mother-in-law won't even talk to Ma. If you didn't grow up in her set, you ain't real. You know what I mean? She thinks she owns America, and she's allowed you and me to come in, and ain't that big of her. She's never invited Ma anywhere. One time they invited us for Thanksgiving, and I said sure we'll come, but Ma has to come too. I can't leave Ma alone on Thanksgiving. So you know what they did? They canceled the whole thing and went out to a restaurant by themselves."

"Good riddance to bad rubbish," I said, but I was thinking about Molly. Her kiss!

"You're telling me. You know what his mother said when Rudy told her we're splitting up? She goes, 'It's about time.' I hope Ma didn't have trouble getting out to the Island. You think she got out there safe?"

"Sure she did. Your limo's got snow chains. What did you think of Nick Meadows?"

"He don't like women, me included. But ain't his boyfriend handsome! He's got this closet upstairs, Harry. Guess what's in it?"

"Did you think she was pretty?"

"Who? Oh, her. Guess what was in the closet. Just guess. You have three guesses."

"Did you see her eyes?"

"What are you, in love or something? Guess what was in the closet."

"Doesn't she have the cutest teeth?"

"Harry, you ain't being no fun at all."

"Because I already know. Nick showed it to me."

We made a can-you-believe-it snort and looked out the window at the snow, lace drifting slowly from the sky. Anita said, "Do we have to give these costumes back to that little midget that visited me?"

Chapter Twenty-Four

Heart pounding, I phoned *Inside Scoop* and heard that Miss Tepper had gone to the Coast and would be working at the Hollywood office for the next several months. It was unreasonable to expect her to let me know. Given her beauty and her job, she probably had dozens of people wanting to know her. How ridiculous I was taking her attention seriously. I was hurt, nonetheless, and sat at my desk with a heavy heart.

A few weeks later, Louie came to town for his big interview, and we met for a late lunch in Times Square across the street from Loew's headquarters, a sixteen-story office tower on Broadway. "Look at them," he said, flicking his head toward the pedestrians we saw through the window, "all bundled up. Is this what you need, freezing weather? When this thing goes through, you'll come to me."

"Louie, you never give up! I love New York."

"Because you love pollution? Because you love crowds? Because you love food that isn't fresh?" He was thirty-four and still wore his armor of swagger.

"Because I love my work, and I think it's beautiful here."

"Beautiful? I'll tell you what's beautiful. The ocean is beautiful." He swallowed and took another big bite. "The desert is beautiful, dry but beautiful in its own way, especially during the sunset."

"The moon above the buildings at night, Louie. That's beautiful."

"The moon above a building is not beautiful, for your information. The moon above the ocean, yes. The moon above the desert? Yes. The moon in Yosemite National Park. Now that's worth seeing. Here's a question for you. When is the last time you saw stars?" I wondered if I should tease him and describe the last time I got punched or the last time I saw a famous actor. "Just what I thought," he said. "And here's another question for you. When is the last time you picked a fig from a tree and ate it on the spot? On the spot. Tell me that. I dare you to tell me that."

I laughed. "You win, Louie. I'm throwing the fight." We ate a few bites thinking our own thoughts, mine being how happy I was that hemlines had gone up because I had an excellent view of pretty legs at the next table.

"It's true I'm just renting. You're right. I don't own my own place out there like your precious William Fox. I ain't saying it's ideal. Did I ever say that? No, I did not. Sometimes the monkeys get out. Is that so terrible? And the lions are noisy at night. Anita has a legitimate gripe about that. We got plenty of horses right there. When we shot *In Old Kentucky*, who knew we ain't in Kentucky? Nobody, that's who. We got thirty acres of scenery. We got palm trees for jungle scenes, caves, African village sets, a eucalyptus grove for sylvan scenes. We also got a building for indoor shooting. I hired Lois Weber to direct. I sent her a telegram saying my unchanging policy will be great star, great director, great play, great cast. You are authorized to get these without stint or limit. Spare nothing, neither expense, time nor effort. Results only are what I am after. Simply send me the bills, and I will okay them."

"She must think you're a millionaire."

"It don't hurt to impress people." We chewed for a while without talking. "You remember that picture of

Teddy Roosevelt's safari that Ray Owen showed at the Bijou in Haverhill?"

"Of course. We played big-game hunter for weeks after that."

"Colonel Selig made that. In Chicago. Teddy Roosevelt wouldn't take him with him to Africa, so he made an African picture of his own."

"What do you mean? I saw Teddy Roosevelt on the screen with my own eyes."

"It was a Chicago vaudeville actor Selig hired for the part."

"But I saw Teddy Roosevelt shoot a lion."

"That was just some busted down old lion that Selig bought from some menagerie in Milwaukee. He killed it for the picture. They put some greenery in a cage—it looks like the jungle. They hire some Negroes to act like gun bearers—one of them hands a gun to the actor, and he pretends to shoot, and down goes the lion."

"It wasn't Teddy Roosevelt?"

"Look at you. You who is now in the business of making up things and calling it news. Forget about it. You're coming to me the minute this thing is settled. When you say no, it's because you don't know what you're talking about. Period." He leaned across the table. "Don't look now, but ain't that Douglas Fairbanks sitting over there?"

"It wasn't Teddy Roosevelt?"

"I said don't look now!"

"Yes. He's in town promoting *Robin Hood.*"

"I'll go say hello." Louie wiped his mouth on his napkin and stood up.

"Do you know him?"

"What difference does that make?" He crossed the room avoiding frantic waiters carrying trays and interrupted the actor's conversation with three other men at a table in the corner. Douglas Fairbanks looked blank, then nodded politely, smiled his famous broad smile, extended his hand, introduced Louie all around. Then Louie returned and sat down across from me. "One day he'll remember that he first met me here. Would you enjoy to have a piece of cheesecake?" He flagged a waiter. "Looks like you don't eat. You're skin and bones. Don't you eat? Why don't you eat?"

"I eat."

"What you need is a girl. You come to me out there, and you'll find the most beautiful girls you ever saw. Not one. Not two. Hundreds. That's how many there are. And do they want to get married? You bet they do. They may be beautiful but they're normal, red-blooded American girls." I was happy to see Louie—he felt like home to me, but I didn't like feeling so young. It didn't seem to make any impression on him that I was not a young boy anymore, and just as I was thinking maybe I was wrong about this, he repeated something he used to say to me when I was in elementary school. "You follow my sainted mother's advice and you'll never get in trouble. Only do it to make babies." He flagged the waiter again and took a slurp of coffee. "The merger of the Goldwyn studio in Culver City, California, with Metro Pictures will create one of the largest film-production companies in the world."

"It's not what you wanted though."

"No. It ain't. You're the only one in the world who would ever say those words to me, Harry." He pushed cole slaw around on his plate with his fork. "I got a late start."

"No, that's not it, Louie."

"What's it, then. You tell me."

"You're tired of owning your own business. You want a steady paycheck, like me. You're tired of coming up short."

"I don't come up short. Who says I come up short." There was no need to answer this. He was in New York applying for a job. He had decided to be someone else's employee.

Louie took a slurp of coffee. "Wasn't easy getting an in-person interview face to face. Marcus Loew makes a fortune of money. Has a mansion on the water in Long Island, a yacht and suits! You should see his suits. I thought I had a good tailor. I do have a good tailor. He's Chinese. Used to work laying track for the railroad. You'll go to him when you come to me—you'll get fitted. You'll look like a million dollars." Louie flagged the waiter again, then used his fingers to pick up some cole slaw that fell out of his sandwich. "I can see why his employees love him so much," Louie said. "I'm with him, what, a couple of hours, and I love him too!" Louie pushed his plate away to signal he was finished. "How can I describe Marcus Loew to you, Harry. He's humble. I go into his office, and I'm trembling. This I can tell to you alone. I'm trembling. Why am I trembling? Because I want this position so much. That is why I am trembling. I'm trembling with want. He's modest, Harry. He don't got a swelled head. He says to me, 'If it wasn't for Sime Silverman, I wouldn't have nothing.' I say to him, 'You mean Sime Silverman the editor of *Variety?*' He says to me, 'I'll tell you what Sime done for me.' His voice, Harry, is deep. I'm surprised. Such a small man with such a voice. Basso profundo. Just between I and you, I am going to take elocution lessons when I get back and make my voice deeper. You can do that, you know. We got drama coaches out there, and they tell me they can make that happen." The waiter cleared our plates, took the order for cheesecake with a quick nod and hurried away into the dish-clanking, order-shouting chaos of the popular New York delicatessen.

"Marcus Loew tells me that every weekend Sime Silverman drives out of the city with his chauffeur. As he motors along, he notices new housing developments. So that no other theater man will have a chance to discover the location, Silverman publishes the news in *Variety*. For instance, something on the order of, 'Marcus Loew is developing a new realty project on the Grand Concourse, and a prime focal point will be a deluxer in the Bronx.' Loew reads the item, goes to investigate, agrees it's a good site and builds the Loew's Paradise. Loew says to me, 'Mr. Mayer, my theater empire was built by Sime Silverman.'" The waiter delivered our cheesecake, banged the plates down and hurried away. "You know what he says to me? He says, 'Mr. Mayer, do you know why all Loew's theaters have such fancy ladies' rooms?' The reason for this, he says to me, is that he grew up on the Lower East Side and remembers what it's like to schlep downstairs to an outhouse in the courtyard. Some of my patrons still live like that, Mr. Mayer, he says to me. Some of them pay the dime just to use the ladies' room, just to smell the perfumed soap." Louie nodded his head thinking about it. "To work for such an individual is not a comedown."

"No, indeed."

"It's an honor. It's a privilege. It's the prize!" Then he leaned way across the table and whispered, "I offered him Hearst."

"William Randolph Hearst?"

"Just a man," Louie said, sitting back with a look of self-satisfaction. "Just a man, Harry." Louie bounced his fist against his heart. "Has a heart that breaks like any of us."

"I take it you found the very thing that breaks his?"

Louie smiled at me. "Yes, I did. And I knew of all the people in the world you would recognize the brilliance in what I have done."

"Do tell."

"I did it through the girl. My reasoning was this," he said. "William Randolph Hearst may be worth four hundred million, but what he really cares about is Marion Davies. This I know from an interesting thing he said once, which is that Marion is the best friend he ever had. Men don't say that about their mistresses. It made an impression. Especially because he's old enough to be her father. So I took this to mean their relationship is deeper than just what you and me think." Louie took a bite of cheesecake and continued, mashed cheesecake on his teeth. "She was threatening to leave him. Everyone out there knew it. And we all knew her gripe too. She don't like the roles Hearst makes her play. The pretty milkmaid, the innocent virgin. He don't recognize she ain't that nineteen-year-old chorus girl he met at Ziegfeld's. She's a grown woman. He gives her an allowance, for crying out loud, like she's a kid! She can see her picture career ain't going nowhere, no matter how many favorable articles Louella writes about her. She ain't dumb. She knows all that publicity he gives her makes her a laughingstock. She don't want to be a laughingstock. Bad enough she's a social pariah and can't show her face in New York."

When Louie finished his cheesecake, he wiped the plate with his finger and licked it off. Then he took two cigars from his vest pocket, bit the ends off both, spit them on the floor, handed one cigar to me, put the other in his mouth and lit them both with his latest, most up-to-date pocket lighter. "I know Marion Davies," he said. "I have had many close conversations with her. She stutters, like my Irene." We puffed our cigars. "She is far from a stupid individual. It is not for nothing that she does not attend parties outside of her own home. She gets snubbed. To Marion, her career is very important. Why? Because it makes her something more than a kept woman. So word comes to me through the grapevine that I have planted that Marion sees the merger of Metro and Goldwyn as her chance to get her career out from under Poppy's mismanagement. Ain't that cute? She calls him Poppy. She thinks some of the writers and directors at Metro might help her persuade Poppy to let her express her comic side. She wants to play brassy dames. But Poppy don't go for it at all. He hears about the merger and says he don't need Goldwyn. He's going to start a company of his own to distribute Cosmopolitan Pictures, and he don't need Metro either. He's going to buy his own theaters and show her pictures in them. So she says she's going to leave him. She could too. She's got dough." Louie flagged the waiter and ordered more coffee. "Between you and I, Harry, I don't approve of a married man, the father of sons, flaunting his mistress in his wife's face."

"But Opportunity knocks."

"It was banging on my door, Harry. Banging. I said shut up Opportunity! I hear you!" We laughed and puffed. "So I make an appointment, and here's the big surprise." Louie leaned across the table. "I like him. Hearst ain't hoity-toity. He's got this squeaky high voice, and the man's heart is breaking. He tells me if he could divorce his wife, he would, but he thinks the marriage vows are eternal. He don't want Marion parading around like a harlot on the screen, and he don't understand why she wants to. Hearst don't want people seeing her like that. Now he's telling me this, and I'm supposed to think it's for Marion's own good, to save her reputation because we all know his sons call her a whore to her face. But my mother, of blessed memory, whispers in my ear, he's jealous. The man is jealous. Fears losing her to a younger man. So now I know how to proceed."

The waiter put down the coffee too fast and it sloshed into the saucer. We both poured it back into the cup and stirred in some sugar and cream. "So I say to him, there's no reason for you to lose control of Marion's pictures. I say to him, you are a person of experience, chief. It is right for you to want to guide her career. So he relaxes. On the other hand, I say to him, Marion is an independent person, and you like that about her. What I think, I says to him, is she should earn a salary and not an allowance. I tell him she has great talent and that he should allow her to work with the best directors and supporting actors. I suggest to him that he merge Cosmopolitan Pictures with Goldwyn and Metro and that he set up a bungalow for Marion right on the grounds of the Culver City studio. I tell him I want to be in charge of the new studio, and I tell him that when I am in charge, I will keep an eye on Marion when Hearst is away on business. I said if I'm put in charge of the combined companies, I'd make sure Marion is treated like a queen and that none of her pictures will have anything dirty-minded in them. So the chief says to me, 'Consider it done, son.'"

We clinked coffee cups. "This morning, across the street—you can see the building from here—I lay my cards on the table to Mr. Marcus Loew himself. I tell him if I am put in charge of Metro-Goldwyn, Hearst will splash articles about Metro-Goldwyn's pictures all over the pages of the *New York Mirror* and the *Los Angeles Examiner*. He will order his columnist Louella Parsons to discuss Metro-Goldwyn players helpfully and ignore the actors of other companies. Hearst has promised that he will build a fourteen-room bungalow for Marion on the Culver City lot if, and I said if with a lot of *if* in it, his friend Louis B. Mayer is put in charge."

A couple of days later, word came through that Louie got the job. He would be in charge of running one of the biggest picture studios in the world. He was staying at the Astor Hotel, and we met there for breakfast. He was not ecstatic. "I want my name included," Louie said to me. "I told Marcus this. I told him. I want my name included. I don't want the name to be the Metro-Goldwyn Company. Marcus says to me, 'Louis, it is not possible. My board of directors will not allow it.' What he don't say to me is the name Mayer don't mean nothing to nobody. All these years, I toil, I move to California, I wake up again, and I toil—and still it don't mean nothing. You ever see my name in *Variety*?"

"Sure, I have, Louie."

"Yeah? As what?"

"Well, as..."

"Go on. Say it. As Louis Mayer of Boston. Metro-Goldwyn, now those names mean something. What am I, chopped liver?"

"What does your contract say?"

"Says when the picture starts, the main title card will be "Louis B. Mayer Presents a Metro-Goldwyn Production."

"What's wrong with that?"

"What's wrong? Who reads the small print? No one, that's who. They read the name of the picture, period.

And there ain't nothing in my contract says how big the letters of my name have to be. They could make the name so small you'd need a periscope to see it."

"What else does your contract say?"

"Says that in all advertising and paid publicity, the name Louis B. Mayer shall be prominently mentioned as the producer of said motion-picture photoplays."

"Isn't that good?"

"No. That ain't good. Who looks at the small print on a poster when they can look at the beautiful actress?"

"Louie. Be happy. You've been hired as vice president in charge of all production activities of the Metro-Goldwyn Corporation, with a salary of fifteen hundred dollars per week. It's right here in the *Herald Tribune.* See? You're mentioned. 'Metro, Goldwyn, Cosmopolitan and Louis B. Mayer in Giant Motion Picture Merger Headed by Loew.'"

He took off his glasses, huffed on them, wiped them with a napkin and put them back on. "Tomorrow that piece of paper you're holding will wrap a piece of fish." He sighed and took a bite of coffee cake. "You'll come to the opening on the lot in Culver City."

"No can do, Louie. George Bernard Shaw's coming to town. We've got cameras to meet him when he disembarks."

"You would rather do that than come see me speak before thousands of people as the head of the biggest motion-picture concern in the country?"

"I wouldn't rather. It's not a question of rather, Louie. You'll be fine. Don't worry about it."

Louie leaned way across the table. "Harry," he whispered, "Only to you could I say my secret plan." I leaned toward him in a conspiratorial way and sniffed that manly smell from my childhood, Mennen aftershave talc. "When I'm up there, when I'm on the podium, after the mayor of Culver City makes his speech, after all the hoopla dies down with the movie stars parading themselves around, I'm going to say that I've been warned that this new company starts off with a handicap, a name that's not easy to say, Metro-Goldwyn-Mayer."

"Louie! You can't do that!"

"Shhh!"

"You can't defy your own board of directors. You're responsible to them now."

He smiled wickedly and gave me the come-hither finger. I leaned in close. "Then I'm going to say we should have a short name, crisp and able to become familiar, like other studios. So instead of saying those long words, we'll shorten it and call the studio M-G-M. Then I'll say MGM is going to be the foremost movie studio in the world." He sat back, highly pleased with himself. Not a rash in sight. "What can they do? Metro-Goldwyn-Mayer. That's it. The papers are going to print what I say."

"And you'll say it in your new lower voice."

He stood up. "Com'ere." We hugged for a long time before I returned to Fox News.

Chapter Twenty-Five

I picked up copies of *Inside Scoop*, brought Molly's byline to my lips, kissed her name and read, "Live way beyond your means...in spirit! That is the code of the woman whose hours are filled to the brim with happiness, friendships and love. It is your code for the New Year if you want to develop your personality and radiate charm and magnetism." She did not write about Niko's party or about Anita. When I phoned her office in New York, I heard that she would be at the California office indefinitely. "Forget about her," Kenny said. "What's the use of having a girlfriend thousands of miles away?" Molly must have agreed with him because she did not reply to the messages I left in New York or at her office in Hollywood. Why would she? Why would a girl like that want me? Yes, she kissed me at midnight, but she'd had a lot to drink. She must have been inundated with attention from college men and wealthy theater men. I felt like an idiot making such a big deal out of a party flirtation.

I went out with Kenny to the speaks where working people spent their time: truckdrivers, manicurists, construction workers, salesgirls. We sat in groups and talked about nothing, and sometimes a girl invited me home with her, and there I would meet her roommates who would politely leave us alone in a tiny living room.

It was May when Etta confessed to me that she had "borrowed" the fabric and fur she used to make the Oberon and Titania costumes for Anita and me. "Have they noticed?"

"Who?"

"Whoever's in charge."

"Shhh. Not from here. From Hammerstein's. It was just lying around back stage. I went over there to get your tights."

"I don't get it. Are you in danger?"

"No. But I think you owe me."

"Name your price."

"I want to go to Jack and Charlie's new gin mill." Another girl would have insisted on the Palm Court, but Etta was one of those rare people plugged in to the coming thing. To Etta, the Palm Court might be delicious and elegant, the service impeccable, but it wasn't hip. Anyone could appreciate the Palm Court, which meant, to Etta, that it wasn't interesting.

We got jammed up in Rudolph Valentino's funeral. We knew it was happening—our cameramen were covering it—but we figured the crowds would have dispersed by nightfall. Wrong. I almost lost Etta in the crush of a hundred thousand sobbing women. "Look at these dames," Etta said, getting jostled by people who didn't even notice her, as happens with children. "They've lost their marbles." Mounted police patrolled back and forth trying to keep order. My impulse was to pick up Etta or, at least, run interference for her, but she didn't need me. She swerved in and out, around people, this way, that way, and often had to wait for me to catch up. We finally arrived at the Puncheon on West Forty-ninth Street.

The owners were the same young cousins who owned the Red Head in Greenwich Village where Kenny and I were so uncomfortable. The Red Head had been demolished to make way for the subway. At this new place in Midtown, there weren't so many college kids. The people sitting in the Puncheon, a small, narrow antique house, looked like they could have been artists, musicians, journalists—people who didn't have to look stiff and formal when they went to work. It was dim inside, smelled of beer, and a Duke Ellington record was on the phonograph behind the bar. I recognized some of the staff from the Red Head: the waiter who said *enjoy* and the seedy lookout who stood at the door, alert to the threat of a raid.

Etta and I got the last available table, sat down and peeked around to see who else was there. "To your right," Etta whispered.

"Where?"

"In front of your eyes."

"Who?"

"The Warner brothers."

"How do you know what the Warner brothers look like?"

"Trust me. That's Sam, Harry, Jack and Albert." Our drinks arrived in coffee mugs, and we added our cigarette smoke to the prevailing cloud.

"Are you telling me," I said, waving her hand away when she offered to drop a cube of ice in my mug, "that you take them seriously?"

"Are you telling me that you don't?"

"I don't think there's any future in talking features," I said. "Who wants to hear photoplayers talk? Can you imagine hearing John Gilbert's soprano voice saying, 'Open the safe, and hand over the cash?'"

"Their intention isn't to make actors talk. It's the music they want. And vaudeville acts."

"But that's only because the Warners don't have moolah. They don't own any decent theaters. Who would go to a picture accompanied by a tinny orchestra on a wax disc when they could go see a feature at Loew's Theaters, hear a live orchestra and see George Burns and Gracie Allen in person?"

We heard a commotion above the general din. A couple who had been waiting for a seat took it upon themselves to sit down at an empty table in the back corner. Jack and Charlie were refusing to let them sit there. The patrons smiled in a superior way to each other and exchanged in-crowd smirks. Etta leaned over to the next table and asked, "What's it about?" One of the men answered, "That's Jimmy Walker's table. No one sits there except the mayor of New York."

The couple found another table, and everything calmed down. Etta said, "Let's say the picture isn't a feature but a short of your friend Nick Meadows singing. People could hear him and watch him at the same time without his being there in person."

"It would end in comedy. The sound and the picture all out of sync. You remember that one we saw at the studio. The dog opens his mouth to bark and out came a canary tweeting. And why would Nick give away his singing for free. If people could go hear him on the screen for a quarter, why would they buy his records? He wouldn't do it. It's a fad. It won't last." We watched the Warner brothers accept their bill, discuss it, pay up and walk out. A tough bunch. You wouldn't want to be on the plains alone and have that pride stalk you. "You saw *Don Juan*. Thirteen reels of John Barrymore synchronized with the sounds of swords clinking, water fountain bubbling, doors slamming. We had that years ago. A man behind the screen. He even read the lines."

"I'm not talking about the feature, Harry. I didn't care about *Don Juan* either. I'm talking about the short subject, when Will Hays comes out and says…" Etta rummaged in her purse, unfolded a piece of paper and read, "Far indeed have we advanced from that few seconds of shadow of a serpentine dancer thirty years ago when the motion picture was born—to this public demonstration of the Vitaphone synchronizing the reproduction of sound with the reproduction of actions."

"Etta! You wrote it down!"

"Harry, this," and she rattled her notepaper, "is the first speech ever recorded for a commercial talking picture. It's history. On that very same screen, we heard Mischa Elman play Dvorak on the violin, Roy Smeck play the ukulele, Marion Talley sing an aria from *Rigoletto*, Efrem Zimbalist play Beethoven's *Kreutzer Sonata*. You don't know the future when you see it."

"It's not practical. It requires a huge phonograph to play the wax discs and a special projection machine that synchronizes the film with the disc, one disc for every ten minutes of film. The discs are fragile and last for only about twenty playings. Then they get gurgly, until the sound seems to be coming from underwater. Not to mention the problem when film prints get torn or broken. You can't repair them by splicing. An entirely new section of film has to be printed as a replacement to preserve synchronization with the phonograph disc. And what about deaf people?"

Etta lit another cigarette and exhaled the word, "Touché."

"And what about the export trade? You would have to produce one feature in English and others in Korean, Flemish, Syrian, Lithuanian and Chinese." Etta let her cigarette dangle from her lower lip and turned her palms upward, meaning she didn't know how to solve that problem. "And what would be allowed? Could the actor say damn or hell?"

I finished my drink and craned my head around to see where the waiter was. There, coming through the door, was Molly Tepper with exactly the kind of man who intimated me—ancestors on the Mayflower, all the right clubs. He could have stepped right off the polo fields: sandy straight hair falling over one eyebrow, straight features, well-tailored clothes and an air of ease. "Oh, my God," I said, heart lurching. "Etta. Let's blow."

"Now? I don't have an edge yet."

"Change seats with me."

"Why?"

"Just do it. Do it."

"Okay, okay, don't percolate." Keeping my chin on my chest, we changed chairs so I was facing away from the door where Molly waited for a table. "Who is it?" Etta asked. "Who walked in?"

"Someone. Nobody. Nothing."

"You know that doll in the cloche hat and beaded skirt?"

My hands were trembling. Etta swung her lips over to the side, nibbled the inside of her cheek and examined my face. I avoided her eyes. She turned in her chair to peer into the dimness across the room. "He's shtupping her, that's for sure."

"Stop."

"If he's not shtupping her, I'll drink my Coco Chanel."

"Shut. Up."

She waved the waiter over, and through the roar in my ears, I heard Etta say, "Bring him another one and me too. Make it a double. Might as well. He's buying." Waiter gone, she continued to peer across the room.

"Must you stare?"

"Yes, I must. I like her outfit. There's pleating on the sleeves. That's why they fall like that."

"Etta."

"Relax." She took a sip of whiskey, blew a few smoke rings. "She's not looking over here."

"I am very uncomfortable, Etta."

"Ah, here's further refreshment. Set 'em down, amigo. Good. You brought more ice." I gulped the whiskey, felt it burning my gut and kept my face averted.

Molly was even more beautiful than I remembered: elegant, poised, radiating a sort of calm. "They don't have that kind of relationship at all," I said.

"Maybe. Maybe not. Relax. They got a table. So did Kenny get shots of that family with the thirty-four children?"

"I'm uncomfortable, Etta."

"Did she dump you?"

"Did who dump me?"

"The doll who walked in." I didn't answer. "You're safest sitting here. We'd have to walk right by her table if we left now. And believe me, she would notice you because you're with me, and everyone stares at me. It's my curse and my gift." We sipped our drinks, inhaled smoke, blew out smoke, sipped our drinks. "Harry, I'm quitting."

"Okay. You get up first, and I'll follow."

"No. I mean I'm quitting Fox."

"What? Why?"

"I'm going out to the Coast. New York isn't the center of the industry anymore. It used to be, but it isn't now. The future is Hollywood."

"It is not, Etta. You don't know what you're talking about. You've never even been to Hollywood. How can you move someplace you know nothing about." She said nothing. "It's cactus and adobe. It's the middle of nowhere. No stores, no theaters, no people, no nightclubs. New York is the hub. It's where all the checks are signed."

"But the signing of the checks doesn't interest me."

"Don't be silly. You wouldn't like wearing chaps."

"It's the future. That much I know."

"You're serious."

"Yes. I already told my roommate. She says I owe her two weeks rent, but I don't. She uses my soap all the time, my shampoo. One time I came home and three eggs were missing out of my carton. Like they just got up and walked away. And she's saying I owe her."

"But Etta. What will you do out there?"

"Work. What else? You know what Mr. Fox said? This is unbelievable. He told me the cost of living in California is so much lower than in New York, it makes no sense to offer me the same salary. I said, 'But moving is expensive—the train ride, getting settled, all of that.' He said he is not prepared at this moment to pay an employee to work exclusively in the costume department of the Fox Film Company. Why? Because there is no costume department."

"How can there be a costume department, Etta? There's no stores there. The costume department is they travel back to New York to buy what they need and schlep it out there."

"I said to him, 'I will create a costume department.' He said, 'Mr. Fox does not need a costume department. The photoplayers are responsible for their own wardrobes.' I said, 'That's why most of them look like shit.' You should have seen his face."

"You said that?"

"He said, 'Is that your opinion, Etta?' I said, 'Yes, that's my opinion.' He said, 'Your opinion ain't worth crap.' The end. He was done. I never saw anything like it. It was like he closed a door in my face. I just stood there. Then I realized, oh, time to leave."

"I'll miss you, Etta. I really will. I'm sorry you're leaving."

"You know, if he were the least bit generous, if he said great, we need talent like yours out there, I'd return those garments I borrowed. But I'm not going to. I'm considering them severance pay. Especially the chinchilla cloak. He owes me."

"Well," I said, holding my coffee mug toward her, "here's to you, my friend."

"And the mink cape."

I wondered if Molly had noticed me. I took a chance, turned and our eyes locked. My heart leaped into my throat. She waved to me in a secret way, folded her fingertips against her palm once. I looked away first.

"Plus that bolt of paisley," Etta added.

My heart was thudding against my ribs. "Time to go, Etta."

"Okay, okay, I've got a buzz." I paid the bill, and we headed toward the door. Etta whispered, "Are you going to talk to her?"

I kept my eyes lowered as long as I could, but I knew she was watching me. I rehearsed a blasé attitude: Why, hello there, how nice... But when we had worked our way through the aisles and past all the other people, I just stood there gawking at Molly, helpless with love. Whatever she said didn't matter. I'd seen the look on her face, I'd felt the touch of her eyes. She was mine. Through the roaring of anxiety, I heard the words "My fiancé" and some name. I clasped hands with the man who stood to greet me, heard the words Fox News, heard the words "It's been a long time" and prayed that the floor would part and swallow me. I should have shaved my mustache off. No one at work liked it. Someone poked my hip. I ignored the jab until it happened again and hurt. "Oh," I said in a croaky voice, looking down at Etta's annoyed face, "allow me to..."

"Raid!" shouted the lookout. "Jack! Charlie! It's the feds!" Suddenly, chaos: drinks being dumped on the floor, people leaping up, chairs turning over, everyone rushing toward the door. Cops burst in as Jack and Charlie activated their system of pulleys and levers, which swept bottles from the bar shelves and hurled the smashed remains down a chute into the New York sewers. Women screamed, men shouted, police ransacked the building, searching behind the bar, in closets, in the ladies' room. I was carried by the tide of people out to the sidewalk where Etta was shouting, "Harry! Hurry up! Run!" I searched for Molly but didn't find her and ran to Etta who had darted across the street. She thought all this was much funnier than I did.

Chapter Twenty-Six

It was a myth that the cigarette-smoking, short-skirt-wearing, free-love-talking girls of the Jazz Age were promiscuous. They were as prudish as their mothers. So I avoided those stylish creatures and kept company with the girls who frequented Paddy's bar. Some of them had fathers in jail. No one was looking out for them, and no one was watching over me, either. We did as we pleased in whatever rooms we could find. But I have drawn the curtain over this aspect of my middle twenties. What was happening at work was more interesting.

Mr. Fox believed that talking pictures were the future, and he invited me and some of his other producers to witness a sound system that might solve the problem of equipment that was too heavy to be portable. He wanted compact equipment that could be carried on a truck and rapidly transported to the site of important events. He wanted his audiences to hear the sound of breaking news.

An inventor from upstate New York managed to record sound directly on film, so it was no longer necessary to synchronize separate discs with the film. Theodore Case had been experimenting with photographing sound waves since his undergraduate days at Yale. His father, also a scientist, converted one of the greenhouses on the family's estate into a laboratory, and it was in that space, with no pressure to earn a living, that Ted Case, at thirty-six, invented what Mr. Fox called us together to see. Selling his invention to Mr. Fox was not Case's first choice. His device has been rejected by both General Electric and Western Electric.

In the screening room, he showed us his demo reels: "Miss Martin and Her Pet Squirrel," "Gus Visser and His Singing Duck," "Bird in a Cage" and "Chinese Man with a Ukulele." The sound was perfectly synchronized with the action. When the bird opened its beak, tweets came out. When the Chinese man plunked his uke, we heard music at the exact same time. Lights up, Mr. Fox sprang from his seat and shouted, "Charlatan! Do you think me stupid, fella? Do you think me so easily fooled? Does William Fox, the founder of the Fox Film Corporation and Fox News, look like a jackass to you?"

Bewildered, Case said nothing. "Don't be impudent with me!" Mr. Fox barked. "What is the trick? I demand to know how it is done. You are in my place of business—I have a right to know."

Case, though surprised by the outburst, remained composed. "Sound waves," he said in his mild voice, "have been changed into electrical vibrations, which in turn were changed into light variations that we photographed onto the edge of the film. When the film was projected, the process was reversed and the re-created sound waves were transmitted from amplifying speakers behind the screen."

"Nonsense!"

Case tried again. "We photograph variations of light intensity on moving-picture film. This is accomplished by collecting the sounds to be recorded through the use of a microphone, which has the property of changing sound variations into electrical variations. These electrical variations are amplified and, in turn, vary the intensity of the recording light. The light contains a filament and a plate, similar to the two-element vacuum tubes we used many years ago in radio reception. The filament is coated with an alkaline earth oxide. The filament and plate are sealed in a small quartz tube from which the air has been removed and helium gas has been substituted. This tube is connected in the output circuit of a transformer, the input of which is connected to…"

"It wouldn't work outside of this room!" Mr. Fox yelled as he strode across the room to the screen, which he pushed aside. "Where is he? Where is the ventriloquist?"

Now Case understood, and his face relaxed. "Oh," he said.

After seeing another demonstration of the system at his own home in Woodmere, Long Island, Mr. Fox bought the patents to the sound-on-film process and set up the Fox-Case Corporation to develop what became known as Movietone. He Movietoned his California studio and, thereafter, only produced sound pictures. Now, instead of working for Fox News, I worked for Fox-Movietone News, and we changed our slogan from "The Mightiest of Them All" to "It Speaks for Itself."

Doubts about the sound-on-film system were swept away at the Roxy Theater when we all saw and heard Charles Lindbergh at Roosevelt Field, Long Island, taking off for his historic flight across the Atlantic. The scene was photographed in a single, continuous-pan shot at the moment of Lindbergh's takeoff on a gray, overcast morning while a group of bystanders milled around expectantly. A shout was heard, and the plane was seen gathering speed to lift off from the field. When the plane roared into the sky, the audience stood up and cheered.

Kenny and I went to Washington to photograph Lindbergh at his homecoming ceremony. Politicians were eager to accommodate us, letting us take apart the stage their people had set up so we could move it into better light, asking us where they should stand and how long their speeches should be and what kind of clothes would photograph best. We used an immobile sound camera set up on the reception stand and simply turned the camera on when President Coolidge began to talk. He was famously taciturn. Audiences had seen his closed-lipped face on dozens of silent newsreels in which he spoke his few words with sincerity to the crowd. This time, instead of speaking to the crowd, Coolidge turned his back to them and spoke directly to the camera lens using weird, robot-like gestures. He was talking to invisible people in invisible dark theaters. Kenny, concentrating on the task at hand, was cranking away while I was awash with a feeling of unease. We were getting between the people and their elected official. The camera, in a sense, obliterated the real Coolidge and presented the public with a poser, an actor. Would this be the new way: politicians wooing the camera rather than the people? Would there come a time when only photogenic people could hold office? Later, Kenny made me laugh by saying there would come a time when movie stars would run for office.

Lindbergh did the opposite of Coolidge. He ignored the camera and spoke directly to the crowd. When he was done, our microphone inadvertently caught an official's order: "Strike up the band!" I left that in the final cut.

The two Lindbergh newsreels, his departure and his return, were an immense financial success. Mr. Fox began to expand his chain of theaters and converted them all to Movietone. "The Fox Theaters Corporation will build up a chain of theaters that will cover the forty-eight states of the Union," he said at a staff meeting when we were sitting around his conference table, "from Maine to California." He spoke to the wall as if watching a film of himself moving his personnel and equipment into various theaters, tearing down the current name and replacing it with Fox. "Amplifiers and speakers must be installed at a cost of approximately twenty thousand dollars per theater," Mr. Fox said. "All our motion-picture stages, here in New York and in California, are being converted to sound. To finance the expansion of theaters, we have borrowed money." He rose, walked to the window, pulled back the shade, looked out on Tenth Avenue and said to the windowpane, "But I rather enjoy being in difficulties. Working them out is a satisfaction to me." He let the shade drop and returned to the conference table. "During the entire history of my picturemaking, I have always been under the impression that I was doing something just a little bit more than making money. I was putting entertainment and relaxation within the reach of all. Now, with Movietone, I have an opportunity to do even more for my fellow human beings. It is my intention to help medical students by documenting correct surgical procedures. On Thursday of this week, Fox cameramen in a Chicago hospital will record a surgical operation while physicians explain the procedure. This is the first time in history that a surgical operation has been thus recorded. It is the goal of Fox-Movietone News to introduce audiovisual teaching in the areas of science and mathematics. Just imagine," he said, "professors at college coming to our studio and delivering lectures on subjects they have studied for years and that they hope to present to a body of students. We photograph the speaker, and at the same time on the same celluloid, we photograph his voice. That lecture can simultaneously be shown in all the universities of the world, so that the speaker's voice may be heard in a thousand classrooms at one time.

Movietone will ultimately be one of the greatest factors for education that it is possible to conceive."

"Are we going to use the amplifiers developed by Bell Laboratories?" one of the accountants asked.

"I have been compelled," Mr. Fox said, "to make a deal with the telephone company to obtain their superior amplifiers. Speakers for our new system are created by Western Electric. Every theater that converts to Movietone must install Western Electric speakers and pay that company a monthly fee. Western Electric has hired and trained hundreds of installation and service personnel and is now establishing networks of regional offices across the country."

There was a knock on his door, and Faye stuck her head in. This was unusual because no one was allowed to interrupt staff meetings. She said, "Marcus Loew is dead, sir."

"What? Who told you that?"

"Mrs. Fox, sir."

"When?"

"Just now, sir. On the telephone."

"When? When did he die?" Faye did not know the answer, just stood halfway in the door, no expression on her face. "Find out the particulars, and send a bouquet."

"The usual, sir?"

"Of course not. It's Marcus Loew. The biggest they got."

"Yes, sir."

"Four of them. Fox-Movietone News, Fox Film Company, Fox Theaters and Mr. William Fox and family. Send a telegram to Caroline Loew: so sorry to hear etc. Send two more, one to each twin. Where's the funeral?" Faye didn't know. "Find out, and rearrange my schedule."

"You leave for the Coast tomorrow, sir." She withdrew.

Mr. Fox went to his desk, picked up his telephone, remembered us and waved us away with the gesture most people reserve for gnats.

Five thousand people attended Loew's funeral in September 1927. We entered the arched wrought-iron gates of Pembroke, his forty-six-acre estate in Glen Cove, Long Island. There, we saw sweeping lawns decorated with Japanese gardens and reflecting ponds. There was a mosaic-tile swimming pool seventy feet in circumference, a garage that held twenty cars and a stable that could accommodate twenty horses.

Two thousand mourners were allowed into the eighty-room house facing the ocean where Loew's yacht was moored with its flag at half-mast. The religiously observant men wore their own yarmulkes held in place with bobby pins at the top of their head while all the other men took a temporary yarmulke from a box at the door and clapped it on their head. The women wore stylish black hats or pieces of lace stuck on top of their hairdos. Whispered conversation admired the home's twelve master bedrooms, twelve baths and stained-glass globes designed by Tiffany, who lived nearby.

I was with the executives representing Mr. Fox, and Louie was with the MGM people, but we did manage a brief exchange as we filed into a marble reception hall. Loew's slight body, a waxy figure embalmed in a tuxedo, lay in its posh coffin surrounded by thousands of floral tributes. Louie, sobbing openly, said to me, "You see this house? You see this house where we are? How big? How grand? He was afraid of it. Marcus was awed by his own house." He blew his nose hard. "I loved this man," he said. "I loved him."

Next to the coffin, greeting guests, was Loew's wife, her adult twin sons and Nicholas Schenck, vice president of Loew's Incorporated. It was curious that Louie, as chief of production at MGM, had not been given a place of honor next to the coffin. He was being treated as if he were just another employee with no more importance than any of the other hundreds of Loew's employees milling about with somber expressions. He tried to remedy this by not moving along when it was his turn at the reception line. He came to a stop next to Schenck and boldly accepted the hand of the next person in line who muttered, "He looks good, so peaceful." Schenck was a tough guy in expensive clothes—muscular, thuggish, implacable. He turned to Louie and said, "Louis, thank you for coming." He took Louie's hand, and the next thing I knew, Louie was not in the reception line but beyond it, again just part of the crowd. I discovered how this happened when it was my turn. I planned to say something sympathetic but only had time to introduce myself. "Harry Sirkus," I said, "Movietone News." I took the extended hand of Schenck, Louie's new boss. He gripped my hand and held it too long, making sure I could feel the strength in his arm. It was a secret contest during which he quickly searched my eyes to see if I understood that he would release me when it suited him. His thrill was feeling the hand in his squirm to get away. My impulse was to win the contest, to not let go when he let go, to just stand and look into his face. But he was prepared for even that because when he felt my hand tighten as his opened, he shoved me with his other hand and the next person in line took my spot as I moved on.

I found myself standing next to Sophie Tucker, the vaudeville singer whom I'd known since the days when

I booked vaudeville acts for Gordon-Mayer Theatrical Company in Boston. Face puffy and red from crying, she said to me, "I performed on the stage of Marcus Loew's first theater. He paid twenty dollars a week for an act with one person, forty dollars for two people, and a three-person act didn't get on."

Charlie Ebbets, the owner of Ebbets Field where the Dodgers played, said, "Marcus used to say to me, 'If you want to make good, never grow tired of your shop.'"

Sime Silverman, the editor of *Variety*, joined us. "He burned out worrying for his stockholders."

The rabbi's service ended with, "To know Marcus Loew was to love him. He was a man without an enemy."

The pallbearers, both sons, Schenck and the actor David Warfield, fit the coffin into the hearse against a backdrop of ocean. We climbed into the limousines lined up outside the door and joined the parade of limousines that followed the hearse to the cemetery. One of the women in my car was a real estate agent who pointed out the Woolworth mansion, J.P. Morgan's estate and the Pratt estate. "That," she said as the car crawled along, "is Mountainview Farm, a thousand acres owned by Adolph Zukor, founder of Paramount. He's got a golf course, a clubhouse that contains a movie theater, a guest house, a swimming pool and a filling station where guests can tank-up free. I sold Mr. Zukor that property. I asked him how he liked being Mr. Loew's neighbor, and he said it was pleasant because they could sit on the veranda and make fun of each other's pictures." We drove along in silence for a while. "He was an excellent tennis player," another woman in the limousine said. "You wouldn't think such a little man would be a good athlete, but he was, God rest his soul."

The limousines made an orderly line at Maimonides Cemetery. As the grave diggers lowered the coffin into the pit, Warfield jumped into the hole screaming, "Don't! Don't! Don't take him!" which made Mrs. Loew wail and her sons cover their faces. Louie reached down to the actor and coaxed him to climb out. I hardened myself and turned away. "I was wondering what my lead would be," a female voice whispered to me, "A distraught David Warfield, long time friend of..."

There, standing right next to me was Molly Tepper. She allowed me to give her a kiss on her petal-soft cheek, and my knees grew weak from her fragrance.

She beamed up at me; I beamed down at her. We might have stayed like that into eternity except someone bumped into us so I took her hand and led her through the crowd to a peaceful glade where ancient gravestones, tipped sideways, were dressed in moss. The leaves had not changed yet, but they were a tired, grayish green, and there was a crisp fall smell in the air.

We stood there smiling at each other. I saw the blaze of dancing light in her eyes, and she saw it in mine. It was as if my insides were standing bewitched before her insides, as if our bodies were transparent. I couldn't find any words to say. This had nothing to do with thought. Then I heard myself say, "How could you?"

She lowered her eyes, and we disconnected. She sat on a garden bench and adjusted her black cloche hat, though it didn't need adjusting. "I'm sorry, Harry. I shouldn't have had so much to drink at Nick's party."

"What are you talking about, Molly? What are you talking about?"

"Harry, you don't know me. You think you do, but you don't. You met me once at a party. We were dressed up—it was New Year's Eve."

"Stop talking like that."

"Harry, I go to a lot of parties. I meet a lot of people. It's my job. I should have been more careful."

"You mean you were engaged at the time?"

"No."

"You met him out there?"

"Yes. He's an attorney for one of the oil companies out there."

"You feel our connection, Molly. You know you do."

"Harry, forget about me. I'm not worth the trouble. Robert and I have an understanding. He doesn't want to get married anymore than I do. We're engaged so our parents will get off our backs about settling down. I don't want to get married. I don't want to have children. I don't want to live my mother's life. I am not the little woman. I earn my own way, and that's how I like it. Robert's office is in London. I hardly ever see him. So now you know."

"Is he in London now?"

"Yes."

"Then have dinner with me tonight."

"Harry, you haven't been listening to a word I said."

"Yes, I have. In between watching your lips move. In between stealing sniffs of you."

We were quiet for a while, feeling the intensity of the tug between us. We watched some chickadees hop around, fly up into bushes, tweet their two notes over and over until their song penetrated and we understood that they were complaining to us. "We're sitting in their synagogue," Molly said, referring to the birds' coloring, the patch of black on top of their heads. "They're having a service of their own, all dressed in little yarmulkes." We touched eyes. "Where were you thinking of?"

"Delmonico's. Tomorrow night." The funeral crowd was breaking up, and people walked heavily to the waiting limousines. We stood up. "It's just dinner, for pity's sake. I buy, you eat. You have to have dinner anyway. Right?"

She agreed to meet me, and we parted with a European kiss on each cheek. But later the next day, a messenger brought me a note saying, "Harry, forgive me. I'm leaving for the Coast tonight."

Chapter Twenty-Seven

The trade papers told us that Loew's estate was worth thirty million dollars. His wife believed that the empire her husband built depended upon his genius, that without Loew's attractive personality, Loew's Incorporated would lose value. Her twin sons agreed that they should cash out, and they instructed Schenck to find a buyer. His commission would be ten percent, more than he could ever earn as president of Loew's Incorporated. The timing was perfect because Schenck at forty-six had come through a messy divorce and was newly married to a young show girl named Pansy. His commission on the sale would allow him to retire, and there was nothing he wanted more than leisure time to spend with his new bride.

The Warner brothers offered to buy and so did Paramount, but Mr. Fox trumped them by offering to pay double the price that Loew's stock was trading at on the open market. Shareholders were eager to sell. The cost to Mr. Fox for the entire block of Loew's stock was fifty million dollars. If the sale went through, Fox would acquire hundreds of movie theaters here and abroad plus the valuable real estate they sat on, a sixteen-story office building in Times Square, a sheet-music company, a record company, and the Metro-Goldwyn-Mayer studio with stars Joan Crawford, Buster Keaton, Norma Shearer, Lon Chaney and the newest sensation, Greta Garbo. Mr. Fox would become Louie's boss.

The negotiations for Loew's Inc. were not secret. We all knew that Mr. Fox imagined himself king of a global entertainment empire. I was probably the only one in the office not wholeheartedly rooting for him because of my allegiance to Louie. The two men were much too egotistical to get along. Also, there was something giddy about the way Mr. Fox was borrowing money to expand his theater empire even before acquiring Loew's. He bought twenty houses in New England, brought his holdings in New York to one hundred thirty and invested fourteen million in cash to buy the Gaumont chain of three hundred theaters in Great Britain.

I had the apartment to myself a lot because Kenny was photographing Herbert Hoover on the campaign trail. He shot Hoover in every town and village. "How many babies do we have to see recoil from him?" Kenny said, but we realized the answer. Mr. Fox was setting up Hoover, and when he won the election, it would be payback time. So when the Justice Department declared that Fox could not merge with Loew's because it would create a monopoly, Mr. Fox went to Washington to remind President Hoover that he wouldn't have won the election if it weren't for all the favorable exposure he had received in Fox newsreels. We heard that Hoover's attorney general had promised Mr. Fox that the Justice Department would not turn its antitrust guns against the merger.

While Mr. Fox believed his backing put Hoover in the White House, Louie believed he himself had done it. Hoover was a favorite with movie executives because he said government should not interfere with private business. When he was secretary of commerce under the Harding Administration, Hoover refused to let the federal government censor motion pictures. Nor would he interfere in the clashes between theater owners and distributors, film crews and producers, artists and studios. Hoover insisted that the film industry police itself.

Louie campaigned vigorously for Hoover, gave after-dinner speeches and organized fund raisers. He believed that with enough publicity, he could turn Hoover into the biggest star of all. To show his appreciation, Hoover invited Louie and his family to the Inauguration in 1929 and to the White House for dinner. Louie stopped in New York on his way back to the Coast, and we met at Lindy's for cheesecake. I expected a description of the White House dinner and a long sermon about the wonders of America, that an impoverished boy like himself, with no education, could dine at the White House with the President of the United States. Instead, there was Louie with a rash across his cheeks, furious, not because Schenck planned to sell the company out from under him but because he had not been told in time to sell his own stock to Fox for twice the market price.

"So I says to Schenck, Mr. Skunk, I built Metro-Goldwyn-Mayer. Me. How do you think we got more stars than there are in heaven? You think that's easy? I tell my talent scouts, go find talent. We'll put them on contract for seven years, even if we don't got a picture for them right away. We'll groom them, we'll give them dancing lessons, singing lessons, get them a drama coach, so they can get rid of their accent. They got a flat chest, we'll build them falsies: they drive drunk, we'll cover it up and keep it out of the papers. We take care of everything, so the public will get what it wants. What does the public want, I says to Mr. Skunk standing there in his big office across the street. I says to him, the public wants idols. The public wants to adore—that's what the public wants. You think the public wants to know Loretta Young got a secret baby? No, they do not want to know that."

"Calm down, Louie. Your rash is flaring."

"Look at this Lucille Le Sueur, nothing but a tramp. What have I done with this tramp? You think Fox has got anything on me with what he did with that tailor's kid? No. What he did for that Goodman girl don't hold a candle to what I done for Lucille. You ever hear about Theda Bara anymore? No. You never hear about her. She's finished. So what did Fox do for her, after all, in the long run? Nothing. She's washed up. Me, I'm more careful. I groom, I polish, I say not ready yet, I trim, I shine, I say not ready yet, I put more studio shots in *Movie News*, another sentence in *Hollywood Reporter*—and then, when it's perfect, when I've spun gold out of straw, I present Joan Crawford." He snapped his fingers. "Lucille Le Sueur? Who is Lucille Le Sueur? No one. She's dead. She don't exist."

"Tell me about your trip to Washington. How was the Inauguration?"

"She comes to me, says she don't want her mother living with her, going to throw her mother out on the street."

"Who?"

"Lucille. Who do you think? I say to her, 'How would that look? You think the American public wants to love a woman who throws her own mother out on the street?' I tell her, 'Buy your mother a house.' She says to me, 'You buy my mother a house. I ain't spending one dime on that piece of shit.' I say, 'It won't look the same if I buy her a house. You got to buy it. And you got to buy her a nice house.' Then I remind her how her career depends upon the public, so if she don't want her mother drinking up her liquor in her house, she should save her pennies, do without for a while and buy her mother a separate house. So we call in *Inside Scoop*, and they write up about the beautiful house Joan Crawford bought her sainted mother.

Mr. Skunk trades the company I built. The company is worth triple since I took over. The fox and the skunk. Well, they've got another think coming."

"Who did you call from *Inside Scoop*?"

"What? Waiter! Get over here! Bring me more coffee!"

"Who did you call from *Inside Scoop*?"

"What are you talking, Harry. What difference does that make? I just come from Skunk's office, and he offers me one hundred thousand dollars. He throws peanuts at me. He thinks he can sell the company I built for fifty million dollars and not give me a piece of the pie? I will move heaven and earth to prevent this merger."

"Just tell me. Who wrote the Joan Crawford piece for *Inside Scoop*?"

"How the hell should I know? I turned it over to publicity. You think I'm going to sit still and be treated like chopped liver? I went to Hoover, and I said to him, this is a monopoly. Don't let this merger go through. He says to me, 'Okay, Louis, I will make sure the Justice Department stops this merger.' Waiter! Get over here! How many times I got to ask you?"

The waiter poured more coffee into our cups and dashed away. "Mr. Skunk don't know nothing about making pictures. The man is a walking ledger book. He says, 'King Vidor costs too much. Hire another director.' I say, 'Another director can't make this picture.' He says, 'Cut back on sets.' I say, 'Without the Viking ships, it ain't a picture.' How can you make a Norway picture without Viking ships? You're filling out, Harry. You ain't so skinny as you used to be. You getting laid?"

About a week later, we heard that Mr. Fox went to Washington. When he returned, he called me into his office. Shades down, cigar smoke everywhere, he kept his eyes away from mine and spoke to the edge of my cheek. "After we had adjourned to his smoking room, I reminded President Hoover of how favorably he appeared in Movietone newsreels. I frankly told him of my great embarrassment. The Justice Department, I said to the President, has done me an injustice. After all, I had been told that the merger would not violate anti trust laws. Before I left, he requested that my attorney go back to the department and have another talk." Mr. Fox opened his humidor and offered me a cigar. He bored his eyes into mine to see if I appreciated that this was a great event. I did. He lit his cigar and tossed the matches to me.

"My troubles with the Justice Department can be traced to your friend Louis B. Mayer," he said. "He has made himself a power in Republican politics." Mr. Fox stood up, took his usual route to the window, pulled the drawn shade back, gazed out and said to the pane, "It is my job now to make him my friend if I can. For this reason, I invited him to Fox Hall." He let the shade drop and returned to his desk. "When he arrived at Fox Hall, I invited him to call me Bill. This he refused to do. Instead, he accused me of underhanded behavior. What is the reason your friend is opposed to the merger? It is because he believes he was treated unfairly. Mr. Schenck assured Louis Mayer that his contract is secure and that everything at the Metro-Goldwyn-Mayer studio will remain the same. Louis Mayer is angry because, had he been given the chance, he, too, would have sold his Loew's shares to me at the elevated price I offered." Mr. Fox smoothed his hair down to make sure it was still covering his bald spot. "When Louis Mayer visited my residence, I told him that I bought Metro-Goldwyn because of his ability. I told him that I have reconsidered the transaction and have reached the conclusion that he has not been treated properly. I said that if we can merge these two companies, I am willing to pay him two million dollars. He said that I have given him a difficult task. He wondered how he was going to change the government's mind back again. That he will succeed in doing so, I have no doubt." Mr. Fox leaned back in his chair and said to the ceiling, "At fifty-one, I will be the head of the largest company of its kind in the world. The Fox Film Corporation, when merged with Loew's, will extend to the far corners of the earth."

Chapter Twenty-Eight

A few weeks later, Mr. Fox called me into his office again. He told me that the only thing troubling the Justice Department was the close connection of Loew's with Paramount. The son of Loew's was married to the daughter of Paramount, and there was fear that unless that connection was legally severed, Fox would be, essentially, acquiring Paramount as well as Loew's. "Do you play golf?" he asked me.

"No, sir."

"I am a champion golfer. I play with one-armed golfers as well as those who have the use of both arms. Trophies line the shelves of my home. Mr. Nicholas Schenck, president of Loew's, and I have decided to iron out the last obstacles to our merger on the golf course. I want you to produce a film of this game, not only because of its historic import but also because I believe that when someone has become as expert as I have, it is his duty to teach others. The film will be used to teach one-armed golfers how to swing, how to stand, which clubs to use. The game will be Movietoned, and you will read into a microphone the script that I write. This is not a commercial venture but a public service. The cameraman will be Kenny Anderson." He told me the date and the time. "You must not be late. Country clubs are strict about tee times."

On the day of the assignment, it was as if New York had a fever. Kenny and I were glad to get away from hot sidewalks and the traffic fumes that no breeze blew away. We were looking forward to a swim in the ocean. Kenny arrived dressed as a golfer, clothes obviously borrowed from a Burberry fashion shoot. He wore knickers, knee-high socks and a plaid cap. At the Fox-Movietone garage downtown, he stuffed his camera gear into the back of one of the trucks, climbed in behind the wheel, and we bounced and rattled away from skyscrapers and sweaty pedestrians, out of the city on the Long Island motor parkway.

There were toll lodges along the way. We stopped, filled the truck with gas and splashed the dust off our faces at the water pump. We had a delicious duck dinner for two dollars. Other motorists were happy to see one of the Fox-Movietone trucks with its logo on the side and asked us questions in a shy, starstruck way.

It took a couple of hours to get to Long Island on rutted roads bordered by farms. We arrived at Fox Hall, an oceanfront white house so imposing that Kenny exclaimed, "Hot dog! Look where the big cheese lives!" He slammed on the brakes so hard we had to brace ourselves against the dashboard. We climbed down next to a marble statue of Bacchus wearing a crown of grapes and a modest fig leaf, one of several Greek statues lining a driveway made of crushed seashells. We stretched our legs, brushed the dust off our trousers and inhaled the delicious breeze blowing in off the ocean that sparkled to the horizon. Moored next to a boat house was Mr. Fox's wooden yacht, the *Mona Belle*, named after his daughters. The grounds were spectacular, with grape arbors and a man-made lake of at least an acre with cabanas around it. Kenny wiped his forehead with one of the clean and ironed handkerchiefs he always carried, then bent down to pet one of about six cats that came to greet us. Mrs. Fox came from the other side of the hedge with a bowl in her hand, saw us and said, "Some are friendly and some..." just as the cat Kenny had chosen to adore swiped at him and hissed. Mrs. Fox set down a bowl of food, and even more cats trotted over to look in it. "We have almost a hundred of them," she said with a throaty laugh. "I called the shack where we keep them the cat house until the girls told me that don't mean what I think it means."

Eve Fox had a commanding presence, not like a queen but like the owner of a shop who knew her merchandise was worth what she was asking for it. You want it? Take it. You don't want it, get out. "Harry I know," she said. "Which one are you?"

"Allow me to introduce Kenny Anderson, Mrs. Fox," I said. "The best of the best."

No handshake. No welcome. Just an appraising look up and down. Would this one give good value? "He's waiting for you in the garden."

"Can't we see inside?" Kenny said.

"Why should I show you the inside of my house?"

"Why not?"

She laughed, checked the watch pinned to her bodice and gestured for us to follow her. Cats pranced along with us, then lost interest and either dashed away or sat down and washed with a paw. The house was a museum, overstuffed with tapestries, brocaded wallpapers, poofed-up drapery and paintings in rococo gold frames. A large portrait of Eve Fox showed her sitting in a ball gown with her hand on a Borzoi. Was it the same Borzoi I met in Theda Bara's tent? She escorted us downstairs to show us their home movie theater with real movie-theater seats. There must have been a part of the house where the family relaxed, but Mrs. Fox didn't show it to us.

Tour over, we followed her through French doors outside to an exuberant flower garden where Mr. Fox—portly belly in a golf shirt, tweed knickers and knee-high socks covering skinny calves—was pumping insect-repelling dust on his flowers. In the distance, there were two women in bathing suits lounging on chairs by the lake. They were almost hidden by the topiary garden near them, a team of gardeners on ladders trimming and shaping.

Mr. Fox greeted us with a lift of his chin, gave a few more pumps of dust, then set the spritzer down on a patio table. "Is there time for iced tea?" he asked his wife.

She looked down at the enamel watch pinned to her bosom. "No."

"What a beautiful place you have here," Kenny said. "Never saw anything like it. So peaceful! How much does something like this cost?"

Mrs. Fox laughed, a throaty sound. "It don't happen all at once," she said. "You get rich little by little." She picked up a pewter bell on the patio table and tinkled it. A maid in uniform answered the bell. "Tell Joe Mr. Fox is ready to go," Mrs. Fox said. The maid nodded and went inside. One of the women by the lake swung her legs over the side of her chaise, put on shoes and a robe and walked toward the house. Was this a daughter?

Kenny was doing his usual, making a camera out of his hands, thumbs touching, and panning the sweep of manicured lawns. When his pretend lens landed on the woman approaching from the distance, she stopped. Her kimono was untied showing a bathing suit of bold black-and-white stripes that ended midthigh. She was carrying a sun hat made of matching stripes. Those stripes, the ocean sparkling in the background, the human shape on the green lawn, made an attractive picture. The woman stood still. I secretly nudged Kenny, and he lowered his hands. Seagulls shrieked above us, and the woman resumed her progress toward the house.

I thought it must have been heat waves rising that made it look as if the woman wobbled. This was definitely one of the daughters. She matched the photograph on Mr. Fox's desk. But the wobbling was not a heat mirage. It was as if her legs were made of jelly, and it was horrible to see her trying to support her top half on limbs that were so limp, that threatened to collapse when she put weight on them. It was almost as if she had no knees. My stomach turned over. Was this the mother of the little cadet? What mysterious sorrows in Mr. Fox's life!

Though I tried not to stare, I must have been because Mr. Fox gestured abruptly and said, "Come on. We ain't got all day." We followed him out to the driveway. "You must be aware," he said as he walked quickly toward the Rolls Royce parked in front of the garage, "that I am working on a revolutionary new process for showing motion pictures. The small screen as we know it today will be a thing of the past. I am experimenting with projection machines that will throw big images upon a wide screen."

"What kind of camera would you need for something like that?" Kenny asked.

"It will use 80mm film," Mr. Fox said. "I am calling it Grandeur. Every theater in the world will be converted to accommodate the wide screen. It is revolutionary, and I own the patents to both the projection machines and the screens."

"Won't the other producers object?" Kenny asked. "They're all going bust converting to sound. Are you going to ask them to convert again?"

"If they want to stay in business, they will have to show big pictures."

Parked in the driveway, the motor purring, was a burgundy Rolls Royce Phantom with white-walled tires.

The chauffeur, about my age, leaned against the car smoking a cigarette until he saw his boss. Then he flicked the butt away and ran to open the back door of the car. "In the future," Mr. Fox said, "do not lean against this machine. It makes smudges. Clean that fender before we leave."

"I just cleaned it."

Mr. Fox pulled himself up and glared. "Make it snappy."

The chauffeur rubbed the spot with a rag, as Mr. Fox inspected the rest of the car, leaning in close when he saw anything amiss—taking off his glasses, putting them back on, then continuing around the car. "How long have you worked here?"

"Two days, boss." Rag in hand, he stood at attention in an exaggerated way, as if making fun of himself.

"When you wax this automobile, it is of vital importance that you get every speck of wax off. This requires elbow grease. Are you prepared to keep this motorcar looking as if it just came out of the showroom?"

"It does."

Mr. Fox jabbed his finger toward a white speck of wax. The chauffeur rubbed the spot with the rag in a sullen way. Then he stood at attention next to the back door as Mr. Fox lowered himself in. "You boys follow me," he called to Kenny. The Rolls headed out of the driveway, and Kenny and I ran to the truck.

"What was the matter with her?" Kenny said, pulling out the choke, revving the engine and putting the truck in gear. "Was that the married one?"

"Aren't they both married?"

"What was the matter with her?"

"I thought she was going to fall. Weren't there two son-in-laws always hanging around?"

"One of those homo-boobians was always hanging around the fashion shoots ogling the dames," Kenny said as we drove past farms bordered by stone walls and cows with heads down, tails swishing. "No. You're right. They were both married and both divorced and both of them have a son named William and Bill adopted both of them and took away their father's names so now he has two grandsons named William Fox."

"Kenny, keep your hands on the wheel. I'll light your ciggy when you want it."

Kenny swerved left suddenly onto a narrow road. "How about signaling when you're going to turn, buddy!" he yelled to his windshield. We could see the back of Mr. Fox's head through the rear window, his golf clubs next to him on the seat. We rattled along past sheep grazing and horses looking up when they heard the racket our truck made.

"I think I'll just shoot it straight," Kenny said. "Get Schenck teeing off, get Bill teeing off, sounds of the ball getting smacked, then a long shot of them doddering away toward the next hole. Maybe a wide shot of the golf course, the caddies lugging their crap around." We drove under a canopy of elms. A bee flew in the window, and Kenny had a fit whacking the air while I grabbed the wheel to keep the car straight. It flew out at last.

"I hate those things. They shouldn't be allowed in New York State," Kenny said, brushing off the cigarette ash that fell on his lap while he was trying to swat the bee. "How does Bill play golf with that gimpy arm?"

Again Mr. Fox's chauffeur forgot to signal, and we had to swerve suddenly. We saw Mr. Fox turn to see if we were following, then turn back again. "Bill ever tell you the story of his arm?" Kenny asked. "He fell off the back of an ice wagon. He was too poor to go to the doctor, so he went to some quack who paralyzed his elbow. He's forever telling me he's going to send me to Mount Sinai to shoot a surgical operation. He wants to aid medical education. I say, 'Sure, okay,' and I'm thinking, 'You put me in that operating room, and you will get zilch. Zero. Because I will be flat on the floor fainted dead away.' I hate the sight of blood."

The chauffeur, apparently, did not know the way because again he turned suddenly, and Kenny slammed on the brakes, which made the camera equipment jiggle and clank. Kenny was craning his head around to make sure the sudden swerve did not damage his equipment, not looking at the road, not seeing that another car was speeding toward us on the wrong side of the road. "Kenny! Watch out!"

He turned in time to see the other car smash into the Rolls head on so hard the Rolls spun into the air while the other car twirled into a ditch. The Rolls dropped to the ground on its roof, the crash making terrible noises—metal on metal, glass breaking. Kenny swerved, brakes screeched, and we skidded to a stop next to the wreck. He put his forehead down on the wheel.

I leaped out of the truck and ran to the Rolls, bending down to peer under the crumpled window frames. Glass was all over the road, blood everywhere. The chauffeur's head was on the seat next to his body. "Oh, my God. Oh, my God. Kenny! Kenny! Oh, my God."

I heard moaning and saw Mr. Fox trying to crawl out, blood pouring from his head. "I'll get help!" I yelled. "Don't move! Don't move! I'll get help! Kenny! Kenny!" But Mr. Fox continued to work his way out from under the wreckage, and when he had crawled all the way out, he tried to stand up, but his knees buckled. He collapsed unconscious, blood pooling around him on the dirt road. I ran to the other car listing sideways in the ditch, the front end pushed in, the windshield smashed, and I saw a woman at the wheel covered in blood, a piece of glass stuck in her cheek. Eyes wild with terror, she moved her lips but no sound came out. "Kenny! Kenny!" I ran back to the truck where Kenny still had his forehead on the wheel. "Kenny! We have to get help. Drive!" He did nothing. "Kenny! Drive! We have to get help!"

He looked up at me dazed. I lost patience and slapped his face, screaming, "Drive! We have to get help!" He put his palm against his stinging cheek, blinked a few times. Then his chin quivered, and he began to blubber. I pulled him out of the truck. "Don't make me look, Harry," he said, keeping his head turned from the wreckage. "Don't make me look."

I ripped off my shirt, tore off a sleeve, ran to Mr. Fox and tried to stop the bleeding from his head. My sleeve was soaked red in seconds. I didn't dare move him for fear I'd break him worse than he was broken. I ran to the other car, but the door felt welded shut. "You stay here!" I screamed at Kenny, who was sitting in the middle of the road with his back to the accident like a helpless child, hugging himself as if freezing. The eerie quiet was pierced by the harsh *wheet wheet* of a cardinal in a tree somewhere.

I didn't know how to drive. I turned the key, and the motor caught, but when I put it in gear, it lurched forward and stopped. I tried again, and the truck lurched, slowed, lurched, and in that way, I made progress past meadows with not a house in sight—endless dirt roads. I came at last to a sign: Lakeview Country Club. All eyes turned when I charged into the clubhouse, blood all over my shirt, screaming, "Call an ambulance!"

* * *

There were so many floral tributes at the hospital that some of the bouquets were in the hall for the nurses to take to other rooms. Mr. Fox lay unconscious, bandaged like a mummy, tubes in his nose, a machine ticking next to him. Whatever blather I had rehearsed disappeared, and all that came out was, "Oh," as I grabbed the back of the nearest chair to steady myself.

The room was full of people, adults and children, relatives probably. "Who's that?" someone whispered, and I crossed the room to Mrs. Fox. Hair in disarray, clothes disheveled, she sat on a chair next to the bed, eyes fixed on her husband. No longer the self-contained proprietor who had given me a tour of her house by the sea two days before, she was haggard. She took my hand, squeezed it very tightly. "You and Kenny saved his life. I'll always be grateful to you both." She kept my hand and seemed to be holding onto it for dear life. "But Joe," she said, "they say his head..." I saw it again, the pulpy neck, felt my eyes fill up, cursed them, looked away. She put her palms on her cheeks and began to keen, "Oy, yoy yoy," rocking back and forth. "Oy yoy yoy, his poor bride, his poor bride."

Instantly, the relatives were next to her, saying reassuring things like, "This too shall pass," and touching her and trying to hug her. "Get away! Get away!" When they backed off, she muttered, "Vultures." I looked around for a chair and noticed the daughters dressed in expensive, stylish clothes, sitting like frightened children on two straightback chairs in a corner away from the others. If they had been Hansel and Gretel in the witch's house they couldn't have been more terrified. Their chairs were touching, and they were holding hands.

"He's had three blood transfusions," Mrs. Fox said. "He lost almost all the blood in his entire body." She smoothed the sheet that covered him. "This morning he was near death—now not so much." She blew her nose on a lace handkerchief.

"She was driving a Ford car," I said.

Mrs. Fox looked up to show she knew that I was referring to her husband's threat to destroy Henry Ford by photographing accidents involving his cars. "Didn't even have a license to drive," Mrs. Fox said. "Didn't even know how." She hunched her shoulders in a gesture that said one is helpless in the face of fate. "She's here," Mrs. Fox said. "Down the hall. Were you there when the ambulance arrived?"

"Yes. I phoned from the club, then went back and waited."

"Kane. Miss Dorothy Kane. Lives in the city. Midtown. Was out for a lark."

Again I saw the glass sticking out of her cheek and her head covered with blood—Kenny shouting, "Don't make me look, Harry. I will not look!" I realized that Kenny's camera was his totem, a kind of Saint Christopher's medal. Holding the camera to his eye for protection, he could view horrible sights without fear. He sent in footage of assassinations, of a man mauled by a tiger. The camera was looking at it, not him. I believed that if I had retrieved one of the cameras from the truck and forced it into his hands, he could have photographed that wreckage, including the chauffeur's head on the car's seat.

A nurse entered the room, and we all fell back. Mrs. Fox stood up, and the nurse yanked a curtain around the bed. "I'll be going along now," I whispered to Mrs. Fox. "When he wakes up, tell him I stopped by."

"Thank you for coming, Harry," she said, chin quivering. "It's a long way out here."

"Your husband's strong as an ox," I managed to say though I was nearly overwhelmed by sadness. I worked my way through the relatives and out the door to the corridor lined with whirring fans that attempted to blow away the July heat but instead just stirred around the sickening hospital smells and warm air. I wanted to extend myself to the poor creature in the other car whose face, with that shard of glass sticking out of her cheek, haunted me. I would not tell her about the chauffeur she killed. I would only say that Mr. Fox was improving, he'd be fine, not to worry. At the nurse's station where fans spun on desks, I asked for Dorothy Kane.

She was in a ward with beds lined up against the walls. Visitors sat on some of the beds, and curtains were drawn around others. A nurse pointed to a mummy wrapped in bandages. "Miss Kane?" I asked, and the bloodshot eyes turned to me.

"Docker, when kuh I go hone?"

"I'm not the doctor, Miss Kane."

The eyes got steely. "Oh," she said. "Cop. Go way." Her hand was, bandaged like a boxing glove.

"I just came to tell you Mr. Fox is okay. He'll be all right, I think."

"Who?"

"The man you hit."

"I hit? He hit me. Yook wha he did to me."

I hurried from the room, down the corridor, past orderlies pushing food carts or rolling stretchers topped with ashen sick people, doctors in white coats wearing stethoscope necklaces and nurses conferring in hushed voices. Let me out of here, let me out of here! I was dead tired, haunted at night by images of Mr. Fox crawling from under the smashed Rolls, the chauffeur, the girl's lips moving on the other side of her cracked windshield, the bucolic dirt road bordered by stone walls, the mechanical sound of an indifferent tractor in the distance.

I had to get back to the studio to see the rushes of the riots in Palestine: Arabs attacking Jews at the Wailing Wall. I would take the caption from the UP wire: "Mufti of Jerusalem issues the call Slaughter the Jews!" If I could just steal some time to sleep, just lay my head down and untangle the turmoil.

The hospital doors opened to a blast of summer heat, and there before me was Molly striding down the entrance path, notebook in hand, summer dress swinging. I was too nauseated to make up a clever or charming greeting. I just stood there. As she approached the entrance, she groomed herself quickly—a hair pat, a sleeve tug—looked up and saw me. She stopped, mouth open, and immediately collected herself so she could say something breezy. Then she understood the expression on my face. I was a mess. "Don't go in, Molly," I said, looking into her eyes, astonished again by how familiar she seemed to me, how close to her I felt, though I hadn't seen her in months. "His family is with him."

She looked away from me. "Are the other reporters here?" I shook my head. She met my eyes again but not fully. "*Modern Screen's* not here?"

I gave up, turned away and headed down the front path. She was next to me, put her hand in mine. We walked together toward the train station, not speaking. Holding hands with Molly, I felt as if I was protected by higher beings, that I was walking along in a momentary state of grace. We sat next to each other on the train, my side mashed up against her side, my arm against hers, my thigh against hers. It was really too hot to sit like that, but neither of us moved. "I saw it," I said after a while.

Molly touched my hand, and I noticed that her engagement ring was gone. "Was that the worst thing you ever saw?"

"No," I said and took her hand in mine. "I saw a bad fire when I was a child."

Chapter Twenty-Nine

"Everyone's calling up," Faye told me when we collided in the hall at work.

"To see if he's okay?"

"No. To find out if he's brain damaged."

"Who says he's brain damaged?"

"Everyone."

"Who's everyone?"

"The people at Chase Bank."

"Anyone else?"

"Someone from the telephone company said she heard he's a vegetable."

"Anyone else?"

"A reporter from the *Wall Street Journal*."

"What did you say?"

"He's expected to recover."

"Have you seen him?"

"Yes."

"And?"

"He could talk."

"Here's what you do. Have public relations meet with reporters. Let's squash the rumors."

All of us at the Hell's Kitchen building were surprised to discover that Mr. Fox's favorite boast, that he was a one-man show and that the whole venture would collapse without him, was not based on fact. Even without Mr. Fox, everything ran smoothly. We at Movietone News—editors, cameramen, sound men, producers, cutting staff, contact men, artists, lab technicians—still met two deadlines a week. We were team Movietone News, touchdown after touchdown. An esprit de corps developed, and I heard no one wishing Mr. Fox would hurry up and come back.

After a few months, he called a press conference, invited about thirty reporters to Fox Hall and appeared before them so they could see for themselves that he was not brain damaged. We read in the papers that he had referred to himself in the third person and greeted them with "William Fox has invited you to his home today to tell you something of his plans for the next twenty-five years." He told them about his new big-screen process, Grandeur, and the first production, *The Big Trail,* starring John Wayne, scheduled to open at the Roxy Theater soon. He told them that he had seen the new invention, television, and said, "If we don't give them a big screen, they will one day sit at home watching radio beams on small screens." He told them about the economies of scale that would happen when Fox merged with Loew's, how MGM would continue to produce high-class pictures, and Fox Films would produce inexpensive pictures. He explained that there would be just one distribution arm instead of two, one home office, one mammoth chain of theaters, and he assured them that he was the only man in the world who could run such a vast operation.

Molly and I were both busy at work, she on the Coast again, doing a piece about Gloria Swanson's wardrobe of skin-tight metallic dresses, and me, doing a piece about the start of construction on the Empire State Building. I would cover both those who were in favor of the skyscraper and those who mourned the loss of the fabulous Waldorf Astoria, razed to make room for it. But in October 1929, all other stories paled compared with the big news. The stock market crashed. A stampede of frantic sellers dumped millions of shares.

The shares of Loew's that Mr. Fox bought for seventy-three million dollars fell to less than half that value. His brokers called his margins. We saw him at the office limping around with a cane, much less of him now inside his suits.

Box-office receipts declined. To lure customers, theaters offered two pictures for the price of one. Double bills required twice the product. To pay for the Loew's shares and for the theaters he had acquired, Mr. Fox depleted the reserves of the Fox Film Corporation, so he no longer could produce enough pictures for double features. He couldn't compete. Customers stayed away. The rumor on Wall Street was that Fox Film and Fox Theaters were about to collapse, that Mr. Fox had mismanaged his companies. His stockholders turned against him. They claimed he misrepresented, falsified records and made up bogus corporations to hide income. We couldn't open a newspaper without reading about Mr. Fox's latest humiliation. No one offered to rescue him. It seemed as if his bankers were happy to watch him drowning.

His partner in Grandeur was a manufacturer and seller of theater equipment. The partner offered to buy a controlling stake of Fox Film. Though the shares were valued at about three hundred million dollars, Mr. Fox was so desperate he accepted eighteen million, and his partner, Harley Clarke, a man who knew nothing about making movies or running a chain of theaters, became president of the Fox Film Corporation. The first thing he did after moving himself into Mr. Fox's office was order the refurbishing of hundreds of Fox theaters, whether they needed it or not. He awarded the contract for installing new seats and carpet to his own company, National Theater Supply Corporation.

We at Movietone News continued to prosper, though an avalanche of debts overwhelmed Mr. Fox. His woes got wide circulation in every big newspaper. When the federal government came after him demanding that he pay three million dollars in back taxes, he declared bankruptcy.

One day I opened the newspaper and a headline screamed: "William Fox, Movie Man, Bribes Bankruptcy Judge." I assumed this was a mistake, that he was falsely accused, that he would be exonerated when the case came to trial. It was impossible to see him to ask him for the truth, because he never came into the office and he would not return my phone calls. I was stunned to read in the paper that he confessed to bribing the judge in charge of his bankruptcy hearing. The judge, according to Mr. Fox's testimony, complained about the expense of his daughter's wedding, said fifteen thousand dollars would help. Mr. Fox sent money to the judge in an unmarked envelope. The judge demanded more. Mr. Fox used his own daughter as a courier, sent her to some hotel with twelve thousand dollars worth of bills wrapped in newspaper. She testified that she put the wad in the hands of some man she was instructed to meet there. Mr. Fox was indicted on a charge of conspiracy to obstruct justice. He was sentenced to prison. The doors of the Lewisberg Penitentiary clanked shut behind him.

Chapter Thirty

In rural Pennsylvania, where the Amish clip-clopped along bucolic roads in their horse-drawn carriages decorated with fringe and thousands of acres of farmland were productive and tidy, there was a chilling sight: a massive red-brick building shaped like a Florentine palace, guard towers and high walls reinforced with barbed wire and daggers of glass. In nearby fields, groups of men, all dressed the same, pitched hay into wagons as guards holding rifles watched them. Pheasants pecked in the grass by the edge of the road.

Freckles, in the black chauffeur's uniform of the company, Classy Rides, that he formed when Prohibition lifted, parked his one limousine in the parking lot next to a row of paddy wagons and said to me in the rearview mirror, "You go in there, Harry, you ain't never coming out."

"Don't worry," I said, though I was reluctant to get out of the car. No one visited my former boss except his wife and daughters. He was a pariah. Others in the industry, when they thought of him at all, gloated. Louie exulted over the collapse of the sale of Loew's. Zukor and the other heads of studios were happy that Grandeur died in infancy, and they wouldn't have to retrofit their theaters with wide screens. And a new player on the scene, Twentieth Century Pictures, had obliterated William Fox by buying his companies.

"You visit someone in there, Harry," Freckles turned from the front seat to warn me face to face, "when they get out, they'll come visit you."

The prison entrance was a metal door that opened by itself. It shut behind me with a finality that made my heart leap. A male voice said, "Do you have any alcohol, drugs or weapons?" Another door lifted, and I entered a concrete yard where another door marked "Control Center" opened. An indifferent guard frisked me, then said my name into an intercom and gestured for me to continue down a wide corridor. The walls were decorated with paintings copied from photographs. All the paintings were the same, covered bridges, red barns, flowers in a vase. I came to the visitors' room where women and children sat at tables. I heard one of the mothers say, "Because Daddy's in the army here." Through bars on the window, I looked down at a courtyard full of inmates, some lying around, others standing in groups. String bags hung from some of the bars on the windows with food brought perhaps by loyal wives.

With the sound of metal on metal, two guards entered and stood fully armed by the door, as prisoners came into the waiting room and went to their families. Mr. Fox was among them, and when I saw how embarrassed he was, a feeling he expressed by walking in an especially upright manner, I regretted this good deed of mine. His hair had been shaved so there was no excess to comb over the top, and his mustache was gone. His head was a perfect egg with sad, heavy-lidded eyes. His uniform was too big and hung on him as if he were a child wearing the pajamas of an older brother. There was a popular observation about the Ku Klux Klan that even though they were hidden by their ghost robes, you could tell they were poor slobs who had nothing because of their shoes. Now I saw the opposite. Mr. Fox's expensive shoes showed what he had lost.

We sat opposite each other at one of the tables. I had rehearsed some cheerful greeting but couldn't use it. This was too real. All I could say was, "They treating you all right?" He did not respond, as if my question was too stupid to merit a reply. I offered him a Cuban cigar, and we sat there puffing. "Movietone News," I told him, "is on six continents now, commentators in every language except Chinese. In China, they put a fellow next to the screen, and he translates my words, screaming to the audience above my voice." Mr. Fox had been embroiled in legal battles so was not part of our latest innovation at Movietone News, commentators instead of titles. We used various voices, one to narrate fashion items, a more hectic voice for sports, a zany voice for feature bits, and mine for the news. Much to my amazement, I received fan mail.Mr. Fox said, "I was betrayed by scoundrels at Chase Bank. They encouraged me to take out the loans they called. They set a trap, and Fox fell in." I said nothing, just nodded my head in a sympathetic way, although I was thinking that everyone in the prison probably thought of themselves as innocent. Mr. Fox had, afterall, confessed to bribing a judge. "Your friend Louis Mayer send you here?"

"Louie?"

"You heard me. The rat who stole my company."

"Why would Louie send me here?"

"He got my theaters. He got Movietone City. There ain't no studio in California can top mine for equipment. He got Will Rogers. He got Shirley Temple."

"In a way, I guess."

"In a way, you guess? What way ain't it true?"

"In the way that Louie isn't Twentieth Century Pictures. Darryl Zanuck is Twentieth Century Pictures."

"There ain't no Darryl Zanuck without the dough Mayer and Nick Schenck put into that company. There's only one reason Twentieth Century Pictures exists on this earth. The reason is this: Mayer wanted to provide for his daughter Edith." Mr. Fox bore his eyes into mine waiting to see if I would argue with him. When I said nothing, he continued. "Well I got news for him. I tried the same thing. I made jobs for my no-count son-in-laws, and it don't work. You think I don't know that kid he made vice president of Twentieth Century Pictures? You think I don't know that son-in-law of his? I know him. Hell, he used to work for me. A two-bit producer. You think Zanuck would have given that kid the time of day if Mayer didn't put money behind him?"

"Might work out, though. So far so good."

"What kind of crap is that? You think I don't know they've scored at the box office? You think I don't know they've done well enough to buy my companies? You think I don't know they've done well enough to put their name in front of mine? What do you think is the reason they've done so good, huh? Tell me that. Go on. Tell me that. The reason is this: your friend and Schenck lent them the big stars at Metro-Goldwyn-Mayer, Clark Gable and the rest of them. Then he puts Twentieth Century in front of Fox. Has the gall to put a mouse ahead of an elephant."

"Seems to me your dream is coming true."

"Yeah? What dream?"

"That the name of Fox would be on the screen in some part of the world every second of the day."

He was surprised by my comment, thought about it, blinked as if seeing me as a real person for the first time, as someone who listened to him and thought about him. He sighed and his posture sagged. "But it ain't me."

"It's bigger than you. It's Fox."

"But it ain't mine." We sat puffing our cigars while the children of inmates ran around the tables, got scolded, sat down, ran around again. Some women were sobbing while their husbands whispered reassurances. "Eve tried to stop the merger," Mr. Fox said. "She done her best."

"The Fox stockholders wanted to sell."

"It ain't like I'm strapped. Hell, I got eighteen million bucks when I sold my shares to that rat Clarke."

"A sizable sum."

"Sizable? You call that sizable?" He tapped his cigar ash, puffed, pulled his posture up. "There is nothing to stop me from putting my name on a new company," he said. "I started with nothing, and I'm not afraid to try again. Imagination and perseverance are what is required to be a success in business."

I thought, getting along with other people is necessary too, but I said, "You took a chance on me, Mr. Fox. And I appreciate that. I owe my career to you."

Mr. Fox looked at me suspiciously, smoothed his dome and said, "I own the patents to the sound-on-film process and to the Grandeur process. The day will arrive when all the others will come to William Fox and be forced to pay a fee for the use of this equipment. Then," he said with a malicious smile, "I'll have them by the balls and don't think I won't squeeze."

He stood up, turned his back on me and walked away past a guard standing at the door.

Chapter Thirty-One

Mr. Fox's art collection came up for auction the same week that Anita moved back to New York. She had a contract with Lux soap, and soon we saw her face on billboards—"Lux Toilet Soap is Hard-Milled! It L-A-S-T-S!" We saw her face in *Ladies Home Journal*—"My Lux Soap Facials Are a Wonderful Beauty Aid!" And on posters in the trolley—"To Pass the Close-up Test, 98% of the Lovely Screen Actresses Use Lux Toilet Soap."

Anita and I took a cab to the former Fifth Avenue mansion of Jay Gould, a robber baron whose home had been leased by Gimbel Brothers for art auctions. "These stories about so many of us being broke," Anita said to me in the cab on the way to the auction, "makes us girls of the silents look so dumb." Her eyes were glued to the cab window; she couldn't get enough of the city. "We haven't been here since repeal," she said. "I never saw such a change. The dirty old speaks have become sidewalk cafés. It's the cat's meow!"

"You're a sight for sore eyes," I said, stroking the sleeve of her sable coat as if it might purr.

"The Talmadges ain't broke," she said. "The Gishes ain't broke."

"Quite the opposite."

"Look at Mary so-called Pickford and Fairbanks. They're rolling in dough." She was more beautiful than ever because the strain was gone from her face, and she had new confidence. She was thirty-eight and knew she had sufficient intelligence to meet whatever came her way. "Ma bought one of them little cameras for making movies you can show at home. Can you beat that? Little projectors for people's front parlors! I said, 'Ma, ain't I in front of the cameras enough without you following me around the house with that thing?'"

"Nick Meadows had one of those."

"You should see his house in Beverly Hills, Harry. It's swell. They wanted me to do a picture with Nick, but I am done with that. Never going to do another picture. Did you see him in *Canada Song*?"

"He looked good as a Mountie."

"But the camera don't love him. It should—he's handsome enough. But it don't. Ain't it funny how that is? You have someone looks like him, or Toby for that matter, and you have someone looks like Norma Shearer—with bitty little eyes the size of rabbit poop, one of them crossed—and the camera loves her, and it don't love them. Ma says I got that certain something."

"You do."

"Nick don't have to worry. With that voice, he'll make dough till he drops."

We entered a four-story mansion and walked into a parade of viewers pausing before each painting during the preview. There were fifty-two paintings, including some by Gainsborough, Van Dyck, Tintoretto, Murillo, Sir Joshua Reynolds and Peter Paul Rubens. We read the artist's name and the estimated sales price. I wondered if Mrs. Fox would be there to see what the pieces brought, to see if she had been correct about their investment value when she bought them to decorate the lobbies of various Fox theaters. She and her daughters now lived close by on Park Avenue in a thirty-five-room apartment. But Mrs. Fox was not there.

Anita and I gave each painting a respectful examination as we saw others doing. Sometimes we heard, "Isn't that

Anita Stewart?" and "Doesn't that woman look like Anita Stewart?" She was the most glamorous woman in the room in her full-length sable coat and high-heel leather boots and that shine that movie stars have. We took seats in the front row, both of us trying to act the part of art connoisseurs by maintaining grave faces though neither of us had ever been to an art auction before. "I don't like having pictures on my walls," Anita whispered, "unless they go with the furniture."

"You mean like the colors match?"

"Yeah."

"Do any of these go?"

"That's why I'm disappointed. Ma told me to bid on the Gainsborough and the Sir Joshua Reynolds. But neither of them go, and we just did the apartment, so I ain't returning that couch. It's sort of lemon-colored. Looks good. You saw it, right?"

"No. Hadn't come yet."

"It's sort of a green yellow. Anyway, I'm going to bid. Why should Louie's daughter be the only one who collects art? I'm as rich as her anyday." She opened a package of peppermint Life Savers, offered me one, and we sat there enjoying the blast on our tongues. "All she does is brag about her Gainsborough. I didn't even know what she was talking about. I thought it was a street someplace."

"Excuse me," a blue-haired matron said shyly. "But could you sign an autograph for my daughter, Miss Stewart? She just loves you."

Anita tongued the peppermint into her cheek and took the auction catalog from the woman. "Sure, darling."

"Make it to Susie."

Anita opened her alligator purse and hunted for a pen. I handed her the one in my breast pocket, and she signed. The woman hugged the catalog as she walked away.

"Who, Irene or Edie?"

"Edie. She thinks she's a big shot since Louie bought her husband that job."

"That's not fair. Goetz has experience. He used to produce pictures at Fox Film."

"Pictures? Spanish language westerns! Louie bankrolled that project so his daughter would be married to someone who earns a living. Now Edie goes around bragging how her husband is vice president of Twentieth Century-Fox."

"They got a bargain when they got Fox. Do you know Darryl Zanuck?"

"I knew him when he was a producer at Warner Brothers. I kissed him one time."

"Bad girl."

"I'm thinking of maybe settling down now, Harry. I got them oats out of me. Ma ain't getting any younger. I'm getting younger, but she ain't. Sends her love to you. And so don't Louie."

"At least they're leaving Movietone alone."

"The most valuable asset Fox has," Anita said, "besides you at Movietone, is Shirley Temple. That is the cutest little girl I ever saw. I asked her, I said, 'Shirley, of all the famous laps they make you sit on, whose do you like best?' She says, 'J. Edgar Hoover because he don't jiggle his knees.'"

Preview over, people filled in the chairs around us while the auction staff took paintings off the wall. There was a lot of chatter in the room, excitement and anticipation.

"Did you know Louie was going to cast me as Jane in *Tarzan the Ape Man*? I said, 'Louie, haven't you noticed I ain't nineteen no more?' He says that I could pass for seventeen. I says, 'Louie, get your eyes checked.' He says, 'You don't want to play opposite Johnny Weissmuller, a U.S. swimming champion?' Did you see the picture, Harry? They're sitting in a tree, and Maureen O'Sullivan introduces herself. She says Jane, he says Tarzan, she says Jane and then, to show he's learned that they're telling each other their names, he says Tarzan and thumps himself with that ape hand he makes, all the fingers together and bent down. Then he thumps her in the chest with them fingers and says Jane—back and forth, back and forth, Jane, Tarzan, Jane, Tarzan. He thumps her chest so hard every time he says Jane, Maureen storms off the set and says, 'I ain't acting with that ape!'"

At the front of the room, the auctioneer stood at a wooden lectern. He was a sweet-faced, gray-haired gent in a suit and a tartan vest, a mild man who might avoid a caterpillar on his path. He spoke calmly. The first lot came up and was sold. Next lot came up and was sold. Tension built as each painting was carried from behind the black curtain, placed on an easel at the front of the podium and then was carried back behind the black curtain when the gavel thwonked and the auctioneer cried, "Sold!"

The Sir Joshua Reynolds portrait of the Prince of Wales was set on the easel. Anita tensed and held her paddle poised. She wanted that picture because she had met the current Prince of Wales when he was touring the United States. The auctioneer said the opening bid. Anita held up her paddle, was outbid, held it up again, was outbid, then turned to see who was bidding against her. I turned too, but a woman behind me in a tall hat with feathers blocked my view. Anita was huffy that anyone would dare bid against her. Wasn't he a fan? Couldn't he see she wanted that painting? She fired bullets from her eyes, turned back to the auctioneer and kept her paddle raised. "Three thousand dollars. Do I have four?" Nodding to the back of the room, "Yes, and do I hear five?" Nodding to Anita, "Yes, and do I hear six?" Anita hesitated. The auctioneer said, "Do I hear six thousand?" Anita kept her paddle down while she did calculations furiously in her head. "Six thousand? Do I hear six thousand dollars for Sir Joshua Reynolds." She hesitated, and he struck the gavel. "Sold. Five thousand dollars to number twenty-two. Thank you." Anita twisted around to glare at the victor, then turned back. "Hey," she whispered to me, "who is that guy? He looks familiar." But I couldn't see.

Some Chinese pottery came up next, some watercolor paintings and the Gainsborough portrait of Mrs. Ralph Bell. The bidding started at two thousand. Anita held up her paddle until the auctioneer said, "Seven thousand, do I hear seven thousand dollars?" Again she hesitated. The auctioneer waited. She agonized. Then, *thwonk*! "Sold to number twenty-two. Thank you."

"Damn," Anita whispered. She twisted around to glare at her competitor.

"Had enough?"

"I should of bid more. I should of kept going. Why didn't you make me keep going?"

"You don't need a portrait of some person you don't even know."

The Peter Paul Rubens painting of Madonna and child was carried to the easel. "I think that baby is so cute. I'm buying this one."

"Does it go?"

"Yeah. I think so. There's sort of a yellow color in the background." The bidding started at two thousand. Anita held up her paddle. "And do I hear three? Yes, and do I hear four? Do I hear four thousand dollars?" Anna hesitated. "I don't know, I don't know," she whispered. "Yes," he said to the back of the room. "And do I hear five? Do I hear five thousand dollars? Going once," he looked around the room. "Peter Paul Rubens, do I hear five thousand dollars? Going twice, do I hear five? Sold! Number twenty-two. Thank you."

"Let's get out of this place. This place ain't fair."

"Let's go meet Molly at the St. Regis," I said. "She's interviewing Alfred Hitchcock. She'll be done now."

We walked toward the exit, Anita doing her movie-star strut as everyone turned to watch her. In the lobby was George Peabody Converse holding paddle number twenty-two. Dressed in a blue cashmere coat with velvet lapels, a cream ascot at his throat, he bowed. "Anita Stewart," he said.

"That wasn't very nice of you," she said. "I wanted them paintings."

"But so did I," he said. He extended his hand to me and said, "Harry," in a way that was meant to sound surprised. Our eyes met in a split second of conspiracy. He was still Molly's boss at *Inside Scoop*, and I had told Molly that Anita would attend this auction. But I didn't know that George would bid against my friend. "You don't remember me, do you?" he asked her.

She met so many people and had such a direct manner that they all expected her to remember them. "Of course I do," she lied. George just stood there smiling. Maybe he was remembering how she felt in his arms. Maybe he was thinking how the years had not made a dent in her beauty. "Oh!" she said, at last. "U.S. Steel!"

He laughed. "At your service."

"Nick Meadow's New Year's Eve party a million years ago!"

He was smitten. He was positively smitten. "You're even more beautiful now, if I may be so bold."

"You can be as bold as you want," she said. "You're U.S. Steel, for Pete's sake."

"And you can be as bold as you want," he said. "You're Anita Stewart, for Pete's sake."

She laughed and said in a coy way, "You took them pictures away from me. That wasn't very gentlemanly of you."

"No," he said. "It wasn't. Let me make it up to you. Come have a drink at my club. It's not far from here. You come too, Harry."

"I ain't sitting in no club with you," Anita said. "Next thing, everything I say will be plastered all over *Inside Scoop*."

"Off the record," George said. He was tanned from Palm Beach, where he played in tennis tournaments. Molly and the rest of his staff were fond of him. He paid well, had a shrewd sense of what was interesting, never published anything malicious, and his magazine was the most popular of its kind on the newsstands.

"Harry," Anita said, "Ma will be sorry she missed you." As she gave me a peck on the cheek, she gave me a secret poke, which meant I should clear out so she could work her magic on U.S. Steel.

Chapter Thirty-Two

In 1935, Will Rogers, the cowboy entertainer, was killed in an airplane crash in Alaska. He was Fox Films' top box-office star, more popular than Shirley Temple or anyone else in the business. The American people loved him and never tired of quoting him: "An onion can make people cry, but there has never been a vegetable invented to make them laugh." "Diplomacy is the art of saying 'Nice doggie' until you can find a rock." "Live in such a way that you would not be ashamed to sell your parrot to the town gossip."

His small airplane made an unplanned stop south of Barrow, Alaska. As they took off again, the plane stalled and plunged into a river. The next day, Movietone News camera crews flew to Alaska for footage to show the mourning nation.

We would cut in existing footage from our archives. I had four research assistants, all industrious youngsters working their way through college. One of them, Joel, an ungainly boy with a sparse blond beard, was so new, he didn't yet know how to avoid going off on a tangent. One interesting fact about Alaska led to another, and before he knew it, he was feeding me images of the Alaska gold rush.

I was a fan of celebrity news as much as anyone else, but it frightened me that the frenzy over the death of Will Rogers inspired more news items than the Nazis in Germany establishing the Nuremberg Laws that stripped Jews of their German citizenship and forbade marriage between "Jews" and "Germans." The German people had elected Hitler, and all books by non-Nazi or Jewish authors had been burned. Kenny flew over there to get shots of a Nazi parade, but he was beaten up by a gang of brown shirts and left for dead in an alley. He was still walking around the studio with his foot in a cast. So my patience was short as I examined outtakes of Will Rogers chewing gum and saying, "Howdy."

Joel was deep into his newfound passion for the Alaska gold rush and brought me still shots of the Alaska-Yukon-Pacific Exposition in 1909. "Look at these," he said. "It's a coming-of-age party for the city of Seattle. This fair attracted four million visitors. Look at this, Mr. Sirkus. This is the parade in downtown Seattle. Look how Seattle looked back then. And look at this. It's an amusement park called the Paystreak. I looked up Paystreak. It's the term they used for the richest deposit of gold that you get when you pan. Look at this. Look at this, Mr. Sirkus. It's an attraction in the amusement park called Gold Camps of Alaska. And look. They had carnival rides. Look at them! Would you ever go on one of those things?"

"Joel."

"I know you're busy. I know you're busy, but look at this. This is a picture of a gold nugget. Look. Come on. Just one look. You've got to see this, Mr. Sirkus. Look. Come on."

I sighed. "Joel, you are driving me crazy." I snatched the grainy old print from him. It showed a slender young man in overalls and muddy boots holding on his palm a piece of gold about the size of a walnut. I was stunned to see a man who looked like my father. I took out my wallet and smoothed the wrinkled photograph I had been carrying around all my life. Same hair, same soulful eyes, same square shoulders, same way of holding himself. A million men probably looked like that. Just because my heart was beating fast, it didn't mean it really was Uncle Sonny. "Joel, find out who this man is."

"Will do, Mr. Sirkus!" He gathered up all the stills and charged back upstairs to the library. I returned to viewing shots of Will Rogers roping calves.

Late in the day, Joel returned with news. "He has your same name, Mr. Sirkus! What are the chances of that! That's not a very common name. You couldn't make up a name like that. He worked in that Paystreak amusement park."

"Go on."

"There's still a list of those people! Can you believe this? I called Seattle. Are you angry?"

"Go on."

"It wasn't that expensive. I talked maybe three minutes. Four, maybe."

"Go on, Joel. Tell me what you found."

"They have a special section in the library. All the history of Seattle. I asked the reference librarian to look him up. Couldn't find anything. I said, 'Do you have obituaries cataloged?' I am a very resourceful person, Mr. Sirkus. Once I'm onto something, I see it through to the end." I lit a cigarette and hoped he didn't see my hand tremble. "He died about two years after that photo was taken. So I said, 'Did he get murdered for the gold?' And the librarian said, 'It doesn't say. His name is just on a list of dead people for that year.' Is he a relative of yours, Mr. Sirkus? What are the chances of that? I couldn't believe she called me back. Isn't that nice? She said there is nothing in the Seattle papers about any murder. So I said, 'What happened to the nugget?' She said she thinks it's in the museum out there and that it didn't belong to him. He was just hired by the fair to show it to people."

"Did anyone bury him?" I managed to say.

"Wouldn't they have to, Mr. Sirkus? Isn't that the law?"

When I could speak, I said, "Thank you, son. You've helped me. Now let's put it aside and make some news."

I phoned Molly and said, "I found Uncle Sonny."

After I told her how this happened, she said, "Good. Now you can really leave the Elizabeth Home for Destitute Children."

"What? What's that supposed to mean?"

"Harry, I'm on deadline."

"You can't just say something like that and go back to work. I ran away from that place when I was thirteen. I put that all behind me a long time ago."

"Do me a favor. Look at your jacket."

"What about it?"

"Describe the elbows."

"There's nothing wrong with them. I put patches over the holes. You can't see the holes."

"But you don't need to put patches on your clothes anymore, Harry. Nothing's going to break your heart now."

Afterword

Anita Stewart (1895-1961) married George Peabody Converse and divorced him twelve years later. She died of a heart attack in 1961 in Beverly Hills, some saying she was fifty-nine, others claiming she was sixty-five. For her contribution to the motion-picture industry as an actress, Stewart was given a star on the legendary Hollywood Walk of Fame in Los Angeles.

Louis B. Mayer (1884-1957) became a Hollywood legend. While he was chief of production, Metro-Goldwyn-Mayer became the most glamorous movie studio in the world, boasting more stars than are in the heavens. It was home to Joan Crawford, Jean Harlow, Clark Gable, Greta Garbo, James Stewart, Spencer Tracy, Fred Astaire, Ava Gardner, Judy Garland, Mickey Rooney, Debbie Reynolds, Gene Kelly and other luminaries. Its logo of a roaring lion was perhaps the most famous logo in the world. Louie was eventually forced out of the company in the late 1950s and failed to regain his position. He divorced Maggie after forty years of marriage, remarried and became an owner of racehorses. He died of leukemia in 1957 when he was seventy-two.

The Red Head speakeasy in Greenwich Village, opened in 1922, moved uptown and was renamed the Puncheon. After Prohibition, the business moved to Fifty-second Street with a new name, the 21 Club.

William Fox (1879-1952) served several months in prison and lived the rest of his life, an additional twenty-five years, in such obscurity that the *New York Times* described him as the late William Fox while he was still alive. His dream came true, just not as he imagined. The name Fox is everywhere now, but no one knows it stands for him.

Kenny Anderson "went Hollywood" after moving there. He dressed in a flamboyant style, drove sports cars, invited pretty starlets to his pool, and won many awards for cinematography.

Harry Sirkus became television's premier news broadcaster. His weekly television show, *Watch It Now*, was a consistent favorite from 1950 to 1970, its popularity matched by only *The Ed Sullivan Show.* Harry interviewed the great newsmakers of his day, always asking the questions viewers at home wished they could ask. He married Molly and lived happily with her in a Dutch colonial house in Larchmont, New York. Harry died of lung cancer in 1972. Thousands of mourning fans lined Madison Avenue outside the Frank E. Campbell Funeral Chapel. The pallbearers were Walter Cronkite, Ed Sullivan, Freckles, Kenny Anderson and Harry's three sons, Richard, Donald and Franklin.

9 780615 343273